Almost *True* Confessions

Also by Jane O'Connor

Dangerous Admissions

The Fancy Nancy series

Almost *True* Confessions

Closet Sleuth Spills All

JANE O'CONNOR

WILLIAM MORROW
An Imprint of HarperCollinsPublishers

P.S.™ is a trademark of HarperCollins Publishers.

HarperCollins books may be purchased for educational, business, or sales promotional use. For information please e-mail the Special Markets Department at SPsales@harpercollins.com.

FIRST EDITION

Designed by Diahann Sturge

Library of Congress Cataloging-in-Publication Data has been applied for.

ISBN 978-0-06-124094-2

13 14 15 16 17   OV/RRD   10 9 8 7 6 5 4 3 2 1

To Jim again, always

Acknowledgments

I'd like to thank my very talented editor, Carrie Feron, for having the patience of a saint.

Almost *True* Confessions

Chapter 1

PEN NAME FOR JOSETTE? THE ANSWER WAS TEN LETTERS LONG.

Staring at all the maddening blank squares in the puzzle, Rannie Bookman faced the fact that she needed a more meaningful goal in life than completing the Saturday *New York Times* crossword. The realization did not, however, compel her to put down the newspaper and take action, not even to the point of getting out of bed or casting off the flannel nightgown with a peanut butter and jelly stain on the sleeve that she'd been wearing for the past forty hours. It was almost three in the afternoon of what should have been a pleasurable tail-end-of-November day, weak sunlight filtering through the closed shutters of her bedroom windows. Yet all she wanted to do was pull the covers up over her head and hibernate. She swallowed hard a few times, testing to see if her throat hurt, just as she used to do eons ago as an excuse to miss school and stay in bed. And actually, now after the fourth try, her throat did feel a little scratchy.

Was she, she wondered absently, the only person in the world who after coming within a hairsbreadth of dying wasn't filled to the overflowing brim with renewed purpose, boundless energy, as well as a humbling sense of life's beauty? Oh sure, for a while she'd felt like a walking, talking smiley-face emoticon. A heady—or maybe just wrongheaded—feeling of invincibility had lasted the entire time she remained the darling of the New York tabloids and morning news shows. Sitting with a camera trained on her, Rannie ("Just think Annie with an 'R,'" she'd explain to interviewers butchering her name) would modestly recount foiling her attacker, a psychotic murderer, with nothing more than her Col-Erase blue pencil, the stock-in-trade of every copy editor. The TV hosts would look at all 102 pounds, five feet, two inches of her; shake their heads in wonderment; and pronounce, "It's a miracle you're here."

But now the media hoopla was over and her life was back to normal, no better or worse than it had been before. On the plus side: she had two almost-grown kids whom she adored—a daughter at Yale, a son in his senior year of high school; a really attractive man seemed to be falling in love with her; all the TV makeup people had said she looked thirty-three, not forty-three; and her three-bedroom apartment was rent controlled. On the minus side: she had two almost-grown kids who drove her crazy; the man in question was a recovering alcoholic with more old issues than *National Geographic;* she often felt she acted thirteen, not forty-three; and she still had no job.

Ironically, the person who best understood her anomie was her ex-husband, an amiable underachiever whose life purpose was simply to play tennis every day under a clear California sky. "You're still looking for meaning, Rannie?" he asked, incredulous. "Just *live.*" When Peter Lorimer started sounding deep, you knew you were in trouble.

Simple truth: Rannie needed work to distract herself.

It was now more than four months since she'd gotten pink-slipped at Simon & Schuster, all because of a mistake made by a junior copy editor and blamed on Rannie, his supervisor. Oh, it had been a beaut all right—an "L" missing from the last word in the title of the first Nancy Drew mystery, a title that was supposed to be *The Secret of the Old Clock.* All fifty thousand copies of the special gold-embossed "pleather" anniversary edition were destroyed, although some managed to pop up on eBay, selling for outrageous amounts.

By now the freelance copyediting assignments that had been keeping her mind occupied and her wallet marginally full had dried up. And her part-time work as a tour guide at the private school her son attended had ended once the deadline for applications had passed. She had too much time on her hands; everyone was unanimous on that score—her kids, her boyfriend, her mother, her ex-husband's mother. And since she was hardly sleeping, she actually had even *more* time to fill, especially those joyous hours between two and four A.M. when there are only two adjectives to describe life—bleak and pointless.

Each night she'd awaken, bolt upright in bed, her scalp tingling, her heart galloping, after another ghastly replay of the rooftop attack that had nearly ended her life. But instead of relief that she was safe in bed, she'd be swamped by guilt. She was still alive only because she'd ended someone else's life. She'd listen to her own heart beating and the fact that she'd stopped someone's from doing that very same elemental act seemed impossible, horrifying, and wrong.

"You are way overthinking this. Self-defense, Rannie. It was you or him. End of discussion." This was what Tim Butler, who

had once been a cop, kept reminding her, lately with an undertone of impatience. "Look, call me if you can't sleep. I don't care
what time it is. I'll come over and take your mind off crazy stuff."

Indeed he could. If not for all those wonderful sex-released
endorphins, Rannie figured she'd probably be on an intravenous
drip of antidepressants. And sex with Tim was fun, unpredict-
able, loaded with raw animal satisfaction. They'd meet, and
all through dinner or a movie or some sports event at Chapel
School, where Tim's son also was a senior, she'd sit counting
down the minutes until they were alone and she could grab him.
Yet never once had she picked up the phone when the night terrors came stalking. She deserved the guilt; it was right to suffer
over killing someone.

"You say you're Jewish. But in another life you definitely were
wearing a parochial school uniform," was Tim's assessment.

Chapter 2

THE RINGING OF THE PHONE ON HER BEDSIDE TABLE STARTLED Rannie. Her hand emerged from the covers and groped for the receiver. Tim, probably, about plans for tonight.

"Rannie? It's Ellen." Ellen Donahoe, a senior editor at Simon & Schuster, always threw whatever freelance copyediting she needed Rannie's way. "I have a job for you. A biggie. We're on a crazy tight deadline. Can you do it?"

"Yes! I'm sharpening blue pencils as we speak! I don't care if it's a tax code manual." Rannie leaped from bed and shuddered as she caught sight of herself in the mirror. Raging bedhead.

"Oh, I guarantee it's a lot juicier than that."

"You have the disk? I'll come right now and pick it up." With her free hand, Rannie brushed her dark baby-fine hair into its Louise Brooks–ish bob.

Ellen didn't. "You have to pick up a hard copy and the disk at the author's apartment. She specifically asked for you, and she'll send her limo to get you."

Limo? This was getting better and better. She sprinted toward the bathroom. "Who's the writer?" The one author Rannie had dated, a guy whose depressing novels never ranked higher than a zillion on Amazon, was always so strapped for cash that he'd mooch MetroCard rides off her.

"Before I tell you," Ellen went on, "you have to agree to a few ground rules. The author is pretty paranoid but justifiably so."

It flickered through Rannie's mind that *paranoia* was by definition never *justifiable;* however, she held her tongue.

"First, you have to sign a confidentiality agreement. You are to tell no one about the book or who wrote it."

"Fine."

"The manuscript can never be left laying around. When you're not actually proofing it, when it's not physically in your hands, it must be kept in a locked briefcase—the author's got that for you, too—and the key must be kept on your person at all times."

On my person? Rannie could almost hear strains of the *Mission Impossible* theme music starting up. Was this a Mafia tell-all? Had somebody finally owned up to being the second shooter on the grassy knoll in Dallas?

When Ellen finally divulged the writer's name, all Rannie said was "No kidding!" Ret Sullivan had written several search-and-destroy biographies of high-wattage boldface names. She'd become a celebrity herself; in fact, stacks of a biography about Ret Sullivan were displayed in front windows of Barnes & Noble stores at this very moment.

Ret's books were always unauthorized and nasty as hell. And she had a blog called dirtylinen.com. Still, Rannie harbored a soft spot for Ret. Years ago, after copyediting Ret's bio of Princess Di, Rannie received a lavish gift basket from a fancy Madison Avenue gourmet shop. How many other authors had ever bothered with even an e-mail of thanks? Exactly none.

Ret Sullivan's most recent book had torpedoed the career of Mike Bellettra, a beloved Oscar-winning actor. What nobody had known about, before Ret made it public knowledge, was his fondness for tween girls. The book was a runaway bestseller, but Ret Sullivan paid a steep price for the top spot on the *New York Times* nonfiction list. Bellettra lay in wait outside her Manhattan apartment house and when she appeared threw lye in her face. Horribly disfigured, Ret Sullivan had disappeared from view ever since, while Mike Bellettra landed in prison with a fifteen-year sentence.

"Oh, God! What's she look like now?" Rannie couldn't help asking. Years ago Rannie used to see Ret in the S&S offices, and you couldn't miss her, she with her retro black French twist, skin-tight jumpsuits, stiletto heels, and lips so red and Botox-inflated they looked like the plastic mouthpiece for Mrs. Potato Head.

"She wore a ski mask every time I went to her apartment. She never goes out. And she won't let friends visit, not that many are banging down the door. Sometimes she has her chauffeur drive her around late at night, just to get out of the house."

"That's no life," Rannie said.

"Agreed. She was hoping for a face transplant like that woman whose face got chewed off by a dog. But every doctor told her the same thing: she wasn't a candidate. And the stuff she dug up on Mike Bellettra was all true. Rannie, the guy was fucking pre-teens!" Ellen went on. "To tell you the truth, I like her. Always have. She's a breeze to work with. Loves to yak. She accepts what she does for what it is. Doodoo of the rich and famous. I'd take her any day over some midlist novelist with delusions of artistic grandeur."

Rannie understood: for some writers, even so much as the deletion of a comma was cause for endless debate. "So who's she skewering this time? Are there any Kennedys left she *hasn't* already nailed to the cross?"

"I'm not allowed to say, not until you sign the confidentiality agreement. But it's someone interesting and not someone you'd expect."

Ellen was dangling a lot of carrots.

"So how soon can the limo be here?" It was a quarter to four.

"Let me call Ret. But listen, this is serious, Rannie. We have kept this project under total wraps. Up to now, I am the only person who has read the manuscript. In-house it's just referred to as *Book X*. All the sales force knows is the book will be embargoed and that it's going to be huge."

An embargo meant that absolutely no copies of the book could be sold before a specific publication date with legal repercussions for disobedient accounts. It was a pain in the ass for a publishing house to coordinate, thus embargoes were reserved for major news-breaking books, memoirs by former presidents, and publishing phenoms such as *Harry Potter* or *The Hunger Games*.

"Stay where you are, Rannie. I'll call you right back."

Ellen was as good as her word. Rannie was barely out of the shower before her cell rang again. The limo was on its way.

And it wasn't just a limo! Rannie could hardly believe her eyes when a caramel-colored Rolls-Royce rolled up Broadway to 108th Street, in all likelihood the first ever to grace her very ungentrified neighborhood, which her daughter had dubbed LoCo for Lower Columbia U. There was something that didn't compute about seeing such a majestic vehicle with the El Yunque Beauty Parlor as backdrop. Too bad neither of her kids was home to see this.

Rannie waited until the liveried driver had opened the door for her before she slipped into the luxe interior, with a muted "thank you," in a tone that she hoped approximated the upper-crust whisper of Jackie O.

"So where are we headed?"

When the driver answered, "Sixty-Nine East Sixty-Ninth Street," Rannie had to stifle a giggle; even Ret's address had a salacious ring. Then she leaned back, savoring the subtle smell of soft leather, in a pale shade of caramel, two bud vases containing a single rose at each rear window and a built-in minibar with crystal decanters and glassware. "Nothing bad can ever happen in here" was what all the accoutrements seemed to guarantee, and Rannie figured that for someone who'd been doused with lye and left scarred for life, no matter what Ret Sullivan had shelled out for this baby, it was worth it.

A legal-size envelope with Rannie's name on it was tucked into the magazine rack in front of her. The confidentiality agreement. Rannie read it over. The standard no-blabbing stuff. So she signed in triplicate and called Ellen.

"I'm in the Rolls. I'm signed, sealed, and about to be delivered. So spill."

"Okay. The book's about Charlotte Cummings."

"No! You're kidding." At Charlotte Cummings's one-hundredth birthday celebration, the mayor declared her a New York City landmark. She was the patron saint of a certain circumscribed Manhattan—the well-bred, moneyed Manhattan where everyone had been old, old friends since their days at Chapin or

Brearley (the girls) or St. Bernard's (the boys) and where all the inhabitants, including Rannie's former mother-in-law, were on a first-name basis.

The most remarkable thing about Charlotte Cummings, besides the obscene wealth of her second husband, Silas, was that she'd outlived all her old, old friends. Recently Charlotte Cummings had been as reclusive as Ret Sullivan, ill health finally catching up with her.

But what dirty linen could Ret possibly air on the likes of Charlotte Cummings? That she once had purchased a knock-off designer ball gown? That she had hosted a dinner party with the fish forks and spoons in the wrong spots?

In far too short a time, the Rolls-Royce glided through Central Park, over to the East Side, and, at Sixty-Ninth Street between Madison and Park Avenues, Rannie reluctantly emerged from the posh cocoon. What stood before her was a postwar white-brick apartment house, set back with microterraces at the corners of the top floors. She had expected, after the Rolls, a grander residence. But probably the board of any exclusive co-op would let out a collective screech at the idea of a neighbor with enemies like Ret Sullivan's. Can't have lye ruining the lobby woodwork, after all.

Rannie gave her name to a concierge in a headphone set, who was perched behind a wraparound counter. He tapped four buttons on a console and blinked, waited, then tried the number again before saying, "Ms. Sullivan must not hear the phone. But it's okay. She called a little while ago saying to let you up."

At the bank of elevators, Rannie watched the digital race of red numbers to see which of the four elevators would reach L first. Then soundlessly and speedily she was whisked to the twenty-sixth floor: 26J—that's where she was going. Signs with arrows for apartments A–K directed her along a warren of maroon-carpeted hallways periodically punctuated with Marriott-style abstract paintings on the walls. To Rannie, hell could be a never-ending version of this. Of course, according to Ellen, Ret stayed hermetically sealed inside her apartment and thus rarely saw these hallways. . . . Poor woman, Rannie thought once again as she reached the front door of 26J. After all, plenty of writers dished out bucketloads of dirt—look at Kitty Kelly. None of them wound up like Ret. Rannie arranged her features in a neutral expression and buzzed. Please, please, let Ret's ski mask be in place!

Rannie buzzed again and waited. Then she rapped on the door, hard. She thought she heard noise inside the apartment. "Hello? It's Rannie Bookman. Your copy editor."

Still no response. Rannie hit the buzzer for an annoyingly extended time. The high-pitched drone could wake the dead. Futilely, she jiggled the doorknob, called out Ret's name again. What if she was hurt, unable to get help? Quickly Rannie retraced her steps through the labyrinth back to the elevators and down to the lobby, where she reported the locked, unanswered door to the concierge.

"Sometimes she takes naps," he said in a suggestive way that put invisible quotes around naps. Was the implication that these afternoon snoozes were drug induced? "Maybe come back later," he added.

No way. She wasn't leaving empty-handed. "Look, I'm here to pick up an important package. And what if something's happened to her? I heard noise inside. You need to check."

"I'll call the handyman."

She waited for what seemed like an annoyingly long time, force of habit making her check her wrist though her watch had been stolen from her at knifepoint right on her block a month ago. Rannie checked her cell. Finally a tall guy in navy work clothes appeared with keys.

Back at 26J he rapped loudly after a long buzz, then unlocked the door to Ret Sullivan's apartment.

They found themselves in an airy, open expanse of living room/dining room/kitchen with wall-to-wall windows interrupted only by French doors opening onto one of the shoebox terraces Rannie had seen from the street. The decor was stark, modern: a gray U-shaped sectional sofa wrapped around three sides of a square glass-topped coffee table. The artwork, by contrast, was all religious. On one wall was an assemblage of crosses centered around a massive stone one that might have once been a tombstone.

"Ret?" Rannie called, then, "Ret Sullivan?" as if adding her last name might elicit a response.

To their right was a hallway that could only lead to the bedroom or bedrooms. "I'm going in to check," the handyman stated. "You stay here." Rannie didn't and was right behind him at the entrance to the master bedroom when he let out a disbelieving "Jesus fuckin' Christ!"

There was only one light on. At first Rannie's eyes were drawn to a painting above the bed of a Madonna tenderly cradling baby Jesus. The painting seemed enveloped in a frame of light.

In the next instant Rannie's gaze dropped to the bed. Ret Sullivan, clad in a black push-up bra and panties, lay stretched almost Christlike on it, wrists lashed by brightly colored scarves to brass bedposts. Her head drooped sideways. Her eyes were open; one of them was made of glass. She had no lips, only a black hole for a mouth, and a bulbous nodule of skin in the middle of her face vaguely resembled a nose. Her hair, normally worn in a sixties French twist, was loose—or had been loose before being tied in two bunches to rungs on the bedstead. Rannie willed herself to look away but somehow couldn't, riveted by the sight of the woman's tongue protruding lasciviously from the black hole of her mouth. One more scarf, long and flowing, was knotted way too tightly around Ret Sullivan's neck.

At some point Rannie must have stopped screaming because later she remembered drinking a Diet Coke the handyman got her from Ret's fridge and also catching sight of a slim, brushed-steel briefcase near the front door. Ten to one, the manuscript.

It was while they waited on the sectional sofa for the police to arrive that Rannie realized two things. Her throat was now really and truly sore. And there was indeed justifiable paranoia.

Chapter 3

WHY WAS EVERYONE—AT LEAST, HER SO-CALLED NEAREST AND dearest—acting as if it was Rannie's fault she'd stumbled on Ret Sullivan's body? The cop who arrived at Ret's apartment had shown more compassion, offering Kleenex and chewing gum while he questioned her. Yet that evening back home Rannie found herself in the unfair position of having to defend herself.

"Rannie, really! This has got to stop!" Harriet Bookman commanded from the sanctity of her Shaker Heights Tudor in an aggrieved tone that implied one more misstep and Rannie would be grounded indefinitely. "Your sisters never find dead bodies!"

"Ma, what are you, some kind of corpse magnet?" Nate asked.

Alice via e-mail sounded almost as outraged as Rannie's mother but more out of literary snobbery. "Mother, what were you doing there? Ret Sullivan writes such trash."

Even Mary, Rannie's blue-blooded former mother-in-law, in whose eyes she could usually do no wrong, seemed upset mainly by the possibility that Rannie's name might appear in the paper, as if finding a dead body constituted an unforgivable breach of etiquette.

Tim Butler was the last to weigh in. His opener was "You can't just stay away from trouble, can you?"

Rannie explained the reason for her appearance at Ret Sullivan's apartment. "She asked for me to be the copy editor on her new book. I was supposed to pick up the manuscript."

"So who's getting smeared this time?"

"Not allowed to tell."

"For real?"

"I signed a confidentiality agreement."

"I'll keep it hush-hush, cross my heart and hope to die."

"Okay, Tim. Make fun if you want." Rannie paused. "What I don't understand is how Ret dug up any dirt this time. Supposedly she hardly ever set foot out of her apartment."

"Doesn't seem hard to me," Tim replied. "She paid somebody to do the snooping for her." Then he fired off a bunch of standard cop questions.

"I'll tell you what I told the cop. Nothing seemed out of place in the apartment. There was no sign of forced entry—the door was locked." Rannie paused and sighed. "So anyway now I'm out of a big fat freelance job . . . at least I got to ride in a Rolls."

No reply from Tim.

"Sorry. That sounded selfish and crass."

"Really? She got murdered and you're no poorer than you were this morning. I wonder who I feel sorrier for?"

The trouble with Tim was he wasn't shallow. Not a superficial bone in his buff body. Of course, considering his stats—he'd been drunk at the wheel of the car crash that killed his wife,

had done a stint in rehab followed by years of AA, and was raising a son who knew why he had no mother—small wonder that
Tim took life seriously. Still, Rannie bet he'd been born that way,
and sometimes she had to bite her tongue to keep herself from
saying, "Lighten up a little."

She described the way she'd found the body, omitting particulars of Ret Sullivan's disfigured face. She felt a pang of guilt.
This *was* serious.

"Maybe it was sex that got out of hand."

"The woman was strangled, Tim!"

"You never heard of the choking game? Space Cowboy?
Rannie, kids have filmed themselves. Go on YouTube and see
for yourself."

"I know about the choking game." But what she'd read involved teenaged boys, terrifying since she owned one. So did
Tim. The formal term for the choking game was autoerotic
asphyxiation. A kid masturbated and then right before orgasm
choked himself, with a tie or noose at the ready, just to the point
of unconsciousness. The brief strangling supposedly produced
a surging rush—and a much more intense orgasm—by denying
and then replenishing blood to the brain. According to pediatri-
cians, some cases of what appeared to be suicide were accidents,
horrible instances of kids masturbating and ending up dead.

"Her hands were tied. She didn't strangle herself. Plus I never
heard of women liking that," Rannie said.

"You're not housebound or freakish looking. Maybe the same
old, same old got boring. If that's the case, it's probably involuntary manslaughter."

"Ooh, I like it when you talk cop."

"I can come over right now and read you your rights."

Rannie begged off. "I'm exhausted. And some friends of Nate's just arrived."

"And what? You're chaperoning?"

Hardly. She'd been dozing when Tim called, her cheek soaking in a pool of drool on her pillow, the television set on. "Look. I'll see you tomorrow."

A second call from Tim around ten greatly improved her peace of mind: the police had already picked up a suspect.

The Offbeat, the West Side bar that Tim owned, was a cop hangout, and often Tim heard about crime investigations before the public did. "Evidently the drill on Saturday afternoons was the regular boy toy at two thirty. According to the doormen, he's been coming every Saturday—for a couple of years now. "

"I thought I heard someone inside Ret's apartment!" Rannie said. "Oh, Jesus. He was still in the apartment the first time I buzzed! Maybe Ret was still alive." Rannie suddenly felt lightheaded. It had taken twenty minutes for the damned handyman to come with the keys.

"The guy's claiming he was out by three thirty and that Ret Sullivan was fine . . . at least, as fine as somebody can be with only half a face. But nobody on the building staff remembers seeing him leave."

"What about security cameras?"

"Several guys in gym clothes with roughly the same build are seen leaving the building late afternoon. Any of them could be him or could be tenants. . . . He has a record, robbery and assault."

"So? This was a robbery?" That didn't sound right.

"Not necessarily. Like I said before, maybe it was rough sex that got too rough."

So . . . case closed or just about to be. Not that it did Ret Sullivan much good. Rannie brushed her teeth—having disgusting morning mouth before midnight seemed in violation of the social contract. The local news at eleven reported that the suspect in Ret Sullivan's murder was Gerald Steele, an instructor at a midtown health club. A camera panned across its mirrored walls reflecting rows upon rows of young buns-of-steel singles, clad in tight tees and spandex, working away on shiny equipment that, to Rannie, appeared to have been designed by direct descendants of the Marquis de Sade. Didn't these people have anything better to do on a weekend night? There was also a brief clip of the guy, in handcuffs, being loaded into the back of a police car; with his back to the camera, all Rannie could make out was his stocky, bowlegged physique. That and a cocky, rolling *Saturday Night Fever* gait.

Rannie turned off the TV and turned her pillow over to its dry side. It occurred to her that she had no business scoffing at gym rats, considering where she was on a Saturday night, though at least she'd had the opportunity for something better. Why *had* she said no to Tim?

Tim had even won Nate's approval, no mean feat, because of shared tastes in eighties music—Squeeze, the Cars, Crowded House. Then, in the past weeks, they'd played tennis together a few times on the courts at Chaps—doubles, with Nate and his friend Ben against Tim and his son, Chris. There had even been one dinner at Tim's bar/restaurant with both their sons. Rannie suspected Nate would not have much problem with Tim staying overnight. Yet she never broached the subject—to either of them. It would make everything, well, much more serious. *Serious.* There was that adjective again. What was her problem? Did she only like shallow people and only want shallow relationships? Postdivorce and pre-Tim, that had certainly been her MO. Men who were fun, both in and out of bed. Even her eleven-year marriage to Peter Lorimer seemed superficial on many levels. When he up and left for California with the girlfriend du jour in tow, she hadn't been devastated, not really. She had ached for her kids, shed tears for what the breakup did to them. And the reason she and her philanderer of an ex-husband could remain friendly, even once succumbing to a shamefully terrific tryst at a New York hotel, was not solely because of their children but also because they'd never been so deeply in love that they had to hate each other once the marriage was over.

Willing her body to relax, Rannie pulled up the covers to her chin and tried her best to push away troubling thoughts about the state of her psyche as well as selfish thoughts about the juicy manuscript by Ret Sullivan, sealed inside a brushed aluminum briefcase now in police hands instead of hers.

Chapter 4

At a little past ten the next morning, Rannie stood in front of a cashier at the Barnes & Noble superstore at Eighty-Third and Broadway and parted with more than twenty-five bucks for a copy of *Tattletale: The Life and Times of Ret Sullivan*. Why did she buy it? Rannie couldn't say for sure, except that she was drawn by the fact that her own prosaic path had, however briefly, intersected with Ret Sullivan's far more lurid trajectory.

This morning's Sunday *Times* had carried a short article about the book and its brisk sales. A "spokesperson" for the publishing company had been quoted as saying, "For quite a while rumors have been floating around that Ms. Sullivan was finishing up a new tell-all so we decided to bring out a biography of Ret Sullivan. She was, after all, a celebrity in her own right. Of course, we are terribly saddened by her demise."

"Demise." It was such a clunky, unconversational word, one that you came across in crossword puzzles yet rarely heard uttered. On the walk home, she picked up a copy of the *Daily News* and ducked into the nearest Starbucks to read it. A long-ago photo of Ret and one of Gerald Steele, the murder suspect, shared the front page. The headline read POISON PEN RUNS OUT OF INK. Rannie sat with a container of coffee and scanned all the stories, including one on Mike Bellettra, the movie star responsible for disfiguring Ret.

> Ret Sullivan's unauthorized biography—*Mike Bellettra: Dark Side of the Moon*—came out soon after his Oscar for best actor in *Moon Landing*. Bellettra's portrayal of an aging U.S. astronaut on his final mission traded on everything that made the 50-year-old star box-office gold—his upbeat American can-do attitude and seemingly rock-solid sense of decency.
>
> Ret Sullivan blew the myth of Mike Bellettra sky-high by revealing what payoffs to the New Jersey police and several hospitals in Camden had kept secret for years: Bellettra was beating and raping underage girls.
>
> Days after the book's publication, Bellettra waylaid Sullivan outside her Upper East Side building and threw lye in her face, blinding her in one eye and burning ninety percent of her face. That night Bellettra was arrested. He is now serving a fifteen-year sentence at the Clinton Correctional Facility in Dannemora, New York.

Almost as soon as she left Starbucks, carrying what little was left of her vente house blend, Rannie's cell rang.

It was Ellen Donahoe. The last time Rannie had spoken to her was from the Rolls en route to Ret's.

"Omigod, Rannie, I freaked when I heard about Ret. This morning when I read 'a concerned friend found her,' I knew that had to be you!" A short pause in which Rannie could practically feel Ellen shuddering. "So listen. Last night I tried calling umpteen times. Was your cell off? And every time I tried the landline it was busy, busy. Don't you believe in call waiting?" Ellen didn't stop to hear the answer, which was no.

"I didn't want to leave a message because, well, because of how sensitive this whole thing is but, Rannie, I need you to get to work right away. I mean this instant."

It took a moment more of Ellen's headlong chatter for Rannie to realize that by "sensitive matter" Ellen was not referring to Ret Sullivan's "demise," but rather to the manuscript Ret had written about Charlotte Cummings.

"Wait! You've got a copy!"

"Yes. I told you that yesterday. Didn't I? The briefcase you were supposed to pick up included the disk in case she wanted to make small, last-minute changes."

"The police have that."

"Doesn't matter. You can work on the printout I have. It's not like Ret was planning any major rewrites. She wanted the book out pronto. . . . So the question is: How fast can you do the job?"

"How soon can I get the copy?"

"How soon can you get here?"

Rannie did a quick about-face and sprinted—well, walked at a brisk pace—to Ellen's apartment on Ninety-Fourth Street off Broadway. Less than half a mile, but that probably doubled her total exercise for the year. In Rannie's mind, sex was all the workout a human body needed. She was naturally thin: no matter how many peanut butter and jelly sandwiches she scarfed down, she remained a size 4. Nevertheless, it surprised her how winded she was by the time she reached Ellen's apartment.

Ellen greeted Rannie at the door dressed in running shorts and a sweat-soaked souvenir T-shirt from a Queens half marathon. She had just returned from her daily run. She was short and dark haired like Rannie, though some years younger and, since recent implants, far better endowed in what Rannie's mother always referred to as "the bazoom department."

"Here, it's all yours." She thrust a briefcase at Rannie, a twin of the one in Ret Sullivan's apartment, and slipped an elasticized bracelet with a key over Rannie's wrist.

"Gee, you act as if it might blow up any second."

"The way Ret died—way too scary for me." Ellen pulled off the sweaty tee. Even in a bazoom-flattening sports bra, she looked bodacious. "All I ask is that you delete my name from the acknowledgments page."

"Come on. The murder had nothing to do with the book. A guy's in custody already."

"Fine. Still do it, okay?" Then Ellen squeezed her eyes shut for a moment. "Oh, God. Poor Ret! I can't stop thinking about her! . . . I hope she made it to heaven."

"Heaven? Are you kidding?"

"Absolutely not. Ret was seriously Catholic. Believed in heaven, hell, the whole deal."

Rannie remembered the collection of crosses and the Madonna painting in the apartment.

"Right after the Mike Bellettra horror show, she considered taking vows, entering a convent where nobody would think twice about her face."

"Maybe that wasn't such a bad idea . . . she'd still be alive."

"Puh-leeze." Ellen waved a hand dismissively. "I told her, 'Ret, you would have lasted a day, tops. No TV? No blog? No phones?'" Ellen smiled ruefully and sighed. "I remember her saying how once this Charlotte Cummings book was out, all the morning news shows would want to have her on. She was considering it too. She thought wearing the ski mask would titillate viewers and boost sales."

Then Ellen glanced at her watch and turned businesslike again. "Look, I need to shower and get ready for a lunch date."

"Date! As in, 'with a guy'?"

"Yeah. An insignificant other. Believe me."

"Name? Stats?"

Ellen dodged the question. "Just somebody who takes my mind off Frank."

Frank was the son of a bitch who had unceremoniously dumped Ellen after a fraught two-year-long relationship.

Ellen patted the briefcase. "With all the publicity around the murder, S&S wants the book out yesterday. Nobody cares, Rannie, if the grammar is wrong in some places. Believe me, as long as Charlotte Cummings's name is spelled correctly, that'll be good enough."

After demonstrating how to unlock and lock the ingenious superslim briefcase, Ellen waited for the elevator to whisk away Rannie. At the last moment, before the elevator doors closed, Ellen uttered the words that were music—the "Hallelujah" chorus—to the ears of all freelancers: "Charge whatever you want."

Chapter 5

RANNIE TURNED THE KEY TO THE FRONT DOOR OF HER APART-
ment. Bursts of staccato gunshot pops and the boom of explo-
sions signaled Nate was playing a video game. What accounted
for him being up already? On weekends, any hour with an A.M.
after it counted as dawn patrol. When she walked past the den,
formerly known as Alice's bedroom, she put her head in to say hi.

Nate sat on the sofa in front of the TV with Olivia Werner on
his lap, their thumbs working away manically at separate video
controls.

"Didn't hear you come in, Ma." Nate's eyes remained glued to
the screen where one muscle-bound guy, riddled with gunshot
wounds, dripping blood, was attempting to behead another with
a chain saw.

"Hey, Ms. Bookman." Olivia took a nanosecond to look up and
offer an appealing off-kilter smile. The greeting evidently cost
her, because Nate was suddenly screaming, "Yesssss! You are so
dead, O!"

Rannie liked Olivia. For a rich girl who was also beautiful, she had a touching vulnerability. Her nails were badly bitten and she had a nervous way of clearing her throat before speaking. And while nervousness wasn't usually an endearing quality, somehow in Olivia's case it was.

In the kitchen, Rannie made herself a PB&J. Almost eighteen, Nate never confided in her, barely communicated at all, in fact. Oh, yes, for a few days following the rooftop attack, Nate would hug her for no reason and gaze at her in the loving, "I'm so glad you're my mommy" way he used to when he was a little boy. But just as Rannie had plummeted from her glad-to-be-alive high, so had Nate swiftly reverted to his characteristic avoidance/contempt mode. Still, Rannie could tell he was going through the throes of whatever was the current word for ceaseless longing, sweet obsession, aching lust, total bewitchment.

"Ma? You got a sec?"

Suddenly, Nate, all six feet, two inches of him, stood before her, shirtless and in cargo pants. He fiddled with one of the refrigerator magnets.

"So listen. Um . . . Is it okay if she stays?"

"Of course. I'll make brunch!" The notion of making pancakes, frying bacon, and putting out nice plates and cloth napkins was immensely cheering.

"Uh, I wasn't talking about now. . . . I meant tonight."

"Oh!"

"Otherwise, uh, she has to stay home alone and it kind of spooks her."

Olivia's home, Rannie knew, was a beautiful town house in the East Seventies.

In the next second, Olivia appeared, did that throat-clearing thing, and explained that her parents were in the country; Carlotta, the housekeeper, was off; and Olivia's grandmother was on a cruise.

"And I'm not speaking to either of my so-called best friends." Then she raised her eyes, amber and fringed with incredibly thick lashes. "It'll only be for one night. Carlotta's back tomorrow."

Rannie smiled and blinked repeatedly.

Ugh! In the damned-if-you-do, damned-if-you-don't category, this one was a doozy. Was saying yes moronically permissive? Was saying no hypocritical? After all, as a teenager Rannie had been 110 percent in favor of teenage sex. And she didn't even know for sure what Olivia and Nate had or hadn't done. Rannie wanted to blow a whistle and cry, "Time out!" Then she'd whisk Olivia aside to ask a subtle question or two, along the lines of, "Do you now or have you ever had an STD?," after which she'd grab Nate and blitz through "the joy of safe sex" lecture she'd delivered awhile back.

Instead, Rannie ended up waffling. "Why don't we see what your mom has to say about this? Okay?" she said, turning to Olivia, who provided a number that began with an 860, northern Connecticut area code.

Surprisingly, Carole Werner, a skinny fashionista with a year-round tan and a toothy smile, signed off on the sleepover right away. "Great. Now I don't have to rush back to the city. . . . Olivia and I need a break from each other. Lately, the further apart we are, the better we get along."

You're referring to distance, so it's farther *apart,* chided the picky grammar cop lodged in Rannie's brain. "Further" was for abstract mulling. But clearly Olivia's mother didn't need to think any *further.*

"I just won't tell her father she's staying over at a boy's."

Carole Werner's sole hesitation was over the location of the roof under which Olivia would be sleeping. "Wh-where exactly on the West Side do you live?" she asked with hesitancy. The correct answer, Rannie knew, would be one of the grand Central Park West palazzos—the Beresford or El Dorado. There was an audible gulp when Rannie supplied her address, a street with a triple-digit number off Broadway.

"Our building has a name," Rannie almost volunteered as proof of some residential cachet, although DOLORES COURT chiseled in stone above the entrance sounded so silly, like the title of a noir-ish Joan Crawford movie.

Half an hour later, Olivia and Nate were dressed and on their way to collect Olivia's belongings. So no time like the present to rack up some freelance billing. Rannie retrieved the brushed aluminum briefcase from her closet, eventually vanquished its lock, and removed the manuscript. Then armed with her weapon of choice, her faithful Col-Erase blue copyediting pencil, she settled down on the living room sofa, overjoyed at not being able to do the job electronically.

Copyediting was an unglamorous job in publishing. Acquiring editors on the prowl for future Pulitzers and National Book Awards dismissed Rannie and her stickler ilk as the Grammar Gestapo, nothing more than human spell-checkers.

Nevertheless, twenty years ago, fresh out of Yale and brand-new to New York City, she'd accepted an entry-level copyediting job with an eye toward moving into editorial. That never happened. However, over the years she'd come to take considerable pride in her career. Maybe nobody dreamed of copyediting the Great American Novel; still, the communication of thoughts in clean, clear sentences free of dangling participles and garbled syntax *was* important.

Then, too, there were all the wonderfully arcane marks and symbols of copyediting. Insertion carets, transposition squiggles, underlining for italics, triple underlining for capitalization. It was like knowing a secret code.

Portrait of a Lady was the innocuous title of the manuscript. The dedication was "To Sister Dorothy Cusack, whose strength has carried me through dark times." Okay, proof of what Ellen had told her earlier about Ret and Catholicism. And it made Rannie glad to know Ret found solace through religion.

The acknowledgments began with "I must express eternal gratitude to Ellen Donahoe, my editor par excellence." Dutifully, Rannie ran a pencil line ending with a deletion curl through the sentence. There were only two other "thankees." "For Audeo, who was my ears and without whom I never could have written this book." Here was the first boo-boo. While Rannie corrected the misspelling—changing "Audeo" to "Audio"—she remembered Tim's hunch about paid information. Was Ret keeping the person's identity secret so her snoop remained exclusively hers or was it for Audio's sake because snooping might prove dangerous? The final acknowledgment was "For Gery Antioch. I have come to appreciate how artful you are." The guy in custody was a Gerald, perhaps known as Gery. But his last name was Steele.

None of this mulling should be on S&S's dime, Rannie reminded herself, and sitting up a little straighter, blue pencil poised, she began Chapter One, which recounted the night in late 1945 when Charlotte's second husband, financier Silas Cummings, proposed.

Charlotte was divorced, with a daughter in college, and work-
ing at Vogue. *(Her column on society events, originally called*

"Doings," was rechristened "Cummings and Goings" after her marriage to Silas.) Charlotte's beauty was fading. Nevertheless for Silas, a boy from the Bronx whose last name had morphed from Cominsky to Cummings, Charlotte was New York Unattainable, a blond Wasp with a pedigree.

What Charlotte no longer had was money. Her first husband had managed to squander both his inheritance and hers.

Then enter Silas Cummings, richer than Croesus.

When he presented Charlotte with a ten-carat square-cut Tiffany diamond ring, she accepted it.

Rannie read on. The book was a breezy no-brainer, best enjoyed in bed with a box of bonbons or, at the very least, a bar of Hershey's finest.

When she next checked a clock, Rannie was pleased to see how many pages she'd copyedited. She rotated her shoulders to relieve the crick in her neck, then laid down her pencil. It probably was time to take a break. The ringing of her cell sealed the deal.

It was Tim. "Hold on a sec," she said, dutifully relocking the manuscript in its aluminum home before sliding the bracelet with the key back on.

"So Ret Sullivan was taking cheap shots at Charlotte Cummings," he said, not bothering to disguise the crow in his voice.

"How'd you find out?" Rannie yelped and then, remembering Ret's own copy of the manuscript had been taken by the police, supplied the answer herself. "I swear, Tim, the New York City cops are as gossipy as a bunch of teenage girls. Well, here's something I bet you don't know. My friend Ellen had a copy of the manuscript so guess who is copyediting it furiously?"

"Okay, good for you. Does this mean your life's on hold till the job's done? Or can we meet up in Riverside Park?"

"I'll be at the usual spot. But run fast. It's nippy out."

Huddled in a duffle coat and wool cap, Rannie sat finishing off another PB&J sandwich on one of the wooden benches by the community garden at Ninety-First Street. Now that it was November, neighborhood people were no longer patiently toiling inside the black iron fence that bordered the garden—a riot of daffodils and tulips in early spring, clusters of hydrangea, phlox, and daylilies in summer, followed by autumnal asters and mums.

The garden, the shape of which from an aerial view would look like a giant exclamation point, was Rannie's favorite place in the park, and while waiting for Tim to show up, she took pleasure in watching the parade of bicyclists, young families with strollers, and dogs playing off leash.

Rannie waved at the small dot of a figure that grew steadily larger as it ran toward her on the promenade. She could spot Tim just from the movement of his body, the easy rhythm of legs pounding up and down, the abbreviated sway of arms held close to his sides. She felt a swell of happiness—or at least something close to that—just seeing him. He was so graceful in a purely masculine, unstudied way.

Once he reached the far end of the flower garden, he slowed to a trot, removed a Red Sox baseball cap, and shook drops of sweat from his forehead. He wasn't tall—five nine tops—and his nose and chin were cut a little too sharply. But the prematurely silver hair, almost punk in its spikiness, and the intense brown of his eyes, hidden now behind a pair of wire-rimmed sunglasses, added up to something better than classically handsome. And then there was his smile, one front tooth just overlapping the other. He was not a man with a sunny disposition, but when he smiled, as he was now—an all-out grin, in fact—it melted her every time.

Tim sat on the bench, careful to stay a couple of feet from Rannie. "I'm drenched."

"I don't mind," she said and moved closer.

"You got anything to drink?"

Rannie produced a Diet Lemon Snapple, which Tim began to swig. She watched his breathing go from ragged to slow and even, and while he finished off the Snapple Rannie filled him in on how she came to possess a copy of Ret's manuscript. "Ellen said to charge whatever I want."

Tim tossed the empty Snapple bottle, *swish,* into a garbage can on the other side of Rannie. Then he stood. "Listen. This boy needs a shower." He cast a questioning look over the top of his sunglasses. "*Your place?*" he was asking.

"Sorry. Nate'll be home soon, if he's not already." Rannie's eyes suddenly widened. "Oh, my God! I forgot to tell you!"

But Tim's only response to the news of Rannie's houseguest was "What I wouldn't have given for a mom like you. So? Want to come home with me, little girl?" Tim rubbed his hands together lasciviously and waggled his eyebrows, so that his sunglasses bobbed up and down comically.

"Jerk," she said with affection and followed him up the hill that led out of Riverside Park.

She made Tim spring for a cab to the brownstone he owned on Eighty-First Street off Columbus, purchased for a song way back when he first moved to New York from Massachusetts. He and Chris lived on two floors directly above the bar and grill, with tenants in four apartments providing income for the part of the Chapel School tuition that scholarship money didn't cover.

Her friend Joan, a Chapel School mom and currently acting head, had remarked, only half in jest, "Of all the unmarried fathers at Chaps—guys who could buy up a small third world country if they felt like playing dictator—you find a guy with credit card debt and no secondary residence."

Very true but who could possibly have a cuter butt than Tim? she asked herself while he opened the door to what he had promised in the cab would be a kid-free apartment. Rannie headed immediately for Tim's bedroom. Although the apartment hadn't come fully furnished, it had the anonymous look of one—just a collection of beige-y bland furniture with no real feel of home; right now, however, decor was not on her mind. Even before Tim had a chance to turn on the shower, Rannie was out of her coat, jeans, and turtleneck and in his bed.

"I shouldn't be doing this," she said, envisioning the hefty manuscript waiting at home.

"I bet you've been saying that since you were sixteen." Then he stripped off his running clothes. A second later, she heard the thrum of water and Tim singing, "You're Sixteen, You're Beautiful and You're Mine."

"Very funny. I should be home working, so make it snappy." Nooners were not something financially strapped freelancers should be indulging in.

"Come on in," he called out. "We can get a head start."

So Rannie did.

As soon as she pulled the glass shower door shut, Tim cupped her face in both hands and kissed her. She wrapped her arms around his neck. It was a wonderful kiss, one that lasted to the point where Rannie was no longer aware of the water rushing down on them. "You taste delicious," he murmured after pulling away from her embrace. He stood a foot away staring at her.

"What?" She was breathing hard.

"I don't think I'll ever get tired of looking at you."

How many men would say that to a forty-three-year-old woman?

She threw her arms around him again, kissed him, and then began to gently soap his back, his chest, slowly moving down the line of hair that whorled around his navel and then led farther down to his cock. She could feel herself starting to throb. "Maybe we should—" She was going to say "get in bed," but Tim was already lifting her up. As he pressed her against the tile wall, her legs encircling his waist, he entered her.

"Still in a rush?"

Rannie didn't answer. Her mind snapped off. She gave in to her body, to the rhythm of his body inside hers, to pure sensation. That terrible, wonderful, demanding pressure, unlike no other, was building inside her rapidly; she clutched Tim tighter so that each thrust reached the very core of her. She started to come a second before he did and only when she found herself standing again, wobbly-legged, orgasm over, water streaming down and plastering her hair all over her face, did she realize they were still in the shower stall.

After they dried off, Rannie nixed snuggling in bed. She dressed quickly, and the guilt trip—put on hold for the duration of the shower—resumed. Well, she told herself, there would be no further distractions the entire afternoon; she'd remain closeted in her room working.

Tim was sitting on his bed, almost fully dressed himself, lacing up sneakers. Well-mannered, former parochial schoolboy that he was, he always insisted on escorting Rannie to a cab.

"Just let me check to see if Charlie made it in," he said once they were downstairs, and he ducked into the bar. "Only'll take a sec." Charlie, one of the many retired cops Tim employed, was someone known for partying too hard on Saturday nights.

"Hey, boss," Charlie called, a cell phone cradled in his neck as he maneuvered around a table setting out silverware. "Gotta go," he told whoever was at the other end of the line. Snapping shut his cell, he gave Rannie a wink then shook his head ruefully. "This is when I really miss the force. You hear what happened in the Thirty-Eighth? Those bozos botched a homicide case."

"The Thirty-Eighth? Where's that?" Rannie asked.

"Upper East Side."

For some reason, the hairs on Rannie's arms began to tingle. "Does this have anything to do with Ret Sullivan?" Rannie inquired.

Charlie nodded. "The guy they picked up? Not him."

"What?" Rannie half croaked, half screeched.

Charlie continued. "The cops pulled the phone log; a call came in to Ret Sullivan yesterday at 3:50. She was alive then; they got in touch with the person she spoke to."

That had to be Ellen, Rannie realized. Ellen had called Ret Sullivan about Rannie coming to pick up the manuscript.

"And the guy," Charlie continued, "he was already with his next customer by then—surveillance cams in the lobby of a high-rise on East Sixty-Seventh Street back him up."

So much for Tim's theory of accidental murder. This was

murder murder. "Are there any leads? Any tips from the guy who was in custody? Maybe Ret Sullivan said something to him? Maybe—"

Tim cut her off. "Come on, Rannie. Don't start grilling Charlie. *Please.*" And before she knew it, he was steering her by the elbow—a little too forcefully—out of the bar. Rannie managed a furtive backward glance at Charlie, who had both hands spread, one still clutching a bunch of forks, in a classic "Sorry, I got nothing" pose.

Tim whistled for a cab, which swerved suddenly from the middle lane on Columbus and pulled to the curb.

"Stay away from this murder, okay? It's *not* your business, Rannie."

"Who said it was? I simply asked a few questions."

But Tim was already off on a minirant. "Homicide is no game. It's not like solving some fucking crossword. Didn't nearly getting killed teach you *anything?*"

"You are way overreacting!"

"Am I? You get night terrors. You carry Mace wherever you go."

Actually, no. True, she had bought a slim metallic blue wand of Mace online. It pleased her that it looked somewhat like a shiny Col-Erase blue pencil. But she never remembered to carry the Mace nor could she figure out how to activate the nozzle.

"You're not Nancy Drew. You're a copy editor. Stick to that," Tim ranted on. She could practically hear the next words forming in his mouth—*Do I make myself clear?*—but before he could utter them, she jumped in the cab.

"Don't talk to me that way. I'm not a child," Rannie said hotly before slamming the door. She stared straight ahead at the Plexi-glas partition while supplying her address for the driver.

The cab took off. She swiveled around. From the rear window, she saw Tim reopening his front door. His back was to her so Rannie did the only sensible, adult thing she could think of.

She stuck out her tongue at him.

Chapter 6

WAS HER CLOCK RIGHT? COULD IT REALLY BE PAST FOUR? SEEMED so, the late-afternoon hour corroborated by the lengthening shadows outside her window, shadows from bare treetop branches that strafed the tenement buildings across the street. Three solid hours of work—too bad Tim hadn't witnessed her discipline and diligence! The whole afternoon she'd managed to erase Ret's murder from her mind and concentrate on the biography of Charlotte Cummings.

Copyediting required a particular kind of intense focus; once her Col-Erase blue pencil was in hand, it was as if she had on mental blinders and nothing existed except the printed page before her eyes. Her cell had been turned off. When she took a break and checked messages, there were three from Ellen. The first: "Rannie? Have you heard? The cops had the wrong guy! They were here at my apartment. I was the last person she spoke to!"

The second: "Rannie, what if Ret was murdered because of something in the book?"

The third: "Oh my God, Rannie, maybe *I* know something I shouldn't, only I don't even know what it is! I'm terrified. What if the killer knows I'm her editor?"

The near hysteria in these last words was practically audible, so Rannie called Ellen.

"Oh, thank God!" Ellen said as soon as she heard Rannie's voice. "I was beginning to worry."

"What? That I was victim number two? Seriously?"

"Where were you anyway?" Ellen sounded annoyed and also as if her tongue were swollen. She was lisping a little.

"Right here. Working on the book. For *you*," Rannie said with emphasis. "Rest assured you no longer are cited in the acknowledgments. Who are Audio and Gery Antioch?"

"No clue. But Ret must have had help with the book. She couldn't exactly go out and do interviews."

"Look, Ellen, the book can't have anything to do with Ret's murder. It doesn't make sense; the killer wouldn't have waited for her to finish writing it."

"Hold on a sec, will you?" When Ellen returned to the phone, she was no longer lisping. "Just needed water for the Ativan. And, okay, yeah, I see your point."

"Ret Sullivan trashed a lot of people. The woman had enemies. That's why Mike Bellettra's wearing an orange jumpsuit. Maybe he arranged a hit from prison."

"No. I've been watching TV all afternoon. He's not a suspect. He issued a statement from jail. He's angry she's dead. He, quote, 'didn't want her misery to end.'"

"Maybe it's somebody from one of Ret's other books. People can nurse grievances forever." Yet even as those words came out of her mouth, Rannie was already discounting this line of reasoning.

Ellen wasn't buying it either. "Don't tell me you think Caroline Kennedy was avenging her mother? Or Prince Charles was still mad about being called a royal twat?"

"Money is still considered a perfectly good motive for murder, right? Maybe somebody in her family didn't want to wait for an inheritance."

"She had no family. Last week she said she'd miss our daily calls now that the book was finished. Like I was her best friend."

"That's pathetic. Unless of course *you* turn out to be a newly minted heiress."

"Fat chance. In the next breath, Ret swore if I said one negative word about her to the press, I'd never work in publishing again. And she meant it." Ellen sighed. "Who knows? Maybe poor Ret was just unlucky and some neighborhood sex fiend randomly broke into her apartment."

This notion seemed to cheer Ellen, so Rannie saw no reason to mention that Ret's apartment had been locked securely. Either Rannie, the Ativan, or both seemed to be having a calming effect on her. "You know who the police asked if I knew—Larry Katz. He used to be an editor at S&S . . . did you and he overlap?"

"Yes, we overlapped." Larry Katz was someone whom her dad would have called "a skirt chaser." He also had been the first man Rannie had slept with after her husband bolted. Larry was more than ten years older than Rannie and chronically depressed in a Woody Allen–ish way, which for Rannie, no poster girl for mental health back then, had the oddly sanguine effect of buoying her spirits. Often she found herself trying to cheer up Larry. All in all, he'd been just what the doctor ordered—sardonic, flattering, attentive for the run of the romance. It ended amicably when he left

Simon & Schuster for a small, independent West Coast publishing house.

"God, what's he up to?" Rannie asked. At S&S, his specialty had been New Age books—feng shui, crystals, all things woo woo—not because of any personal belief, far from it, but because the books sold like crazy and, according to Larry, all the authors were lonely women desperate for sex. "Why would the cops ask about him?"

"No idea. He was in California for a long time but back in the city now. He's at Dusk."

Dusk Books was a fourth-tier publishing house. "Dusk published the bio of Ret that's out."

"Larry's executive editor there."

"For real?" The Larry who Rannie had known was smart but terminally lazy.

"Funny, right? At S&S, whenever I'd go into his office, he'd always be doing a crossword or playing Scrabble on the computer."

Ellen's assessment was right on the money, and something in Ellen's voice—a mix of amusement and exasperation—made Rannie wonder whether Ellen and Larry had also "overlapped."

"Thank God for Ativan. I feel better now. Sorry for wigging out before . . . how are you doing with the manuscript?"

"Chugging right along. And I plan to put in many more hours tonight. So tell me, when do I get to the bitchy parts? Was Charlotte Cummings doing lap dances at her one-hundredth birthday party? Because so far she comes across as genuinely nice, if not the brightest gem in the jewel box."

"There are no bombshells. It's clear Ret admired her. Silas

takes a few hits. The book's gossipy but more in a Liz Smith than a Kitty Kelley–ish way," Ellen replied. "It's a fun read, isn't it?"

"Then all the more reason to believe this book has nothing whatsoever to do with Ret's murder," Rannie said. And on that reassuring note, the conversation ended.

When the phone rang again almost instantly, Rannie expected Ellen with some postscript. Instead it was Nate. Olivia couldn't find her keys. They were locked out of the Werners' town house. "So we still haven't picked up her shit. Some friend of her mom's has spare keys. We're trying to find her."

The plan for key retrieval was all very Byzantine. Typical teenage flakiness. "We're just hanging now." The two of them were going to grab a burger and be back with Olivia's "shit" around dinnertime.

Rannie strolled back into the living room and dutifully plowed through another chapter of the manuscript. But she found her mind wandering. Rannie leaned back on the sofa and kneaded her neck. Why *had* Ret Sullivan chosen to write about Charlotte Cummings? she wondered. All Rannie could come up with was vicarious pleasure. Perhaps in chronicling such a long, gilded, and mostly happy life, Ret—housebound and lonely—felt almost as if she were experiencing the events herself. And any envy might have been tempered by the fact that at the point in time Ret Sullivan began writing the book, 102-year-old Charlotte was in essentially the same boat Ret was. A shut-in waiting to die.

Of course, dying peacefully in bed, as Charlotte Cummings undoubtedly would do in the not-too-distant future, was a far cry from being trussed to a bed and strangled. And what was the hair thing about? It was not mentioned in the newspapers; both Rannie and the handyman had been told—emphatically told—not to share any information, especially that detail. There was something almost sacrificial, ritualistic—at least to Rannie's mind—about the murder. Also debasing and sadistic. Rannie found herself hoping Ret had died quickly, before being tied up. Forensics could establish the sequence of events—if Ret were still alive when tied to the bed, she would have struggled; most likely there would be bruise marks or cuts on her wrists. If already dead, Ret couldn't have put up a fight. But if that were the case, why would the killer have bothered with the kinky tableau? To make it appear a sex game gone wrong? To make it *look* like a more sadistic crime? All so puzzling... and, Rannie had to confess, morbidly intriguing. Rannie wished there was a way to get Tim's take on the crime. What did his gut tell him? But calling him for that reason would anger him ... and anyway why hadn't *he* called? He knew she was ticked at him, so wasn't a make-nice gesture in order?

The siren song of sleuthing was calling. There was no sense denying it—although right away Rannie could hear her mother's voice. "Sleuthing? Please! Concentrate on finding yourself a real job. You're a middle-aged woman, Rannie, not some *fekokte* girl detective."

As the youngest of the three Bookman girls, Rannie had been her father's darling. From him, a lawyer felled by a massive heart attack at fifty-two, came her love of books, respect for language, and addiction to peanut butter and jelly. As the least obedient of the daughters, Rannie was a puzzlement to her mother, Harriet, a practical-minded woman who bought at Loehmann's, had her hair "done" once a week, always carried a plastic rain bonnet and breath mints in her purse, and now returned from every far-flung jaunt with widow friends firm in the belief that there was no better place on earth to live than Shaker Heights, Ohio. She and her mother simply didn't get each other.

These days for uncritical love Rannie turned to her former mother-in-law. Their relationship had not only outlasted Rannie's marriage but also deepened after the divorce. Rannie picked up the phone and dialed, then waited to hear the familiar cultured voice. If Daisy Buchanan's voice sounded like money, Mary Lorimer's sounded like old money.

"Rannie, dear! My friend, Mrs. Satterthwaite, is here and we were just talking about you. You remember her, don't you? Daisy Satterthwaite?"

Rannie had met Daisy Satterthwaite umpteen times, a Daisy who bore no resemblance to Fitzgerald's glamour girl. But perhaps Mary thought Rannie's memory was as faulty as the memory of her doddery dowager friends.

"We're having tea," Mary continued, which Rannie suspected did not feature buttered scones and Earl Grey. "Tea" was probably "T" as in "Tanqueray." "We're about to go for a little walk to visit an old, old friend of Daisy's."

"Mary, it's dark out." In broad daylight and stone sober, Mary was tentative navigating city streets yet still unwilling to use her cane. "Please take a cab."

Mary made a scoffing noise. "It's only a few blocks away. We need the exercise." In the background Rannie could hear Daisy say, "Cheers to that!"

Uh-oh. The blind drunk leading the . . . It was most unusual for Mary to venture out on a Sunday evening and miss *60 Minutes*.

"Can't you wait to visit Daisy's friend? It's dark out. Why not go tomorrow?"

"Daisy is leaving for Fisher Island tomorrow. To be frank, dear, she's worried if she doesn't pay a visit this evening, she may not have another chance."

"Her friend is dying? I'm so sorry."

"Yes. The poor thing has been a vegetable for a quite a while, and now suddenly she's taken a turn for the worse. Of course, she won't even know we're there. She's over a hundred."

Say what? Suddenly Rannie felt prickly all over. Mary went on about how lovely the woman had been to Daisy at a particularly trying time in Daisy's life and how Daisy was "absolutely religious" about visiting. But Rannie's brain was fixated on "over a hundred."

"Is Charlotte Cummings Daisy's friend?"

"Why, yes. Do you know her?" Mary never seemed to grasp that many people in her circle were familiar names to the general public.

"I know of her." Were Rannie's next words altruistic? No. But there were times when selfish gain and a good deed neatly dovetailed. "Look, I'm just sitting here. Nate won't be home for hours. I'll come by and visit and then walk you both over."

"I'd love to see you! What a darling you are!"

"No, I'm really not. Do you think I'll get a peek at the house?"

"Oh, it's something to see. Just mammoth," said Mary who occupied, *toute seule,* ten vast rooms on Park Avenue. "So we'll expect you in a little while . . . and dear—" Mary's voice lowered to a confidential whisper. "I didn't mention anything about your mishap to Daisy."

Mishap? Then it hit her. The dead body thing—*that* mishap.

Right as they hung up, Rannie heard Mary reassuring Daisy that "Yes, of course there's time to freshen your glass."

Chapter 7

RANNIE MADE HERSELF PRESENTABLE, SWITCHING FROM JEANS to a pair of tweed trousers and pulling a brown wool turtleneck over the ratty tee she'd been wearing. In her handbag were a few blue pencils and the last of her nifty, name-engraved S&S notepads. Scribbling "I went to Grandma's," Rannie tore off the top sheet and left it on the front hall table where chances were fifty-fifty that Nate might spot it and less than zero that her whereabouts were of even mild interest to him.

Her faux Barbour jacket at the ready, Rannie constructed another PB&J sandwich, which she scarfed down en route to Mary's.

The doorman at the limestone fortress on Eighty-Third and Park Avenue where Mary Lorimer had resided for the past fifty years picked up the receiver on the brass intercom console. His ringing announcement that "Ms. Bookman" was on her way up made Rannie straighten her shoulders and rise to her full five feet, two inches as she proceeded toward the elevator.

Mary was at the door of her apartment to greet her. Stately, slender, and silver haired, Mary called to mind a tall Tiffany sterling candlestick, especially so this evening, outfitted as she was in pearl gray slacks and a silk blouse of the same color that tied at the neck in a bow. Rannie kissed her mother-in-law. There was always a lovely cloud of scent, warm and spicy—with a hint of cloves—hovering about Mary, yet she wore no perfume. Rannie's kids still called it the "grandma smell."

Mary's friend Daisy Satterthwaite, as stocky as Mary was slim, was on the phone, enveloped in one of the blue-striped armchairs in the smaller and less formal of the apartment's two dens. She was holding a gold shrimp earring in one hand along with a highball.

"Some wine?" Mary asked Rannie.

Daisy turned and scowled. "Sorry, Barbara. Say that again. I couldn't hear." A pause. "We'll pop over and only stay a minute. Yes, yes. It'll be lovely to see you too, Barbara."

"It's all too *ghastly*," Daisy said a moment later while clipping her earring back on. Then she drained her highball and lit a cigarette. "I love Charlotte to pieces. She was better to me than my own mother. But, *really*, she ought to die already. Everybody else does. Why won't she?"

Mary, ever the solicitous hostess, replenished the highball that Daisy was jiggling impatiently, then poured white wine for Rannie—a babyish drink to these hollow-legged ladies, the alcoholic equivalent of training wheels.

As a tray of classic Wasp canapes—Triscuits with WisPride—made the rounds, Daisy reported that what had initially appeared to be "really and truly the end" was yet another false alarm. A few minutes ago, Charlotte Cummings's fluttering 102-year-old heart had once again returned to a steady rhythm.

"Charlotte's like the boy who cried wolf!" Daisy declared with considerable annoyance. "I almost said so to Barbara."

"Barbara is Charlotte's granddaughter," Mary informed Rannie. "A very capable gal, owns a darling store on Madison called Bibilots. Whenever I need a gift, I go there. And she is so devoted to Charlotte. She has a hairdresser and manicurist come every week."

Daisy turned her jowly face to Rannie. "If you ask me, it's ghoulish. Dressing up Charlotte as if she were some giant-sized doll."

On the face of it, Rannie tended to agree and, in addition, gave props to Daisy for her correct use of the subjunctive "were."

Daisy crushed out her cigarette in an overflowing crystal ashtray and stood so that she could dust Triscuit bristles and ashes off her slacks and blouse, which was Smurf blue and misbuttoned.

"Well, we'd better be going. Finish your drink, Rannie," Daisy ordered, as if scolding a child dawdling over dinner. She reached for her purse and smeared on more lipstick, then finding no comb patted her coarse blond coiffure into place.

In the front hall, Rannie helped the ladies into their coats—Daisy's an Autumn Haze mink circa 1955 with a rip in the lining. Whereas Mary had a soft, cool, soothing elegance, Daisy, even richer and with a far grander pedigree, fell just short of slattern, a genetic trait that Rannie liked to picture running back over generations all the way to Goody So-and-So stepping off the *Mayflower* in a rumpled mobcap and stained apron.

Once outside on Park Avenue, the ladies linked arms with Rannie and began a slow march southward. Practically every ten steps either Daisy or Mary waved a fluttering kid-gloved hand at other old people doddering by, everyone interconnected through family, marriage, or club membership.

On Eighty-First Street they made a right turn and headed in the direction of Fifth Avenue, Mary nattering on about Charlotte's granddaughter. "Barbara never had children, such a shame." A freak accident in Vail had left Barbara a widow. "I don't think her husband was even forty. He skied straight into a tree, smashed his head wide open, just like that son of Ethel Kennedy's."

The side street was poorly lit. Daisy lost her balance and nearly fell. "Oh Lord, that's the second time today," she said, gripping onto Rannie. "I really should use a cane." Then she sighed. "You never think you'll get old. Sometimes I look in the mirror and wonder who's that staring at me?" Daisy peered across at Mary. "Mims, I realized the other day that I've known Charlotte seventy-five years. Isn't that astounding?"

Quick mental math told Rannie that Daisy, though over eighty, was still a generation younger than Charlotte Cummings. "Was Charlotte a friend of your mother's?" Rannie inquired.

"No. I was great friends with Charlotte's daughter, Madeline. We met the first day of kindergarten at Spence."

"Poor Madeline," Mary said. "Melanoma. They found a tiny mole, no bigger than a freckle. Three months later we were all at Saint Thomas's for the funeral."

It never ceased to amaze Rannie: when it came to cause of death, her mother-in-law had astounding recall, able to recite chapter and verse what had done in even the most casual of departed acquaintances.

"I was bereft, but Madeline's death just about killed Charlotte," Daisy said. "That's when we—Charlotte and I—became close. It was as if she adopted me." They had reached the corner of Eighty-First and Madison Avenue just as the light turned red.

"And then about a year later Charlotte saved my life! I'm not exaggerating. Charlotte Cummings . . . saved . . . my . . . life!" Daisy uttered each word separately for added emphasis. "I was very sick."

"Throat cancer," Mary elaborated as they crossed the street. "Stage three. Daisy had had an *agonizing* sore throat for months but refused to do anything about it."

"I couldn't bear hearing a doctor tell me that I had cancer. When I finally did go to a specialist, he gave me a year, two at most, and that was only *if* my whole pharynx was removed. Charlotte was with me when I got the news. We went straight from the doctor's office to the Carlyle, and as painful as it was for me to swallow, we did not leave that bar until I'd finished three martinis." Daisy relayed the last fact as if it were an especially heroic achievement, her refusal to let pain interfere with her intake of vermouth and gin.

"The very next morning Charlotte appeared at my apartment with a large box from Bergdorf Goodman. I thought, 'Oh Lord, it's something depressing, a bed jacket for the hospital.' But it was a painting. A painting of St. Godelieve—she's the patron saint of sore throats. It was from Silas's art collection. The painting is five hundred years old. Charlotte insisted I keep it because I needed a miracle.

"So I hung Godelieve in my bedroom—she's a creepy, little pasty-faced thing, yet I wouldn't part with her for the world. I started praying to her every night. And right away I started feeling better. When I went for a follow-up MRI two weeks later, the tumor had shrunk by half. And a month later it was gone. Vanished. Absolutely no trace of it. I have been cancer free ever since."

"The doctors at Sloan-Kettering were baffled, absolutely stupefied!" Mary confirmed.

"So-so you consider this a-a miracle?" Rannie stammered.

"What else would you call it?" Daisy asked querulously.

"I don't know." Miracles were so un-Jewish. The only miracle ever discussed at Anshe Chesed Fairmount Temple Sunday school in Cleveland was the one connected to the story of Hanukkah in celebration of the tiny amount of oil in the temple lamp that kept on burning for eight nights. As a child, Rannie had always found the story a little disappointing. On a miracle scale, it barely rated a two and was nothing next to walking on water or raising the dead.

"And you still smoke?" Rannie said in wonderment.

"Why on earth not! Saint Godelieve is protecting me. I'm cancer free. She's also the patron saint of bad marriages. But I got her too late to help out there. After I'm back from Florida, you must come over to see her, Rannie."

Rannie was nodding and saying that, yes, she'd like to when Mary pointed out that they'd just walked right past the entrance to Charlotte Cummings's Fifth Avenue mansion. So Rannie maneuvered the ladies into an about-face.

Two weeks ago she'd accompanied Tim on a walking tour of Upper Fifth Avenue mansions. The guide had paraded them past the former residences of Andrew Carnegie, Henry Frick, and other robber barons, which were all museums or schools now. Only one remained a private home, the Palladian-style villa where Charlotte Cummings currently resided.

Now, bathing in the glow of street-level spotlights trained on its pale stone façade, the building had a ghostly beauty: to Rannie it truly seemed like an apparition from a bygone era. She wished Tim could be here until she remembered she was annoyed at him, so she revised her wish—if only he could see her waltzing into a Manhattan mansion, an honest-to-goodness mansion with no denigrating "Mc" prefix.

The waltzing had to wait until Daisy remembered the entry code on the security panel by the door; they listened for the answering you-got-it-right buzz and gained entrance.

Rannie blinked. She found herself inside a rotunda all in marble, yet not one square inch was in classic Carrara white: the different marbles made for a riotous eyeful of color—the intricate geometric floor and the circle of gilt-topped pilasters and columns were all in sumptuous shades of apricot, rose, rust, ocher, and olive green.

"Daisy! You're a love to come."

A tall blonde who could have been on either side of fifty had materialized and strode toward them, arms outstretched. She was dressed simply but chicly in black velvet slacks, a black cashmere V-neck, chunky gold jewelry, and—in lieu of a belt—a hot pink silk scarf jauntily knotted around her waist. On her feet were black velvet Belgian loafers. She exuded a high-energy confidence that brought to mind legions of lean girl jocks from Rannie's class at Yale, the ones who wore gold signet rings from boarding schools on their pinkie fingers and whose natural habitat was a hockey field. Even now, twenty-odd years later, the type still intimidated and intrigued Rannie.

"And Mary. May-ree. It's been ages!" The woman spoke in a

loud ringing tone, although as soon as Rannie introduced herself she realized that all the marble was amplifying sound, sending every word reverberating off the walls.

"Rannie Bookman?" the granddaughter asked. Her broad smile had vanished, replaced by an expression that wavered from "Do I know you?" to "What are you doing here?"

"The ladies insisted on walking over from Mary's, so I served as escort," Rannie explained quickly and nervously. "I used to be married to Mary's son, Peter."

The smile returned, although its wattage was lower. Rannie took no offense. Charlotte's granddaughter had every right to seem perturbed by the intrusion of a total stranger. "I'll be leaving now."

"Oh, no, don't. Stay a bit. I'm Barbara Gaines. But call me Bibi," she instructed. "Everybody does except Grammy and Daisy."

"Then Bibi it is," Rannie obliged.

After disposing of everyone's coats, she motioned for Daisy and Mary to come along and wrapping an arm around Rannie, almost conspiratorially, as if they were old chums, said, "Grammy's just waking up from a little snooze. Lord! She gave us a scare before." Bibi patted her heart with her free hand and, yes, she had classic boarding-school fingernails, unpolished yet baby pink with perfect white half-moons.

A small elevator tucked behind the marble stairway in the rotunda disgorged them on the second-floor landing. For Rannie it was an otherworldly sensation to walk through rooms she'd been reading about not even an hour earlier—the library and its Tiffany glass ceiling, the music room with a harpsichord that Mozart had played on. In a gargantuan salon whose walls were lined in bottle-green velvet, Rannie caught a fleeting glimpse of a world-famous altarpiece depicting the Crucifixion. It was by a fifteenth-century Flemish artist known as the Master of the Agony.

"I wrote a paper on that painting for an art history course in college," Rannie told Bibi.

"Really! I'll show it to you later. Personally I find it sickening."

Rannie smiled and wondered what would be her Yale professor's reaction to this blunt critique. An entire lecture had been devoted to the "brutal, frenzied genius" of the crucifixion scene.

"Here we are—Grammy's suite," Bibi announced, opening a door into a sitting room with feminine furniture à la Marie Antoinette, everything in pale tones of blue and yellow water-marked silk.

"I'll duck in and see if Grammy's ready for visitors. The nurse was just getting her in her evening gown."

"Evening gown!" Daisy huffed under her breath. "I ask you!"

Morbid as it might be, Rannie was yearning for a face-to-face with the real, just-barely-alive Charlotte Cummings. A moment later, after a stout woman in full Nurse Ratched regalia exited the bedroom, Rannie found out.

In the center of a canopy bed worthy of Sleeping Beauty lay a tiny form, eyes closed. A faint, soggy-diaper smell lingered in the room that mammoth arrangements of yellow roses couldn't mask entirely.

"Grammy, you have visitors," Bibi murmured softly, bending over the bed.

Rannie was mesmerized.

Oxygen tubes were affixed to tiny nostrils. And evidently a

heart was still beating under the gauzy layer of yellow chiffon; otherwise there was no sign of life. Not even a tic of an eyelid.

"Yellow is Grammy's signature color," Bibi said as if an explanation was in order.

Drenched in diamonds, dazzling canary-yellow ones, Charlotte was certainly all dolled up, as if ready for a night on the town. Yet, Rannie thought, if this frail, humanlike object was chauffeured anywhere, the most fitting destination would be Madame Tussauds in Times Square.

Bibi motioned to a loveseat, on which Daisy and Mary arranged themselves, frozen smiles on their faces.

"Daisy is here, Grammy. And Mary Lorimer. And Mary's daughter-in-law. You've never met her. But you remember Mary, don't you?"

Did Bibi actually expect her grandmother to reply? Like Daisy, Rannie was put off by the creepy charade and hard pressed to imagine the purpose of it.

"Why don't we let Daisy and Mary spend a little time alone with Grammy. Come with me. Would you like to see the altarpiece?"

"Absolutely!" Rannie replied far too loudly in her eagerness to escape the confines of this weirdo boudoir, and then, because it seemed rude not to, she waggled tentative fingers, murmuring "Bye" to the wizened little odalisque in bed.

"I'm on an early flight to Florida. We can't stay long, Barbara," Daisy trumpeted an imperious warning as Rannie was led past the sitting room where the nurse was stationed with a book of KenKen puzzles.

"I'm so grateful to Daisy. I know she dreads coming," Bibi said in a confidential tone as she and Rannie walked down the hall-way. "When Grammy first began to fail, all her friends would drop by. Then, of course, as time passed, far less of them."

Rannie held her tongue while the grammar cop chided, *No, no, no. "Less" is an adverb, not an adjective. Far fewer friends visited, and they came less often.*

"I know it's wretched for Daisy seeing Grammy the way she is now." Then Bibi smiled ruefully. "You should have seen her in her prime. . . . And by prime, I mean late eighties. She was still going to opening-night *everything*."

Rannie nodded in reply but again found herself wondering if the bling and designer duds truly made it easier for Bibi to cope with her grandmother's snail's-pace march to the grave?

"Here we are," Bibi said shortly and with a flourish of her hand motioned Rannie into the green velvet expanses of the salon where the Master of the Agony altarpiece took pride of place. "Supposedly the artist went mad, completely bonkers while painting it, and hung himself before the paint was even dry."

Only half listening, Rannie approached the three hinged panels that ran at least twelve feet across the wall facing them. Until this moment, Rannie had only seen it miniaturized in the pages of art history books. In reality, all the main figures—Christ on the Cross, the Virgin Mother, John the Baptist in animal pelts, a frizzy-haired Mary Magdalene—were larger-than-life, NBA-size giants, arranged in a horrifying and yet mesmerizing death-scene tableau.

"When I was a little girl, I never came in here. The painting scared me silly."

Rannie could understand why. She was staring at the cruci-fixion scene now. This was no patiently suffering Christ biding his time on the cross, stoic in the knowledge that soon the bad stuff would be over and he'd be on his way to heaven. Here was a naked, earthly man being tortured to death.

"Those are the donors." Bibi was pointing at a man and woman depicted on the narrower side panels. "Jan and Berthe Meister. He was a jeweler from Bruges. She was his second wife."

"You seem to know a lot about the painting."

"Only because so many curators and art historians ask to come see it. For years I've had to listen to them going into absolute fits of rapture over it. Funny, but the more I look at Jan Meister, the more I see how much he looks like Silas. I wonder if Silas noticed that too."

Bibi told Rannie that Jan Meister had commissioned the altarpiece to prove what a good Catholic he was. "There were rumors he was Jewish, and you can understand why. Just look at his nose." Then Bibi touched her own, straight and thin, a plastic surgeon's dream.

Rannie felt herself stiffen. Was it an offhand remark? Or anti-Semitic? Or offhand *and* anti-Semitic? Even after all these years among Wasps, even being married to one for eleven years, Rannie was still never sure when she was being hypersensitive versus picking up on subtle, ingrained prejudice. She was, after all, her father's child. Besides owning a good-size schnoz himself, he was a man who always had his radar out, scanning for any and all possible slights to his people. In a show of loyalty, Rannie decided to dispel, right here and now, any misconceptions Bibi might harbor as to Rannie's own forebears.

"You know, he actually bears a resemblance to *my* dad." Rannie paused, adding, "Irving Bookman."

Not even the slightest "oops" flinch crossed Bibi's face, which made Rannie decide she had been in defensive-Jew mode.

"As soon as Grammy dies, the altarpiece gets packed up and carted over to the Met. Along with all the paintings of saints in here." Bibi waved an arm around the room. "They'll all be exhibited in a special gallery. But I'll let you in on a little secret," she said, again speaking with a just *entre nous* intimacy. "The altarpiece is the only thing the museum wants. They could care less about the rest of the paintings. In fact, no one would mind if they fell off the back of the truck."

"Really?" From Ret's manuscript, Rannie had learned that the other paintings, all from the 1400s and 1500s, were gruesome depictions of martyred saints. Still, they must have considerable value. "May I take a look?"

"Be my guest. I hope you have a strong stomach." Bibi crooked her arm through Rannie's and walked her around the room. On one side of a mammoth fireplace, big enough to roast a bull or burn a heretic, was a painting of a golden-haired maiden in a bloodied bodice holding a silver tray upon which lay her breasts, like twin mounds of pink jelly topped by nipples instead of cherries.

"That's Saint Barbara. My namesake."

By the time she'd viewed about five paintings of martyred saints, each one more "ewwww yuck" than the one before, Rannie'd had her fill. St. Lawrence roasting on a spit, St. Bartholomew being flayed alive, St. George crushed between two wheels, St. Somebody having his nails pulled out by an oddly cheerful medieval manicurist.

"Daisy was telling me before that your grandmother gave her a painting of a saint. Saint—" The name was escaping Rannie. "She's the patron saint of sore throats. Was she in here too?"

"Yes, St. Godelieve. Silas's tastes were—shall we say—eccentric. After dinner parties, Silas would serve brandy here. He enjoyed watching his guests squirm," Bibi went on. "From the day Silas died—oh, that has to be thirty years ago—Grammy never stepped foot in here again. I can't tell you how many times I tried convincing her to put the art in storage or to let the museum have the whole kit and caboodle now." Bibi paused for a moment and glanced at all the paneling and gloomy furniture. "It could be such a handsome room. But Grammy was unmovable. She'd always say, 'Silas insisted everything should stay here, just as it is, until it goes to the Met. I'd never dream of going against Silas's wishes.'" Bibi shrugged and shook her head. "I guess I understand. Otherwise, I certainly wouldn't be doing what I'm doing."

"I'm sorry. I don't understand."

"It's not *my* idea to dress up my grandmother. I assure you of that."

"No?"

"My grandmother spelled out her wants—to the letter—when she was still sharp as a tack. At six o'clock every evening she is to be dressed as if for a black-tie affair. There are written instructions for what jewels and which handbags go with each gown. She said, 'Barbara, even if I'm a vegetable, you cannot let anyone visit and find me in a nightgown. I want to look gorgeous.'"

"No! Honestly?" Rannie wondered how many people besides Daisy Satterthwaite were giving Bibi a bum rap.

"I loved my grandmother dearly. I lived with her after my mother died. So how can I not do what she asked?"

The question was rhetorical. And even if it hadn't been, Daisy—with Mary in tow—suddenly appeared at the arched entrance to the salon.

"Barbara, didn't I tell you we had come for a *short* visit? I'm not packed yet."

"Oh my. And I haven't even offered you anything."

"Another time," Daisy said.

Refusing liquid sustenance? Clearly Daisy was desperate to blow this Popsicle stand.

"I'll leave you the number where I'm staying in case—well, in case there's any change with your grandmother." Daisy rummaged around in her purse and came up with a pen but kept making impatient noises, mumbling about never finding what you need.

"Here." Rannie produced her S&S notepad for Daisy.

"Oh, I see you work at Simon & Schuster. How interesting," Bibi said to Rannie; then she was polite enough not to press the issue after Rannie's terse reply of "No longer."

Moments later, back in the baroque rotunda, everyone slipped into coats and gloves again. As the massive front door opened, light was cast on two people sitting cross-legged on the balustrade. Even from the back, one looked familiar, and as they turned, Rannie saw why.

It was Nate and Olivia.

"Ma!" he said.

"Mrs. Gaines!" Olivia said, addressing Bibi. She and Nate both jumped up and nervously tossed cigarettes into the street.

Nate was smoking again! So much for her son swearing up and down that he'd quit, not because of Rannie's nagging, he'd made sure to inform her, but because it was hurting his tennis game. It was such a believable lie. But she'd deal with that later.

"My son, Nate," Rannie said.

"My good friend's daughter," Bibi countered. "Olivia Werner."

Rannie wasn't all that surprised. Yes, the five boroughs of New York City contained nine million people; however, Manhattan, at least within a certain radius, was a tiny hamlet.

"You told me the entry code, but I forgot it," Olivia said sheepishly to Bibi and tapped her forehead as if nothing stayed in there for long. "I tried your cell. . . . I'm so sorry to bother you about the spare keys."

Okay, now the pieces were starting to fit together. Olivia didn't have her house keys; Bibi Gaines had the extra set.

"Honey, I'm the one who should be sorry, making you traipse all over. I was just so flustered after the nurse called. I had the keys in an envelope all ready to leave at the concierge desk." Bibi turned. "I'll be back in one second, sweetie."

In the interim, introductions were made all around.

"Mrs. Satterthwaite and Nate's grandmother are old friends of Mrs. Cummings, who lives here," Rannie informed Olivia. "Nate and Olivia are in the same class at Chapel School," Rannie added for the ladies' benefit.

"School friends. Why, that's lovely," Mary enthused for no apparent reason, then after Bibi returned with the keys for Olivia, Mary extended an invitation to one and all for dinner at her apartment.

At the panicked look on Nate's face, Rannie came to the rescue. "That's so kind, Mary. But Nate was saying earlier that he has a test to study for. Isn't that right, honey?"

Manic nodding, after which Olivia and Nate bade quick adieus and made a getaway.

More good-byes with Bibi. Then Rannie waved down a cab

and helped the ladies into it. "Rannie dear, Daisy and I can't thank you enough for walking us over," Mary said through the window.

"Nate and I will be over either Tuesday or Wednesday, I'll let you know which night," Rannie promised. Dinner at Mary's was a weekly ritual, although the food that Mary's devoted cook, Earla, whipped up was just shy of inedible. That there was never enough was actually a blessing.

As Rannie checked her jacket pocket for her MetroCard and began walking toward the crosstown bus, she smiled at her kids' long-standing joke. They referred to the tiny desiccated fowl their grandmother served at holiday time as "the Thanksgiving sparrow."

Chapter 8

ON THE BUS, RANNIE WHIPPED OUT HER CELL, LONGING TO TELL Ellen about seeing the real, barely alive Charlotte Cummings, but her phone was out of juice.

Ellen, it turned out, had been trying to reach Rannie. At home, a message from Ellen was on the landline.

"Okay, Rannie, so I'm a nut job but I've got a week of vacation left and I'm booked on a flight to Martinique tomorrow at one. I'll be back Sunday and by then the cops better have the right guy in custody. My assistant's expecting the manuscript from you; just remember she knows nothing except it's BIG and SUPER SECRET. So don't you dare even mention Ret's name or gab about the murder." Then just before she clicked off, Ellen added, "Think of me on a beach with a strawberry daiquiri and some cute cabana boy oiling me up."

Although Ellen was striving to keep her tone light, Rannie detected the undercurrent of anxiety in her voice, and when she tried Ellen's number, it went immediately to a recorded message. "Ellen, it's Rannie. I just came from Charlotte Cummings's mansion! I saw her! What a creep show! I have a feeling you're home, so please pick up."

But Ellen didn't, perhaps worrying that either Rannie might scoff at Ellen's nervousness (which she might) or else try to dissuade her from leaving (which Rannie definitely wouldn't). A week in Martinique? Who could argue with that?

Paid vacation. Now there was a concept that rated among the high watermarks of modern civilization. Rannie ambled into the living room, tossing her jacket on the sofa and surveying the premises with a hypercritical eye. When exactly had shabby chic crossed the border to just plain shabby? In the brief time since she'd set out for Charlotte Cummings's palatial digs, her apartment seemed to have acquired an extra layer of dust, new patches of damp plaster had bloomed on the ceiling, and a mammoth water bug had gone belly up by the coffee table.

Rannie plopped down on the couch, a hand-me-down from Mary, and ignored the fact that the chenille throw over the back was as worn as the rose toile upholstery underneath. A low-level funk descended: it wasn't a question of not appreciating how fortunate she was compared to practically every other out-of-work single mother on the planet: child support from her ex came like clockwork worthy of the Swiss; Mary generously footed the tuition bills; and—touchingly—several checks had arrived recently with a note, penned in her mother's graceful script, that the "enclosed is a little mad money." But, dammit, what she wanted was a job, the beauty of a bimonthly check, direct deposit, 401(k) deductions, to tend to spindly office plants and have an in-box stacked with manuscripts, all labeled RUSH. Even rush hour—she'd almost come to miss that too. It meant you had somewhere to rush to; you had a place in the wider world.

Then, cutting short her "woe is I" lament, Rannie forced herself off the couch and headed for the kitchen, the departed water bug shrouded in a Kleenex, bound for the trashcan. It was time to start dinner.

While she was excavating in the pantry cabinets for olive oil, balsamic vinegar, and other stuff, Rannie's thoughts turned again to Bibi, who one day soon would be phenomenally, absurdly, filthily rich. What would it be like to become chatelaine of a mansion on Fifth and never have to worry about upkeep? It wasn't a question of jealousy; jealousy, Rannie decided, was for the attainable—a job like Ellen's, a week of vacation in the sun. The kind of wealth the Cummingses owned was simply beyond fathom.

Suddenly a picture of Brooke Astor's oh-so-proper-looking son, heir and executor, popped to mind. At eighty-four, Anthony Marshall had been convicted of bilking his mother out of millions before her death. Was it possible that Ret had caught Bibi's hand in the Cummings cookie jar, dipping into money that wasn't rightfully hers yet? Rannie had spent all of an hour with Bibi. She hadn't appeared to be tapping a foot impatiently waiting for Grammy to finally flatline, but you never knew.

Of course, Rannie was assuming that Bibi was sole or chief beneficiary to the estate. And as Rannie's seventh-grade English teacher loved to remind students, "The word 'assume' makes an 'ass' of 'u' and 'me.'" There might be siblings, half siblings, cousins, or fond old retainers also waiting in line for their slice of the Cummings pie.

Rannie persevered in the kitchen. Then as soon as the chicken breasts, awash in Peter Luger steak sauce the way Nate liked, were braising, the sweet potatoes were baking, and the salad was ready for dressing, Rannie sat down and unlocked the aluminum briefcase, determined to learn a little more about Barbara, aka Bibi, Gaines.

Since the only disk for the book was in the hands of the police, Rannie had to resort to the more laborious route of leafing through the manuscript page by page, her eye on the lookout for "Barbara," "Bibi," "grandchildren," "inheritance," "will," "heirs," "executor," and so on.

All copy editors developed sharp, un-electronic "word search" skills, and in a few minutes Rannie had gleaned the following information: Barbara Beauchamp Gaines, now forty-eight, was the daughter of Charlotte's only child, Madeline—the Madeline who had been Daisy's good friend—and her husband, Frank Beauchamp, a charmer from a poor but old-line Lexington, Kentucky, clan. After divorcing Frank, Madeline traipsed down the aisle two more times but never had more children, making Bibi her grandmother's only direct descendant.

One little wrinkle: upon her grandmother's death, it did not appear that Bibi would take up residence in the Fifth Avenue mansion. Ret devoted several paragraphs to the house's history. Built by Charlotte's steel-rich dad, the house was left to Charlotte upon her mother's death. Unfortunately, Charlotte's first husband frittered away most of her money as well as his on ill-fated, dawn of the Depression land deals, and Charlotte was forced to sell the family manse. For many years, it operated as a posh hospice facility. Charlotte did not return to the Fifth Avenue address until after her marriage to Silas Cummings.

According to the spiel given by the walking-tour guide, Silas had bought back the mansion as an anniversary present for Charlotte. Ret said otherwise. And Rannie trusted Ret, who had a reputation for getting her facts straight. The manuscript said that Silas had only leased the mansion; the medical center that had run the hospice would reclaim it upon Charlotte's death. In would come hospital beds and medical equipment and out would go the countless antiques and costly furnishings that Charlotte and Silas Cummings had snapped up over the years from cash-strapped castles and châteaus. All the costly furnishings were destined for the Met and other museums around the country.

So Bibi Gaines was losing out on a hefty chunk of prime Manhattan real estate. Rannie couldn't even begin to guess at its worth. One hundred million? Two? More? Nonetheless, on balance Rannie didn't feel too sorry for Bibi. There was still Charlotte's fabled jewelry collection, including the knockout canary diamonds Rannie had glimpsed at the comatose invalid's throat. No doubt the bling would be Bibi's.

The tidbit of real estate trivia seemed like a good reason to call Tim and boast where she'd been.

"Guess who just spent an hour at Charlotte Cummings's house," she gloated in a purposefully annoying singsong. "And our guide on the walking tour—little Miss Columbia know-it-all grad student—didn't have all her facts straight. Silas didn't buy back the family digs for his beloved wife. The place is a rental!"

"Well, la di da . . . How'd you worm your way in there?" He sounded amused.

"No worming! No worming at all." She told him about Daisy and Mary.

"So escorting tipsy old ladies around, that counts as a mitzvah?" Tim's wife had been Jewish: he mock-prided himself on his knowledge of Yiddish, limited though it was and pronounced

with an accent that owed far more to Irish Boston than to Eastern Europe. "The Cummings mansion." He whistled softly. "I
forget you hang with a swanky crowd."

Tim had yet to meet Mary. There was no reason for him to,
not yet. Maybe not ever. And more to the point, Rannie knew
Mary's drinking would trouble Tim. That, in turn, would bring
out his stern, tight-lipped side. End result: neither one would
like the other.

"Listen, I was about to call you," he said. "You have any interest in hearing me qualify tonight? I'm speaking at an AA meeting at eight o'clock. It's over on the East Side."

Traipse back across town again? No, truthfully she really
didn't want to. Tonight she wanted to bill hours on the manuscript. Nevertheless, Rannie's response was an automatic yes.
He'd told her what made him stop drinking fifteen years ago.
Tim had been behind the wheel—"shit-faced," he admitted—in
the crash that killed his pregnant wife. Their son, Chris, was
only three at the time. The first cops on the scene were bud-
dies of Tim's who covered for him so he could avoid conviction
and raise Chris. Quid pro quo—he resigned from the force and
entered rehab. But what had come before the fatal accident, he
never discussed beyond alluding to his former self as "one sick
angry fuck." Asking Rannie to hear the story of his drinking was
a significant offer, one she couldn't turn down, although Rannie
suspected there might be things that she'd just as soon not know.

"I'll pick you up at seven thirty," he said.

A minute later the arrival of Nate and Olivia brought the conversation to a close.

"You honestly like Hostess CupCakes?" Rannie heard Olivia
saying to Nate.

"I didn't say 'like,' O. What I said was, 'There has never been a more delicious food experience than the Hostess CupCake.' The second I heard the company went bust, I, like, went into every deli and supermarket on the West Side and bought them all up."

"That's crazy. For me it was always about Ring Dings. The creamy part . . . Mmmm."

"But no chocolate icing with the squiggles. That's key to the Hostess CupCake. You can peel it off whole and eat it separately."

Was this what passed for lively debate between Chapel School seniors—almost seventy percent of whom would wind up at top-tier colleges?

Rannie, holding plates and cutlery, greeted them.

"Hey, Ms. Bookman," Olivia said, followed by Nate lugging a ridiculously large Louis Vuitton suitcase for a one-night stay.

Exactly which room would their overnight guest stay in? Rannie quickly made an executive parental decision. "Just put the bag in the den." Her rationale: let Olivia and Nate sneak around after she was asleep. "We're going to eat in two minutes."

It was lovely having a girl at the dinner table. Such a change from Nate, who, even under duress, would part with no more than grunts or monosyllabic answers to all Rannie's conversational gambits.

Olivia was chatty without being a nonstop talker. She was hoping to enroll at FIT—the Fashion Institute of Technology—which was near the Garment District. "My great-grandfather came over from Odessa and was a tailor on the Lower East Side," she informed Rannie. "I guess it's in my genes. Our housekeeper taught me to sew when I was six."

Rannie nodded, smiling back around a forkful of chicken

while noting to herself that in three generations, Olivia's family had come a long way from Delancey Street. Her father was a hedge-fund something and her mother, she of the brittle, overly wide smile, worked at Sotheby's.

By dessert, the conversation worked its way around to the coincidence of meeting up at the Cummings mansion. "How funny that you know Mrs. Gaines," Olivia said.

"Actually I never met her before this evening."

"Oh. She's one of my mom's friends. When Grant was in bad shape, she helped get him in the place where he's living now."

Rannie was aware that "the place" referred to was a rehab facility in New Haven. Olivia's older brother had been expelled from Chaps his senior year for dealing cocaine on school grounds.

Olivia was sitting beside Nate, the two of them directly across the table from Rannie; every once in a while Rannie stole a look at Nate stealing a look at Olivia. It was as if a thought balloon floated over his head. "You are a goddess," it said.

It made Rannie simultaneously happy—what was more pure and intense than love at seventeen?—and scared—what was more painful than getting your heart ripped to shreds at seventeen?

It wasn't fair. Nobody ever told you that being a parent meant living through the aches and disappointments of growing up all over again. And guess what? You didn't acquire any perspective just because you were twenty years older and this time the hurt wasn't actually happening to you; completely the opposite in fact: watching your child suffer was twice as painful. Rannie remembered times when a supposed best friend suddenly ganged up against Alice or Nate wasn't invited to a birthday party that all his friends were going to. Rannie's reaction: pure and simple, tear the offending child limb from limb. Anything less extreme meant you weren't a devoted mother.

After dinner, while Nate and Olivia cleared and did dishes, Rannie managed to squeeze in more pages of copyediting, ones on Silas Cummings's art collection. Ret's manuscript corroborated what Bibi Gaines had told Rannie earlier: the Metropolitan Museum of Art would place all the paintings of saints on permanent exhibition in order to win the prize—"The Master of the Agony alterpiece." Rannie cringed at the misspelling and made the correction just as the intercom buzzed.

Her recovering alcoholic was waiting.

"I was thirteen years old the first time I got drunk. I came to lying on the sidewalk with vomit all over me, my wallet gone, and a black eye, and I thought, 'Wow! When can I do this again?'"

The audience at the Church of the Heavenly Rest on Fifth Avenue and Ninetieth Street, laughed, several men nodding in recognition. Rannie was sitting alone toward the back of the room. Fifty or so people had assembled on gray folding chairs in the church's basement. It was a mixed crowd—there were many prosperous-looking men and women. There were just as many who looked down on their luck and seemed especially grateful for the cookies and hot coffee. It had touched Rannie that the "greeter" at the door—a man in his seventies from among the well heeled—knew everyone by name. Alcoholism was evidently a great social equalizer.

Tim had been talking for five minutes. Posters on the wall behind him said, "Easy Does It," "One Day at a Time," and "Keep It Simple." His "drunkologue" quickly filled in his stats—he was from an Irish Catholic family south of Boston outside Plymouth, Massachusetts, seven kids, all girls except for Tim, who by age six was sipping beer from his dad's can of Schlitz.

"He thought it was funny to hear a little kid slurring." His father, a plumber, was a disappointed, bitter man who limped from polio contracted in the very last outbreak before the Salk vaccine. "Polio, according to my dad, was the reason for everything wrong with his life. Bum leg, bum luck, that's all I heard. The only way we 'bonded'"—Tim put air quotes around the word—"was over booze. And I *loved* to drink. Loved the taste. Loved holding a glass or bottle. Loved waiting for the buzz to kick in."

Lots of nodding from everybody in the audience. It was then that Rannie happened to notice a well-coiffed blond woman in black, sitting a couple of rows ahead, doing needlepoint. Even from the back, there was something familiar about her, the perfect ruler-straight posture.

"I don't even remember losing my virginity," Tim went on as he rubbed his cheek and smiled ruefully. "Totally missed out on that. The girl filled me in. At least I was smart enough to stay sober the second time."

More laughs, then Tim cut to the chase—the car accident that killed his wife, cop friends who covered for him, his stint in rehab, and the postrehab move to New York, where "I started piecing together a life for me and my son, Chris, who was three." He looked around the room for a moment. "This program saved my life, sitting in rooms like this, listening to people's stories and not being too stubborn to ask for help." A moment later, he ended with a shrug. "There's no magic; for anyone new in the program, I'm staying sober the same way you are, one day at a time."

Right after that, everyone joined hands and recited the Serenity Prayer. "God grant me the strength to change the things I can, to accept the things I cannot change, and the wisdom to know the difference."

As she unclasped the hands of her neighbors, Rannie once again took notice of the blond woman who'd been needlepointing. Rannie watched her turn to gather up a tote bag and black wool jacket, then rise and walk toward the exit.

It was Bibi Gaines.

Seeing her here was surreal. Rannie blinked; it was almost as if a life-size image of Bibi had been cut out and manipulated into the wrong background with Photoshop. Bibi didn't belong in this dingy gray basement. Then Rannie stopped to remember what she'd been thinking just minutes ago about the democratic spirit of AA. *Everybody* here belonged here.

Encountering Bibi would be awkward, so Rannie ducked down and pretended to be fishing around for something in her bag and didn't budge until she figured Bibi was safely beyond the exit door.

The room emptied slowly. Rannie waited in her seat while several people thronged around Tim, men shaking his hand, women offering hugs.

Of all the uncanny coincidences. Charlotte Cummings's granddaughter exuded an air of "I'm in charge" confidence, something that to Rannie often seemed the birthright of tall, blond women with silly nicknames. Yet obviously there were demons lurking, and somehow knowing this about Bibi made Rannie like her better; it humanized her. Rannie's gaze turned to Tim again. She watched him wrap an arm around a teary-eyed young woman. AA was a big part of his life. For all she knew, Bibi was one of Tim's AA friends.

Tim strode toward her and together they walked up the stairs and out a side door of the church. The brisk night air underscored how stuffy, smoky, and overheated it had been in the basement. Rannie took in a couple of deep head-clearing breaths.

"Charlotte Cummings's granddaughter was at the meeting," Rannie said as they walked to his car. "She took me around the mansion, acted like we were old chums from boarding school. Do you know her? Her name is Bibi."

Predictably, Tim said, "If I do, I'm not saying. And remember, whatever you heard—or saw—in there stays in there. Understood?"

"I know that, Tim. You don't have to lecture me."

He put a hand on the back of her neck and they continued down the street.

"So now you know all my secrets," Tim said. As he unlocked the car door for her, Rannie decided that no, she was pretty sure she did not.

Tim dropped her off with a quick kiss. There had been no offer to take her back to his apartment nor any request to come upstairs to hers. Now, lying alone in bed, she felt deprived . . . or to put it more bluntly, horny. Being around Tim primed her body for sex, sometimes without her mind even being consciously aware of it.

And what were Nate and Olivia doing behind the closed door to the den? "Studying" had been their chimed, pat-sounding response to her "I'm back" announcement.

Rannie briefly considered putting in another hour of freelance work. But even sharpening her blue pencils seemed too strenuous a task. She simply didn't have the mental acuity right now for copyediting. Instead she got under the covers and skimmed through *Tattletale*, the bio of Ret Sullivan that she'd purchased at Barnes & Noble that morning. It turned out to be a complete hoot.

The author, someone named Lina Struvel, had turned Ret's life into an over-the-top rags-to-riches story. The adjectives most frequently used to describe Ret were "raven-haired," "sultry," "curvaceous," and "luscious-lipped."

As for the facts: Ret (born Kathleen Margaret) Sullivan had been orphaned at a young age and grew up in a Westchester convent, where Sister Dorothy Cusack had taken the girl under her wing.

Ah, thought Rannie, *the nun to whom Ret had dedicated* Portrait of a Lady.

After high school, Ret worked for *U.S. Enquirer* dreaming up weird UFO stories, including ones about an alien stalking Elizabeth Taylor. "Ret Sullivan had a real gift," a former boss was quoted as saying. "She *never* underestimated the stupidity of our readers."

A stint at *Entertainment Weekly* led to appearances on Fox Network gossip shows, which in turn led to her first book contract. In the past twenty years she'd cranked out twelve celebrity bios. A workaholic who never married "despite countless offers" and had no close friends, she enjoyed "a dream life attending movie premieres, press parties, and glamorous charity galas almost every night."

There were a couple of howlers: Ret was described as "a consummate journalist" and a "crusader who spoke truth to power."

Silly as the book was, the more she read of *Tattletale*, the sorrier Rannie felt for Ret. Okay, in reality the stuff that "the consummate journalist" wrote was scuzz but she worked so hard at it. And until she crossed paths with Mike Bellettra, she had carved out exactly the high-profile life she had longed for. How many people could say that?

At eleven, Rannie channel surfed but none of the stations had anything newsworthy about the murder. Every channel replayed the same archival footage of Mike Bellettra's arrest after the lye incident, the same shots of Ret's apartment building, and old photos of Ret herself in her heyday.

Rannie lay in bed, thoughts free floating, zigzagging from the horrifying sight of Ret Sullivan dead in bed to the slightly less horrifying sight of Charlotte Cummings nearly dead in bed. Rannie's gut, which she usually trusted, judged it unlikely that the manuscript about Charlotte Cummings had anything to do with Ret's murder. Yet *somebody* out there, somebody who might be asleep in his or her bed right this very minute, hated Ret enough to end her life brutally and sordidly. Tim, she knew, would argue whether hatred was the motive behind most premeditated murders. She couldn't remember his exact words; however, he'd once said that murder was at bottom a selfish act. He didn't believe most killers hated their victims; for whatever reason, they simply wanted them out of the way, permanently gone.

As she was about to turn off the light, the spine of *Tattletale* caught her eye. Dusk Books. That was the publishing house where Larry Katz worked now. As executive editor, no less.

Rannie hadn't thought about Larry in eons, not until Ellen mentioned him earlier in the day. Maybe she should give him a call. Who knew? Dusk might be another source for freelance. Or maybe Larry had some idea what leads the cops were following.

Chapter 9

THE THRUM OF HEAVY RAIN WOKE RANNIE. WHEN SHE PEERED bleary eyed at the clock on her night table, she was startled to see it was eight fifteen. She sprang from bed. Olivia and Nate had departed for school long ago, so she was free to check out both Nate's bedroom and the den.

No telltale signs anywhere. The Vuitton suitcase was gone. Nate's bed was unmade, with the covers balled up frenetically into what looked almost like a makeshift punching bag. In the den it was impossible to tell whether the convertible couch had ever been pulled out to bed mode or not.

By eight thirty, Rannie's workday began. She stationed herself at her desk. An hour and a half of coffee and copyediting brought Rannie well past the halfway mark in the manuscript. Still no eye-popping disclosures about Charlotte Cummings. Yet it interested Rannie to learn that Charlotte and her first husband had adopted Madeline through the Gladney Home in Texas, legendary for its "crops" of blond, blue-eyed babies, the go-to place for all barren rich Wasps. That meant that Bibi, sole offspring of

Madeline, was not actually a blood relative of Charlotte Cummings's.

During a break for an open-faced PB&J, Rannie reconsidered her plan to get in touch with Larry Katz at Dusk Books. In the light of day it still didn't seem like a bad idea.

She called the general number at Dusk, was redirected to Larry's extension, and ended up leaving a message. "Larry, it's Rannie Bookman. I know this is out of the blue. I'm a freelancer now and hoping you might need a good copy editor. . . . And of course it'd be fun to see you and catch up."

Hearing Larry Katz's voice on the prompt with its nasal Long Island accent made Rannie smile. "I'm either away from my desk or out of the office," it said. Rannie looked at her watch. Ten thirty. If he still kept to the same hours as in his Simon & Schuster days, Larry probably hadn't yet made it into the office.

Ten minutes later the phone rang. It was Larry's assistant asking if Rannie could come into Dusk at eleven o'clock.

Yes, ma'am! She certainly could.

Rannie arrived at Dusk with yet another cheapie black umbrella blown inside out. Dependably, the heavy rain and winds let up just before she entered a nondescript office building on Fifty-Ninth Street. Though it was after eleven, Rannie had made it in before Larry and waited in the reception area. Copies of Dusk books stood behind a wall of glass-fronted shelves—*Tattletale* as well as many celebrity confessionals, sex manuals for all persuasions, and self-help titles.

At eleven fifteen Larry came bursting in.

"Rannie! Sorry I'm late. I—I had a meeting outside the office."

Words undoubtedly uttered for the benefit of the receptionist. "With the rain it was impossible to find a cab."

Larry looked pretty much the same, with wild Brillo hair, shorter now and only nominally grayer since the last time she'd seen him. He had to be in his midfifties by now but didn't look it. Tall and rumpled, he was a big bearish guy. His raincoat was dirty; so were his shoes. That was Larry, a mess but an appealing mess.

Larry placed his hands on her shoulders, kissed her lightly on the cheek. "You still look like a grad student. I always think of you with glasses perched on your head and a pencil stuck behind one ear."

Behind one of his ears, the right one, Rannie was now startled to notice a hearing aid, almost imperceptibly tiny, the expensive kind marketed to boomers. Fallout from too many rock concerts, probably. Rannie remembered that Larry once showed her a photo from his college days at Columbia. Back then he'd sported a full-blown "Jewfro" and a Fu Manchu mustache, and he looked stoned out of his gourd.

Larry led her down a cubicle-lined hallway to his office. As for decor, bare essentials summed it up. Gray walls, a metal credenza and filing cabinets, a desk and a wall of shelves displaying many of the same titles as in the reception area.

"Welcome to the glamorous world of Dusk Books."

Rannie sat down in the chair facing Larry's desk. She produced one of her business cards—"Have Pencil, Will Travel," it said at the top—and handed it to him, their fingers briefly touching.

He looked at the card. "I remember hearing you left S&S."

"You're nice to be so tactful." The entire publishing world had been privy to the reason for her abrupt, involuntary leave-taking, thanks to an article in *Publishers Weekly* about the Nancy Drew recall.

"If it makes you feel better," Larry replied, "I know of worse bloopers . . . or ones that are just as bad."

"By now I've heard them all." In attempts to console her, industry pals kept e-mailing "contenders"; her favorites thus far were a literary first novel about Mozart that landed on bookshelves entitled *Rectals for the Emperor,* an indictment of the educational system called *Why Pubic Schools Don't Work,* and a children's picture book called *Whales: Gentile Giants of the Sea.*

He leaned back, arms folded across his chest, smiling at her. He had a dimple in his chin to rival Kirk Douglas's. Rannie had forgotten that.

They played catch-up; Larry had returned to New York about a year ago from California, single again after a brief marriage. "My first and last. It lasted a minute and somehow I'm paying alimony." He lived in the Meatpacking District now.

Then he said, "I caught you on one of the morning shows, right after you killed that psycho. Amazing what you did. I remember thinking, 'This is the same Rannie I knew?'"

"I had no choice. I don't even remember doing it."

"The stuff about the blue pencil, that was all true?"

Rannie nodded.

"Must have been damn sharp."

This was not the conversational avenue Rannie wanted to stroll down. She cleared her throat and Larry seemed to pick up on her discomfort. He put his feet up on his desk and leaned back farther. The soles of his shoes were caked with mud.

"I almost called," he said. "I was surprised to hear you say you were a single mother. So you never remarried? I thought for sure somebody would snap you up right away."

"Nope." Rannie was not sure what to say next. Larry was looking at her so intently, she had to resist the urge to squirm. "Funny but just yesterday your name came up. I didn't know you were executive editor here. Congratulations."

Larry shrugged. "The pay ain't bad—in fact much better than at one of the big houses—but there's absolutely no cachet when I present my business card."

"I'm curious. . . . Did you edit the book about Ret Sullivan? *Tattletale?* I saw it in the reception area."

"Yup, I confess. Want a copy? There are ten sitting on the shelf behind you."

"Actually I already bought one."

Larry dipped his head in thanks. "It's horrible to say, but Ret getting murdered was the best thing that could've happened for the book. Last time I looked, *Tattletale* was 77 on Amazon," he continued. "We're going back to press for another fifty thousand copies."

"So you're the 'Dusk spokesperson' quoted in the *Times!* The one talking about Ret Sullivan's 'demise'?"

He nodded. "I thought 'demise' had a nice respectful sound. And wherever Ret Sullivan is now, I guarantee you she's having a good laugh over the whole thing—the cops looked at me like I was crazy when I told them that."

"Cops!" Rannie feigned surprise and hoped she seemed convincing. "The cops talked to you?" Rannie paused. "I read how she died and, I gotta say, Larry, it didn't strike me as riotously funny either."

Larry acknowledged her point with a shrug. "Poor choice of words. What I told the police was that Ret would be digging all the headlines."

"Were you two friends?" she asked.

"Nah. Years ago I used to run into her at author parties, restaurants, conventions. She once told me, 'I started out in tabloids and I bet that's where I end up.' She was right. She was a true believer in the power of publicity—good or bad." Larry paused for a moment. "If an autopsy discovers Ret had terminal cancer, I wouldn't put it past her to have staged her own death."

"Get out! Paying someone to strangle her? Some sort of perverted euthanasia?"

"Not seriously. But I bet what drove her nuts about being disfigured, maybe more than anything, was being off the radar screen. And you have to admit her death is a Rupert Murdoch wet dream. She would get perverse pleasure in that."

Rannie refrained from commenting that Larry seemed to know Ret awfully well for someone claiming to be simply a long-ago acquaintance. "So listen, Larry. I came down here in pouring rain. And while it's great to see you, please don't send me away empty-handed."

"No, no. Of course not." He removed his feet from the desk, swiveled around to the credenza, and, sifting through a pile of manuscripts, rattled off the titles of three projects. "Take your pick." He swiveled back and looked at her with concern. "So? You managing to get by freelancing?"

"Squeaking by is probably more accurate. Ellen Donahoe's been great about giving me work. You remember Ellen."

"Yeah. Brunette, looks a little like you. How's she doing?"

"Fine, and she'll be even finer in a couple of hours when her plane lands in Martinique."

Soon after, Rannie left Dusk with the company's backlist catalog and a manuscript entitled *Cutthroat: Do Psychopaths Make Successful CEOs?* Larry hugged her good-bye; the embrace felt so familiar. A great big enveloping hug.

"You happy now?" Larry wasn't talking about the freelance job. She shrugged. "I'm not the basket case I was when you knew me."

On the way home, Rannie debated whether she'd felt any re-kindling of the attraction she used to feel. Her first reaction on seeing Larry was to tell him to comb his hair and send his rain-coat to the cleaners. But then, part of Larry's charm was that he needed mothering. He also never expected more or less of him-self than he delivered. That probably explained why he had such a forgiving nature. A trait that Tim Butler sorely lacked.

Chapter 10

DONE AND DONE! LATE THAT AFTERNOON, RANNIE FINISHED copyediting the final pages of *Portrait of a Lady: The Life of Charlotte Cummings*. She put down her blue pencil and rolled her shoulders to uncrick them. Whoever Audio was, somehow he—or she—had gained entry to the Cummings château on Fifth Avenue. Rannie was sure of that. The description of the place read like an eyewitness account, not something pieced together from old articles in *Vanity Fair* or *Architectural Digest*. What ruse had permitted Audio to pass through those giant wrought-iron gates? The book also included an insert of photos, many taken inside the mansion. The copyright was in Ret's name, but Rannie guessed the shots had been taken by Audio.

As for revelatory stink bombs, none had been lobbed. Charlotte emerged a doting mother and grandmother, a caring wife, and a woman who was fiercely loyal to friends, loved a good party, and enjoyed doling out vast sums of money to worthy causes. Ret, again via Audio or perhaps Gery Antioch, had ferreted out a few bitchy tidbits from disgruntled former employees—the weekly supply of custom-made Egyptian cotton diapers Charlotte now wore, hand-delivered from an East Side lingerie shop; a beauty regimen that included facials made from oatmeal and feline uric acid. One maid had resented ironing Charlotte's paper money so the bills were always crisp; another groused about polishing the soles of her shoes black to keep them looking out-of-the-box new.

The cheap shots were saved for Silas. He was no looker. The photo confirmed the accuracy of Ret's unkind description: "a major schlub—fleshy lips, drooping jowls, overhanging belly—an Alfred Hitchcock look-alike minus the mischievous twinkle." Even worse, according to an old unnamed friend of Charlotte's, "Silas was afflicted with farts that could wake the dead and so much body hair that, in a bathing suit, he looked like King Kong." Yet Silas appeared to love Charlotte or at least treasured her in the same way he treasured owning the famous Master of the Agony altarpiece.

Rannie tapped all the pages of the manuscript together into a neat stack. It seemed more and more far-fetched to attribute a link between the contents of this book and Ret Sullivan's murder. Once again she glanced at the corrected acknowledgments page. She'd love to know who Gery Antioch was and learn the identity of Audio. Rannie's guess—Audio was a woman. If frenemies and old retainers of Charlotte's were going to spill secrets, it was harder to imagine them dishing with a man.

Suddenly, it crossed Rannie's mind that Ellen might have been Ret's "ears." After all, Ellen and Ret had been in constant touch while Ret was writing the book. More to the point, Ellen excelled at coaxing secrets from people. At S&S she was everyone's confidante, the first to know who was getting divorced, giving notice, about to undergo chemo. It was to Ellen's office that Rannie had

fled upon first learning of the Nancy Drew recall. You trusted
Ellen when she promised to keep "in the vault" whatever had
just been divulged. Rannie could envision a system whereby Ret,
in the confines of her apartment, researched names of Charlotte
Cummings's friends, employees, and such, then sent Ellen out to
do the pumping. Yes, Ellen had a sympathetic ear; she'd make a
talented "Audio."

Rannie tallied her hours of work and, since Ellen had probably already landed in Martinique or Mustique or whatever fan-
tastique island she was headed to, Rannie put in a call to Ellen's
assistant.

"I'm done. Want to send a messenger to pick up the manuscript? I'll enclose a bill." She was not at all eager to return to
S&S; the wound of her firing, though no longer gaping, still felt
much too fresh to visit corporate HQ.

"Sorry, Rannie. This is *Book X.* No messenger. Ellen was very
clear: you have to hand-deliver it."

Rannie didn't bother asking if a limo would be coming this
time. She said okay, then secured the manuscript in its aluminum case and headed out, MetroCard in hand. The nearest
subway station was at Broadway and 110th Street; however, just
as Rannie was about to descend into its bowels, she stopped and
eyed the Kinko's copying store on the corner. Instead of continuing down the subway stairs, her feet redirected her into the store.

"I need a copy of something that's long and I need it fast,"
she found herself saying to the elderly clerk and after his "no
problem" response, she went through the laborious process of
unlocking the case.

"Jesus, lady, what's in there? State secrets? I don't need Home-
land Security busting in here."

Rannie smiled winningly. "No. A book manuscript. The author is very protective."

In five minutes, to the tune of $50.25 charged to Visa, she had her copy nestled in her tote. Why had she done this? As the number 1 train sent her hurtling downtown, Rannie was hard pressed to fathom her own reasoning. *I am a mystery to myself,* she blithely told herself, as if that settled the matter. Was part of her hoping that this soon-to-be bestseller *did* have a connection to Ret's murder? That somewhere, buried in its pages, was a clue that she and only she might ferret out upon rereading? Yeah, that sounded a lot closer to the mark.

It was otherworldly being back at Simon & Schuster, whose offices were housed in one of the art deco citadels in Rockefeller Center. It had always lifted her spirits to pass through the gilt and mosaic portal of this landmark building. Now she felt demeaned having to sign in at the lobby security desk and present ID to a guy who knew perfectly well who she was, who had seen her trudge in and out of the building for ten years.

Upstairs, one former coworker ducked down a side hall on spotting her. "It's not like cooties. I'm not contagious," Rannie almost hollered. Others greeted her either way too heartily, exclaiming how great she looked, "so relaxed," or else evinced a surplus of furrowed-brow concern.

Rannie kept it light. "So far, I'm remaining solvent with freelance," she said over and over again, although passing her old office, which now belonged to some marketing hotshot, was hard. Very hard. For a decade she had dutifully parked her butt in that same gray-upholstered swivel chair behind that same blond-wood desk that now sported several professionally taken photos of a curly-haired toddler as well as a miniature Zen sand garden with rocks and a little rake. Never in her life had Rannie ever owned an office toy!

To be sure, she had copyedited a lot of dreck in the course of her career, but this was also the office in which she had proofed the pages of a first novel nominated for a National Book Award as well as countless other worthy books, books that people took seriously. Corporate playthings did not belong here. Then Rannie stopped herself. No. She was the one who didn't belong here.

Tears about to prick her eyes, Rannie hurried off to the cube just down the hall where Ellen's assistant sat. What was her name? Rannie looked unsuccessfully for a nameplate.

The assistant was on the phone but held up a finger indicating the call was ending. "She's not back till next Monday. And she wants a real vacation." A pause. "Yes, from you too." A half-exasperated, half-indulgent sigh escaped from the assistant. "That's not true! I *am* diligent about phone messages. Yes, especially yours. Look, Larry, I think she gets home sometime over the weekend. Try then."

Call over.

"Hey, Rannie. Thanks for getting here so fast." The assistant—Diana? Dana?—took the aluminum case. "So? Can you at least give me a hint what's in here? Everybody is saying Ret Sullivan wrote it!" She waited expectantly.

"Sorry. Can't say. Ellen made me swear on a stack of bibles." Rannie handed in her bill. Then she made tracks for the elevator. It couldn't come fast enough.

At first there had been countless consolation calls and e-mails from colleagues, all to the same tune of general outrage caused by her dismissal. If Rannie could be booted out after ten years for some jackass's mistake, then nobody was safe. But of course nobody *was* safe, not in this economy. Now four months later, general outrage had been supplanted by discomfort at her very presence. And it didn't surprise Rannie, not a bit. In the world of an office, once you were gone, you were *so* gone. At least she had presented a cheerfully sane, "I'm okay—really!" demeanor to one and all, she consoled herself. Then her eye caught something hanging off the sleeve of her sweater. A long thread?

No. It was a spiraling length of dental floss.

The elevator door swished open. Well, everyone knew she was still orally hygienic.

Chapter 11

ON THE UPTOWN NUMBER 1 TRAIN RANNIE STOOD AND GLARED down at a man reading the *Post*, his knees spread so far apart that he took up almost three seats. Rannie could tell he saw her; still he didn't budge. What was with these guys? Were they trying to tell you their balls were so ginormous that it was physically impossible for them to sit like a normal human being?

Undaunted, Rannie wedged herself next to him. The front page of the *Post* was practically in her face, the headline story something about an attack that morning in Central Park. A woman dead. How swiftly Ret Sullivan had been knocked off the top spot in the tabloid hierarchy. Rannie wondered how long the *Post* would even bother to keep running articles on her murder without any breaking news.

It wasn't until the train was pulling into her stop at 110th Street that Rannie thought about the snippet of conversation she'd overheard at S&S. Ellen's assistant had been talking to a Larry. All Rannie could think of was Larry Katz. Of course, there were other Larrys in the universe. Yet the assistant's tone of voice, annoyed yet entertained, was exactly the reaction Larry elicited from women.

Strange that Ellen, Larry Katz, and Rannie herself were all a mere one degree of separation from Ret. Of course, no world was smaller than that of publishing. And on the surface, the connections among them seemed perfectly innocuous, as plain as overlapping circles in a Venn diagram.

Walking home, Rannie made a stop at Gristedes and soon was lugging three heavy grocery bags down 108th Street when her cell buzzed. Weighed down as she was, Rannie waited until she was in her apartment to retrieve the message. Nate. Reminding her that he had a long yearbook meeting after school and wouldn't be home for dinner.

Rannie speed-dialed Tim. "How does dinner for two sound?"

It sounded fine to him, and as promised he arrived on the dot of six, tulips in hand. "Found a spot right in front of your building!" he crowed, his parking karma being something he continually bragged about. Rannie set the flowers in a green pottery pitcher on her dining table. Then, while water boiled for linguine and white clam sauce simmered on the stove top, emitting a pleasant garlicky aroma, they watched the local news. The top story echoed what Rannie had glimpsed on the front page of the *Post*, the Central Park attack.

A reporter in a down coat, a wool scarf knotted noose-like around her neck, intoned solemnly into her mic, "Living in New York City, crime is no rarity. Yet a brutal murder shocks us all." The mangled grammar caused Rannie's nose to wrinkle involuntarily, as if she'd smelled something rotten—"crime" didn't live in New York City, people did.

"A bike rider discovered the body around ten thirty this morning. The police are still not saying how the victim died," the reporter continued, brushing away a strand of blond hair blowing across her mouth. "The attack took place only a few yards from where I am standing, here in Central Park by the Ross Pinetum."

Rannie knew the area well from when Nate was in Little League; the Pinetum was a half-acre stand of evergreens bordering the northwestern edge of the baseball fields.

"According to police, the victim was white, dark haired, in her thirties. She was wearing a red running suit. If anyone has information, please call this NYPD hotline number or go to WABC.com."

The Pinetum was not a secluded spot, although the heavy rain in the morning would have kept away everyone except fanatic joggers. Still, had no one been nearby to hear screams? Rannie turned to Tim with questioning eyes, but he shook his head. "Sorry. All I know is what we're hearing right now."

Rannie had been the victim of a mugging herself, at knifepoint. Her purse was taken as well as her father's Rolex wristwatch, one that she'd worn every day since he'd died. Still, she had to count herself lucky, especially since she'd been foolhardy enough ("fucking insane" was Tim's blunt assessment) to be walking alone down her sketchy block late at night. This woman was out during daylight hours when Central Park was considered an urban playground. After the reporter mentioned that no identification was on the body, Rannie turned to Tim again. "You think this was a robbery?"

"No. Who goes for a run loaded with cash?"

Rannie nodded, acknowledging the logic. "But isn't midmorning a little early for violent crime?"

"Go figure what sets off some whack job." Tim reminded her

of a similar attack in the park, years earlier. "Nice spring day, a woman is out for a walk, enjoying the weather, and suddenly she gets her head bashed in by some psycho who's off his meds. It was right near a playground, filled with kids, mothers, nannies. No one heard anything. Horrible but it happens."

Over dinner, Tim turned to more mundane topics and recounted his recent trip to Amherst with his son, Chris, a good student and an even better basketball player, who was applying there. Tim had tuition worries and was contemplating part-time security work to bring in more money. "I've already got a second mortgage, and the bar is way down for the year." He smiled ruefully at Rannie. "I mean, you *know* the middle class is hurting when cops are cutting back on their booze. . . . Amherst better come through with a nice hefty scholarship."

Rannie nodded and held up crossed fingers.

Tim was about to take another forkful of linguine. "You can uncross your fingers. I got something way better going. My mom's at Mass every day, lighting a candle to St. Aloysius. He's the guy who looks out for students."

"Chris doesn't need a miracle. He'll get a good package." Then Rannie remembered Daisy Satterthwaite's miracle and, while Tim finished off a second helping of linguine, she told him about the painting of St. Godelieve.

"Saint who?"

"She's the patron saint of sore throats."

"Hold it right there. That's St. Blaise's gig. After twelve years of parochial school, one thing I know is my saints. And I never heard of this—"

"Godelieve. Her mother-in-law strangled her." Rannie started clearing the plates. Tim followed her into the kitchen with the glasses and silverware. "Daisy seemed very sure of her facts. She believes praying to St. Godelieve cured her throat cancer."

"Probably some *Protestant* saint," Tim said dismissively.

"And what? That means she's a knockoff, like a handbag?"

"Exactly." He said it with such finality that Rannie had no choice but to slap him, except that he caught her wrists before she could land a blow. "Uh, uh, uh. We don't hit. We use our words, Miranda."

Then after swatting her with a dishcloth, Tim returned to the dining room where he wiped crumbs off the table. "You make a decent clam sauce," he said.

"*Grazie*, signore." Rannie curtsied and blew out the candles. Cleaning up after dinner—it was all so ordinary and yet somehow a turn-on. Tim was relaxed in a way that few men were, or at least the ones Rannie knew. He wasn't out to prove anything. He was what he was—utterly himself.

Since her son would not be returning anytime soon, Rannie was all ready with a corny come-on—"And now for dessert—*moi!*"—when the phone rang.

"Rannie, listen, it's Dina."

Dina? A couple of synapses fired. *Dina*—that was the name of Ellen's assistant. "Oh, hi!"

"I need you to tell me I'm being crazy."

"What about?"

"I'm worried about Ellen. After you left the office, I tried reaching her. I texted, called, e-mailed. I swore I'd let her know as soon as you handed in the manuscript. I left like a zillion messages."

"Maybe she didn't think a reply was necessary." Or else Ellen may have hooked up with a cabana boy *tout de suite* and the manuscript was no longer her number one priority. "Where is she? Martinique?"

"Yeah. Look. I called the B&B. She never checked in. Her flight landed on time. So she should have arrived an hour later, an hour and a half tops."

"You're sure about the name of the B&B?"

"No, I wasn't. So I tried googling anything that sounded even vaguely like Island Winds and called the places." Dina's voice rose an octave. "And then after work I was at a bar and something came on TV about a woman who got killed in the park this morning. It would be like Ellen to make sure she got in a run before a long flight. . . . Rannie, please, tell me I am being crazy."

"Everything okay?" Tim asked from the couch, where he was leafing through the newspaper, but Rannie batted away the question with her free hand. Suddenly she could feel a couple of clammy sweat beads trickling down her armpits. Anxiety was *the* most contagious disease, bar none. As for whether it was crazy to worry about Ellen, Rannie was not the best judge. Leaping to worst possible consequences was the only sport at which she excelled. Years ago, whenever one of her kids disappeared from sight at the playground for more than a moment, she'd instantaneously picture their face on the milk carton and herself on TV tearfully pleading for their return. Nevertheless, she took a calming breath now and tried to think rationally. Ellen could certainly be at some other, ungoogled B&B or maybe Ellen had gone to Martinique with a guy—the unnamed insignificant other—and the room was registered under his name. She tried out that one on Dina.

"I don't think so."

"Or maybe Ellen never left the city. Maybe she felt she deserved a week of mental health days and is holed up in her apartment as we speak, watching DVDs, eating ice cream from the carton, and blissfully ignoring all communication from the outside world." Rannie was on a roll now. "Have you called her building?"

"Yeah. The guy on duty buzzed up but got no answer and I felt weird asking him to check the apartment. Maybe I should have. You think I should have, Rannie?"

"I think there is probably some perfectly innocuous reason to explain all this."

"The body was found around ten thirty. On nonworkdays that's when Ellen would be out for a run. The woman had dark hair. They said she was in her thirties."

"Look. I'll call Ellen's building. Maybe somebody has seen her since you called. If not, I'll ask the doorman to ring her bell."

"Would you? Oh, Rannie, thanks! I know it's probably nothing. But after Ret Sullivan . . ."

"We're absolutely not going there." Rannie had to hand it to herself: she really could pull off sounding like a soothing voice of reason, and happily Dina couldn't see how Rannie's hand was sort of trembling as she took down her number.

"What's up?" Tim asked. She could see he'd started filling in the Monday crossword. After hearing the gist of the conversation, all he said was "Call her building."

Rannie did. The four-to-twelve P.M. guy hadn't seen Ellen, and when he called back a few minutes later, the news was not what Rannie had hoped to hear. He'd checked the apartment. It was empty and he found a half-packed suitcase in her room. Even more upsetting, a neighbor had reported seeing Ellen that morning. She was heading out for a run.

"What now?"

Tim didn't answer. He was at her laptop. He scribbled down something and handed it to her. "The hotline number. Look. In all likelihood your friend is okay. But call and put your mind at rest." Rannie took the piece of paper. "Think of things that'll disqualify her as the victim. A chipped tooth, an odd birthmark, scars, a tattoo, a piece of jewelry with initials. Anything like that."

Rannie nodded. Disqualify. Up until this very moment, the word had always carried a strictly pejorative meaning. Like "exile," it seemed harsh, punitive. Now disqualification was the hoped-for goal, although Rannie found herself hard-pressed to list Ellen's singular physical attributes: she was the sort of woman whose looks were pleasantly unremarkable. Okay, Ellen had brand-new boobs. But would they count? Who knew how many brunettes in their late thirties had the same silicone accessories. "She always wore one of those Irish rings with clasped hands," she told Tim.

"A claddagh; I gave one to all my high school girlfriends. You need to do better than that."

"Okay, she used to wear a nose ring. But she stopped when she turned thirty-five. You could still see a tiny hole. And she had a whitish scar over one eyebrow. She told me her brother bashed her with a badminton racket when they were kids."

Tim sat beside her on the couch while she dialed the hotline number.

"My name is Miranda Bookman and I am calling about the murder in Central Park this morning. I'm hoping to rule out any possibility that the victim is a friend of mine." Then she launched into a long-winded, roundabout, and overly detailed account of what prompted her worry, only to be interrupted and told, "Please hold while I transfer you to the hotline."

After robotically repeating everything to a cop, Rannie was comforted—somewhat—when told that calls to the hotline had been pouring in all evening. "It's unlikely, ma'am, that your friend is the victim. So," he said crisply, "what I need is for you to describe her as best you can, anything unusual about her, a scar, a birthmark, tattoo, things of that nature."

Rannie did. She completed her description of Ellen, adding one more detail that suddenly came to her: the nail on Ellen's left thumb had a permanent split in it. There was a second of silence; the moment seemed to stand still and stretch out interminably, like the second before you heard the results of a scary medical test. Rannie's throat began to close, almost in a gag reflex, as the cop in a much graver tone said, "Ma'am, I'm sorry, but I'm afraid I'll need you to make an identification."

A street address was supplied, but Rannie didn't fully register anything except that the word "morgue" was uttered. Tim must have taken her cell because he was speaking into it, saying, "Yeah, she'll be down there as soon as possible. Yeah, I know where it is."

He got her coat and helped her into it; both her feet felt like they had fallen asleep and her arms didn't seem to be working properly. "I don't want to do this."

"Nobody does."

Tim's Toyota was, true to his earlier claim, parked smack-dab in front of the Dolores Court. Rannie climbed in on rubbery legs and, as soon as the engine was running, turned on the heat full blast, which did nada to stop her teeth from chattering.

Rannie didn't say a word during the entire car ride. Instead she played pointless obsessive-compulsive games—Neurotics' Solitaire—with herself. . . . If Tim could drive ten blocks before having to stop for a light, if she could hold her breath until he spoke to her, if her cell phone rang before they reached their destination—the NYU Hospital complex—well, then the body she was about to see would belong to somebody other than Ellen.

The medical examiner's offices were housed in a building on First Avenue and Thirty-Third Street. The viewing room was on the second floor, which seemed odd to Rannie: Didn't a subterranean tomblike location seemed more fitting for the activity at hand? A large picture window, with a shade-like contraption pulled across it, was cut into an interior wall. Rannie clutched Tim's hand as a doctor, a light-skinned black woman with freckled cheeks and a space between her front teeth, came in to explain what Rannie would see—a body lying on a stretcher with a sheet draped over it to the neck—and emphasized that it was important for Rannie to take a careful look. "I understand why folks want to get this over with fast, but you want to be sure when you say yes or no. Okay?"

Rannie nodded obediently. Tim told her to take a couple of deep breaths and then said, "She's ready."

The doctor pressed what appeared to be a doorbell button by the window. The shade began to open. Involuntarily, Rannie's eyelids snapped shut. But then she forced herself to look.

Ellen. It was Ellen. Rannie was 110 percent, beyond-a-shred-of-doubt sure. Ellen had been an angsty, antsy person, her hands always in motion, her face continually changing expression, registering any slight degree of emotional change. Now, under pitiless fluorescent light, her features were arranged in an imperturbable, solemn expression, immobile in a wholly permanent way; there was no rise and fall of the sheet covering her body.

"Yes," Rannie managed. Her eyes fixed on the small beauty mark on Ellen's upper lip, something that Rannie had forgotten in her list of possible "disqualifications." "Yes. I'm sure."

Rannie sank into a chair. Tim, squatting down next to her, awkwardly wrapped an arm around her. Rannie shrugged him off. She didn't want to be touched, comforted. She wanted to be left alone. A tall, pleasant-looking guy—someone her dad might have described as a "long drink of water"—entered the room, flashed a badge, and identified himself as Sergeant William Grieg. As he questioned her, carefully taking notes, Rannie realized that for all the years she and Ellen had worked together, for all the umpteen million hours they'd spent in each other's offices or over sandwiches, dissecting and analyzing the smallest bit of drama at S&S, she could actually provide few facts about Ellen. Rannie had to take a pass on Ellen's exact date of birth, middle name. Still, the effort to supply answers postponed thinking about the only question that really mattered. Why was Ellen dead?

"I know Ellen grew up in Ann Arbor and has an older brother," Rannie told Grieg. "As far as I know, both her parents are alive. I think they live in Connecticut now. Beyond that"—Rannie shrugged—"I'm sorry."

When he was done, he said, "I don't want Ms. Donahoe's identity released until we've notified the family, understood?"

Rannie nodded obediently. "How did she die?" There were no bruises on Ellen's face.

"She was stabbed. Death occurred almost immediately."

Maybe she was supposed to say "Well, that's a blessing." All she did was nod again.

"Ms. Bookman, I'm going to let you go home in just a minute. But first, can you tell me if your friend received threats of any kind recently? Any bad breakup? A jealous ex?"

"A long-term romance ended a few months ago. But the guy ended it, not Ellen."

Grieg asked for the name anyway. "Now take your time on this—is there any reason, no matter how far-fetched you think it might be—for Ms. Donahoe to be worrying about her own safety?"

Ooh, that was tricky. "Well, she was the editor of a new book by Ret Sullivan that will be published very soon."

He kept on writing but cocked an eyebrow.

"Ret's murder really shook up Ellen. . . . Me, too," Rannie added. First Ret. Now Ellen. Bad luck came in threes. How good were the odds that sometime in the near future she'd be lying in state on the other side of that fake window? "I was the one who discovered Ret Sullivan's body on Saturday."

The writing stopped. "*You?*" Maybe it was all in her head, but suddenly he seemed to be giving her the hairy eyeball.

"Yes. I was sent to Ms. Sullivan's apartment to pick up a book manuscript. I'm a copy editor." Rannie pressed her lips together, recalling Ellen's frightened voice messages. "Ellen worried that Ret Sullivan was murdered because of something in the book. Ellen was scared that perhaps she was in danger too. But I don't—"

The cop cut her off. "What's the book about?"

"I'm not supposed to say."

The idiocy of her reply struck Rannie even before Tim said, "Rannie. Come on." Homicide, after all, trumped a confidentiality agreement, so she divulged the subject of the book. "But believe me, the—the book is quite flattering. Nothing like Ret Sullivan's other books. A lot about Charlotte Cummings's social life and her jewelry and her dogs." Suddenly a passage from the book describing Charlotte's beloved doxies, Himsy and Hersy, at their weekly beauty parlor appointment caused a loony giggle to erupt from Rannie. All she could picture were the dogs under tiny metallic helmet-shaped hair dryers. She clapped a hand over her mouth and bit down on her lower lip, but that only made things worse. More convulsive tittering. Oh, God!

Tim placed both hands firmly on her shoulders. "It's okay. You're in shock. It's natural. Can I take her home now?" he asked the cop.

The cop nodded. He gave them each a card. "We're going to want to question you again, Ms. Bookman. But it can wait."

"You don't think that the two murders are linked?" The childish plaintiveness in her voice embarrassed Rannie. But she wanted to be offered some kind of escape hatch.

"They are being treated as separate investigations."

Would what Rannie had just told him change that?

"Come on. Let's get out of here." Tim maneuvered her into her coat and steered her to the elevators.

"Ellen, poor Ellen. She just got new boobs. They were still under warranty." Rannie started sobbing loudly in the elevator. Why remembering this set off a crying jag, Rannie couldn't fathom, except that people like Ellen didn't get murdered.

After her first visit to the plastic surgeon, Ellen had called Rannie. "I can't believe I'm doing this! But I've always hated my body and I'm going for it, Rannie." Before hanging up, Ellen had giggled and then warbled off-key, "BORN TO BE W-I-I-I-LD!"

Back in the car, his eyes on the traffic, Tim said, "I want to stay over tonight."

It would be a first. In all the years since her divorce, no man had ever spent the night.

"Chris is staying at a friend's tonight, working on some physics project."

Rannie remained silent. After their linguine dinner, she'd wanted nothing more than to see who could get naked the fastest. Now all she wanted was to swallow an Ativan and see how quickly it knocked her out. Of course she understood that Tim wasn't looking for a night of go-for-broke fucking, but—perversely—knowing that his intentions were selfless made her defensive, contrary, and irritable. On the other hand, what if Nate was still out? Did she really want to go back to an empty apartment?

"So?" They had reached 107th and Amsterdam. "Do I drop you off or look for a spot."

"Oh, I don't know. Look for a spot, I guess," she muttered ungraciously.

Chapter 12

As they entered the apartment, Rannie composed herself. No way in hell was she letting Nate know where she'd been. And what would she say anyway? "Where was I? Oh, just had to dash down to the morgue to identify a murder victim. No, sweetie, not the woman I found the other day. Someone else."

Fortunately, Nate had the typical teenager's interest in her work life—zilch. He'd never met Ellen. So even if Nate heard about a murder in Central Park, he'd remain ignorant of any link it had to Rannie as long as she kept her trap shut.

"Honey, I'm home," Rannie said plastering on a smile that felt like a cross between June Cleaver's and the Joker's. It was all for naught. No Nate, only a note, a scolding one at that: "No food here so I went out."

"What's he talking about?" Rannie said to Tim as she pointed to the dining room table, where the serving bowl with linguine remained half full. Ditto for the salad bowl. And Nate knew there was always a ready supply of Skippy's superchunk peanut butter, Smucker's raspberry jam, and Wonder bread, which together provided nourishment as well as comfort any time of day.

"Know what? I'm desperate for a PB&J."

"Make it two." Tim followed her into the kitchen.

Rannie slung her bag and coat on a counter and began constructing two perfect sandwiches with exactly the correct ratio of peanut butter to jam. Focusing on mundane tasks, getting out plates, pouring glasses of milk, pushed away, at least for the moment, where she'd been and what she'd seen. But she hadn't even taken bite one when her cell started trilling inside her bag. She fished it out. The number wasn't instantly familiar.

"Oh, God, what if it's Dina. Ellen's assistant. What'll I say?"

"Don't answer," he said and took the phone from her. "You've been through enough tonight. Besides, the cops have to notify the family first."

Rannie nodded. They sat at the counter, eating in silence. According to the clock it was only ten after ten. Exhaustion made it feel hours later. Tim was yawning.

Rannie looked at him. "I better leave Nate a note." Then she made a face. "How do I put it—about you staying?"

"Keep it simple, Rannie. Say 'Tim's here.' Nate'll get it."

So she said exactly that on a Post-it that she stuck on top of Nate's note. Tim was right, of course. Keep it simple: Don't answer Dina's phone call. Don't overexplain to Nate. Tim did his best to live by the touchstones of AA. The problem was that, for Rannie, *nothing*, with the possible exception of making a peanut butter sandwich, ever seemed simple.

When she returned to the kitchen, Tim's plate was clean. "Come on, kiddo. Finish up. I'm beat."

"Okay, but I want to turn on the news. Maybe there's an update. Or something on Ret."

She saw Tim's face grow red.

"Never mind! Forget I said it! Bad idea!" she said.

Too late.

Tim's fist came pounding down on the counter. "I don't get you, Rannie! I really don't!" he erupted. "We just came from the fucking morgue. Can't you give it a rest?"

This wasn't the first time he'd blown up at her; nevertheless, it always caught her off guard. Tim angry was scary. And he was incapable of being merely a little pissed off or somewhat irritated; he always went straight from zero to enraged.

"Ellen was my friend! I want to know why she's dead. Why is that so crazy?"

"Oh, no! I know you! There's more to it than that! You remember the last time you decided to do a little investigating? Huh? Do you? You nearly got tossed off your roof."

Rannie didn't reply. Tim continued to stare at her, shaking his head, but already she could see the fury had subsided. He looked repentant. "You make me nuts. You really do," he finally said, rubbing his forehead and raking a hand through his hair. "I just don't want anything happening to you."

"I know." Then suddenly Rannie grew alarmed. "Hold on. Is there stuff you're not telling me that you've heard? 'Cause if there is—"

He cut her off. "No. I'm just trying to explain how I feel and doing a shit job of it." Then with her napkin, he came over and wiped peanut butter off the corner of her mouth.

Right then the front door opened.

"Ma?"

"In the kitchen," she called with false cheer.

A second later Nate appeared. "Hey," he said to Tim. He took in the open jars of peanut butter and jam. "So Ma has you hooked?"

Had he seen the note? Maybe so because Nate avoided eye contact with Rannie and beat a hasty retreat to his room.

"Come on. No more dawdling," Tim said a moment later. Rannie took the hand he extended and followed him to her bedroom. They took turns brushing their teeth and flossing. Then they undressed, Tim stripping down to boxers.

"I'm warning you. I'm a covers hog," Rannie said as she pulled back the quilt. "And I feel about as sexy as I look." She was wearing a Chapel School T-shirt, XX-Large, which came down to her knees. That and a pair of white cotton socks.

"Understood."

In a minute they were both settled in bed, Tim behind her with an arm cradled around her shoulder. She could feel his breath on the back of her neck.

"Sorry I lost it before. Didn't your mama warn you about the Irish?"

"Lucky for you, I never listened to anything she said."

He held her closer and kissed her hair.

Rannie let out a long, slow sigh and in a little while her eyelids grew heavy and her body began to relax, her muscles unknotting one by one. Here in the darkness with Tim beside her, she could almost trick herself into believing that the world outside the bedroom, where such horrible things happened, didn't exist. There was nobody else she wanted to be with.

Then—was it five minutes or five hours later?—she awoke. Her mouth was dry and she was shivering; somehow the quilt had migrated to the other side of the bed and morphed into a cocoon with Tim inside it, in an annoyingly peaceful sleep. Rannie fumbled for her glasses and peered at the clock. Almost three. She drank a glass of water in the bathroom and padded back to bed, where first she gave Tim a gentle tap, and when that didn't work, poked him hard in the back.

"Wake up, Tim."

"Wha?" Only a faint stirring.

Rannie shook him by the shoulder. "Wake up!"

His head emerged from the cocoon, his hair spikier than ever. He blinked and as he returned to a conscious state smiled groggily at Rannie.

"*You're* the covers hog! I'm freezing."

"Sorry." His voice was raspy from sleep. He managed to unfurl part of the quilt and held it over her tentlike. "Come on in."

Rannie nestled beside him. Almost immediately the heat radiating off his body enveloped her.

In no time, Tim fell back asleep. Rannie did not.

How odd . . . When she'd gone to sleep a few hours earlier, Tim's presence had been nothing more than comforting; now it was arousing. She swallowed hard as she felt a familiar tingling in her breasts and farther down, deep inside her. Oh, the magic of endorphins; when all else failed, you could at least count on pure animal drive to restore some glimmer of hope about life and the future. Rannie peeled off her T-shirt and socks, snuggled closer, hooking a foot around Tim's leg.

"Hey, you," she whispered, kissing him on the neck, on the ear, on his jawline.

Instinctively, Tim reached out and drew her closer. As soon

as he felt her bare skin, he murmured, "When did you lose that hot negligee?"

"Listen. I can't get back to sleep and it's your fault. So you owe me."

He was wide awake now. Tim sat up and shimmied out of his boxers.

"Lie back," Rannie said, and, straddling Tim, began flicking her tongue back and forth over his right nipple, then the left, then the right again. Tim murmured something unintelligible. When he started to maneuver himself inside her, Rannie pushed his hand away. She wanted to call the shots tonight, and she wanted to stretch out the "intro."

Tim understood. Obligingly, he raised both hands over his head, signaling "I'm all yours."

With one hand, she traced the outline of his eyebrows, the rim of his eyelashes, and the curve of his nose and lips. It was like she was drawing a picture of his face, a face that was better than beautiful to her. When she bent down to kiss him, his mouth opened and she ran her tongue over the place where one of his front teeth overlapped the other. Then she leaned back and stroked Tim's chest with one hand, while with the other, she stroked her breasts. However and wherever she touched Tim, she touched herself as well.

Tim was watching her. "You are something," he said.

Yeah, this was one thing she was good at, something that had always come naturally. Rannie closed her eyes, slipped in Tim's cock, and started rocking back and forth, slowly at first, squeezing him inside her, ratcheting up the rhythm little by little. Every time she felt herself edging too close to an orgasm, she'd lean back, not moving until the tension in her body lessened a bit; then she'd start moving again. Tim met her thrust for thrust. He wasn't a talker; he didn't ever make a lot of noise. He was purposeful, intuitive, and almost calm about fucking.

Brushing away Rannie's hands, he cupped her breasts. Even their breathing was in sync, quickening at the same instant. One part of her wanted to hold back; if she didn't, this would be over. But she couldn't and so there was nothing to do except go with the moment.

One of them came a nanosecond before the other but who— Tim or Rannie—she had no idea. She remained stone still until the last little waves had finished rippling through her, then lay beside Tim.

He held her hand in both of his. "So it was me instead of an Ativan," she heard him say. Already her eyes were closed: she felt peaceful. The last thing Rannie remembered was Tim carefully arranging the quilt over her.

She slept deeply but not nearly long enough. The next time her eyes opened, the room was filling with a harsh and cheerless gray light. Shreds of an upsetting dream floated before her but were disintegrating rapidly; in the dream Rannie was somewhere with Ellen and Ret, who were dead but neither one realized it. Dream Rannie was in anguish, unable to decide whether to break the news or leave them happily ignorant.

It was nearly six o'clock. The police must have called Ellen's parents by now. Was there any news worse than hearing your child had been murdered? How did a parent go on for even a minute, much less a day, a month, a year? Rannie no longer expected good luck; nowadays a glass somewhat less than half full seemed acceptable. All she asked from the God she didn't believe in was to avoid life-shattering bad luck.

All at once an icy, irrational panic seized hold of her, forcing Rannie out of bed, back into her T-shirt and socks and down the hall, where she peeked in on Nate, her pulse slowing at the sight of him asleep on his back, mouth open, safe and sound.

She was up for good. After grabbing her bathrobe, a pink terrycloth number from Mama Bookman, she made a pot of Zabar's house blend and sat in the living room with her mug, waiting for the caffeine to kick in. On the coffee table was the *Times* crossword puzzle that Tim had been working on last night. A Monday puzzle and almost half was blank. It irked Tim that Rannie dismissed the early weekday puzzles as being too easy to bother with. And it irked her just as much that he actually liked the word scrambles in the *Daily News*. The snob in her wondered if such a difference could count as the root problem of their relationship.

Rannie gathered up all the sections of yesterday's paper for recycling. Underneath them lay the copy of *Tattletale*, Ret Sullivan's face suddenly staring up at her. It was unsettling.

The photo was from Ret's red lipstick, French twist glory days. A sly taunting smile played on her lips, a smile that said, "I know lots of secrets." Rannie found herself picking up the book. For some reason, the credit line caught her eye. "Written by Lina Struvel." The longer she looked at the name, the phonier it started to sound. A pseudonym?

Rannie located a yellow legal pad and a Bic. First she wrote out the name backward and came out with Anil Levurts. No cigar. After that, she tried a code that she and her friends used for passing notes in elementary school, a code that had seemed so "top secret" to ten-year-olds. Rannie rewrote the name, substituting B's for A's, C's for B's, D's for C's, and so on. She wound up with Mjob Tusvwfm. No cigar, not even cigar ash.

Then all of a sudden certain letters in the author's name started jumping out at her, calling attention to themselves. The "R," the "E," the "T."

To be sure, Rannie wrote out "Lina Struvel" first and then wrote "Ret Sullivan" underneath and began drawing lines between matching letters. Well, what do you know! A word scramble!

Ret had written *Tattletale,* every over-the-top flattering word of it! It wasn't a biography at all; it was Ret's autobiography, actually more like a really long mash note to herself.

Rannie sat back on the couch, sipping coffee, and mulled. She bet the idea had been Larry's. It was so like him to play a game like this. "Who better to write it?" Rannie could almost hear him saying to Ret. "It'll be a hoot. Say whatever you want about yourself." Why wouldn't Ret have jumped at the offer?

So everything Larry had said yesterday about being out of touch with Ret for years was a bunch of baloney. Rannie tried to be objective about his deception. She hadn't seen Larry in ages. There was no earthly reason for him to tell her who wrote *Tattletale* . . . was there? Nevertheless, Rannie wished he hadn't lied so blatantly and so convincingly.

"You okay? Whatcha doing out here?"

Startled, Rannie turned. Tim was standing behind the couch. He was unshaven but already had on the khakis and polo shirt he'd worn last night. He leaned over and, clasping her around the shoulders, nuzzled the back of her neck.

"Mmmm. You smell good." Rannie, closing her eyes, was settling into his embrace when abruptly his hands pulled away.

"Aw, come on!"

Her eyes flew open. She turned and saw Tim pointing at *Tattletale*. "That's what you're reading first thing in the morning?"

"I wasn't. Scout's honor. I was just sitting here with my coffee and the cover caught my eye. C'mere. Look at the author's name." Rannie moved over and patted the sofa. Tim didn't move.

"Then look." She proffered her sheet of yellow paper. "I thought there was something strange about the name. Lina Struvel."

Tim glanced at it. This was when Tim, dedicated fan of word scrambles, was supposed to marvel at her cleverness. Instead all he did was nod and say, "Yeah. I get it. So Ret Sullivan wrote her own biography."

"I know the editor. I saw him just yesterday. For freelance. We were talking about Ret. But he never said a word. He told me he hadn't been in touch with Ret for years. The police have already questioned him."

"What's the guy's name?"

"Larry Katz. Why?"

"No reason. Don't even know why I'm asking."

Tim was not a practiced fibber. Once again, the unnerving thought occurred to Rannie that Tim might be more looped into the investigation than he was letting on. But she didn't press the issue. Instead, she offered breakfast, which he declined, claiming that a meat delivery truck was arriving at seven. He was gone five minutes later. No good-bye kiss.

Chapter 13

AFTER ONE MORE CUP OF COFFEE, RANNIE MADE THE BED AND then turned on the shower where—global warming be damned— she remained for a good fifteen minutes. As hot water drubbed down on her skull full blast, it seemed that all her brain could think about was murder. Tim was right. The urge was sick. It was like mental scab picking, but Rannie couldn't help herself.

Did the murders appear to be more alike than different? One was private, an at-home crime; the other, in Central Park, occurred in as public a place as was possible to find in New York; both were violent crimes but one was a strangling, the other a stabbing. One seemed planned, the other appeared random. The murders happened at different times of day, though only two days apart. Except for the author-editor connection, there would be little reason to link the crimes. Of course, that single word "except" deserved to be printed in fifty-point type and in bold-face. All of which brought Rannie back to one conclusion: both women had been murdered by the same person. What bound

Ellen and Ret together, like consecutive signatures in a side-sewn binding, was the Charlotte Cummings biography.

Rannie was dressed and in the dining room with a bagel when Nate hove into view.

"Want breakfast?"

He shook his head. "I'm meeting Olivia at Dunkin' Donuts." Nate was trying to be subtle but Rannie saw him shifting his glance to the living room and then the kitchen.

"Tim left already," she told him.

"Oh," Nate said.

She was all set to be parentally responsible and have a discussion on the matter of Tim staying over and how exactly Nate felt about it when he blurted out, "He's a nice guy, Ma." Then quickly he shouldered his backpack, a tennis racket sticking out of the top, and was already in the front hall before turning and in a rush adding, "You deserve somebody nice."

Rannie broke into a wide smile, one that Nate didn't see. The door had already slammed behind him.

A few minutes later Rannie heard the paper land with a thunk. Ellen's murder qualified as not-quite-top news: the story—with Ellen's name withheld—appeared below the fold on page one. Reading it, Rannie was able to piece together a rough time line of events. From eight fifteen to nine a group of dog walkers had been in the Pinetum, their dogs off leash. One man was quoted as saying, "Believe me, if there'd been a body around, the dogs would have found it. We were there until the rain started coming down really hard." They'd left about nine thirty, nine forty. At ten thirty a bike rider discovered Ellen's bloody, muddy body.

Ellen was such a creature of habit that even Rannie knew her regular running route. She always jogged to Eighty-Fifth Street and Central Park West, entered the park, continued around the reservoir twice—what in Ellen's mind counted merely as a "little fun run"—and started heading for home from the park exit at Ninety-Fifth Street. The Pinetum was no more than a hundred to two hundred yards from the Eighty-Fifth Street park entrance. So Ellen had just begun her run when the murderer waylaid her.

There wasn't a word for how unjust Ellen's death was. It had been raining so hard: if only once, just once, Ellen had stayed home and let a little cellulite build up, she would have finished packing and boarded the plane to the Caribbean.

By the time Rannie finished the paper, the little hand still hadn't reached the eight. She was depressed and jumpy—a terrible combo. She thrummed her fingers on the dining table. Her brain was jazzed from all the caffeine. There were simply too many hours in the day looming emptily before her. Her good angel, perched primly on one shoulder, ordered her to work on the manuscript on the CEO mentality for Larry and then call Mary to meet for lunch and a movie. Her bad angel had other ideas, whispering tantalizingly in her ear, "Call Larry. Call Larry. He knows more than he's telling."

So who would she listen to?

"Hello, Larry. It's Rannie."

"You heard about Ellen?"

Okay, word was out. "Yes" was Rannie's reply.

"I can't talk. The cops want me down at the precinct."

A second trip?

As she hung up it crossed Rannie's mind that Larry referring to "Ellen"—and not the more formal, acquaintance-worthy "Ellen Donahoe"—suggested Larry was on fairly familiar terms with Ellen in addition to Ret. Was he the Larry on the phone with Ellen's assistant?

Cutthroat was in full view on her desk, and partially to atone for listening to her bad angel before, Rannie worked her way through the first chapter and part of the second. Still, while trying her hardest to stay focused on the pages, Rannie kept thinking about Larry.

Larry Katz, at least the Larry Katz Rannie had known, seemed constitutionally incapable of murder, not because he was such a paragon of humankind but because carrying out something premeditated required traits that weren't in Larry's genetic code. He was smart enough, for sure, but he wasn't purposeful, aggressive, detail oriented, or remotely good at follow-through. Yet the cops clearly considered him a person of interest.

Giving up on the manuscript, Rannie searched her desk drawers for her date book—a Sierra Club special with gorgeous photos of places she'd probably never get to visit—and opened to the current week, almost hoping to see in the Tuesday space "Annual checkup" or some other obligation that would take up a goodly chunk of time. Tomorrow Nate had his interview at Yale. That, however, didn't solve the problem of today. Then Rannie's eye traveled down to the December month-in-review box where she'd circled a date and written, "Mary's birthday!!"

Okay, now here was exactly the kind of good angel errand she'd been hoping for. She would find the absolutely perfect present and spend hours doing so.

In the estimation of her former mother-in-law, Saks Fifth

Avenue bore the closest approximation to the hallowed B. Alt-
man's department store, which had been closed since 1989 yet
whose demise—there was that word again!—Mary had never
ceased to lament.

Saks opened at ten. Rannie watered Tim's tulips, called and
left a message saying how much it meant having him with her
last night, then washed whatever dishes were in the sink; after
dispensing with recyclables in the back hall, she made it to the
bus shelter on Broadway and 108th Street by nine fifteen.

Traveling aboveground in midtown Manhattan was an exercise in frustration unless you went on foot or took a cab between
the hours of midnight and dawn. Today, however, time was not a
consideration, so Rannie patiently waited for the 104 bus, which
lumbered through traffic, wheezing to its assigned stops every
two blocks along the avenue. At one point a lady of indetermi-
nate age came on board carrying a copy of *Tattletale*, which kept
her engrossed for the course of her ride. A pity, really, that Ret
didn't know what a hot topic she was once again.

A crosstown bus ride later, Rannie arrived at Fifth Avenue
and Fiftieth Street and at 10:01 began cruising the aisles on the
ground floor of Saks, already decked out as a silvery holiday
wonderland. In one of the mahogany and glass display cases she
spotted a pair of gray kid gloves. Before dwelling on the price
Rannie whipped out her charge card and paid.

The day was warmer than its predecessors by at least ten degrees, so Rannie headed one block east to Madison and then
continued north on foot through the Fifties, which in recent decades had become a dispiriting stretch of banks, costume jewelry
stores, and bland clothing boutiques. Rannie had reached the

posher Sixties, where art gallery owners and fashion designers had set up shop when it hit her: she had given Mary gloves last Christmas, maybe even gray ones.

Irritated with herself, Rannie waited for the light then crossed to the other side of Madison Avenue so that the return trip to Saks would at least offer different shop windows to inspect. She hadn't walked more than a couple of blocks before she came upon a tiny gift shop sandwiched in between a Belgian chocolatier and a place that sold nothing but antique glass paperweights. Rannie stopped. The name of the boutique was Bibilots—it was the one owned by Barbara Gaines, the one Mary had described as "so darling." And no wonder; it looked like Wasp retail heaven. In the front window were artfully arranged needlepoint pillows with clever sayings, shell-encrusted wall mirrors and picture frames, toile place mats and matching napkins, painted Italian pottery candlesticks, leather travel jewelry cases in fruit sorbet colors, and eyelet lace handkerchiefs, the kind that almost nobody except Mary still carried in their purses.

Rannie buzzed and waited for the answering buzz to enter.

Bibi glanced up from behind a pair of half-frame glasses perched on her nose. She'd been reading in a small armchair tucked in the far corner of the store, but at the prospect of a customer, she shut the book. "Hello. Please have a look around and—" A startled expression crossed Bibi's face and stopped her well-modulated voice in midsentence. She rose. "Rannie?" She came forward to greet her. "Rannie Bookman, right?"

"I'm impressed. Nobody ever gets my name straight."

"Maybe it's because I'm saddled with a funny nickname too," Bibi said.

"Mary's birthday is coming up. She mentioned your store, what terrific taste you have. And just from a quick look in the window I saw about ten things she would love."

"Browse to your heart's content. Everything is twenty percent off."

The interior was small almost to the point of claustrophobic and doubly hard to navigate what with so many highly breakable items displayed on the glass vitrines, demilune side tables, and small chests that were also for sale. One false move and a collection of art deco perfume bottles would be nothing but very expensive shards. Still, it seemed impolite not to take her time browsing, especially since Bibi kept chatting, filling Rannie in on the history of Bibilots—she'd opened it shortly after her husband died—taking pains to make certain Rannie understood that financial necessity had played no part in the venture. "From the start, it's been like a hobby. I have no head for business." She tapped her forehead. "I'm thick as a plank, but whether I have a good year or a bad year, well, it doesn't matter terribly much. You would not believe the rent now, absolutely as-tro-nom-i-cal." Bibi enunciated each syllable separately. "Still, this place keeps me out of trouble."

These last words, spoken so airily, were uttered at the exact moment Rannie's eyes fell on a lacquered cocktail tray atop which were six art deco martini glasses. Considering Bibi's affiliation with AA, Rannie wondered whether her glibness about running a gift store was merely for a stranger's benefit. According to Tim, steady work—the responsibility of showing up for a job day after day—helped alcoholics stay sober. And it didn't matter if you were punching a time clock or on Goldman Sachs's payroll or handing checks to yourself, as Bibi was.

Rannie nodded as she picked up an address book covered in watermarked silk. "Everything in here practically screams 'Mary wants me,' but I saw some handkerchiefs in the window."

"Of course! They're initialed. I'll get you ones with an embroidered M on them. How perfect!"

In a flash, Bibi retrieved the handkerchiefs. They *were* perfect and not "as-tro-nom-i-cal" in price. Rannie could imagine them acquiring the lovely "grandma smell" and taking their rightful place inside Mary's ladylike black leather handbags.

Rannie watched Bibi's large capable hands cut off exactly the right-sized square of hot pink-and-white polka-dot gift paper for the box and then snip off a length of lime green ribbon. So very Palm Beach.

Force of habit, Rannie checked her left wrist for the time.

"Sorry. I'll hurry."

"No, no. I'm not in a rush. I—uh, I lost—my watch, so of course now I find myself always obsessively checking the time."

"I bet it'll turn up. Just recently I found a bracelet that vanished years ago. My grandmother had given it to me. One day I was taking the cover off a tennis racket and out it fell."

"I'm afraid my watch is gone for good." Then Rannie added, although why was anybody's guess, "I got mugged—at knife-point."

Bibi had finished wrapping the box and was affixing a Bibilots label onto it. She looked up, aghast. "You poor thing! Where did it happen? You must have been terrified!"

Rannie didn't relish recounting the incident, particularly since it had been her own damn fault, but mentioning it now had also been her own damn fault. "It happened one night right on my block."

Bibi seemed relieved after learning Rannie's address, which, in all likelihood, was many zip codes from hers.

"Well, I know that you can get fab-ulous space up there," she said. Her "up there" made it sound as if Rannie had chosen to live in the frozen tundra with only starving wolves for neighbors.

Bibi handed Rannie the wrapped gift. "Hang on just a sec. I have something for you. Not a replacement for your watch but . . ." Next to the tray with martini glasses was a stack of coasters. Bibi took four for Rannie. On each was a clock face, the painted hands set perpetually at five, an unstated allusion to the Wasp rallying cry "It's always five o'clock somewhere!"

Rannie laughed. "That's so nice really, but—"

"It's nothing. I thought these would sell like hotcakes and I way overordered. So think of it as relieving me of inventory." Bibi slipped the coasters into a small shopping bag along with Mary's handkerchiefs.

Rannie was ready for the return trip to Saks when a pang of guilt forestalled her. Her mother's birthday was in early January. Normally Rannie made do by sending the newest Rosamunde Pilcher or Nora Roberts novel via Amazon. But now Rannie told herself that it wouldn't kill her to put in a little more effort. And there was a picture frame that her mother would love.

Different in temperament as they were, Rannie and her mother, both native, landlocked Midwesterners, shared a passion for the ocean; among her happiest childhood memories—or at least happy memories involving her mother—were those of shell collecting on Bookman family vacations in rental houses on Cape Cod.

"Would you mind showing me a picture frame in the window? The one with scallop shells."

"I hope you're not feeling obligated to buy something else."

"No, of course not," Rannie replied, though actually she did, a little bit. "My mother's birthday is coming up, too."

"I've got those frames already boxed in back. It'll just take me a sec to find one." Bibi told her the price, which even minus twenty percent was far more than Rannie had expected to spend. Bibi grabbed her book before disappearing on the other side of a pink-and-white polka-dot curtain. The book that Bibi had been reading was *Tattletale*.

Bibi returned and in a minute crafted another expertly wrapped gift.

"Thanks so much." Rannie waved good-bye. Her smile felt a little pasted on. Bibi's choice of reading matter had startled her. Yet really why should it? After all, *Tattletale* was turning into an instant bestseller. It seemed like everybody and his mother had a copy. There seemed no imaginable way that Bibi Gaines could know of Ret's book about her grandmother. Unless—was this beyond crazy to think?—Bibi was Audio.

Walking back to Saks, Rannie tested out the possibility. No one was closer to Charlotte Cummings or knew more about her than her granddaughter. And *Portrait of a Lady* was completely unlike Ret's other books—it cast Charlotte Cummings in almost sanctified light. Bibi would be gratified by the portrayal.

Even so, would Bibi agree to lay out her grandmother's life before the likes of Ret Sullivan? Rannie recalled Tim's remark about Audio being a paid snitch. But Bibi Gaines surely didn't need the money. What other incentive was there? Might Ret have called and said something like, "Look, I'm writing a biography of your grandmother, whether or not you agree to help." The news wouldn't have made Bibi happy, not if she knew of

Ret's previous search-and-destroy biographies. If so, then Bibi Gaines was caught in a thorny beggar's bargain. Perhaps she concluded it was better to be the primary source for the book. Maybe she had even wangled manuscript approval, though that seemed doubtful knowing how Ret Sullivan operated. Certainly Bibi would have been dead set against *any* acknowledgment of her participation in the book. Yet Ret gave props to somebody she called "Audio."

A car horn honking put a sudden stop to all her theorizing. Rannie suddenly realized she was crossing against the light; a taxi swerving onto Madison Avenue had narrowly avoided her. Rannie smiled apologetically and held up a hand in thanks. Behind closed windows the cabdriver was shouting something and she was sure it wasn't "You're welcome."

She was only half a block away from Saks. As she went in the Fiftieth Street side entrance of the department store, Rannie ended up deciding to burst the trial balloon of Bibi as Audio. It wasn't so much a rational judgment; it relied more on Rannie's being unable to conjure Bibi and Ret together in any sort of association, even a semiforced one. If Ret had contacted Bibi, Rannie imagined her likely response would have been on the order of, "You're writing a book about Grammy? *Bonne chance!*" and then slamming down the phone.

Chapter 14

ON THE HOMEWARD-BOUND BROADWAY BUS, RANNIE CHECKED her cell. There were text messages from various S&S folk, all understandably in shock over Ellen's death. Only Ellen's assistant, Dina, thought to connect the dots between Ret's murder and Ellen's. *"Please say the big secret book isn't by Ret."*

A text from Larry simply said, *"Call."* That would wait until she was home.

One by one, she deleted texts. There were also old voice messages; Rannie was all set to clear them en masse when she realized some were from Ellen on Sunday. A chill slithered up from the nape of her neck and across her scalp. She shouldn't delete them, should she? Not before informing the police of their existence. All she remembered about the messages was the increasing note of panic in her friend's voice. Was there anything more? Should Rannie listen to them again?

No. She couldn't bear to.

In her wallet was the card of the policeman from the morgue. William Grieg. As soon as she was in her apartment, Rannie called. Grieg arrived half an hour later and, after listening to Ellen's messages, said, "Ms. Bookman. You think you're up to answering some questions now?" Immediately Rannie wished that she had a hand to hold, specifically one belonging to Tim Butler. "One sec," she said and called Tim again, leaving a message to get in touch; right after, she felt babyish and so, facing Grieg with a look of resignation, told him, "I'm not eager. But since you're here . . ."

Over Diet Cokes in the living room, Rannie talked while Grieg studiously took notes.

"What time did Ellen Donahoe usually go for a run?"

"On days she wasn't at work, around nine thirty."

"Had Frank . . ." He leafed back in his notebook. "Frank Meeker tried to contact her recently?"

"Not that I know of. He's married now." The SOB.

"Was Ms. Donahoe seeing anyone new?"

"Yes. But she didn't say who. On Sunday she was meeting the guy for lunch. She said it was nobody special."

Grieg asked about colleagues from S&S and what Ellen's job entailed, so Rannie used Ellen's relationship with Ret as an example of an editor's function. Grieg seemed surprised at how much day-to-day involvement and confidence boosting were required in the job.

"Had they worked together before?"

"Yes." Rannie explained that Ellen had been Ret's editor for many books, including *Dark Side of the Moon,* the biography of Mike Bellettra. "Ellen was devastated about what happened to Ret. I don't know if you remember—"

"Remember? Who could forget, Bellettra attacking her like that? Lye—nasty stuff." He shook his head in distaste. "I once followed up on a 911, a domestic, a woman screaming how her husband was threatening to kill himself by swallowing lye. He did it too, right as I came in the apartment. It took two days for the poor bastard to die." Grieg paused and his brow furrowed. "You know, actually now that I'm thinking about it, it wasn't lye. It was Drano." He nodded to Rannie. "Yeah, definitely Drano."

Rannie refrained from comment. Lye. Drano. Lemon-scented Clorox. What did it possibly matter which lethally corrosive cleanser the poor schlub had taken?

The cop consulted his notes again and, looking up at Rannie, asked, "Do you know Lawrence Katz?"

Strangely, it took a half second for Rannie to compute that Larry and Lawrence Katz were one and the same.

"Larry? Yes! Why?"

Grieg avoided the question. "How do you know him?"

"He used to work at Simon & Schuster, where I once worked. That's where I first met him."

" 'First' met him?" Grieg repeated.

"Years ago, after my divorce, Larry and I saw each other for a short time . . . socially." Grieg kept his expression neutral, she noticed. "Larry left New York. We lost touch. It was a short romance." Rannie frowned. "We connected at an unhappy time in both our lives, and for a while being unhappy together seemed better than being unhappy alone." Rannie could hear herself and mentally winced: Why did she feel it necessary to blather on about her neediness to a member of the NYPD?

"When were you last in touch?"

Rannie crossed her legs. "Well, coincidentally I saw Larry yesterday. It was the first time in ages." How suspicious did that sound?

"You ran into him?"

"No. I had a meeting with him at Dusk Books." That sounded professional, aboveboard.

"Why suddenly reconnect?"

The short-form answer was "I hoped he'd have freelance work for me." Then Rannie drained her Diet Coke and added, "Well, truthfully it was more than that." Jesus! Why had she used the word "truthfully" as if up till now she'd been lying like a shag rug? Rannie wet her upper lip, which felt stuck to her gum. "Dusk, where Larry works, just published a book about Ret Sullivan. It's called *Tattletale*." Rannie paused. "And I have to confess—" Shit! "Confess"? What was wrong with her? "I have to confess that morbid interest made me call Larry. I was curious if he'd kept up with Ret."

"So he knew Ms. Sullivan?"

Grieg had to be aware of that already since he was part of the homicide investigation and Larry had been questioned, twice now. "Publishing is a very small world," Rannie replied.

"And had he?"

Rannie looked at him blankly. "Had he what?"

"Had Mr. Katz kept up with Ms. Sullivan?"

Ooh. This was getting stickier and stickier. "He said no."

He stopped writing and looked up. "Any reason not to believe him?

Rannie owed no allegiance to Larry Katz, not when she was being interviewed about a double homicide. Yet she wished giving a forthright answer didn't feel quite so much like ratting out someone whom she'd once been genuinely fond of. "Larry is the kind of guy who loves crossword puzzles, anagrams, any kind of word game. I mention this because the author of *Tattle-*

tale is called Lina Struvel." Rannie showed him her copy of the book. "I'm not sure why but this morning, I began fixating on the author's name. All of a sudden I saw that if you take all the letters in 'Lina Struvel' and move them around, you come out with 'Ret Sullivan.' Ret Sullivan wrote the book."

Grieg eyes were still fixed on the book cover. "A word scramble. You figured this out yourself?"

Rannie tried to smile modestly, although the obnoxious smart girl in her never ceased craving recognition of her cleverness.

"And Lawrence Katz's involvement in this book would be what?"

"I don't know this for sure, but I'm guessing he was the editor. Suggesting to Ret that she use a word-scramble pseudonym would be a very Larry thing to do."

"Why bother? It seems like everybody and his brother has a memoir out. Ret Sullivan was a big-time author. So why not have her write the book and use her own name?"

Rannie shrugged. "Maybe just for a goof." She could see Grieg was not getting the humor.

"So if Larry Katz was the editor," he pointed at *Tattletale,* "then he'd have been in touch with her, Ms. Sullivan, quite a bit, if I'm following your drift."

Rannie didn't feel a nod was even required. She sank back into the couch. Jesus, she'd just made Larry sound like a sophomoric, games-playing twit. And while he sort of was, he was also a decent guy. Larry's signing up Ret to write *Tattletale* could even be construed as a good-hearted gesture in a certain, off-kilter light. No doubt he saw profit in the book, yet handing Ret the project was a mitzvah of sorts. Rannie tried explaining this line of reasoning to Grieg. "He was throwing a lifeline to a woman who spent her days holed up in an apartment with her press clippings for company. He gave her something to do."

"Did Ellen Donahoe know Larry Katz?"

Publishing was hands-down the most incestuous business. "Yes. We all knew each other from Simon & Schuster."

"So just professional colleagues?"

Redundancy alert! Rannie's brain signaled. Colleagues by definition connoted a professional relationship. "Yes, they were business acquaintances," she said. "Ellen and I were more than that. We were friends, and she was great about giving me freelance work after I lost my job at S&S."

"Ms. Bookman, do you mind saying why you were let go?" He was tactful enough to avoid saying "fired." But Rannie could tell a whole raft of creepy reasons for dismissal had instantly occurred to him. . . . Had Ms. Bookman been stealing? Engaging in inappropriate behavior at the office—oh, maybe like getting caught having sex with the entire sales force? Or perhaps threatening another employee?

Rannie recounted in detail the ludicrous story of Nancy Drew that led her to file for unemployment. He tried to suppress a smile.

"It's okay. I'd think it was funny too if it had happened to someone else," Rannie said. Would he bother to verify her story with S&S human resources? Probably.

"Pretty harsh if you weren't the one who screwed up."

Rannie shrugged in a "whatever" way.

After that, his questions returned to Ellen. "When did you last see her?"

"On Sunday at her apartment. I picked up a copy of the manuscript about Charlotte Cummings so I could start copyediting it.

Ellen had the only hard copy besides Ret's." Uttering those last words jogged Rannie's memory. "Ellen told me that the copy she gave me and the one the police took from Ret Sullivan's apartment might not be identical."

"How so?"

"I don't know. According to Ellen, Ret Sullivan might have made some last-minute changes that would be entered on her disk. I was supposed to check over that final version. But once it was in police custody, Ellen said I should just work on the printout she gave me: she was quite sure that Ret wasn't adding new chunks or making major changes."

"But Ms. Donahoe didn't know that for certain."

Rannie frowned and suddenly started to conjure up a new scenario. Maybe Ret's final manuscript did contain a bombshell and somehow the murderer found out about it. Could Ret have been engaging in a little prepublication blackmail on the order of "Pay me to leave out the dirt, or else"?

"I don't know what to think. If the disk with you guys is meaningful, why didn't the killer take it? It was in a briefcase right in plain sight—it seems to me a briefcase would strike anyone as a logical place for the disk."

He nodded. "How familiar are you with the manuscript, the version you worked on?"

"Very."

"So you'd notice differences between the two?"

"Anything substantive, absolutely."

He asked if she'd mind coming down to the precinct.

Armed with her photocopy of *Portrait of a Lady*, Rannie accompanied the cop to his car and rode to the Twenty-Fourth Precinct on the Upper West Side, about a mile and a half from her apartment. It was a white-brick sugar cube, four stories high. Somehow the scraggly, three-quarters-dead plantings in front made the building look even uglier.

She was left at the desk of a detective on medical leave. It took two hours to read Ret's final manuscript on his PC. Phones jangled constantly, announcements came over a loudspeaker at frequent intervals, and the cops' preferred means of communication was shouting across the room to each other. None of it bothered Rannie. It was gratifying to think that her expertise was needed and valued. She was not snooping, she was aiding an investigation. And she felt completely safe inside the precinct building, safe in the same way that she'd felt when her dad would tuck her into bed before turning on her Tinker Bell night-light.

When she was done, Grieg thanked her. "I appreciate you giving up your time."

The problem was that she'd turned up bubkes. Exactly as Ellen had predicted, the two versions were essentially the same. On Ret's disk there was a more detailed description of Charlotte's Northeast Harbor "cottage," which, after her death, would become a research center for a vast wildlife preserve created from the acres of shoreline property that she owned. Again, Rannie found herself wondering if Ellen might have been Audio. She mentioned this to Grieg and showed him the acknowledgments. Ret trusted Ellen as much as she trusted anyone. They worked well together. Somehow it seemed likelier that Ellen had been killed for snooping than for editing. And yet nothing scurrilous appeared in the manuscript. Grieg scribbled all this in his pad but didn't seem impressed with Rannie's reasoning.

Once outside, Rannie took Grieg up on his offer of a ride. It was rush hour, therefore horrendous traffic.

"Actually could you hold on a sec?" she asked when they reached the sidewalk. Rannie texted Nate. *"Going straight to Grandma's. Meet me there."* It was better to avoid a phone conversation. Dinner at Mary's was the source of untold arguments between Rannie and Nate, who rightfully resented the almost inedible fare that was served. Usually they both wolfed down a quick burger or slice of pizza beforehand, but time didn't allow for that this evening.

"Instead of home, would you mind dropping me off at Eighty-Third and Park Avenue?"

"Whatever you say." Grieg opened the car door for her. "Want a real-deal police escort?"

"Absolutely!"

In less than a minute he had a flasher attached to the roof of his car and away they went, siren blasting. It was even better than riding in Ret's Rolls . . . well, maybe that was going too far. They sped through the Eighty-Sixth Street transverse and down Park Avenue in record time. So in addition to walking and two A.M. cab rides, there was yet a third way to travel aboveground in NYC unimpeded—police escort!

She thanked Grieg as Mary's white-gloved doorman extended a hand to help her from the police vehicle. Certainly this was not the usual mode of transportation for residents of the building or arriving guests; nonetheless, the doorman's smile was as cordial as ever.

"I wished I'd turned up something," Rannie said.

"I would have been amazed if you did. Double-checking is ninety-nine percent of my job."

"Same with copyediting."

The doorman was about to shut the door behind her when

Grieg held up a hand to forestall him. "One more thing." He was addressing Rannie. "By any chance, were you Audio?"

Come again? "*Me!* No! Of course not! What makes you—"

Grieg cut her off. "Just asking," he said and then, motioning for the doorman to shut the door, he took off, leaving Rannie standing under the canopy, mouth open, eyes as round and wide as in a cartoon double take.

Analyzing what prompted Grieg's last question, delivered with an undertone of accusation, had to be put on hold. The elevator door opened. There was Mary, waiting to greet her.

"Come in, come in, Rannie dear. What a day! I'm in quite a dither!" Mary exclaimed. In the past year Rannie had noticed how increasingly minor nuisances—a mix-up in a delivery from the dry cleaners, a misplaced electric bill—could send Mary into a tailspin.

The phone started ringing and Mary's hands flew up.

"Oh, Lord! It'll be Daisy again! This must be the tenth time she's called. I'd better dash off and get it."

"Dashing off" now translated to proceeding with great caution, Mary making her way haltingly from the large entry hall, through the living room, and into the small den. Mary had a cane. Rannie wished she'd use it.

"No, Daisy dear, I'm not hard of hearing," Mary was saying and motioned to Rannie to sit down. "It sometimes takes me a little while to reach the phone."

The TV was on mute in the den; however, from images flashing on the screen, all of the same tiny, fashionably dressed, anciently old lady, Rannie understood why the day had been so dither-making for Mary.

Charlotte Cummings had exhaled for the very last time.

Rannie raced to Mary's bedroom and turned on the TV. The mayor, in front of City Hall, was speaking before reporters, full-bore somber: "New York has lost a true icon," he intoned.

The coverage focused on the extraordinary length of Charlotte Cummings's life, someone born before World War I. The NBC anchor signed off, saying, "Now the life of this extraordinary lady has at last come to an end." His demeanor and tone were appropriately grave too; yet hearing a slight stress on the words "at last" made Rannie think of the Oz Munchkins warbling about the Wicked Witch, who was "really most sincerely dead."

When commercials came on, Rannie returned to the den. Mary was still on the phone.

"Oh, you managed to book a direct flight?" Mary was saying. "At this time of year and such short notice, well, yes, I *am* amazed."

Mary nodded several times in silent response to whatever Daisy was telling her. She opened an end table drawer and took out a notepad from Piping Rock Country Club, on which she began writing in her neat Chapin School print. "Yes, dear. I have everything down, though I still say Charlotte would want you to stay in Florida."

A moment later, Mary hung up. At the same time Rannie's phone pinged, announcing a text. Nate. He was bailing. "Bio test. Gotta study."

Yeah, right.

"Daisy got a call this afternoon from Charlotte's granddaughter. The first thing Daisy asked was, 'This isn't another false alarm, is it?'" Mary giggled. "But now it's all over the news."

"When and where is the funeral?" Rannie asked as Mary freshened her drink.

"Saint Thomas on Saturday morning."

A neo-Gothic structure the soothing color of chocolate pudding, Saint Thomas Church sat at the corner of Fifth Avenue and Fifty-Third Street and was famous for its boys choir. The church also boasted two walls of giant stained-glass windows, more than a hundred years old. However, over time the metalwork holding the glass had disintegrated to the point where hundreds of pieces were threatening to burst from their frames. From copyediting *Portrait of a Lady,* Rannie now knew that Charlotte Cummings had come to the rescue, coughing up three million dollars for their restoration.

"The first year we were married, Peter took me to Saint Thomas on Christmas Eve to hear the 'Hallelujah' chorus. It was transporting."

Oops. Mary's smile suddenly tightened.

Rannie rarely brought up her ex-husband, yet never mentioning him only made the elephant in the room grow more enormous. "Charm can only take you so far" had become Mary's terse and pretty much on-the-money appraisal of her youngest son. She had never really forgiven him for leaving Rannie and their kids.

Quickly Mary turned the conversation back to Charlotte Cummings's funeral. "There's a guest list and reserved seating. Can you imagine? As if it's a wedding." Mary paused to jiggle ice cubes and imbibe. "Well, I suppose a lot of important and fancy people will be there. Oh, how Daisy hates crowds since she broke her hip. She's terrified of someone knocking her over." Then all at once Mary looked "dithery" again. "Will you look at me! What an *awful* hostess I am!" Mary rose from the silk striped armchair and moments later Rannie had a glass of white wine in her hand. She sipped it tentatively. It tasted okay. Mary kept white wine in the minifridge under the bar solely for Rannie's pleasure. However, the number of visits it took to polish off a bottle meant the wine always turned sour before the bottle was empty.

"Terrible to live so long," Mary said. "Although, really, you wouldn't say Charlotte Cummings was living, would you? She just wasn't dead."

Rannie nodded and as she sipped her wine she thought more about Charlotte Cummings. It was a shame that Ret Sullivan wasn't around to dash off a last chapter on the funeral, which undoubtedly would be loaded with pomp and full of famous faces. A celebrity sendoff was just up Ret's alley. Would anyone at S&S even bother including a short preface in the book, something along the order of "Charlotte Cummings died on blah blah and was buried at blah blah"? Always conscientious Ellen certainly would have seen to it. Suddenly the wine turned sour in Rannie's mouth. Ellen too was "most sincerely dead." It wasn't even twenty-four hours ago that Rannie had identified her body. She shut her eyes as if that could block out the memory of the morgue, Ellen on the gurney.

"Dear, you look unhappy."

"No, no, I'm fine. Just tired." Rannie stopped then and blurted out a request, the words sounding strange even to her own ears. "Mary, I'd take Daisy to the funeral . . . that's if she'd like me to."

"Lord, volunteering for a funeral! I try to avoid them like the plague!"

Rannie tipped her head in acknowledgment. "It's horrible to admit. But the voyeur in me wouldn't mind seeing the turnout—*and* the restored windows." There was more to it than that, of course. A homicide detective had just accused her of being Audio, Ret's snoop. Well, the snoop in Rannie wanted, pure and simple, to check out Charlotte Cummings's funeral. She had no expectation of picking up some telltale clue in the pews of Saint Thomas that would solve either Ret's murder or Ellen's. Nevertheless, Rannie felt an urge to go, and here was the perfect excuse to do so.

"Well, I'll certainly mention it to Daisy. The windows *are* something to see now."

Mary offered a tray of withered baby carrots. "I had absolutely no idea that airlines give a 'bereavement' discount," she said brightly. "Otherwise Daisy would have had to pay more than thirteen hundred dollars for a plane ticket!"

Rannie dipped a carrot in a small bowlful of something that bore a faint resemblance to salsa and yet tasted more like unheated tomato vegetable soup. Then she broke the news about Nate.

"Well, isn't that too bad? But I understand. I told Nate I'll be there when the Chapel tennis team plays Collegiate. That's in just a week."

Here was one of the reasons Rannie loved Mary. She accepted without a particle of rancor her fairly bit part in Nate's life now. Rannie's mother, on the other hand, seemed almost to revel in taking umbrage over any slight from her grandchildren . . . or her daughters.

The news over, Rannie and Mary watched *Jeopardy!*, another of Mary's sacred rituals, most evenings in Earla's company as well. "Ooh, phooey." Mary scowled upon seeing the categories pop up. "I'm hopeless at baseball." As usual, after every correct response from Rannie, Mary declared that Rannie should try out to become a contestant because she'd win "a bundle."

After Final Jeopardy!, Mary stood and collected the carrots and dip. "I'll be back in a moment. I need to heat up one of the dinners Earla left. We have a choice. Tuna tetrazzini or chili. Which do you prefer?"

"Ooh, that's hard," Rannie said. As she'd sampled both in the past, the truthful answer would have to be "neither."

"Well, since we had salsa for hors d'oeuvres, shall we do chili and make a Mexican night of it?" Mary suggested.

"Olé!" Rannie answered gaily, consoling herself that Skippy in all his wonderful chunkiness would be at home, waiting for her.

Chapter 15

A MAN IN A TRENCH COAT WAS STANDING (OR DID IT QUALIFY AS lurking?) inside the vestibule of the Dolores Court, his back to Rannie, probably hoping someone would emerge from the elevator and let him in. Obviously not a tenant or he'd have a key. Fruitlessly Rannie felt for the slim wand of Mace that she never remembered to carry. She decided to open the door just as the man turned.

It was Larry.

"What are you doing here?" she cried.

"Waiting for you."

"What do you mean? How do you know I still live here?"

"Who gives up a rent-controlled apartment? I buzzed but nobody's home. Listen, I need to talk."

Rannie blinked and didn't answer. Exactly how wrong was this, Larry just showing up at her door? And why wasn't Nate home? So much for his selfless dedication to biology.

"Look, I'm sorry if I startled you." He took a step toward her. Rannie shrank back.

"What's the matter with you?" she said. "Haven't you heard of that nifty little invention called the phone?"

"Rannie, I spent an hour and a half at the Twenty-Fourth Precinct today." If it were possible, his shoulders slumped even lower than usual. "I'm a murder suspect! Me!"

Curiosity got the best of her. Rannie found herself relenting. "All right. There's a coffee shop a block away. But I can't stay long."

They took one of the faux red leather booths at the Acropolis, where Rannie ordered a cheeseburger with bacon, fries, and a Diet Coke. "I haven't really had dinner," she explained—the chili at Mary's had looked unnervingly like cat food. Then looking quizzically at Larry, she asked, "So? What's up?"

"The cop was asking all about Ellen Donahoe, acting like I killed Ellen *and* Ret. Just because I knew them both. I tried explaining how everybody in publishing knows everybody."

So the investigations weren't separate any longer. "Was the cop named Grieg?"

"Yeah. Looks like Ron Howard's double."

The resemblance hadn't occurred to her till now, yet Larry's description was apt. "Ret was murdered Saturday afternoon. You were out of town. You told me that."

"I was at my mother's house in West Islip. But it's only fifty minutes away and I had my car."

"Surely your mother will vouch for you." Although how much credence did the police give to an alibi that came courtesy of Mom?

Larry was shaking his head. "My mother is eighty-seven and has dementia, Rannie. She thinks I'm twelve and about to have my bar mitzvah. All she worries about is whether Leonard's of Great Neck will be available for the reception."

"Well, then she's not living alone, right?"

Their order arrived. Immediately, Rannie tore into her burger—bliss! artery-clogging bliss!—while Larry stared balefully at his decaf.

"After lunch, I let Consuela go to a movie. My mother is terrible to her. Calls her a spic to her face, accuses her of stealing. I live in fear that she'll quit. So I'm at the house, I figured why not give her a break. She was gone for four hours. So all Saturday afternoon I'm basically unaccounted for."

Rannie looked at Larry and attempted an objective assessment of the man. Here sitting across a Formica table from her, one with cigarette burns from the distant pre-Bloomberg past, was a guy who already wore a hearing aid and judging from the raw nick on his chin still hadn't learned to shave properly. He'd had one quickie marriage, no kids, and seemingly his only deep and abiding relationship was with his gaga mother. Rannie had always placed filial devotion squarely in the mensch column of Larry Katz's personality traits. "I hope my kids will be half as good to me," she remembered saying to him more than once. But what about all those movies where guys with charm turn out to be knife-wielding serial killers with really big unresolved mommy issues?

Larry's next words made Rannie wonder if a ticker tape ran across her forehead broadcasting every inner thought. "I'm the same guy you knew way back when. I promise I didn't turn into some kinky killer."

Rannie remembered the noise she'd heard inside Ret's apartment. Could she imagine it being Larry on the other side of the door? Honestly, no. He was a garden-variety neurotic, a man who'd gone through years of talk therapy. He wasn't psychotic. Yet Larry had not been forthcoming about his relationship with Ret. Rannie decided to toss out a little bait.

"It makes no sense, Larry. You hadn't seen Ret in years. Why should you be a suspect?"

Larry stalled with a long sip of coffee. Then he sighed. "I actually knew Ret better than I led you to believe."

Rannie cocked an eyebrow in feigned surprise. In her kids' estimation, it was one of her few talents, something that neither of them had yet been able to master. "The police know this?"

A nod. "Yeah. That's one reason why a big neon finger is pointing at me."

Rannie waited for Larry to continue.

"For starters, the biography about Ret—*Tattletale*. She wrote it."

Okay, Larry was spilling. And oh how Rannie longed to cry out, "I already know that! Your little word scramble didn't fool me." But she congratulated herself for pulling off a credible stammer."Wh-what—what do you mean, Ret wrote it?"

"Look." Larry pulled a paper napkin from the dispenser and in a replay of what Rannie had demonstrated to both Tim and Grieg only a couple of hours earlier, Larry wrote out Ret's name and the pseudonym, pointing out to Rannie how the letters matched up. "And by the way, last time I looked, *Tattletale* was seventeen on Amazon," Larry informed her.

How typical of editors. In front of a firing squad, they'd forgo a cigarette if they could check Amazon rankings one last time. "Okay, great. So why a word scramble?"

"The pseudonym was Ret's idea. Then I suggested a word scramble, like the ones in the *Daily News* you see morons doing on the subway."

Inwardly Rannie cringed. Tim liked word scrambles.

"Ret didn't want her own name on *Tattletale*. She said, 'It's better if readers think someone else is saying wonderful things about me.'"

As she raked a french fry through ketchup, Rannie nodded. That definitely had the ring of Ret, the "raven-haired, sultry crusader who spoke truth to power."

"Another reason was she'd already started writing the big hush-hush book." Larry made air quotes around "hush-hush." "She didn't want two books by Ret Sullivan in stores at the same time. She worried they'd eat into each other's sales."

Rannie nodded. That too sounded like Ret. Shrewd and savvy.

"Sure, you get it. But when I tried explaining about the pseudonym, showing the cop the whole word-scramble thing, I could tell he thought it was just weirdo games-playing."

Ah, so it seemed Rannie hadn't revealed anything to Grieg that he didn't already know.

"Did Ret tell you who the hush-hush book was about?" Rannie asked.

"No. But it wasn't hard to guess. For all the Mata Hari drama and secrecy, she left a lot of stuff laying around about Charlotte Cummings, articles from *Vogue, Vanity Fair*. Clippings from the one-hundredth birthday."

Rannie managed to keep a poker face at the mention of Charlotte Cummings's name; nor did she bring up her own visit to Ret Sullivan's apartment. Instead she asked, "So you were over there, you actually saw Ret?"

"Only with a ski mask on—like she was about to go schussing down Park Avenue—and not in the last month, not since *Tattletale* went to press. Her cleaning lady must do one shitty job because my fingerprints are still all over the place. Another reason why I'm a person of interest." Larry pointed at the little white paper cup of coleslaw on Rannie's plate.

"Sure. Take it." Now it came back to her, Larry's annoying habit of underordering for himself and then mooching food.

"Look. Ret craved company. Could you blame her? So we'd work on the book there. She used a tape recorder for a lot of *Tattletale*. Then I'd have the stuff typed at the office. Ret was crazy for corned beef. I'd bring over sandwiches from PJ Bernstein's. She'd never eat in front of me, though—always waited till I left. She didn't want me to see her with the mask off."

"Did Ret tell Ellen about writing *Tattletale*?" Rannie asked.

Larry polished off the tangle of coleslaw in a single forkful. He swallowed and said, "No. I doubt it. Ret got off on that being our little secret, although I'm sure she leaked news of the book to *Publishers Weekly*. They ran something online about a book on Ret's life coming out." He snagged a couple of her french fries. "She kept calling *Tattletale* 'our' book . . . not that she offered any share of royalties."

"She was falling in love with you. She was, wasn't she?" It was a question but not a question. Rannie was sure she was right. She remembered the first time she'd slept with Larry. They were at his apartment. "What's someone like you doing with me? Frankly, you could do better," he'd said while Rannie undressed. Self-deprecation, however, was just part of his shtick; most women found him appealing and he knew it. Ret had a guy who came and serviced her once a week—former Suspect #1— but sex with Larry would have been entirely different.

"In love? Ret? *Please.*" Larry finished wiping his mouth with a napkin, the one he'd been writing on a minute ago. Then he caught Rannie's expression. Suddenly he looked incredulous. "Jesus Christ, Rannie, you think I was fucking Ret!"

"I didn't say that," Rannie replied lamely.

"Oh no! Hold it right there. I'll admit to a few pity fucks in my time. And I'm not saying Ret wouldn't have been up for it. She'd call late at night, ask what I was doing. She sent presents, a cashmere robe, caviar from Petrossian. But it wasn't going to happen. And not because of her face . . . or not just because of that. It was the extreme Catholic thing. Her apartment spooked me."

"What do you mean?"

"Crucifixes everywhere. The living room, the dining area. Even in the bathroom, there was Christ staring down every time I took a piss."

Rannie had seen the display crosses in the living room and the Madonna smiling down on Ret's corpse.

"It wouldn't surprise me if Ret kept hair shirts in her closet and went in for a little nightly self-flagellation." He shook his head. "I've never been turned on by Catholics. Unitarians are about as Christian as I can take."

"Ellen told me that at one point, right after Ret was disfigured, she considered taking vows."

Larry shrugged. "Maybe so. She grew up in an orphanage run by nuns. So she knew the drill. But there's nothing in *Tattletale* about becoming a nun." He went for another fry, but Rannie slapped his hand away and told him to order his own, which he did.

"Okay, Larry, so you're pretty sure that this hush-hush book is about Charlotte Cummings—"

"And I bet I can guess who's copyediting it."

"—so did Ret ever say who was doing the groundwork for her,

finding sources, you know, doing the digging that Ret used to do herself?"

Larry shook his head.

"You think it could have been Ellen?" Rannie had to wait for an answer. Larry's fries had arrived. He salted them sparingly, as if under doctor's order to limit sodium. Then he studiously drizzled an abstract pattern of ketchup over them.

"Ellen never said so."

"You two were in touch?" In his office Larry hadn't lied outright about Ellen; still, he'd misled Rannie. And why had Ellen been secretive about Larry? Was Larry Mr. Insignificant Other?

"Ellen called about *Tattletale*. She'd seen the mention in *Publishers Weekly* and was curious to read it. This was maybe, oh, a week or so before the book came out. So I went over to her apartment with a bound galley. I was going to leave it with the doorman. But he buzzed Ellen and she said to send me up. We had a little wine, caught up on life, and I left."

"Did the police find your fingerprints at Ellen's?"

"Oh, yes! I have this incredible talent for showing up at all the right places at the wrong time." The fries seemed to have lost their allure: Larry hadn't touched them. "And then there were a million questions about my *whereabouts*—Jesus, don't you hate that word?—on Monday morning. I explained I got up, went to work, couldn't find a cab, so I arrived late—even later than usual for me."

Yes, Larry had kept her waiting at the Dusk offices. "So you're unaccounted for that morning."

He heard the "oy vey" sympathy in her voice. He nodded.

Larry was in some pickle, as her corporate lawyer father used to say about clients who were on trial for forgetting to report a boatload of income to the IRS or sharing a little privileged info with investor "friends." Only this was homicide. Double homicide. Pickles didn't come big enough to describe the pickle Larry was in.

"Rannie, I look suspicious even to myself. . . . It's all so crazy. Why would I possibly want to kill either of them? And murder? I'm not physically capable of it. I get light-headed from razor cuts." He pointed to his chin as evidence.

That was true. Once Larry had cut his hand slicing tomatoes while helping Rannie make dinner. It wasn't a bad cut but oh! how he had carried on, insisting on going to the Lenox Hill emergency room.

Rannie remembered the trip vividly, not solely because Larry, his hand in a kitchen towel tourniquet, kept moaning about nerve damage and dangerous loss of blood in the cab, but also because, by strange coincidence, it was Rannie's second trip to an emergency room that week.

Nate had fallen off the top of a jungle gym in a Riverside Park playground and torn his frenum, which Rannie learned from the ER doctor was the term for the bridge of skin connecting the upper lip to the upper gum. Nate, with blood-smeared mouth and cheeks, looked like something out of a Grade Z horror movie; still, her son had been more stoic than Larry about getting stitches. "The police now think the same guy killed Ret and Ellen?" she asked.

"Seems so. And they'd like it to be me." Larry caught Rannie looking at the clock, so he signaled for a check and as soon as it came handed the waiter a twenty.

"Thanks, Larry."

"Tell me the long arm of the law will reach out and haul in the right guy."

"You're innocent. The police will find who did it."

Larry smiled. At first she read the smile as a sign that her words had offered Larry reassurance, but then he said, "You still remind me of Leslie Caron."

"It's the overbite," Rannie said, attempting to dismiss the compliment. She did not want to rekindle any old sparks. So why then was her hand, as if it had a life of its own, suddenly extended across the table, giving Larry's hand a squeeze? The sensation of holding Larry's hand triggered another memory: Rannie was in her office at S&S, rolling and unrolling her shoulders, stiff from a day at the computer that had been interrupted only for a stressful lunchtime appointment with her lawyer, signing divorce papers. Larry had passed by in the hallway, saw her, and said, "Stiff neck? I can fix that." He came in, closed the door, and gave her the best back rub of her life. "Magic fingers," he had bragged, waggling them as he left her office. Less than a week later she'd ended up in bed with Larry.

They both got up at the same time, Larry a step ahead of her. She noticed that his trench coat, so mud spattered yesterday, had taken a quick trip to the cleaners. Maybe Larry was becoming more fastidious in older age.

However, as he held the door open for her, Rannie noticed something else and stifled a giggle. The blue cleaner's tag was still stapled to the belt. Once a nerd, always a nerd!

Chapter 16

"YOU DID WHAT?" RANNIE SHRIEKED.

Nate was at his desk, a biology textbook open. A gauze pad held in place by adhesive strips bisected his left arm a third of the way between his wrist and elbow.

"Don't hemorrhage. It's just a tattoo." He shut the book. His calmness was infuriating.

"You're a minor. It's—it's illegal!" Rannie sputtered.

Nate didn't respond. It wasn't necessary. He knew that she knew about the fake ID with his photo on it. Rannie had stumbled upon it months ago when she was doing laundry. Stupidly, Nate had left it in a pocket of his jeans. And instead of destroying it right then and there as she should have, Rannie stupidly believed her son when he swore up and down that its only use was gaining entry into bars where, at most, he'd have one beer. End result: Nate Lorimer hadn't gotten inked; the fictitious Darryl Schmidt had, Darryl who was twenty-five according to his birth date and a student at Queens Community College.

College! A thudding realization.

"Your interview at Yale is tomorrow! Oh, Jesus! It looks like you tried slitting your wrist only you aimed too high!"

"So that's what this is about, whether I get into Yale or not?"

"Oh, no, mister, don't try switching the subject on me!"

Rannie felt like she should yell and carry on some more; the situation required it. Yet all at once every bone in her body felt like lead. She crumpled on Nate's bed. It was too much. Hadn't Nate ever heard about dirty needles and HIV? She cradled her head in her hands and thought, *No, no, no.* Or maybe she actually uttered the words because all at once Nate was sitting beside her. "Come on, Ma. Don't get so worked up." He sounded, well, not contrite exactly but at least concerned. "The bandage can come off in an hour."

Rannie looked up. She could feel that her eyes were wet. It wasn't simply because of the tattoo, although she had no intention of telling him that. She was crying from exhaustion, from being at the morgue, being at the precinct, being at Mary's, being with Larry. . . . And *not* being with Tim. Why no call from him?

She sniffled. "So what am I going to see?" *A topless hula girl? A bleeding crucifix? Maybe "Mom" written in scrolling letters? No, definitely not Mom.*

"Here. Look." Carefully Nate lifted off two of the adhesive strips. Rannie took note that he winced and didn't feel at all sorry for him. The patch of skin underneath was angry looking, swollen.

"Is that a lightning bolt?"

"Yeah, and below it says 'TCB.' That stands for 'Taking—' "

"I know what it stands for. Taking Care of Business. I don't get it. What possessed you to do this? You're not even an Elvis fan."

She managed to stand up, and because nothing came to mind

as far as what additional statement she might make, she made do with "This conversation is not over, Nate. And there will be consequences."

As she walked down the hall to her bedroom, Rannie realized what she wanted was someone to commiserate with. Who else had a teenager with raging testosterone and no common sense? Her ex-husband of course. But Peter at forty-five had recently begun sporting an earring. So his response might be "A tat? Cool!" In fact, it wasn't totally beyond the realm of possibility that the tattooing was some nutty father/son bonding experience, with Peter in California also nursing a swollen arm right now.

She tried Tim again and left a message. Was he incommunicado because (A) he didn't want to speak to her. Or (B) he didn't want to speak to her.

There was Joan, the mother of Nate's best friend, Ben. As acting head of Chapel for the current year, Joan was far less accessible than in the past, her days spent handling faculty concerns and budgets, her nights taken up with fund-raising events and mandatory socializing with parents at Chapel functions. Rannie and Joan had met in the Riverside Park playground when Nate and Ben were toddlers and they, like their sons, had grown up together, celebrating good times and offering solace during bad stretches. Joan was a sensible parent, whose inclination was to look on the bright side.

Rannie dialed. "Hi, Joanie," she said.

Immediately on hearing Rannie's voice, Joan let out a shriek, a shriek nearly identical in length and pitch to the piercing one that Rannie had let out only a few minutes earlier.

"Ben got inked too?"

"What a fucking moron!" Joan yelled. "Japanese pictograms on the inside of his arm. Ben doesn't even eat sushi!"

Joan supplied some details. After school, the boys had gone down to the East Village near St. Mark's Place. "Some place that does piercing, tattoos, and—oh, I almost forgot!" Joan paused for effect. "They also sell used shoes. Ben let that slip."

Joan was not making Rannie feel better. Used shoes? Did that mean it wasn't even a successful tattoo parlor but one with old rusting needles, a place that needed to branch out into other equally unhygienic businesses in order to stay afloat? Rannie knew that particular stretch of the East Village from years past when she'd escort Nate, usually Ben, too, to their favorite comic book store on St. Mark's. Back then the raunchy tattoo parlors and stores with sex toys had intimidated the boys: they'd walk fast, heads down, as if wearing blinders, until they were through the front door of Comicazi. Oh, how times had changed.

"Ben's got his interview at Wesleyan tomorrow. For all I know the tattoo says, 'Wanna fuck?'. . . . Oh, God! What if his interviewer is Japanese!"

It turned out that Ben's interview was at two. Joan's husband had planned on taking half a day off to drive Ben to Middletown, Connecticut; however, since Nate's noon interview in New Haven would certainly be over by one o'clock latest, Rannie offered her services.

"Really? Howard's not eager to take the time off. And I have a board of trustees meeting."

"Then it's settled."

Joan was still hesitating—"I feel like I'm imposing"—and

mentioned that Ben knew somebody else from Chaps was also having an interview at Wesleyan tomorrow. "I could find out who it is and give a call."

"I *like* it that you're imposing. You'll be indebted to me. Okay?"

"Since you put it that way." Then right before they hung up, Joan said, "Is it really true that you let Olivia Werner sleep over the other night?"

"Um, am I speaking to my old friend or to the acting head of Chapel School?"

"Both, I guess."

"In that case, tell Ben to be at our house at eight thirty."

The next morning, when Rannie pulled up in front of the Dolores Court in a red Honda, rented from Avis on Seventy-Fifth Street, Ben was there as promised. She buzzed 6B on the intercom. Nate didn't answer but a minute later he emerged from the building. He looked tired and grumpy.

Well, that makes two of us, thought Rannie, who had not slept well. Another phone call to Tim last night had produced nothing except his voice message.

Ben and Nate greeted each other with a nod; both slid into the backseat, earbuds attached to separate iPods, and were asleep in five minutes.

The drive to New Haven normally took an hour and a half unless there was traffic. Then all bets were off. "Leave at eight thirty! That's nuts," Nate had muttered last night. "The interview's at noon. What? Are you gonna drive like ten miles an hour?"

"Departure time is not up for discussion." On Rannie's last

trip in September to drop off Alice and all her paraphernalia, road work on the Merritt and an accident near Milford had resulted in a three-hour ordeal.

Today the trip was a breeze. Once or twice Rannie turned to steal a quick look at Nate in back. As a little boy he'd been sweet almost to a fault. Rannie remembered the feel of his sticky, chubby hands cupping her face before he bestowed a kiss, a kiss not even asked for, one given freely and gladly just because he loved her. The divorce had toughened him up, a sad fact but probably not a totally bad thing, steeling Nate for the emotional roller coaster of puberty.

They reached the outskirts of New Haven by ten after ten. It was too early to call Alice; her daughter's first class was at noon, so in all likelihood she was still asleep. Calling to mind the address of a good breakfast joint, Rannie followed the lights into New Haven and cut through campus to reach State Street.

Like clockwork Ben and Nate both woke up just as Rannie turned off the ignition. Hefty servings of French toast, sausage, and hash browns kept conversation to a minimum—mostly Ben and Nate debating the progress of some new song that Spiteful Muse, their band, was practicing. "Admit it. We suck," Nate said. There was nary a mention of tattoos and nary a single "I told you so" comment from Nate to Rannie about their early arrival. All in all, a pleasant enough start of the day.

Rannie parked on Hillhouse Avenue by the Admissions Building and watched Nate stride up the steps while Ben, with directions from Rannie, headed off to Old Campus, where nearly all freshmen at Yale were housed and where he planned to hang out with a couple of friends who'd graduated from Chaps last spring.

This left Rannie with more than half an hour before meeting Alice in front of the Yale University Art Gallery Museum for her noon art history lecture.

For Rannie, walking around campus never ceased being odd, and she could never quite decide whether on balance it was happy odd or depressing odd. Four years at Yale had seemed like an eternity while living through them; now on the time line of her life, college counted for such a small blip of time in comparison to marriage, motherhood, career. Yet Yale had been a turning point; sometime during freshman year, Rannie began to realize that Shaker Heights, Ohio, was not going to be the locus of her future.

Woolsey Hall was on the way to the art museum. Rannie decided to pop in. It epitomized the best of Yale for her. An auditorium with a world-class organ, it had been built in celebration of Yale's bicentennial in 1901. On the marble walls of the vestibule were carved the names of every fallen soldier who'd gone to Yale, starting with the Revolution and ending with Vietnam, when space ran out. Rannie had stood here for the first time flanked by both her parents during their visit to New Haven for Rannie's interview. That was twenty-five years ago, she now realized. She remembered her mom and dad slowly turning, silently taking in all the names of dead young men, both awed and moved. The emotional power of Woolsey Hall had eluded her back then, preoccupied as she was with her choice of outfit and whether her class ranking was good enough for Yale. But while a student she found herself returning to this place again and again, most often for concerts but also for no other reason than to feel part of something grand and big, something that was historical and yet also very personal.

Alice was waiting by the entrance to the museum.

"You sure you want to sit through this?" Alice said after accepting a hug. "It's about art restoration."

Rannie nodded and followed her daughter to the side entrance of the museum, where, up a flight of stairs, they entered a wood-paneled lecture hall. Copies of the curriculum vitae of guest lecturer F. Anthony Weld were handed out, like playbills, by a TA who stopped Alice to ask if she'd caught some exhibit on Manet. He was happy to take her if she hadn't.

Alice was even smaller than Rannie and blond with large, soulful eyes that had worked their magic on boys since middle grade. Her "delicate creature" looks were deceiving, however. Alice was a pretty tough cookie, far more pragmatic and thick skinned than her six-foot-two hulk of a brother.

"Nate got a tattoo!" Rannie said as they took their seats. She glanced at the curriculum vitae—the guy had a formidable reputation for restoring Old Master paintings. "I'm furious."

"Oh, Mother, honestly!" Alice said in a dismissive way that made Rannie worry that both her children had permanent artwork on their bodies. "And by the way, I heard Olivia spent the night. You never let me have boys stay over in high school. Never!"

Rannie shrugged.

"I think it's subconsciously sexist on your part," Alice went on. "It's very double standard. Like it's fine for your son to have sex right in the next room but your daughter . . . oh no!"

Happily at that moment the auditorium lights began to dim so Alice, who was also taking a course called Feminism Redux, had to shut up.

The guest lecturer, a guy with longish hair and glasses, was too far away for Rannie to really get a good look at him. He had an urbane air about him and came equipped with plenty of art world anecdotes as well as before-and-after slides of restored paintings to show. "The restorer's task is simple: it's to erase the ravages of time while avoiding doing further harm to a piece of art. The work is painstaking, time-consuming, unglamorous. I can recommend it as a career only to those of you who are fanatic about art preservation and who also suffer from obsessive-compulsive disorder."

Some polite laughter from the crowd. Alice yawned, unamused.

"I remove, fleck by fleck, mold on portraits left rotting for years in damp cellars. I wash off soot from church frescoes subjected to centuries of candle smoke. Ninety-nine percent of what I do is run a very high-priced cleaning service."

He paused a beat longer than the audience's reaction—a weak smattering of chuckles—called for.

"However, repainting savagely damaged artwork, paintings that have been torn or burned, is an altogether different proposition, one requiring a peculiar talent for reconstruction and mimicry. It's no coincidence that some of the most audacious forgers started their careers as art restorers. The restorer's hand must act as if it belonged to the original artist. I am right-handed and personally would never attempt to repaint artwork by a leftie. My rhythm would be off.

"In the cleaning business of restoration, there is an arsenal of twenty-first-century weapons at one's disposal; with repainting, the restorer must forsake modern technology and travel back in time."

A slide popped up of a round-cheeked Madonna cuddling a round-bottomed baby. "I became expert at mixing egg tempera paints while restoring the lower left quadrant of this fifteenth-century painting, school of Fra Angelico, damaged in the Florence flood of November 1966. It resides in Ospedale del'Ognissanti," he said in mellifluous Italian.

Another slide appeared.

"I learned to paint with a brush made of just a few ermine hairs in order to repaint a tiny portion of this Flemish School painting, early fifteenth century. It depicts St. Lawrence and is part of the Silas Cummings Collection."

Rannie poked Alice and whispered excitedly, "I saw that just the other day. I was in Charlotte Cummings's mansion . . . you know who she is, right?"

Alice startled. Her eyes flew open. "Whaa?" she mumbled.

"St. Lawrence is being roasted alive, and the story goes that he was so eager for martyrdom that he cried out, 'This side is done. Turn me over!' My mission was to repaint four of the floor tiles in the painting, each of which was smaller than a square inch and yet each portrayed a scene from the life of Christ. The flight into Egypt is represented here."

An enlargement of one floor tile was shown.

While the lecture continued, Rannie took note of the students in neighboring rows. Although some dutifully tapped away at laptops, many more, like Alice, were slumped in their seats, down for the count. And who knew? Maybe most of those with open laptops were e-mailing or on Facebook. And this was Yale.

"You fell asleep!" Rannie said, dismayed, as they emerged minutes later into the sunlight, both squinting. "I found him enthralling."

Alice shrugged indifference. "Let's find Nate and get lunch. I'm starved. Maybe Modern Apizza since you have a car."

"Sweetie, we can't." Rannie explained about Ben and the Wesleyan interview, which Alice accepted with the proviso that she wasn't going to walk all the way to Hillhouse just to wave at Nate and watch them drive off. "Tell him to call me later. I really want him to come here," Alice said, then took off to catch up with friends. "Love ya!" she shouted back at Rannie.

Nate was sitting on the steps outside the Admissions Building and offered no particulars about the interview other than to say, "It went fine." As soon as Ben rejoined them, they got in the car; even with a quick stop for Rannie at a gas station restroom off Route 17, the Honda pulled into Middletown less than twenty minutes later.

Rannie had seen the Wesleyan campus only once before, several years earlier, when Alice, then a junior at Chapel, was checking out colleges over spring break. Rannie had liked Wesleyan's ambience then; she liked it now.

Far smaller than Yale and with more green open space, Wesleyan had its own distinct laid-back appeal. The architecture was a mishmash—a sleek glass and granite art center, a few gingerbread Victorians, a scattering of nondescript dorms, some sternly Romanesque brick buildings, and some houses, like the yellow clapboard colonial where Admissions had offices, that would have made charming weekend homes. Yale in all its Neo-Gothic grandeur was either imposing or pretentious, depending on your viewpoint. Wesleyan looked more welcoming, a place where you could quickly feel at home, at least as long as you were of an extremely liberal persuasion. Gone were the chalk messages on the sidewalks that Rannie remembered from visiting with Alice, all of a political/sexual bent. But the kids were still a walking testament to the school's rep as PCU—Politically

Correct University—and as a haven for all gender permutations. "Former Cunt" and "Former Dick" buttons were worn on the parkas of several students.

Instead of spending quality time with her, Nate chose to wait for Ben inside the Admissions Building.

"I'll be back to pick you guys up," she said. She drove to a diner, drank a sip of coffee that must have been sitting in the pot since breakfast, paid and returned to campus, lucking into a parking spot near Admissions. She tuned the radio to a classic rock station and opened the copy of the *Times* that she'd brought along, turning right away to the long obituary of Charlotte Cummings. It began on the front page and took up an entire inside page in the first section, accompanied by several photographs. Charlotte as a little girl wearing high-button shoes and an enormous bow in her Goldilocks ringlets. Charlotte at the Stork Club, looking 1940s glamorous in a cocktail dress and mink stole. Charlotte at her centennial bash. In addition to the obituary, there were two full columns of "tombstones," paid expressions of sympathy from all the many New York institutions that had benefited from Charlotte Cummings's largesse.

Only one sentence in the obit didn't totally conform to what Rannie knew. It was a small point: Silas Cummings's art collection was described as a "trove of valuable fourteenth- and fifteenth-century Northern European and Italian religious artwork," including the renowned altarpiece. Bibi had made it sound as if all the paintings of martyred saints were no better than third-rate religious porn. But then "valuable" was such a relative word.

Rannie leaned back against the headrest, about to zone out for a little while, when she spotted a guy across the street checking a campus map and looking lost. It was Tim Butler. In the flesh.

A smile, a big unconditionally happy one, spread itself across her face. At the same time she wished she'd washed her hair this morning before racing off to Avis.

Rannie rolled down the window. "Tim! Over here!"

He looked up, stowed the map, and crossed over.

Rannie said, "What are you doing here?" Then she recalled Joan's remark: "another kid from Chapel" had an interview at Wesleyan today. It never occurred to her that it might be Chris Butler.

"So Nate's got an interview too?" Tim bent down closer to the window. "Or are you keeping tabs on me?" He said it teasingly, yet his smile seemed forced.

"Hey, I called you yesterday, more than once as a matter of fact." After explaining why she happened to be parked in a rental car in Middletown, Connecticut, Rannie reached over and unlocked the passenger side door. "Hop in."

He made a point of checking his watch. "I really should try to connect with Chris."

Something was going on here. "Oh, come on."

He slid into the passenger seat and tossed the newspaper, still open to the obituary, in the back. "A hundred and two. Nobody should live that long."

She was about to ask why he said that; instead she said, "Why didn't you call?'

Tim kept his eyes averted. "Yesterday. Jesus, what a day. Out of the blue the health department shows up and—"

"No, Tim. Really why?"

He breathed out slowly. "I'm not sure." Just then "Every Breath You Take" came on the radio. "Still a great song. Reminds me of steaming up car windows as a kid."

Without thinking, Rannie leaned over and kissed Tim. He started to kiss her back, but stopped and turned off the radio. He looked outside at the Wesleyan kids walking by before facing Rannie again. "I'm too old for this."

Rannie had a horrible feeling that he was talking about much more than making out in a car.

"Listen to me, Rannie." Tim sounded too serious.

Rannie started shaking her head no. "I'm not going to like what you're going to say. I know it."

"The problem is I see you and I want you. We're in a stupid parked car and all I'm thinking is how fast can I peel your clothes off."

"That's a bad thing?"

"I'm too old for casual sex. To be honest I never was into it: even as a kid, I always fell hard."

"Casual sex? How can you say that? About us!"

"That's not what I meant. Fuck! I'm getting this all wrong." He looked at her. His next words were spoken in a sad and defeated way. "I can't see you anymore. We're not right for each other."

"I don't understand."

"With you, I'm up one minute, down the next. It's like being a teenager again. You make me crazy happy sometimes. But most of the time you just make me crazy. I hate how mad I get at you."

She cut him off. "Tim. Listen to me. I was so happy you stayed over. I want you. I *need* you. . . . Yesterday morning, Nate on his own said I deserve somebody like you, somebody nice. He's right." Rannie stroked his cheek. "I can be infuriating. I get that."

"I'm scared for you."

Oh, God. Now she wanted to clap her hands over her ears and

start babbling nonsense words to drown out what he was saying. "Don't say that! Please don't, Tim. It terrifies me."

"Look, I'd do anything to protect you. Say the word, you and Nate can move in—"

"I'm not ready for that." The words slipped out before she even realized it. "Not yet."

"The point is, I *am*. Rannie, I'm in love with you. No matter what you say right this second, you're not in love with me."

"How do you know that? And even if you're right, it doesn't mean I won't be. It's only been a couple of months."

"You remember me telling you about the time I almost had a slip?"

Rannie nodded. At age five, Tim's son had come down with Reye's syndrome. Thanks to a swift diagnosis by a young ER doctor at Roosevelt Hospital, Chris recovered. But while Chris was undergoing an MRI and the prognosis was still iffy, Tim had gotten as far as ordering a double Scotch at an Eighth Avenue bar before calling an AA friend.

"The night I stayed over, I woke up and started getting myself nuts, thinking about what I'd do if anything happened to you. It made me want a drink. I got the itch and started wondering if maybe there was beer in the fridge. So I went in the kitchen and phoned my sponsor instead." Tim started to take her hand, but Rannie yanked it away and held both behind her back.

"I know that move. It's a breakup move."

Tim smiled. "You're too smart for your own good."

Quick! she commanded herself. *Capitalize on the smile.* "Tim, I'll be different once I get a regular job. I won't be crazy. I'll—I'll be seminormal."

"Maybe so." He smiled again, and when he spoke, she saw

how full of regret the smile was. "I can't handle this, Rannie. I'm sorry. I just can't."

Next thing he had the car door open. He looked at her with such intensity, it was as if he were memorizing her face. "You take care," he said. "Stay out of trouble. I mean it."

Then the car door shut and off he went, his jacket collar turned up again the wind.

When she was a junior in high school, a pseudopoetic guy who was a senior broke up with her. They were parked in his car right across from her house. Truthfully, she hadn't liked him all that much except for the fact that he bore a faint resemblance to John Lennon, one that he played up by wearing granny glasses. At least that time, since there was another hour before her curfew, they'd made out to beat the band.

Chapter 17

ON THE DRIVE BACK TO MANHATTAN, RANNIE'S PHONE BUZZED several times.

"Want me to check who?" Nate offered.

"No, sweetie. It can wait." More to the point, remaining ignorant allowed Rannie to indulge in the hope—okay, fantasy—that Tim had immediately regretted dumping her and was now repeatedly calling, desperately calling, to say not only was life without her meaningless but that he had booked a hotel room for the night. Oh, and since this was a fantasy, Rannie decided to go whole hog . . . she and Tim would be staying somewhere très swanky. The Carlyle or, better yet, the Peninsula.

By five thirty, they had whizzed past the exits on the Saw Mill River Parkway, driven through the Riverdale section of the Bronx with its un-Bronx-like mix of gracious Tudor homes and riverfront high-rises, and now were being funneled into the Henry Hudson Parkway. The George Washington Bridge loomed ahead, twin swags of lights strung across the towers, twinkling against a pigeon-gray sky. It was a gorgeous, glamorous, always-uplifting sight that proclaimed to Rannie, "You're home. You're back where you belong."

After depositing both boys in front of the Dolores Court, Rannie returned the rental and en route to the subway checked messages.

Just as her rational self had expected, nothing from Tim. Still, it was a letdown.

One call was from Ellen's now-former assistant, Dina, with the sorrowful news that tomorrow at four there'd be a gathering at S&S to remember Ellen. "Really hoping you can make it, Rannie." Dina sounded as if her nose was stuffed up, probably from crying.

The number for the other calls wasn't instantly familiar nor had any message been left. Then it clicked. The number belonged to her mother's cell phone, a device rarely used yet always kept in Harriet Bookman's handbag in case of an emergency.

Uh-oh!

"Mother, are you okay?"

"Yes. I'm fine." Her answer sounded tentative.

"I was driving back from Connecticut," Rannie went on. "Nate had his interview at Yale or I would have called sooner . . . you sure you're okay?"

"I was hoping to come visit."

"Oh! Wonderful!" Rannie could hear the false cheer in her voice and she bet that her mother, who was nobody's fool, picked up on it too. "When were you thinking?"

"In about twenty minutes."

"Mother! Where are you?"

"The lobby of the Peninsula Hotel. It's on Fifth Avenue and—"

"I know where it is," Rannie answered. Her mom at the fantasy locale for her night with Tim? "What are you doing there?"

Her mother exhaled an atypical world-weary, I've-seen-it-all sigh. "It's a long story."

Rannie waited in the lobby of the Dolores Court for Harriet Bookman. In twenty minutes she emerged from a taxi, all four feet, eleven inches of her, in a sensible brown wool coat, signature salon-stiff hairdo, marshmallow-white Nikes, and sunglasses. While Rannie took the wheelie suitcase that the cabdriver hoisted from the trunk, her mother cast an anxious glance up and down the block before hurrying into the lobby.

Her mother's wariness was not unwarranted and stemmed from her inaugural visit to the neighborhood. Three months after Rannie's graduation from Yale, her parents had driven her and her belongings from the leafy environs of Shaker Heights to New York City, where Rannie was to join two college friends who'd already moved into apartment 6B at the Dolores Court. While her dad remained in the car, parked illegally by the front entrance, Rannie's mother helped her unpack, muttering about "the funny smell" and the threadbare furnishings. Finally ready to leave, Harriet went into the living room and yoo-hooed through the open windows, "Irving, I'm coming down now." Rannie's father did not hear nor was he aware that at that same moment, as he sat in air-conditioned comfort still listening to an Indians game, a homeless guy was squatting on the El Dorado's rear bumper taking a dump.

That turd remained embedded in Harriet Bookman's psyche like a fly in amber, tainting forever the image of her daughter's life in New York, and though never once openly discussed in all the ensuing years, the episode was frequently alluded to in comments such as the one Harriet now uttered.

"I read somewhere that this neighborhood was becoming gentrified. I don't see it." Then right away she zeroed in on Rannie's bare wrist. "You're not wearing your father's watch."

"It's being repaired. The crystal cracked," Rannie lied, and although her mother didn't look convinced, she let the matter drop. It wasn't until they were in the elevator that Harriet removed her sunglasses to reveal eyes red from crying. "Oh, Rannie, I hate to impose but all the late flights to Cleveland were full and the thought of staying in the hotel, even if a single was available . . . well, I couldn't!"

Suddenly Rannie found herself in the unusual but not unwelcome situation of trying to comfort her sobbing mother, although as she murmured soothing words and kept both arms wrapped around Harriet's small frame, she did take note that her mother must have been staying in a double room at the Peninsula. . . . With whom was the question.

The answer came over tea and cookies after Harriet had reached up to hug Nate and after Rannie, in a furtive whisper, warned him, "Don't you dare let Grandma see the tattoo!"

"I met a man," Harriet began, sitting beside Rannie at the kitchen counter, although Harriet, so round and birdlike, seemed not to be sitting so much as roosting on the stool.

"On JDate," Harriet added.

Immediately Rannie choked, spraying English breakfast tea all over the counter.

"Go ahead. Laugh. I deserve it," Harriet said, mopping up tea with her napkin.

Still coughing, Rannie managed to wheeze, "I'm not laughing, Mother, really. I'm surprised, that's all." Surprised? Defibrillator-induced shock was more like it.

"I should have never listened to Amy."

Ah . . . So it had been Rannie's oldest sister's idea. That made sense. Amy possessed a disastrous matchmaking gene; as a little girl she was always staging mock weddings in the backyard, and to this day she pestered Rannie every time an "available" man of Amy's acquaintance was coming to New York. "Hey, you never know" was her sister's mantra.

Harriet nibbled at a cookie. "But I'm lonely, and frankly I can only take so much of the girls."

The "girls," now all in their midseventies, were the gaggle of ladies who sat around the same mah-jongg tables as Harriet, prayed in the same pews at Anshe Chesed temple and traveled on the same cruises to far-flung destinations.

Harriet set down her teacup. "We met a few months ago. And he seemed like such a lovely man. He's from Cincinnati. A widower. His wife was a cousin of Edith Einziger's and his apartment in Palm Beach Gardens is in the same complex as the Bachs. He plays golf with Phil."

"Was this—uh—the first time you went away together?" Rannie ventured. Had senior sex reared its head?

"No. It was *not* the first trip we've taken," Harriet declared huffily. "As a matter of fact we went to Chicago last month and had a marvelous time." Shrewdie that Harriet was, her eyes narrowed. "I can tell what you're thinking, Rannie, and you're wrong. We were quite compatible that way."

Ooookay . . . "So what happened?"

Tears began trickling down her mother's cheeks, so Rannie

did something unexpected. She reached for Harriet's manicured hand and held it, a hand so small and plump that the deep red nail polish seemed almost like a five-year-old's attempt at playing grown-up.

"He arranged for a ménage," her mother said and then added, unnecessarily, "à trois."

Rannie was literally struck dumb. She blinked several times and wondered, between JDating and a ménage à trois, which was the more preposterous term to associate with her mother.

"We had just returned to the hotel after seeing a matinee of *The Book of Mormon*—which by the way I don't understand what everybody is raving about—when there's a knock at the door and in comes this attractive Asian woman, all smiles, who introduces herself as Janine and says, 'Just let me know what will make you happy.' Those were her exact words—I thought maybe we were being offered a room upgrade until she took off her coat and I saw what she was wearing."

"It wasn't a mix-up? The wrong room?"

"That was my first reaction until George started asking why I was getting so upset. He said that we'd discussed this the night before and we'd both agreed it'd be fun to try something different, something spicy, something Asian. I'm such an idiot. I thought he was talking about restaurants!"

"Why did he have to go and pull a stunt like this?" Harriet pulled her hand from Rannie's grasp. "It was such a lovely change being with a man instead of listening to Edith go on about whether she should have an eye lift. Or Helen. Rannie, I honestly think Helen's gone a little kooky. Have I told you how every time she sees a penny on the ground, she thinks it's a signal from Bill? That he's saying hello from heaven? She invited me down to Florida in January but I said no. I can take only so much of that nonsense."

At that moment, Harriet wriggled off the counter stool and announced she was going to call the airlines to see what was available first thing tomorrow morning.

"There's no rush, Mother. Why not stay a couple of days? I haven't seen you since summer." And just what did it say about their relationship that Harriet had come to New York and in all likelihood wouldn't have called if the trip had remained ménage free?

"Yes? You really want me to?"

Rannie nodded.

"Just swear to me you will never breathe a word of this to Amy or Betsy . . . what am I saying? Don't breathe a word to anyone, not a living soul!"

"It's in the vault, Mother," Rannie promised, locking her lips.

While her mother unpacked, Rannie phoned in an order for pizza, then joined her mother in the den.

"The news'll be on in a minute," Harriet said, turning on the TV and catching the tail end of a local talk show.

Lo and behold! There on Rannie's low-definition screen was Larry Katz sitting in a curvilinear white swivel chair that looked way too small for him. Rannie wasn't even that surprised. It had been that kind of day.

The host, a woman who had once been an Eastern European Olympic gymnast, was holding a copy of *Tattletale* and saying, "Dusk Books recently published *Tattletale,* a biography of Ret Sullivan, the disfigured journalist murdered last Saturday in her Upper East Side apartment."

While old photos of Ret flashed on the screen, the TV host first recapped the Mike Bellettra episode with a publicity shot of him shown from prepenitentiary days; then she brought viewers up to speed on the current investigation, basically saying there was no new news. Larry kept nodding emphatically as if verifying every word spoken. He was wearing a tie that was knotted off-kilter, and he didn't seem to know what to do with his long legs. Not only that, he kept fiddling with one of his hearing aids, although to the viewing audience it must have appeared that he was digging out wax. Oy!

"Wait a minute!" Harriet exclaimed. "Isn't that who you found, Rita what's-her-name?"

"Ret. Ret Sullivan. That's right, Mother." *And I used to fuck Larry Katz, small world, no?* Rannie almost added.

"*Tattletale* has shot to the top of bestseller lists, isn't that right, Larry?"

Larry cleared his throat. "Yes, Ilyana. We've gone back to press three times. Ret and I were friends and I know the book's success would please her very much."

Harriet's face registered surprise. "Who knew Rita Sullivan was such a big deal . . . although Edith loves her books."

The host was now smiling conspiratorially. "And you're going to let viewers in on a secret, aren't you, Larry, about *Tattletale*."

Rannie sat forward on the couch. Come again?

"Personally I can't be bothered reading that kind of trash," Harriet continued.

More throat clearing from Larry. "The publishing world has been buzzing. There have been all sorts of rumors circulating online about *Tattletale*."

"Really?" Rannie asked herself.

"The author credit on the book is Lina Struvel but actually this isn't a biography at all. It's an autobiography. Ret Sullivan wrote her own life story under a pseudonym . . . or as she preferred to say, 'a nom de plume.'" Larry let his words hang for a moment to allow the host's raised-eyebrow look of astonishment its full measure of drama.

"You're telling me people really care about this?" Harriet said with a dismissive shrug at the same time the host was waving her arms around and exclaiming, "No! Why did she do that?"

"Ret thought of it as a game." While Larry demonstrated for the host and viewing audience how the pseudonym was an anagram for Ret's name, Rannie tried her best to tune out her mother's chatter and figure out the subtext here. Her conclusion: this was a publicity stunt. Larry had engineered the TV appearance. If there were online rumors about who wrote *Tattletale,* and Rannie doubted there were, the odds were Larry had planted them. In fact, it wasn't far-fetched to envision Ret and Larry at some point concocting the whole scenario together—the ruse of the nom de plume and then, to boost sales of the book, the reveal.

Nom de plume. Suddenly a little buzzer went off in Rannie's head. That was the answer to the crossword puzzle clue that had stumped her—"pseudonym for Josette?" Too late now. She'd already tossed the Saturday paper.

Then a real buzzer sounded. The intercom. It was the pizza delivery guy. Rannie sent Nate downstairs with money. By the time she returned to the den, Larry had disappeared from the television screen.

All during dinner Harriet and Nate, her decided favorite

among all eight grandchildren, gabbed away. It turned out they played bridge together online—who knew! Since the only card game Rannie had ever been good at was "Go Fish," she was left to her own thoughts. Larry was a wily guy, all right; the schlemiel persona made you forget that. Once again Rannie remembered Ellen's assistant fielding a call from a Larry.

Time to check out her hunch, Rannie decided, and she called Dina right after dinner.

"Just letting you know that I'll definitely be there tomorrow," Rannie began.

"I figured you would. Ellen's brother will be there. I still can't believe the whole thing. It's a complete horror show." She paused. "Rannie, would you like to speak tomorrow?"

Oh, God! Rannie had a horror of public speaking. Even conference calls intimidated her. But this wasn't about her. "Sure. Something short, okay?"

"Fine."

"Listen, Dina. I thought of a few alums from before your time who'd want to know about tomorrow." Rannie rattled off the names of some former employees. "And of course Larry Katz."

"Oh, he was like the first person I called."

Rannie paused before going fishing. "Larry must be devastated. I know how much he cared about Ellen."

"He's a complete wreck."

Really? He had looked perfectly functional an hour ago on TV. Rannie went a giant step further. "Um, how long exactly were he and Ellen seeing each other?"

"Whoa. I thought I was the only one who knew."

"Yeah, well, Ellen told me, but she swore me to secrecy," Rannie lied.

"Hmmm... let's see. It wasn't long after Ellen and Frank broke up," Dina went on. "So that's, what? Two, three months ago. God, what a number that shit did on her. Larry was more like a time filler, poor guy. I feel really badly for him."

No, you feel *bad* for him; Rannie couldn't stop from mentally chiding Dina. There's nothing the matter with your sense of touch.

"But oh my God," Dina went on. "Larry won't stop calling. 'What did the cops ask you? Are there leads?' Like the cops are gonna share with me?"

"The cops? They want to know about the men in Ellen's life?"

"Oh yes. But basically for the last two years there was just Frank. And I told them he broke up with her."

Frank. One of those charmers who swear up and down they're never getting married, and then after dumping Ellen, suddenly he's sporting a gold wedding band.

"And you told them about Larry?"

"Sure. I wasn't gonna hold back from the cops. But"—Dina made a dismissive *pfft* sound—"I mean Larry Katz. A murder suspect? Come on!"

Rannie heard the click that signaled Dina's call waiting. "So anything else, Rannie?" Dina asked.

"Just curious about when *Book X* will be out."

"Last I heard, maybe as early as this Saturday."

Perfect timing Rannie thought as she hung up. Saturday was the day of Charlotte Cummings's funeral.

And, yes, Daisy Satterthwaite was indeed counting on Rannie to accompany her to Saint Thomas Church, Mary called to inform Rannie a few minutes later. "She's already made sure your name is on the list of attendees. The church will be packed, just throngs of people, and Daisy lives in mortal fear of rebreaking her hip." Then Mary asked if Rannie had a hat.

"I take it you don't mean baseball hats or ski caps," Rannie replied, knowing full well Mary was referring to something that would fall squarely in the chapeau category.

"Bibi Gaines is asking that all the ladies wear hats."

"Oh, sort of an homage to Charlotte Cummings?" As attested to in myriad society-page photographs, Charlotte's daytime apparel always included gloves and a ladylike hat, usually something featuring a brim and wide band of dark ribbon.

Mary assured Rannie that she owned many from which she could choose. "Are you wearing your navy suit? You look darling in it and I have something that will go perfectly."

Rannie made a mental note to check whether the suit in question needed cleaning. Then before saying good night, Rannie mentioned Harriet's visit, saying only that it had "been spur of the moment."

"Well, isn't that lovely. If time allows, perhaps she and I can get together for lunch."

"I'll certainly suggest it."

The rest of the evening was spent companionably in the living room, Harriet deep into a Rosamunde Pilcher novel, Nate writing a English paper on his laptop, a long-sleeved T-shirt covering up the tat, and Rannie racking up copyediting dollars on the Dusk book on CEOs as sociopaths while keeping one ear out for a phone call from Tim that never came.

By ten, Harriet appeared flat-out exhausted, her open book facedown in her lap. She was by nature a peppy woman, someone who bustled about, efficiently attending to the logistics of daily life, so it was upsetting to see her so done in.

"Mother, would you prefer to sleep in my room? The pullout in here is fine for me."

Harriet's eyes fluttered open. "Absolutely not. This is where I'm staying." She rose, kissed Nate, and headed for the hall bathroom to take a quick bath before turning in.

Harriet reappeared in bathrobe and face cream just as Rannie was finishing putting fresh sheets on the bed. From the wheelie suitcase her mother fished out a small black case that she snapped open.

At first Rannie thought it was for jewelry. Then she watched her mother place two tiny budlike devices into it. Hearing aids.

"Mother, when did you get those?"

"A couple of months ago. I hate them, but your sisters said I was driving them nuts making them repeat everything. And these miserable things do help. They should—they cost almost six thousand dollars." Harriet snapped the case shut. On the top, in a silver high-tech font, was stamped AUDEO.

Audeo.

Rannie sank on the bed stunned.

"My doctor says they're state of the art."

The acknowledgment in Ret Sullivan's book. It had been "Audeo" with an "e" until Rannie had—incorrectly, she now realized—changed it to "Audio".

"What's wrong?" Harriet asked.

"Nothing, really. Just tired, too." Rannie kissed her mother's moisturized cheek. "Sleep well, Mother. I'm glad you're here."

In her bedroom Rannie found the printout of *Portrait of a Lady*.

The acknowledgment to Audeo/Audio read, "Who was my ears and without whom I never could have written this book."

Rannie's hands trembled. Larry was Audeo. He had done the fieldwork for Ret's book on Charlotte Cummings. The reason that the descriptions of rooms in the Cummings mansion seemed so vivid was because Larry must have somehow wangled his way in there. And not only was he involved with Ret up to his hearing-impaired ears, Dina confirmed he'd also been carrying on with Ellen. Rannie tried to untangle the implications of all this. Did Ellen know Larry was Audeo? Probably so. Did Larry know Rannie had copyedited *Portrait of a Lady*? Yes, he'd intimated as much. Did he know that Rannie had found Ret's body? Yes, odds were Ellen had told him.

Ellen's sudden urge to hit a Caribbean beach had been motivated by fear . . . fear that Larry had murdered Ret? But if that had been the case, surely Ellen would have told the police. Then it occurred to Rannie. Perhaps Ellen had.

Rannie slipped on the same oversize T-shirt she had worn when Tim slept over. She curled into bed. She was frightened, and her hand, almost as if it had a life of its own, kept creeping toward her phone, fingers primed to punch in Tim's number. But she restrained herself. Instead, she tried to make sense of what she knew, but it was like trying to fit together puzzle pieces that kept changing shape.

She'd gone to the Dusk offices on Monday around eleven, then much later that same day dropped off the copyedited manuscript to Dina at S&S. That was when Rannie overheard Dina fielding a call from a Larry. Ellen was already dead by then, murdered hours earlier in Central Park.

The memory of Larry entering the Dusk reception area in his mud-splattered trench coat flashed before Rannie and made her scalp tingle. Was Larry fully aware that Ellen was already lying on a slab at the morgue? Was calling S&S to speak to Ellen a ruse to support his innocence for later on when police questioning began? Nowhere near a foolproof alibi, to be sure. Still, she could hear Larry saying to the cops, "Why would I be trying to get in touch with Ellen if I'd murdered her that morning? Just ask her assistant, she'll tell you I called."

Of course the far bigger, capital W why was, Why would Larry have any reason to murder Ellen? Or Ret. Rannie remained in bed and forced herself to shut her eyes, though it took all her willpower not to race into the den, screaming, "Mommy, I'm scared!"

Chapter 18

THE FIRST THING RANNIE DID UPON WAKING WAS TO CHECK her suit. Unsurprisingly, the skirt had shmutz on it, shmutz that didn't come off with a washcloth scrubbing. A trip to the dry cleaners, however, would have to wait until after Ellen's gathering at S&S.

Except for the highest-level suits, who wore exactly that, and the publicity department fashionistas, who were always chicly clad in black, standard publishing company attire was pretty much casual Friday every day. Yet Rannie felt compelled to look presentable and grown up today at Simon & Schuster. She was paying respects.

It was only seven thirty, but the smell of coffee perking was unmistakable, and a real breakfast of scrambled eggs and toast, prepared by Harriet, was waiting for Rannie, when she shambled into the kitchen.

"Grandma, I don't get it; you'll eat ham but you won't cook bacon?" Nate was asking over his baconless plate.

"I don't eat ham, darling. I said I eat prosciutto."

"Your grandmother follows very strict dietary laws. They just happen to be her own and not the Bible's. . . . Ummm, yum," Rannie murmured as she tucked into the eggs, peppered to perfection, that Harriet had spooned out for her.

"Are you still seeing that policeman?" her mother asked once Nate had left for school.

Rannie scowled. So either Amy or Betsy—or both—had blabbed.

"Former policeman. He has a restaurant now in the brownstone that he owns." Rannie stopped herself. Why did she feel compelled to make Tim sound more white-collar haute bourgeoisie than he was? "Actually it's a bar, a cop hangout called the Offbeat. And, no, I'm not seeing him anymore. He broke up with me. Yesterday as a matter of fact."

"I guess neither of us is doing so well in the romance department." Harriet paused. "Nate was talking to me about college before. I told him to think twice about Wesleyan. My friend Lois Berman's granddaughter goes there and evidently all the kids do there is smoke marijuana. I hope he ends up at Yale. Remember when Daddy, you, and I first visited?"

"I was thinking about that yesterday when I was in New Haven."

"When you started college, suddenly we were empty nesters. Empty is the word, all right, and I had your father, remember."

Rannie squirmed. Suddenly she had an uncomfortable feeling that she knew where this conversation was heading; however, she gave her mother the benefit of the doubt.

"Once Nate leaves for college, would you ever think about moving back to Shak—"

"Mother, don't start! Please!"

"But you're not working. You'll be living alone. What would keep you here?"

"Nate won't be leaving until September! And believe it or not, I do have marketable skills. I'm making do with freelancing right now." Rannie left the word "barely" out of the sentence. "So it's not entirely inconceivable that by fall I'll have a full-time job!"

"Don't get so huffy! Forget I said a word." Harriet turned and began cleaning up plates, mugs. "I just want you to be happy. Is that so wrong?" she said from the sink, her back to Rannie.

"Mother, moving home is not the answer." That was a diplomatic alternative to saying, "Go back to Cleveland? Over my dead body!"

While her mother went to bathe and get dressed, Rannie grabbed a yellow legal pad and tried to jot down things she might say about Ellen. Ret murdered. Ellen murdered. Who besides herself was as closely connected to both women? Only Larry.

She glanced at clock on her cell. What kind of hours did cops keep? Rannie didn't know, but she called Grieg anyway. When he didn't pick up, she left a message to call her and within a minute her cell rang.

"Listen, I'm probably not telling you anything you don't already know," Rannie began, "and maybe this means nothing, but I'm practically positive Larry Katz helped Ret Sullivan write the book on Charlotte Cummings."

"Yes."

Rannie couldn't decide whether the yes was statement or question. In any case, she chose to interpret the answer as an invitation to continue. "In *Portrait of a Lady* there's an acknowledgment to Audeo. Ret says that she could never have done the book without Audeo's help. I think Larry Katz is Audeo."

"Ms. Bookman, why wait till now to tell me this?"

So this wasn't news to him?

"I—I just figured it out late last night," Rannie stammered. "My mother is visiting. I saw the case for her hearing aids. The company is called Audeo. Larry Katz wears hearing aids, too. I bet anything his are the same brand."

"Okay. Understood."

Was that all Grieg was going to say?

"When I was copyediting the manuscript, I mistakenly corrected the acknowledgment and changed it to 'Audio.'" "Mistakenly corrected"—did that count as an oxymoron like "jumbo shrimp"? Grieg, Rannie concluded, probably wasn't interested in discussing that. . . . But Larry's mud-stained raincoat, certainly that was pertinent. Squealing on anyone, but especially someone she'd always liked, felt *über*creepy but in for a penny, in for a pound. So oink oink!

"There's something else I think you should know. When I went to Larry Katz's office on Monday, I arrived at Dusk before he did, Dusk meaning the publishing house, not the time of day," Rannie clarified.

Silence.

"You there?" Rannie inquired.

"I'm here."

"So as I was saying, I was waiting for him, and when he arrived, I noticed—"

"What time was that?"

"Um, elevenish. His raincoat was a mess. It had been raining hard that morning. But Larry looked like he'd stomped in every mud puddle on the way in. He said that it had been impossible to get a cab and of course a car speeding by could have splattered him but . . ."

"Hold on, Ms. Bookman, I want to make sure I'm understanding this. Are you saying that you think he might have killed Ellen Donahoe in Central Park and then continued on to his office to meet up with you?"

Yes, that was what had occurred to Rannie, although hearing Grieg's paraphrasing, it sounded either totally absurd or somewhat conspiratorial. "Well, truthfully, I don't know what I think."

Maybe paranoia was setting in, but was Grieg considering the possibility that she and Larry were in cahoots—plotting and carrying out Ellen's murder and Ret's too? Only now Rannie was turning on Larry, to throw suspicion off herself. It was such a ridiculous 1950s noir reading—Larry in the Robert Mitchum role and herself standing in for Lana Turner—and yet actually no more ridiculous than Rannie suspecting Larry Katz of double homicide.

"Listen, Sergeant. The Larry Katz I knew wouldn't murder anyone." True, although now it sounded like unconvincing backpedaling. "I simply thought it was important to tell you what I saw."

"Ms. Bookman, did you know Larry Katz was involved with Ms. Donahoe?"

"I had my suspicions. But I found out for sure just yesterday" . . . although if the sergeant questioned Dina on this point, Dina would say that Rannie was already aware of their relationship. Didn't Mother Bookman always say lying got you in trouble?

Rannie could almost see another scenario playing out in Grieg's head. This one starred Rannie as a psychopathically jealous ex-lover of Larry's—Glenn Close in *Fatal Attraction* minus the boiled bunny—who murdered Ellen and, oh hell, might as well throw in Ret, too! Jilted and vengeful, Rannie was now scheming to frame poor Larry.

Whatever you do, don't start proclaiming your own innocence now! Rannie commanded herself, so when Grieg asked if there was anything else to tell him, all Rannie said was no.

After they hung up, Rannie sat staring at her phone. Well, that certainly hadn't gone well!

A moment later Harriet emerged, announcing that she was meeting Mary at the Metropolitan at ten on the dot, when the museum opened, in order to avoid the crowds.

"You're welcome to join us, of course," Harriet said stiffly, Rannie understanding that her mom was trying to put salve on the sore feelings from before.

"Thanks but I can't."

Instantly, Harriet looked aggrieved.

"I have work that has to get done this morning." Namely the eulogistic paragraphs about Ellen. Harriet, however, seemed to construe the reply as both a convenient excuse as well as "see-I-told-you-so" proof of Rannie's wage-earning prowess.

"Have fun!" Rannie said, handing her mother the spare set of keys. "Maybe we'll go out for a bite tonight. There's that Mexican place you like so much."

"No. Tonight I'm making dinner—my special chicken dish—for you and Nate, and Mary, too, if she's free. I insist." With that, Harriet Polichek Bookman bustled out the door.

"I am wearing the pair of earrings that Ellen gave me as a farewell present when I left Simon & Schuster." Rannie tucked her hair behind both ears to reveal them to the audience. "Ellen said, 'They are silver commas,' although I debated this, arguing in favor of single quote marks . . . whichever, I love them. I mean, what better gift for a copy editor? And along with the earrings was a note in Ellen's inimitable jagged print."

Several heads nodded. Everyone was gathered in the largest of S&S's conference rooms, the gigantic eight-section burl-top table removed to accommodate rows of chairs. Rannie was facing the crowd of about a hundred people; surprisingly Larry Katz was not one of them.

For a second, Rannie turned to take another look at the photo of Ellen projected on a screen behind her. It had been taken at a sales conference somewhere tropical, Ellen lounging on a chaise poolside, smiling happily and lifting a tall glass with a paper umbrella toward the camera.

"Sadly, I no longer have the note and don't remember it word for word. But its meaning has stayed with me. Ellen said that although we'd known each other for ten years and were privy to stuff that absolutely no one else knew about us, she was worried that we might drift apart. Often a work friendship seems deep and indestructible. Day-to-day proximity fosters a closeness that feels real and binding, and then once two people no longer collect paychecks from the same company, well—" Rannie shrugged. "I know I've experienced that and I imagine many of you have too. At the end of her note Ellen wrote 'Please let's stay friends. I'll be so disappointed in both of us if we don't.'

"That was four months ago. So far Ellen and I had been getting together about once a week. Even if it was just for coffee. She was a good friend; she had such a good heart."

Suddenly the door to the conference room opened and in

came Larry Katz, late as usual and in his signature trench coat. His entrance was enough of a distraction for Rannie to lose her train of thought. Larry remained standing at the back of the room, unable to find a seat. He was staring at her, but so of course were approximately a hundred other pairs of eyes. Flustered, Rannie shuffled through her scribbled notes and then opted for a speedy wrap-up. "All I want to say is that I won't ever stop missing Ellen."

Rannie returned to her seat and tried listening to the last speakers instead of fixating on Larry Katz.

At the end, as she made her way out of the conference room, past a shelf of bestsellers all acquired by Ellen, Larry waylaid her and, in a voice that Rannie wished wasn't so loud or so angry, said, "We need to talk. Now."

They settled on the Sixth Avenue Deli, just far enough from the Simon & Schuster offices that other attendees from Ellen's gathering were unlikely to show up. Rannie was hungry. No, make that famished, so she ordered a Rodney Dangerfield—a triple-decker on rye with pastrami, corned beef, roast beef, tomato, and coleslaw. Larry made do with coffee and a Danish.

"Rannie, you honestly do think *I* murdered Ellen!" Larry was trying hard to keep his voice low. He sounded equal parts angry and mystified. No, actually much more angry than mystified. "I told that sergeant, 'I'm happy to take a lie detector test, swab all the DNA you want from me. I'm innocent.' "

Well, Sergeant Grieg certainly didn't dillydally. Instead of responding to that, Rannie said, "You're Audeo."

"If you say so."

"Oh, come off it, Larry."

He leaned back in his chair. "All right, for argument's sake, what if you're right. Without doubt Ret would have made damn sure I signed a very binding nondisclosure agreement."

Rannie nodded in a "point taken" way. Their order arrived, and once the waiter was out of earshot, Larry continued. "Ret never shared a byline or author credit in her life. You know that. Once the new book was out she was going to make sure the publicity spotlight was on her and nobody else."

Rannie prepared to take the first bite of her sandwich, no mean feat, as it was almost three inches thick. Instead she put it down. "Hold on. Didn't you tell me Ret was really on the fence about doing personal appearances?"

"Yeah, I did. But my own guess is once the book came out, she would have jumped at any TV, *Sesame Street* included." Larry took one bite of Danish and immediately put it back on the plate, which he pushed aside, muttering, "Stale." Then glowering at Rannie, he spread out his hands. "Okay, who am I kidding? Yes, I'm Audeo."

"The police know?"

He nodded sullenly and reached for one of Rannie's pickle spears.

"And Ellen, she knew too?"

Another nod. "How'd you figure it out?"

"My mother has the same hearing aids. Audeos."

Larry looked embarrassed. "So much for their bullshit claim to be invisible." He grabbed another pickle off Rannie's plate. "Look. All this stays between us, Rannie. Right? Nobody at Dusk can know about—about my arrangement with Ret. You understand how fucked I'd be."

Indeed she did. Larry had been paid to help Ret write a best-seller for another publishing house. If his bosses knew, he'd be out on his ear faster than you could say "conflict of interest." Had Ret ever held this over Larry's head?

"I worked with her, on and off, for about six months. Took a few personal days. Used up some vacation time. It was fun. I interviewed a lot of people, even got inside the mansion on Fifth Avenue and got all the photos Ret wanted." Larry laughed. "I had a phony ID saying I was an NYU art history professor. So I call and—easy peasy—in I go and get a private tour from the fancy-shmancy granddaughter. Buffy. Binky. Some shiksa name. But no matter what I did, it was never enough. Ret bitched how she was overpaying me, that I was cheating her, billing more hours than I worked. . . . The only person she ever trusted was the sister."

"Sister? Ret had no immediate family."

"Sister as in nun. Sister Dorothy Something."

Of course. Ret's book was dedicated to her. Sister Dorothy Cusack.

"Larry, do you happen to know who Gery Antioch is? Gery with a 'g' and just one 'r.' He's in the acknowledgments, too."

"Nope. She never mentioned that name. I know the nun is up in Westchester. Sisters of the Traveling Pants? Ret drove up regularly to see her. The funeral is tomorrow, by the way, at the nunnery—is that what you call it?

"Convent, more likely," Rannie replied. She was attempting to work her way through the first quarter of the Rodney Dangerfield.

"They're getting the entire estate. Every nickel. I said to Ret, 'What on earth do nuns need with a Rolls? Leave it to me.' Maybe if I'd shtooped her, she would have."

A grim flashback—Ret, half naked and tied to her bed—suddenly assaulted Rannie. Ret's tongue lolling from a hole that bore no resemblance to a mouth. Rannie put down her sandwich—suddenly the sight of all the sliced, fleshy-pink meat, not to mention the oozing coleslaw, was revolting. Larry, however, was eyeing the Rodney Dangerfield hungrily. She was not feeling generous toward him, yet there was no possible way to finish this behemoth, so she sighed with irritation and pushed the plate toward him.

Once he finished it, his expression turned contemplative. "Listen. I'm sorry I didn't catch all of what you said about Ellen before. What I heard was nice, from the heart."

"I came right after the CEO. All she talked about was the end-of-year forecast for Ellen's books, how this was her best year ever for the company. She actually quoted gross versus net revenue."

"I don't understand why Ellen didn't leave Simon. They never even made her a VP."

"I know Penguin made her a good offer not long ago." Then Rannie waited a beat and said, "I also know you two were seeing each other. You never said."

"No, I didn't." Larry licked a shred of mustard-infused coleslaw off his pinkie finger. "And really, is it any of your business?"

"Fair enough, Larry, but then don't act as though it's crazy for me to be suspicious of you. You've been keeping a lot of secrets."

"Okay. I'll tell you this. It was Ellen who didn't want to go public. Initially, we got back in touch because of Ret's book . . . then, well, it kind of went from there. Ellen was up front about that dick Wall Street trader, how she wasn't over him. So I guess you could say she was using me. Fine. I didn't mind."

Larry, arms crossed, gazed hard at Rannie and said, "You

know what I always liked about you? You have a gleam in your eye as if you're about to get in trouble. A born cutie pie."

The compliment came out of left field and made her squirm. "I'm forty-three. Way too old for cute."

"I'll rephrase—I still find you very appealing and I'd jump into bed with you again in a heartbeat. But I don't need to prove my innocence to you. The only people who need convincing are the police."

"When did you last see Ellen?"

"Sunday for a late lunch. She was freaked out about Ret and scared for herself. I thought she was being overly neurotic. I tried to talk her into staying at my place for a few nights, rather than running off to the Caribbean. If she'd listened to me, maybe she'd still be alive."

The waiter passed by and Rannie asked for the check, waving away Larry's offer to pay. She didn't want to be indebted in any way, shape, or form. It was queasy-making to hear him talk about still being attracted to her, right after leaving a memorial get-together for Ellen. As she grabbed her coat from the wall rack, she turned businesslike, assuring him the freelance work he'd assigned would be done by Friday, Monday latest.

Larry squeezed out of the booth and glanced at his watch. "I didn't realize how late it was. . . . I guess I should head back to the office. Or I suppose I could just go home." He smiled a languid smile at Rannie, letting the last sentence hang.

Was this an indirect invitation to his apartment? If so, Rannie chose not to get the hint and instead suggested a different destination. "Maybe now's the time, Larry, to pop by the Twenty-Fourth Precinct. Take the lie detector test or do whatever to clear your name once and for all." Then with a "see ya" wave,

Rannie strode to the corner of Fifty-Fifth Street in the direction of the Broadway subway entrance at Columbus Circle.

Rannie beat her mother home. She changed out of her suit and after dropping it off at the dry cleaners, picked up a bottle of the merlot that, in recent years, her once-abstemious mother had come to favor. Rannie put it in the fridge. "So what if it's gauche," Harriet would always declare. "I happen to like red wine cold."

The message light, which had not been blinking on her earlier return to the apartment, now was.

It was Tim!

Rannie was initially thrilled and then not so thrilled. She listened to the message several times to parse its meaning.

"Rannie, listen, I need to talk. Don't bother trying me. I'll call again, probably sometime tonight."

Needing to talk had to be construed as a good thing, right? It meant he wasn't done with her completely. Yet there was a businesslike brusqueness to his words that didn't sound like he wanted to kiss and make up. If Tim had kept lots of stuff at her house, she might have interpreted the call as figuring out when he could come by to retrieve it. However, except for a paperback thriller he'd finished on a recent Sunday and maybe a ratty running shirt or two, there was nada belonging to him.

Also, why call on her landline? His modus operandi was to call her cell, usually several times on the fly, until the game of phone tag ended and they'd finally connect in real time. This landline message seemed so purposeful, like setting up an appointment.

If only she could call Ellen to help dissect every single syllable of Tim's message. This was exactly the kind of situation—romantic upheaval—that Ellen relished. She could almost hear Ellen giggling and saying how they were still seventh-grade girls at heart. At Simon this afternoon, Rannie had mentioned how much she would miss Ellen; yet right now was the first real instance of that. Up till this very moment, the horror of Ellen's death had blotted out any normal feelings of loss.

By four thirty, Nate—along with Olivia—arrived. "She's gonna stay for dinner," he said.

"I better call Grandma. She's going to cook—"

Nate cut Rannie off. "No need. We texted. She knows and it's fine."

Harriet texting. Okay, add texting to the "most unlikely to" list that already included JDating and ménage à trois.

Soon the intercom buzzer rang. It was Harriet.

"I'm downstairs and need help with the groceries."

"Grandma, you way overtipped the cabdriver," Nate was saying a moment later as he, Olivia, and Harriet, all toting bags from Fairway, came through the door and proceeded to the kitchen. Harriet also was holding a drum-shaped Saks hatbox, circa 1961, which she handed to Rannie. "From Mary," she said. "You never mentioned you were going to Charlotte Cummings's funeral Saturday. How la di da! Imagine who you'll see."

"Wish I could sneak you in," Rannie replied. Harriet was a devotee of *Vanity Fair* and the upscale boldface names covered in its pages. "The only reason I'm—"

"Oh, I heard why you're going and 'what a *darling* you are,' 'what an *absolute* angel' to take Mary's friend." Harriet had always been a pretty good mimic and now managed to capture the cadence of Mary's speech, the way Mary underlined certain words.

"The friend—Daisy, is it?—arrived for dinner just as I was leaving; it wasn't even four thirty and she was half crocked!" Harriet harrumphed softly while unpacking grocery bags. "Maybe she'd be steadier on her feet if she drank less."

As Rannie retrieved cutting boards, mixing bowls, and the spices needed for the chicken dish that Harriet was preparing—within the family known as "Poule à la Harriet"—Rannie wondered whether she hadn't caught wind of something else, jealousy maybe over the relationship Rannie shared with her former mother-in-law.

"Nate and I try to have dinner with her once a week. Mary's been so lonely since Walter died," Rannie said, hoping to imply that duty trumped enjoyment. "It hasn't even been a year and a half."

Harriet nodded and seemed mollified. "I know. We had lunch in the museum cafeteria after the Degas exhibit and all we discussed was being widows. I said, 'I wish I could tell you it gets better. It doesn't, but it does get easier.' She's such a lovely woman. I mentioned that travel helps. Maybe if she learned mah-jongg, she'd like to come on a cruise with the girls and me."

Rannie looked up from the garlic she was mincing. Yes. Her mother, although never known for a sense of humor, had been kidding.

All during dinner Rannie kept an ear cocked for Tim's call. It didn't come until an hour later when all the dishes were done, casserole dish soaking in the sink, and Harriet, Olivia, and Nate were deep into Settlers of Catan, a board game that had utterly confounded Rannie the couple of times she'd tried to play, but that Harriet seemed to pick up with no problem.

"Sweet move, Grandma!" she heard Nate cry.

Rannie was in her bedroom trying on the loaner funeral hats, trying to decide which of the three looked least ridiculous on her. Definitely not the teensy navy velvet beanie with a veil. Maybe a tall svelte type could pull it off. It made Rannie look eerily like Mamie Eisenhower.

The phone rang and Rannie lunged for it, then forced herself to wait until the middle of the second ring to pick up.

"Hello," she said, her voice distinctly aquiver, but when Tim said, "It's me, Rannie," he sounded nervous too, so they were even.

"Now a good time?"

She really did love the sound of his voice, Boston Irish accent and all.

"Now's fine. I'm glad you called. I've been wanting to call you. The only reason I didn't . . . was, well, I was scared you didn't want me to, after what you said in the car."

"I appreciate that." Tim cleared his throat. "Look, this is important. I wouldn't have gotten in touch otherwise."

Her stomach took a dive. He wasn't calling because of a change of heart.

"Okay, there's no easy way to say this, so I'm just gonna spit it out. For your own good, you should stay away from Larry Katz. Don't get involved with him."

Rannie's brain went into hyperdrive. Was Larry under surveillance? Was she? Had a cop been watching them today? What about the other night at the Acropolis coffee shop? And Tim. His claims to being totally in the dark about the murders, was that bullshit? If so, why share now?

"I'm, I'm not involved with him!" Rannie finally said. "He used to work at S&S ages ago. I told you about him—I know I did. We had a brief—I don't know what to call it! A brief fling.

It was right after Peter and I split up. Larry made me feel like I wasn't a total loser. I think the police have got it all wrong, suspecting him of anything." That last sentence was spoken with more certainty than she felt.

"You know he was involved with your friend Ellen?"

"As a matter of fact, I do."

"And his marriage? You know about that too?"

"I know it didn't last long."

"He married a woman with a seventeen-year-old daughter. His wife threw him out of the house and took out an order of protection. Rannie, she said he was hitting on the kid."

Poule à la Harriet lurched in her stomach. "I don't believe it."

"It's a matter of public record." Tim paused. "Also, he was at Ret Sullivan's apartment the day she was killed. That morning."

Larry had told her he hadn't seen Ret in a month. Another lie.

"Everything I'm telling you I heard just this afternoon. No more than a few hours ago."

"Someone saw me with Larry today, right? Someone who knows me from the bar."

"Yeah. The cops are keeping an eye on him."

After they hung up, Rannie went straight to the bathroom and threw up every bit of poule.

"Rannie, are you sick?" Harriet was suddenly shouting from the other side of the door.

Jesus Christ! With her mother here, it was impossible even to vomit in peace. "I'll be all right. Just give me a minute."

"Can I get you some ginger ale, some tea maybe? I'm sure it wasn't the chicken. Everybody else is fine. Listen, let me check my purse. I always carry Alka-Seltzer."

Rannie splashed water on her face and sat on the rim of the

tub, taking deep slow breaths to calm herself while trying to block out everything Tim had told her. "Take care." Those had been his parting words on the phone. He might as well have said, "Have a nice life." But that was Tim. Once he made a decision, he stuck with it. Like quitting drinking or training for a marathon. His inflexibility often worked in his favor; in this particular situation, it worked against hers. Tim would not see her again. Of that she was sure.

A moment later Rannie forced down the glass of Alka-Seltzer that Harriet appeared with. Easier than arguing with her mother, and oddly enough it did help settle her stomach.

Ushered into bed, Rannie allowed her mother to feel her forehead with the back of her hand. "Cool as a cucumber," pronounced Harriet. "Probably one of those twenty-four-hour things. Get a good night's sleep. You know where to find me, if you need anything."

Harriet blew Rannie a kiss and turned off the overhead light as she left. Then, just as she'd done on umpteen million nights as a kid when she wanted to stay up late reading, Rannie counted to fifty, turned on her bedside lamp, and reached for her copy of *Tattletale*. She remembered a long chapter on the convent where Ret had grown up and where now she would be buried. Rannie was interested in the convent's exact location.

Previously Rannie had skimmed the chapters on Ret's childhood; now she read them with greater attention. It was a dispiriting story. Ret had never known her father. She was an infant when he went out to buy the proverbial pack of cigarettes and split for good. At age five, upon the death of her mother, Ret was sent to live at the Sisters of Mercy orphanage in Pound Ridge, New York, which was only about an hour or so from Manhattan.

By Lina/Ret's account, the orphanage was a caring place, a safe haven with bucolic grounds. And yes indeed, Sister Dorothy Cusack had played a major role in young Ret's life. Rannie immediately grasped what had first drawn Ret to her. Sister Dorothy was a celebrity nun. Before taking vows, she'd enjoyed a brief career as a movie star, costarring in two Elvis movies. The nun came across as smart, warm, and energetic. Ret saw her first Broadway musical courtesy of Sister Dorothy; Sister Dorothy encouraged Ret's interest in writing; Sister Dorothy told the children, "This world is yours. Get involved!," and proudly wore JFK buttons on her habit throughout the 1960 campaign. And far from doing a hard sell on the joys of becoming a nun, Sister Dorothy had convinced Ret that "a different path awaited her."

As Lina Struvel, Ret quoted herself as saying, "Sister Dorothy is a beautiful human being. No one knows me better than she does. No one. She is the only person who truly loves me and though that may sound sad, I feel incredibly fortunate. Her love is so great that it equals the love of hundreds of lesser people."

In spite of herself, Rannie started wondering exactly when tomorrow Ret's funeral was, whether it was open to outsiders, and how long it took to get to the convent by train. Was there even a remote possibility that Sister Dorothy would speak to her afterward?

Of course, there was Harriet to take into consideration. That stopped Rannie cold. Maybe she wasn't the world's most dutiful daughter. Still, in good conscience she couldn't see herself ditching her mother to go on some cockamamy sleuthing expedition. Tomorrow they'd spend time together, whatever Harriet wanted to do.

With that she turned off the light, and when sleep refused to come, an Ativan did the trick. . . . Out went the lights.

Chapter 19

IT TURNED OUT THAT HARRIET WAS DITCHING RANNIE.

The next morning over coffee when Rannie said brightly, "Mother, I am at your disposal. Whatever you'd like to do today, just name it."

"Ooh. I'm so sorry. I made plans last night with Olivia."

"Olivia? As in Nate's Olivia?"

"We're spending the day shopping. She can get into all the wholesale places. Designer stuff at a fraction of the price. And we'll have a car and driver at our disposal."

"But it's a school day."

"She told me all seniors have a certain number of personal days."

True, but they were meant for traveling to college interviews, not for chauffeured shopping sprees.

"You're welcome to join us if you'd like."

Rannie loathed shopping, as her mother well knew. Everything about it was anathema to her, prying apart hangers in jam-packed racks of clothes, waiting in line for a hot, claustrophobic dressing room with harsh lighting, getting in and out of dresses or trousers that were always the wrong size, the wrong color, the wrong price.

"One place sells perfect knockoffs of St. John suits."

St. John suits were, in her mother's eyes, the ne plus ultra, the last word in elegance. That St. John suits were themselves basically knockoffs of Chanel designs was never an issue.

"You two go. You'll have more fun without me."

At ten o'clock Olivia buzzed up for Harriet. Across the street, Rannie spotted a silver Jag, double parked, Olivia in the backseat, taking a final drag of a cigarette before chucking it out the window. A minute later Harriet came scurrying out to the car, casting furtive glances left and right, on the lookout for early-rising hoodlums. The chauffeur jumped out and escorted her into the safety of the Jaguar.

Door closed, they were off!

Alone at last. Rannie looked up the phone number of the convent and called. "My name is Miranda Bookman. I'm calling about the funeral for Ret Sullivan. I used to work at Simon & Schuster, that's how I knew Ms. Sullivan. Could you tell me, please, is the funeral open to—" What was the appropriate term here? Non-nuns? Unbelievers? Outsiders?

The friendly voice on the line came to her rescue. "Friends of Miss Sullivan's are most welcome. Will you be driving?"

"No. I'll be taking the train from Grand Central Station."

"Then when you arrive in Mount Kisco, just call and one of the sisters will pick you up."

"No, no. Please. I don't want to inconvenience anyone. I can get a cab."

"And your name again."

Rannie supplied it then hurriedly stammered, "Um . . . There is something else I wanted to ask. Afterward, is there any chance that I might be able to speak with Sister Dorothy Cusack?"

"I couldn't say. That's really up to Sister."

How promising did that sound? Not very. "Of course. Well, thank you," Rannie said and pressed End on her phone screen. Since seeing Ret Sullivan laid to rest was not the true purpose of schlepping to Mount Kisco, Rannie decided to stay put and copy-edit the book about sicko CEOs. And, no, she wouldn't deliver the manuscript in person; she intended to follow Tim's advice and steer clear of Larry. Dusk could spring for messenger pickup.

"The guy has a history of preying on vulnerable women." That's how Tim had put it on the phone last night. It made Larry sound like a complete psycho. According to the personality profile in *Cutthroat*, a predatory nature was a hallmark of all psychopaths. They trained their sights on a target and—through manipulation, charm, quick-wittedness—not only persuaded the victim to do their bidding but also to consider doing so a singular stroke of good fortune. Witness Bernie Madoff, whose clients begged to fork over all their money to him. But Larry? Preying on women, coming on to an underage stepdaughter? Rannie didn't buy it. Nevertheless, as for "vulnerable," objectively, she and Ellen—Ret, too—all qualified as "vulnerable" at the time Larry Katz first shambled into their lives. According to Larry, however, he'd had to fend off Ret's advances. As for Ellen's involvement with Larry, Rannie's hunch was that Ellen viewed him in much the same way Rannie had after her marriage combusted: Larry was an amusing, intelligent, unserious man whose attentions were flattering, pleasant diversions. If it even rated as romance, it was romance lite.

Rannie was unaware that her hand still held the phone until its jangled ringing startled her and she dropped it.

"This is Sister Dorothy Cusack. Am I speaking to Miranda Bookman?"

Holy guacamole! "Yes, Sister. Yes, it is." Rannie didn't know what was more surprising—talking to a former movie star or the fact that a convent had spy phones with caller ID.

"I called before because I knew Ret Sullivan. Not very well." Rannie explained her function as copy editor. "But I liked Ret— in a weird kind of way."

Those last words had popped out unbidden. However, Sister Dorothy seemed to understand. "Yes, Kathleen—or Ret as she came to call herself—didn't always make it easy to like her—or love her. But I did."

"I know. And I'm truly sorry for your loss."

Rannie listened patiently to Sister Dorothy's recital of all the masses, novenas, rosaries being said in Ret's memory. "We've all been so upset!"

"Yes, Sister, I understand. Ret's death has been very upsetting for me too. I was the person who found her."

An audible intake of breath. "How awful! Oh, that must have been awful."

"It was. And then two days later a close friend of mine was killed in Central Park."

"The runner?"

"That's right. The thing is, she knew Ret too. Much better than I did. She was Ret's editor at Simon & Schuster. They'd worked together for years."

"Ellen something?"

"Ellen Donahoe. Yes."

"God have mercy! I read about a woman getting attacked in Central Park but didn't make the connection."

"You couldn't have. The police have kept her name out of the papers."

"Why? Don't tell me they think the murders are related!"

"They may be.... I think they are. Ret has a new book coming out."

"And you think that's why Kathleen was killed? Because of something in it?" There was another audible intake of breath. "Lord! Not again."

Rannie realized that by "not again" Sister Dorothy was referring to what Mike Bellettra had done to Ret. "Sister, if I may, I'd like to attend the funeral for Ret. But I'd also very much like the chance to speak to you afterward."

"You think I might know something?"

"No, probably not, but you knew Ret better than anyone else."

After a moment's hesitation came a decisive reply. "Yes, come. Of course, come. Though I can't imagine I'll be able to shed light on why Kathleen came to such a vicious end."

Within fifteen minutes Rannie showered, had the train schedule written down, and, since she was still waiting to be reunited with her navy suit, borrowed a black wool jacket of Alice's as well as a pair of charcoal pants.

"Now," she told her reflection in the mirror, "Get thee to a nunnery!"

Even on a blustery day with not a ray of sunshine, everything about the convent appeared silvery and serene—stone walls that enclosed a now-leafless apple orchard, a weathered barn and chicken coops and several rustic buildings clustered around a church so small it looked to Rannie more like a children's playhouse than a house of prayer. Sister Dorothy Cusack was waiting for her at the double doors of the church. Under a mannish black overcoat, she wore a full habit and signature lace-up nun shoes, possibly the least attractive footwear known to humankind. She was extremely tall and thin with pale, goyishe blue eyes; and although she had to be roughly the same age as Harriet, her complexion still had a creaminess that Rannie was positive owed nothing to Estée Lauder. Who knew . . . maybe chastity was the secret to perfect skin.

As she led Rannie into the church, she almost seemed to be gliding under her ankle-length skirts like Miss Clavel in the Madeline books.

Rannie was thankful to have worn her duffle coat, which had a hood. It was bone-chillingly cold inside.

"The heat has been very cranky," Sister Dorothy explained by way of apology. "We'll have tea after the burial. The mass should be starting in just a few minutes." After bestowing a sorrowful smile on Rannie, she turned and left.

Rannie huddled in a pew at the back and, even with wool gloves on, needed to keep blowing on her hands. The interior was stark. Plain windows, no stained glass, whitewashed walls adorned with nothing except plaster bas-reliefs of the Stations of the Cross. Rannie sat nearest the one with Jesus dragging his own cross up to Calvary.

Soon recorded organ music started up. A trolley wheeled in Ret's coffin, a white cloth with an embroidered gold cross draped over it. A priest swinging a censer entered, followed by about twenty elderly nuns, among them Sister Dorothy.

For the next hour Rannie, the sole "civilian" here to mourn Ret, listened to murmured prayers and chanted recitations; she rose each time the nuns did, sat while they genuflected, and watched in fascination as each waited obediently in line to receive a Communion wafer from the priest. What did the wafer taste like? How long did it take for one to melt in your mouth? Faster than an M&M? And who baked the wafers? Did one company have a monopoly on the business?

This was a first for Rannie, a funeral mass. A high mass. Although the priest mentioned Ret by name a couple of times, how the soul of Christ's servant Kathleen Margaret Sullivan was entering the kingdom of heaven, Ret's role seemed incidental. No more than a cameo appearance. It was the rite that held significance, the person not so much.

Her father's funeral had been so different. Amy's husband had played piano, a medley of Irving Bookman's favorite Sinatra songs, and after the rabbi's eulogy, many people shared memories of her dad, including her uncle Morty, who suddenly choked up recounting a long-winded saga that involved buying halvah candy, of all things.

Rannie stood once again while the coffin was rolled down the center aisle and maneuvered outside. The cemetery was only a short distance away, beyond what looked like a dormitory—perhaps Ret had lived there as a young girl—and before the first rows of the apple trees.

Unlike the funeral mass, the graveside ceremony was brief, Ret interred with final words from the priest, "May her soul and the souls of all the faithful departed, through the mercy of God, rest in peace." A few minutes later, Rannie was sitting in the parlor of the convent's guest cottage, accepting a steaming mug of tea from Sister Dorothy as well as a Nilla Wafer (more wafers!) from a plate painted with holly berries around the rim.

"Kathleen often stayed overnight here in the guest cottage,

especially after she was disfigured," Sister Dorothy began. "She felt safe here. At ease."

"You knew her practically her entire life."

"She came to the orphanage when she was five. Poor little thing. So unloved. A father who abandoned her. A neglectful mother who up and died. Right from the start she tried very hard to be a good Catholic. Too hard, actually. I think she worried that if she didn't obey every single rule of the church, God wouldn't love her either."

"She loved you and knew you loved her back."

"Well, at first she was fascinated by me, nothing more. 'Sister, what was Elvis like? Sister, did you go to the Oscars? Which stars were your friends?'" The nun shook her head and laughed. "I take it that you are aware of my former career?"

Rannie nodded. "I am."

"At one point—this was years later after she'd moved to New York—Kathleen got it into her head to write a book about me. She had a romantic notion that I was some kind of latter-day Mary Magdalene, a glamorous Hollywood sinner who found Christ and then gave up her wicked ways. 'It has bestseller written all over it,' she kept saying."

"Yes, that definitely sounds like the Ret I knew."

"I told her, 'First of all, there is no dirt. No scandal. I was a good little Catholic girl even back then.' I also said, 'And I won't forgive you if you publicize my life.' I probably would have forgiven her, but Kathleen couldn't afford to take any chances."

"Ret considered taking vows herself, didn't she?"

"Yes. When she was about twelve or thirteen, she went through a stage, like some girls do, where that was all she talked about. But it would have been a mistake. I advised against it."

"Do you mind saying why?"

"Well . . ." Sister Dorothy paused for a moment, fingering the long chain from which her crucifix dangled. Her fingers were painfully arthritic. "To put it plainly, I don't think she loved God. Not truly. It wasn't the glory of religion, the joy, that drew her; it was the suffering. All the other little girls would tape pretty pictures by their bed of the Virgin with the Christ Child. Not Kathleen. She kept pictures of martyred saints. It wasn't healthy. I prayed a lot for Kathleen back then."

Rannie blew on her mug. The tea was scalding. "Her new book is dedicated to you. It'll be out shortly."

"I knew she was finishing up another book, nothing more than that. She wouldn't even say about who."

No, no. "*Whom.*" *About* "*whom.*" But because she liked Sister Dorothy, Rannie granted her a grammatical dispensation. Then, deciding that divulging a secret to a nun didn't count as blabbing, Rannie said, "The book is a biography of Charlotte Cummings, the socialite and philanthropist." Then she added, "She just died a couple of days ago," guessing a convent nun might not be a celebrity newshound.

"Oh, I know who Charlotte Cummings is . . . or was. I met her once when she and her husband came to visit. I'm not exaggerating when I say Silas Cummings saved this convent."

Sister Dorothy seemed amused by the look of surprise on Rannie's face. "This was—what?—probably forty years ago. The diocese had been forced to cut funding for us. Our buildings were falling into terrible disrepair; we had to let go of all the lay teachers. It got to a point where sometimes there was barely enough money to feed and clothe the girls.

"And then one day, Silas and Charlotte Cummings appeared

in a chauffeur-driven Rolls-Royce. Kathleen and a bunch of girls were outside gawking. I remember her asking, 'Sister, that car is funny looking. If they're rich, why don't they have a Cadillac?'" Sister Dorothy laughed. "Well, Kathleen changed her mind about Rolls-Royces, didn't she?"

Rannie smiled, marveling more over the fact that there was an actual connection, however slim, between Ret Sullivan and Charlotte Cummings.

"Kathleen was dazzled by Mrs. Cummings, who must have looked like royalty to her. As soon as she emerged from the backseat of the car, Kathleen made a beeline over to her, curtsied very dramatically, and said, 'Welcome to Sisters of Mercy.'"

Rannie laughed.

"Oh, yes! Kathleen was some little operator. Mrs. Cummings gave her a great big hug and asked to hear all about her life here. I'm sure Kathleen had visions of being adopted, like Little Orphan Annie. For weeks she kept asking when 'the rich lady' was coming back."

"Had Mr. and Mrs. Cummings heard that the convent was in financial trouble? Did they want to make a charitable gift?"

"No. Silas Cummings wanted to buy a painting we owned. We kept it in the library and Kathleen would often go there and stare at it, just mesmerized.

"How he learned we owned the painting, I have no idea. But he knew who painted it, how old it was, and what he was willing to pay for it—two hundred thousand dollars! He said that was a very fair price and Mother Superior didn't argue. Can you imagine! Within two weeks, the painting was his and this convent was saved. Does Kathleen mention this in her new book?"

"No, she doesn't." Nor was there a word about it in *Tattletale*.

"Well, I certainly hope she doesn't say nasty things about Silas Cummings," Sister Dorothy said protectively. "Every now and then I still say a rosary for him. I think of him as our guardian angel."

Rannie thought about the passages on Silas's intestinal troubles but said, "There's nothing awful in the new book. Nothing scandalous. It's quite different from Ret's other books."

"I'm happy to hear that, yet something was preying on her mind the last time she visited. I thought it might have something to do with her new book. Kathleen told me that she'd sinned, grievously sinned, and she said although she was ashamed of herself, she was glad."

"She didn't give you any idea what she'd done?"

"No. She said something to the effect that she was settling a score with a person who'd cheated her. She was getting even." The plate of Nilla Wafers was proffered again and Rannie obliged.

"I told Kathleen, no matter what she'd done, she had to go to confession, make amends for her sin, and undo it if she could. I pray to God she listened to me." The nun closed her eyes, and suddenly her face contorted, as if she was in pain. "I'm so worried she didn't. And now she's dead."

It wasn't until Rannie was back on Metro North, thinking over their conversation, that she grasped the full implication of Sister Dorothy's words. Her anguish was not solely over what damage Ret might have done to somebody else, but over what damage Ret had done to herself, more specifically to her immortal soul.

Chapter 20

THE SHOPPERS HAD RETURNED TRIUMPHANT—A MOUNTAIN OF generic brown shopping bags were piled on the living room couch. Harriet was modeling one of the outfits she'd purchased, a dressy number with a cap-sleeved top covered in bugle beads and a chiffon skirt in the same rusty reddish color. She twirled around in it, revealing the marshmallow-white sneakers she'd set out in this morning, and spread her arms.

"Wow!" was Rannie's noncommittal reaction. Floor-length dresses made her mother look even shorter, verging perilously close to "little people" status or whatever the currently correct euphemism was for midget. Then seeing Harriet was waiting for further comment, Rannie added, "The dress matches the color of your hair exactly. . . . It'll be perfect for Captain's Night on your next cruise."

"It's perfect for tonight," Harriet replied.

Come again?

"Nate. Your mother's home," Harriet called in a loud voice.

"Fuck. I have no clue how you tie this," Rannie heard her son grumbling a moment later as he entered the living room. "And the pants are a deal breaker."

"You bought Nate a tuxedo!" Rannie exclaimed.

"It's borrowed, my brother's." Olivia went over to Nate and with amazing dexterity, for a teenager, knotted a perfect bow tie. Then she took a step to the aside and made a voilà! gesture. "Does he look hunkalicious or what? I'm talkin' total stud muffin!"

"Funny, O. Keep it up and I won't go."

"Go where?" Rannie asked mystified. "Where are you going?"

"To a black-tie affair at the museum. Tonight. We're all going. You included," Harriet informed Rannie. There was a familiar undertone, something besides excitement in her voice, a trace of "and no arguing."

Olivia filled in the holes. She had four tickets to a party in the Temple of Dendur at the Metropolitan Museum, tickets that her parents weren't using. "Once we found this dress for Mrs. B—"

They beamed at each other like BFFs.

"Well, what's the point of buying a party dress," Olivia continued, pausing to clear her throat, "unless you have a party to go to?"

"Rannie, last month I saw this same dress in Nordstrom. I won't even tell you what it cost there. I paid less than a third. It's a knockoff, of course."

"Even the designer wouldn't be able to tell," Olivia assured Rannie's mother and supplied more backstory for Rannie. By three they had finished shopping, so the Jag made a stop at Olivia's house to get the tickets, something for Olivia to wear, and the tux for Nate, the pants of which, now that Rannie examined her son more closely, were too tight in the crotch and short in the legs, revealing the sneakers *he* was wearing . . . black high-tops that had seen far better days.

"So ditch the pants, dude. Wear jeans. That'll look cool," Olivia told him.

Now was the moment to take her stand. "Listen. You all go without me. I have nothing to wear. And much as I hate being a killjoy, really all I want to do tonight is eat ice cream straight from the carton and watch—"

Nate was shaking his head vehemently. "Oh no. No way. If she bails, just forget the whole thing."

"Darling, don't call your mother 'she,'" Harriet chided, then she dealt with Rannie. "Don't be ridiculous. Of course you're coming. Alice must have something suitable you can wear. That closet is so stuffed with clothes, I could barely squeeze my few things in. Come." Harriet had Rannie by the hand and was heading for the den.

Olivia followed while Nate slunk back to his room.

"Oh, whoa!" Olivia said when she opened the closet door. Right away she began sifting through the tightly packed contents on double racks, pulling out various items for Rannie, who sat balefully on the couch, to consider.

After trying on a couple of dresses that Olivia immediately deemed, "Not really you, Ms. Bookman," Rannie zipped herself into a short strapless black dress that seemed to be made of the same material as Spanx.

Olivia tore at a cuticle on her pinkie finger while tilting her head to get various perspectives on the dress. "Yeah. This has definite possibilities."

Harriet pursed her lips in a moue of disapproval. "Awfully

plain, don't you think?" said she of the bugle-bead-encrusted bosom.

"No worries," Olivia replied. "We'll accessorize. Stay right where you are, Ms. Bookman, I'll be back in a jiff."

"Isn't she adorable?" Harriet whispered. "And Jewish, too, you know."

"Actually, I didn't."

"Well, only half. But the half that counts."

For Harriet, the sole consolation of Rannie marrying Peter Lorimer, a lapsed Episcopalian, was that "in the eyes of Israel" and therefore in the eyes of Harriet Bookman, Alice and Nate were still considered Jewish because their mother was. More than once Harriet had reminded them of their eligibility for a free birthright trip. "Remember, you've got till you're twenty-seven!" she'd exclaim brightly.

"Oh, we had such a ball shopping today. Olivia's grandfather started a very successful company that made coat linings. That's how Olivia has entrée to all the wholesale places. She told me in such a serious voice, 'Seventh Avenue is in my blood.'"

"Well, no wonder you bonded!" Rannie replied. Before migrating to the Midwest in the 1930s, Harriet's Polichek forebears had also worked in the New York garment industry. "I'll tell you this, Mother. Olivia's mother doesn't play up her garmento past. She's some big muckety-muck at Sotheby's now and very snooty."

The conversation stopped as Olivia reappeared with an overnight bag, made by the minions at Louis Vuitton.

"Stand, please," she requested, and for the next few minutes experimented on Rannie with various items of costume jewelry—a gold snake bracelet, long ropes of black pearls that dangled past Rannie's waist, many pairs of earrings—though nothing seemed to Olivia's liking. Then her eye glommed onto the scarves and shawls hanging from the back of the closet door. Once again it was Alice in absentia to the rescue.

"Yes!" Olivia cried. She wrapped a long six-inch-wide swath of hot pink silk around Rannie's waist, obi-like, and tied the ends in a giant poufy bow. Then she stood back to survey her handiwork. "Now *that* makes a statement."

"Just as long as the statement isn't 'My mom's my date tonight.'"

"You're funny, Ms. Bookman. No, the statement is very *Gentlemen Prefer Blondes*, wouldn't you say, Mrs. B?"

Harriet was "putting on her face" in front of a magnifying mirror. "Maybe, if the brassiere straps go," she said, pulling down the corner of an eye to apply mascara.

Olivia chewed the inside of her cheek. "You know what would really rock this? A pair of elbow-length gloves."

"Look in the bureau," Rannie said.

In addition to the long black gloves, worn with twin rhinestone cuff bracelets over them, Rannie was soon gamely teetering atop sparkly slingbacks. Olivia gelled back Rannie's dark hair into a severe, behind-the-ears bob, and in one sitting applied more makeup to Rannie's face than she had probably used in an entire year. "How old is this mascara? When did you last use this liquid base?" Olivia kept asking.

"My best guess, sometime during the Giuliani administration," Rannie said.

Olivia giggled again.

"Always with the smart remarks," Harriet muttered.

After adding a pair of giant emerald-cut rhinestone earrings, Olivia lost all her cool and, clasping her hands together, started jumping up and down. "Yes! Perfect!" she crowed. "Take a look!"

The end result was both startling and intriguing. "It's like looking at my evil twin!" Rannie marveled, the kind of no-good woman who appeared out of the blue on soap operas, staying just long enough to steal away husbands, wreck lifelong friendships, and have a hysterical pregnancy.

By six o'clock they were nestled in the Jag, ready to party down, Olivia in pencil-thin black velvet pants, stilettos, and a silvery camisole top; Harriet already grousing that her low-heeled pumps were killing her; and Nate black-tie appropriate from the waist up. Rannie ordered herself to put everything disturbing on hold. For the duration of the evening, she was going to follow her mother's sage advice and have a good time.

They mounted the imposing stone steps leading to the main entrance of the museum. The long trough-like fountains on either side were lit up, water dancing in syncopated spurts.

Olivia and Nate exchanged conspiratorial looks. Rannie guessed why. Among Manhattan private school teenagers, the steps of the Met were a notorious nighttime gathering place on weekends, the best location to scope out parent-free parties and to get buzzed before going. A concerned Chapel mom who lived in an apartment directly across the street on Fifth Avenue had gone so far as to take zoom lens photos of the kids, then mass e-mail them to other parents. "Is your child here?" her message heading had read. That had diminished the crowds, the ID'ed kids grounded. But only for a while.

Inside the museum, right away Olivia spotted someone she knew, a girl with wild hair in a not-from-nature color. "Wertheimer! Stop right there!" she cried, then grabbed Nate by the hand and disappeared into the crowd.

"He's in love," Harriet said with a wistful smile. "I know about the tattoo, by the way. TCB, it stands for 'taking care of business.' . . . It was Elvis's motto."

"Yeah, I know. I could kill Nate."

"Olivia has the same one. But at least hers is somewhere you don't normally see it. Right above her tush. I saw it while we were trying on clothes."

Okay, so one minor mystery solved. "How adorable, his and hers tats."

"She's a lovely girl but such a nervous wreck. Those fingernails!" Harriet shook her head. "I advised trying hypnosis: it worked wonders for Edith's granddaughter. You should see the talons she has now!" Harriet suddenly turned all business, yoo-hooing at a passing waiter balancing flutes of champagne on a silver tray. For some reason she carefully inspected all the identical glasses before choosing two. "I hope she doesn't break his heart."

Rannie accepted one of the flutes from Harriet. "She does and I'll break those gorgeous gams of hers."

"No, you won't. All you can do is suffer along with him." Harriet was eyeing her glass suspiciously as if it might be loaded with a date rape drug. "I'll never forget when that twerp Steve Cohen broke up with you. You wouldn't eat. You weren't sleeping. All you did was lie on your bed staring at the ceiling, crying. Your father had to hold me back; I wanted to go over to his house and tear him limb from limb."

"You did? I never knew that." That twerp was the first boy

Rannie had sex with. He was in a garage band, hardly ever washed his hair, and favored plaid flannel shirts with only one sleeve rolled up. The height of cool to fifteen-year-old Rannie.

Rannie smiled and toasted her mother. "I'm so glad you're here," she said with feeling and leaned forward to bestow a kiss.

"No! You'll shmear lipstick on me," the ever-pragmatic Harriet said, averting her face.

Rannie took a sip of champagne and realized that her mother could not have turned up at a more propitious time. Not only did having Harriet around distract Rannie from brooding about Tim—there'd be plenty of time for tears and self-flagellation once Harriet was winging her way back to Cleveland—but also Rannie could half trick herself into believing Harriet's presence provided a protective shield of sorts. Like a flu shot. Mommy's here. So I'm safe. As a child, Rannie had never confided in her mother. It was her dad she always turned to for comfort, for advice. Yet Rannie seriously considered telling Harriet, not now but later, about Ellen and the flashing neon arrows that all seemed to point straight at Larry Katz. Rannie needed someone to listen and maybe Harriet was the one to offer a sensible, Audeo-enhanced ear.

Harriet was glancing around at the swank crowd milling about in the vaulted great hall. Not all that subtly she pinched Rannie's arm and cocked her head in the direction of an emaciated woman with a mane of blond curls. "Sarah Jessica Parker," she mouthed, then smiled smugly. "Oh, I wish George could see me here."

Rannie peered over the rim of her champagne flute. "George?"

"My gentleman friend . . . ex-gentleman friend. He's e-mailed twice. Doesn't have the nerve to call. I haven't replied nor do I intend to."

For the duration of the cocktail hour, they promenaded around the crowded hall, sampling hors d'oeuvres, Harriet continuing to pinch Rannie every time she ID'ed another celeb. Then once Harriet's bunions started screaming for mercy, they sat on one of the long elliptical benches and nursed increasingly flat champagne.

Harriet rallied for the tour of the Costume Institute's new exhibit, which was the raison d'être for the gala. It was called "Hollywood Heroines" and featured costumes from legendary movies on featureless, toothpaste-white mannequins. Audrey Hepburn's black-and-white Ascot outfit from *My Fair Lady*, Scarlett's green velvet number fashioned by Mammy from Tara draperies, Marilyn Monroe's white halter dress from *The Seven Year Itch*, Faye Dunaway's *Bonnie and Clyde* gangster-chic garb, several Muppet movie ensembles of Miss Piggy's on smaller mannequins with the witty addition of snout masks and hair bands with pig ears.

They ran into Nate and Olivia by a glass case containing ball gowns worn by Greta Garbo in *Anna Karenina*. Olivia looked entranced. Nate was at his iPhone, thumbs going a mile a minute, what Rannie liked to call digital (pun definitely intended) calisthenics.

"Gerta must have been as tall as me," observed Olivia.

Rannie winced reflexively. "*As tall as I am.*"

Harriet winced too. "It's *Greta*. Greta Garbo. You never heard of her?"

Olivia lifted her shoulders in a "sue me!" gesture. "I can't even begin to guess how many yards of lace went into the skirt on that black dress."

"Now *that* was a face, the most gorgeous face you ever saw," Harriet said.

The exhibit's grand finale was a barge with a Cleopatra mannequin decked out in a gold gown, gold headdress and collar, gold everything. From there, everyone was shepherded upstairs and into the Temple of Dendur for dinner. On two sides of the reflecting pool surrounding the temple, tables had been set up with gold cloth and towering floral arrangements mixed with curled strips of movie celluloid film. Harriet collapsed in the nearest faux bamboo chair, one without an evening purse placeholder on it, and put Rannie's clutch, well, Alice's clutch, on the seat next to hers.

"What a gorgeous setting for a party," Rannie marveled. For years, she'd seen photos of this annual shindig in the Style section of the Sunday *New York Times*. Now she was here! Rannie smoothed her femme fatale hairdo in case the society photographer Bill Cunningham was lurking about and might want to snap her pic. "I'm just going to take a quick look around. Back in a flash."

So many times, on family excursions to the Met, she had made a stop here in the airy expanse of the little Temple of Dendur, where tolerant guards had always let young Alice and Nate scamper around its perimeter. Yet viewing Dendur at night, lit from within, two torches on either side of the entrance gate, was a completely different experience. It was hard to keep in mind that just on the other side of a soaring diagonal wall of glass was Central Park, and that only thirty or so yards beyond, cars and buses were whipping through the Eighty-Sixth Street transverse.

Rannie covered the full measure of the pavilion in which the temple was housed, stopping at the south wall to read the captions accompanying large photos that explained how in 1965 it had been transported, block by sandstone block, from Egypt, a gift from the country and also a rescue effort of sorts as the new Aswan Dam was about to permanently submerge the small temple under thirty feet of Nile water.

Rannie gazed at the somewhat stubby columns with their papyrus capitals. Nowadays would any country part with an important piece of its patrimony? Rannie doubted it, although according to Joan, who spent seven days cruising the Nile, Egypt was crawling with temples. Maybe one more or less didn't matter.

Someone was tapping her on the shoulder. "No! What are the odds?"

The Beantown vowels were the tipoff. Still, it was unsettling to turn and see Tim Butler right in front of her.

"Maybe it's fate," Rannie said and shrugged, careful not to raise her shoulders too high and risk exposing her breasts and their Band-Aid-protected nipples. "It's definitely fate. We're the opposite of star-crossed lovers. We're meant to be together. So try all you want; you still won't get rid of me."

Tim didn't respond. He was wearing a tuxedo. Until this moment, she'd never seen him in anything dressier than an old sports coat and cords. Her heart hammered at the sight of him. Nevertheless, she had to admit, it took a taller man to really carry off formalwear.

He was giving her the once-over too. "Some dress!" His words were intended to sound complimentary but Rannie wasn't fooled. At launch parties, how many times had she exclaimed "Some book!" to an author whose deathless prose she'd been forced to copyedit. It was obvious Tim wasn't digging the vampy getup. Suddenly it was as if she could see herself through Tim's eyes and it was mortifying: she no longer felt glamorously sinister; she felt ridiculous, comical, as unself-aware as Miss Piggy or that outlandishly overdressed character in children's books, Fancy Nancy. "What are you doing here?" Rannie sputtered in response.

"Me? I'm here courtesy of Elsie King."

Elsie King? Had he ever mentioned an Elsie King?

Bending toward her, he said in a low voice. "That's L. C. King. As in L. C. King Security Company."

"Oh! You're working the party?"

"It's easy money. Making sure everyone leaves with all the bling they came with."

"So are you packing heat?" she asked teasingly, eyebrow arched.

Tim looked uncomfortable being flirted with; nevertheless, he played along, pointing a finger pistol at Rannie and saying, "Kapow." Then he waited a beat. "Who'd you come with?"

It did not escape Rannie's attention that Tim, while attempting to sound friendly-casual, had started rocking back and forth on the balls of his feet, a nervous habit she'd witnessed before.

"You're not going to believe this." She smiled ruefully and paused for effect. "I'm here with my mother."

"She's in from Cleveland?"

"Yeah." Rannie was about to launch into the improbable story that had brought Harriet to her doorstop, then refrained, not solely because of her vow to keep the reason "in the vault," but also because Tim, with his strict sense of right and wrong, would consider blabbing about her mother's sex life inappropriate, and definitely not something you shared with a guy you no longer were seeing. Instead she said, "Nate and Olivia are here too. It's sort of a quadruple date. . . . Want to meet Harriet?"

She had regaled Tim with more than a few Harriet anecdotes;

however, he was shaking his head, saying "maybe later," which Rannie had no trouble translating as a definitive uh-uh.

It was a moot point in any case because now out of the corner of her eye, Rannie caught sight of her mother heading in their direction. Ooh, she looked pissed. "That's her!" she warned Tim. "She's spotted us!"

"Where were you? You said you'd be back in a minute," Harriet said querulously. "I've been sitting all alone like a lump." Then she turned to Tim and without waiting for the intro Rannie was about to make, said, "I'm Harriet Bookman. Miranda's mother."

"Tim Butler." He clasped her hand. "A pleasure to meet you, Mrs. Bookman."

As soon as she heard his name, Harriet's body language changed. Shoulders back, head erect, almost seeming to grow an inch or two, she pursed her lips and bestowed a glacial smile on Tim. It was what the Sisters Bookman referred to as the "Contessa of Cleveland" look, Jewish noblesse oblige. It was never a good sign. "Yes, Miranda has told me about you. Well, an edited version, I'm sure. Miranda's very good at that—editing, I mean."

Tim looked amused. Rannie was not. You could never predict what would pop out of the Contessa's mouth. . . . And what was with the Miranda thing? "Mother, it looks like they're starting to serve dinner. We should get back to our table."

"Please, join us, won't you?" Harriet offered. "There are plenty of seats free at our table."

"Thanks. But I can't."

"What a pity. I rarely get a chance to meet Miranda's New York friends. Well, then good evening, Officer Butler."

"No, no. It's not 'Officer' anymore," he replied pleasantly. "I left the force years ago."

"My mistake. I thought it was like being a doctor or professor or general; you got to keep the title for life."

"Bye, Tim!" Without ceremony, Rannie turned her mother about-face and, pinching the turkey wattle under Harriet's arm harder than necessary, exclaimed as they walked away, "Look, Mother. I think it's Madonna. And over there, is that Liz Taylor?"

"Can't be. She's dead."

"So are you," Rannie hissed. As she forcefully steered Harriet to their table, Rannie cast a backward glance. Tim's eyes were scanning the pavilion, then head tilted downward, he nodded ever so slightly. Rannie realized he was listening to somebody—L. C. King related—via earphone.

"So what was that for?" Rannie fumed once they were seated.

"What was what for?"

"'Officer Butler'? I clearly remember telling you he was no longer a cop." Naturally she had deleted the minor detail that killing his pregnant wife while driving drunk was what ended his career in law enforcement.

"I was being polite!" Harriet glanced up at the waiter hovering at her shoulder and shielded her plate from the arugula salad being offered.

"Come off it, Mother. Being disingenuous doesn't suit you."

"Oh, you and your fancy five-dollar words."

"Okay. I'll put it more plainly. It was a put-down and he knew it because one thing you're not is subtle."

"I don't know what you're talking—"

"You do too! He's not Jewish. He's not a professional. He's not from Shaker Heights. So in your book he doesn't rate." Rannie scowled at her salad plate and savagely speared a slice of Bosc pear.

The rest of the meal was eaten in silence, Rannie somehow staining the hot pink sash with the dill sauce that accompanied the salmon.

"Yoo-hoo!" Immediately Harriet flagged a waiter and attempted to remove the stain with a napkin soaked in the club soda that was brought to the table. Rannie swatted away her mother's hands. "Stop it! I'm not ten!"

"Suit yourself!" Harriet said. "But you'll regret it. . . . Nothing works better than club soda. Nothing!"

Their nearest seatmates—two elderly couples, the ladies sparkling in the sort of important jewelry that Tim was here to protect—averted their eyes from the squabbling.

"You love him," Harriet stated.

Rannie didn't reply. Was that true? She certainly didn't like getting dumped. But love? Interesting that Harriet didn't say, "You're *in* love with him." Harriet was astute, give her that. After the divorce, Harriet had summed up Rannie's attraction to Peter Lorimer succinctly: "He was the anti-Cleveland." Rannie had spent all her thirty health-insured therapy sessions parsing that one sentence.

"He loves you."

"Please. You met him for all of a minute."

"Some things are obvious."

"It doesn't matter. It's over." In fact, if Harriet was right, Rannie was even surer of that. "I loved booze, really loved it," he'd admitted early on to her. "And I miss it every single day." Equating herself with alcohol sounded overly dramatic, but there were parallels. Once Tim made a decision to give up something that he'd determined was bad for him, he stuck to it, no backward glances.

At almost the exact same time the quartet of tablemates left, Nate and Olivia appeared and occupied two of the empty seats. "Some old guy took our picture! Said he was from the *Times*," Olivia told them excitedly as she and Nate proceeded to dig into two plates of profiteroles. "We had to give him our names and sign a release."

All chitchatting ceased the moment Thomas Campbell, the boyish-looking director of the museum, rose first to thank Anna Wintour, the editor of *Vogue* sitting on his left, for organizing the event, and then turning to his right he continued, "Museum-goers have the Cummings family to thank for funding the dazzling exhibit—'Hollywood Heroines'—you all had the pleasure of previewing earlier this evening. Charlotte Cummings supported the work of the Costume Institute since its beginning in 1980. Without her unflagging generosity we would not be here tonight." These last words had been addressed to his other dinner companion. Bibi Gaines.

"Barbara Gaines told me that her grandmother would insist on her being here tonight. Thank you so much for joining us."

Bibi nodded and remained seated while en masse the crowd stood, Harriet grousing about her bunions, and offered up tribute applause. Among the assembled, nearly every woman under fifty was buff enough to have bare arms. Bibi, however, was appropriately subdued in a long-sleeved black gown with a high neckline.

Campbell leaned down for a moment to exchange cheek kisses with Bibi. "I was privileged to share a glass of champagne with Charlotte Cummings on several occasions," he said, "and so I propose that we all raise a glass to that grand, unforgettable lady."

Immediately a squadron of waiters distributed flutes to all. Nate and Olivia downed the champagne before the toast was even over. Rannie didn't bother scolding; her attention was focused on Bibi Gaines, who was clinking glasses with the museum director and downing the contents of her glass as well.

Of course her flute could have been filled with sparkling cider or ginger ale. In all probability it was.

Ten minutes later, Rannie and Harriet left the Temple of Dendur, in advance of the entertainment portion of the evening, a West Indian rapper whom Nate and Olivia were eager to hear. Rannie scanned the crowd for one last glimpse of Tim Butler. It was in vain.

In less than hour both Rannie and her mother were asleep, having retreated to their separate beds, the air between them still full of frost. The last thing Harriet said was, "I'll be leaving tomorrow. I'm on the nine o'clock flight."

Chapter 21

"I DON'T DO WELL AT FUNERALS," DAISY STATED OMINOUSLY AS Rannie assisted her up the church steps, one by one, slowly and tentatively. At the top, Daisy stopped. She was leaning on her cane, breathing heavily. Somehow, in the process of getting out of the cab, her hat, a black velvet newsboy cap, had tilted sideways; it was an unusual look. Sort of Dowager in the 'Hood. Rannie made sure her own hat—she'd ended up in the Mamie Eisenhower yarmulke after all—was in place and in they went.

While Daisy rummaged through her handbag for the tickets, Rannie had a moment to take in the soaring Gothic expanse of Saint Thomas Church. Sequins of colored light from the panels of stained glass along the north wall spangled the tile floor. Crimson, sea green, turquoise, deep sapphire blue.

It was a little surreal to be attending Charlotte Cummings's funeral, almost like stepping into the pages of *Portrait of a Lady*. Here Rannie was at the very event that should have served as the final chapter in Ret's book except that Ret had gone and gotten murdered before she could write it.

"Here." Daisy thrust an envelope at one of the ushers, an envelope with "Mrs. Dorothy Satterthwaite and Guest" written in calligraphy on the front. The usher, dressed in a morning coat with a yellow freesia pinned to the lapel, glanced at the tickets and beckoned them down the center aisle of the nave. Maroon velvet ropes cordoned off the rows nearest the altar and the canopied pulpit, all of carved wood. He stopped, however, well short of the restricted VIP area, at a row that in a Broadway theater would have corresponded to rear orchestra.

"You and your guest have the aisle seat and one in, Mrs. Satterthwaite," he murmured in a hushed tone.

"Oh, no. There must be some mistake!" Daisy informed him. "I'm sure that Charlotte wouldn't want me back here."

The usher, looking flummoxed, had no answer.

"I see two of Charlotte's nurses several rows ahead." Daisy motioned with a gloved hand. "Has Barbara Gaines taken it upon herself to change the seating plan?"

Rannie touched the sleeve of Daisy's Autumn Haze mink. "Sitting here will make it much easier to leave once the service is over. You won't have to walk far or deal with the crowd."

That mollified Daisy somewhat. The usher handed them each a memorial program with a photo of Charlotte Cummings on the front and beat a hasty retreat.

Once free of her fur, Daisy settled herself in the pew and with a suspicious eye surveyed the mourners streaming into the church—the men in suits that were all small miracles of tailoring, the ladies in hats and somberly chic dresses and jackets. Rannie spotted Olivia's parents, her dad with his slicked-back, hedge-fund hair and Carole Werner, whose toothy smile was subdued for the occasion, pausing to say hello to people she knew. A velvet rope was unhooked to allow the Werners entry to seats way up in front.

"I don't recognize a soul. They must all be people Barbara knows." Implicit in her tone was that "people Barbara knew" did not measure up. Then complaining that "it's like an oven in here," Daisy began fanning herself furiously with the funeral program, pausing only to draw in a loud noseful of air and exhale it dramatically.

Between her mother and Daisy, Rannie had had quite enough of crotchety old biddies. Nevertheless, she made a game attempt to distract Daisy with small talk. "Oh! Isn't this interesting? The program says Charlotte Cummings was born the same year that construction of this building began. The old church had to be rebuilt after a fire."

Daisy paid no heed. She stopped fanning for a second and turned to the back of the program. "Lord, no! The reception is at the University Club. I don't know what they do there to make all the food so constipating."

At eleven on the dot, church bells started to toll, momentarily silencing Daisy. When the ringing ended, Bibi Gaines was escorted to her front-row seat. Whereas last night at the Metropolitan Museum she had worn stark black, this morning she was outfitted in a bright yellow wool suit and hat.

"She looks like a stick of margarine!" Daisy muttered.

Then the rector entered from the back, in richly brocaded vestments, followed by eight pallbearers who carried the coffin on a brass-railed litter. Among the pallbearers, Rannie immediately recognized two former mayors and a world-famous tenor.

The church was filled to capacity; even the galleries upstairs were packed. An organ began playing something somber and magisterial, the notes reverberating off the stonework in a way that made Rannie feel as if the music was echoing inside her.

It was beautiful, all the pageantry, yet Rannie experienced no spiritual stirring any more than she had at Ret's bleak, no-frills send-off at the convent. In fact, not since Yale when she'd taken a course called Religion and Existentialism had Rannie spent any serious time pondering Big Questions—Does God exist? Do I have a soul? What is the meaning of life? At forty-three she found it hard enough just dealing with the here and now without stopping to worry about the hereafter. "I am a deeply shallow person," she once told Tim and meant it.

The service was a soup-to-nuts Anglican requiem mass. Throughout it, Daisy kept complaining. The men's choir wasn't singing any of the hymns she liked. The rector was mumbling, it was impossible to understand a word out of his mouth. Not until the reading of the Twenty-Third Psalm did Daisy finally zip it for a while.

It was the only psalm that Rannie knew by heart, required to memorize it her first year at Anshe Chesed temple Sunday school. "Why does it say 'Yay' in the part about 'walking through the Valley of Death'?" seven-year-old Rannie once had asked in the car on the way home. "What's there to cheer about?"

Betsy had cracked up. Amy said, "It's not 'Yay' like 'Hip, hip, hooray,' you moron!"

"Amy, don't speak to your sister like that! Betsy, stop laughing this instant!" Harriet had commanded from the driver's seat before clarifying the meaning for Rannie. "I love the Twenty-

Third Psalm. It's about how God is always there to comfort and protect us."

The funeral for Charlotte Cummings had begun at eleven. So right about now Harriet was touching down on the tarmac at Cleveland airport. This morning, Rannie had awakened at a little past seven to find her mother already dressed with suitcase packed and the pullout returned to sofa mode, all the used bedding neatly folded and stacked on an armchair.

They were stiffly cordial over breakfast.

"I'll wake Nate so he can say good-bye."

"No. Let him sleep. Who knows what time he came in last night."

Soon Harriet was checking to make sure all essentials were in her handbag. "I don't know what I did with my little hairbrush; it's a collapsible one, white plastic. If you find it, keep it till the next time we see each other, whenever that may be."

This was not how Rannie wanted the visit to end. All of a sudden she remembered the picture frame with seashells, the one from Bibilots.

"Wait. Hold it a sec!" The present was on a shelf in her bedroom closet.

"For you." With a flourish Rannie presented the pink-and-white-wrapped box to Harriet. "It made me think of those days on Cape Cod, shell hunting."

Rannie watched a look of surprised pleasure spread across her mother's face when she opened the box. "I love it!" she exclaimed. "Weren't those vacations wonderful? Remember the house with the big porch and all the rosebushes out front? The one in Chatham." Harriet pressed the frame against her bosom.

"I know just the picture to put in here; it's one of you jumping waves with Daddy." Suddenly Harriet looked uncharacteristically contrite. "Oh, Rannie, last night. It was such a stupid, rude remark. I don't know what gets into me sometimes. I'm turning into a mean old lady. And I won't blame it on my feet, though they were killing me."

"I overreacted. It's forgotten, Mom. Truly."

Harriet put down the frame and they hugged. "This visit was special," Harriet murmured.

Rannie pulled back a little and planted a kiss on her mother's well-moisturized cheek. "Yes, and we have JDate to thank for it."

Downstairs, as she stepped into a cab, Harriet spoke words that sounded rehearsed. "I will keep reminding myself that what I want for you is not what you want for yourself." She buckled her seat belt, then looked up and cocked an eye at Rannie. "Just one thing. Is Dad's watch really being repaired?"

Rannie bristled, then caved. "Okay. Full disclosure. I got mugged. Right on this block."

To her credit, Harriet managed to hold her tongue. She blew a kiss to Rannie and the taxi took off.

The Gentlemen of the Choir, in their white surplices and black robes, were midway through "Amazing Grace" when someone in the row behind tapped Rannie on the shoulder. She turned. A man was whispering something to her. He was attractive in a generic way with longish shiny brown hair and tortoiseshell glasses.

"Excuse me," Rannie whispered back.

"Your friend." He motioned to Daisy.

Daisy had listed to the side, her eyes at half-mast, only the whites showing. Her breathing was ragged. Was she asleep or having a heart attack? Oh my fucking God. What was the protocol here?

(A) Try not to make a scene.

(B) Try not to let Daisy die.

Rannie gripped Daisy by the arm and shook her. In a moment, Daisy startled and her lids fluttered open. She trained an unfocused gaze on Rannie. "My purse," she slurred. Rannie grabbed it, expecting to discover a nitro tablet. Nope. Only a lipstick tube, a silver flask, a twenty, and an almost empty pack of Camels. Then, hallelujah, under a wrinkled hankie, a little brown glass vial. Smelling salts, the same kind Mary carried with her.

Once uncorked and passed beneath Daisy's nostrils a couple of times, the smelling salts did the trick. Daisy sat up straighter and began fanning herself again with the program.

"I'm calling 911," Rannie stated.

"Don't be ridiculous. Just get me outside. All I need is some air."

The choir sang on while the guy with the good hair came to their aid. He hoisted Daisy to her feet and, with remarkable ease considering he was dealing with at least a hundred and sixty pounds of almost deadweight old lady, maneuvered Daisy down the aisle and through the doors, where he lowered her into a sitting position on the front steps.

"Put your head down. Take deep breaths," he instructed while Rannie stood by with Daisy's things.

"Oh, honestly, stop the fussing," Daisy said and snatched her purse from Rannie.

All it took was an open flask and a lit cigarette to fully restore her, Daisy alternating between sips, actually snorts, from one and deep Tallulah Bankhead drags from the other. "I'm ready to leave now," she announced. "And, Rannie, don't dare utter the word 'hospital.' I'm going home."

The guy and Rannie looked at each other and shrugged simultaneously. "One last favor," Rannie asked. "Would you call a cab for us?"

"Take my car. I insist."

Even before Rannie could launch into an obligatory "Oh, we couldn't possibly" refusal, his phone was out and he was instructing someone to drive around to the front of the church on Fifth Avenue. "You're to drop off two ladies at . . ." He turned to Rannie questioningly.

Rannie supplied the address.

"Seven Forty Park Avenue. Then come back to the church and wait till I call again."

While listening to these brisk directives, it struck Rannie that although the guy's face wasn't familiar, his voice—well modulated, faintly British, rich in timbre—was. Where might she have heard it? . . . Maybe he did voice-overs for ads on TV, ones for investment banks or high-end automobiles . . . or was he the host of some NPR radio show?

Less than a New York minute later, a car service SUV pulled to the curb. A husky driver in a black coat jumped out, bounded up the steps, and, sizing up the situation, took charge of Daisy. "Just lean on me, ma'am. I'll have you in the car and home in a flash."

That left Rannie to offer thanks. "Considering where we are, I guess it'd be sacrilegious to call you our savior."

He awarded Rannie with a tight smile, which instantly made

her feel gauche for punning. "Seriously, I'm awfully grateful for your help with Mrs. Satterthwaite," and then she added, "I'm Miranda Bookman, by the way." At Charlotte Cummings's funeral, only her proper name would do.

"F. Anthony Weld." He pronounced Anthony in the British fashion with a hard T.

It wasn't until the SUV was making its way up Park Avenue, Daisy sucking on another Camel, that Rannie put it together. The name. The voice. And the face that Rannie had seen from a distance in a darkened auditorium at Yale. It was the guy whose lecture Alice had snoozed through. The art restorer.

Chapter 22

"SO THAT MUST BE GODELIEVE, PATRON SAINT OF SORE THROATS," Rannie said, bearing forth a tray with the requested tumbler of gin and plate of buttered saltines on it. The painting, positioned between two windows in Daisy's bedroom, was much smaller than Rannie had expected, not all that much bigger than a cereal box, and judging from the deep crack that ran through Godelieve's blue gown, it had never been subjected to the TLC of F. Anthony Weld. *F.* Anthony? How many people used a first initial when introducing themselves?

Daisy motioned impatiently for the gin. "Ghastly painting. But there's no way I'll part with it." She was reclining on a chaise lounge covered in faded chintz, the back of her free hand pressed against her forehead, very southern Gothic, very late Tennessee Williams.

Rannie set down the tray and went over to inspect Daisy's miracle worker. Godelieve was no beauty but who looked their best hanging from a tree? Besides bulging eyes and death's head grin, Godelieve had wispy hair and an unnaturally broad expanse of forehead, as if she was suffering from the early onset of female pattern baldness. Rannie had once read somewhere that in the 1400s, upper-class ladies plucked their hairline way back for a noble-looking brow. Oh, the vagaries of fashion!

"All the poor thing wanted was to become a nun. Prayed day and night. But she got married off when she was still a child and had a mother-in-law from hell. She tried to behead Godelieve. Then tried drowning her. Finally hanging did the trick. Do you see the mother-in-law peeking from behind a tree?"

Rannie squinted. "No . . . Oh, maybe."

"The painting's a wreck. It's my fault. For years I kept it right over my bed in direct sunlight. Then when it cracked, I moved Godelieve. She and my grandmother traded places."

That accounted for the frame of brighter floral wallpaper around the actual frame, evidence that a larger painting had once occupied this spot. Suddenly Rannie experienced a disorienting flash of déjà vu, then it fled, and she turned to look at the painting over Daisy's four-poster, a sizable portrait of a jowly dowager, circa 1920, in a lavender dress and formidable pearls.

Rannie was about to comment on the startling resemblance Daisy bore to her grandmother when Daisy said, "I don't care what happens to that painting. My grandmother was dreadful. She *terrified* me. When I was small, if I misbehaved, she'd rap my knuckles with her cane."

Moments later, Mary arrived with lunch for everyone in Tupperware containers.

"Earla's cod balls?"

Mary nodded.

"Oh, Mims, how you spoil me!" Daisy exclaimed.

They repaired to the lugubrious elegance of the dining room (dining "ruhm" in these ladies' boarding school parlance) where more portraits of Daisy's ancestors surrounded them and watched disapprovingly as they ate. More gin for Daisy and a "well, if you insist" drink for Mary.

"I'll tell you this, I have simply had it with funerals," Daisy declared. "The next one I attend will be my own. That's a promise."

"Poor Rannie. Daisy must have given you quite a scare."

Rannie was eyeing her cod ball. She doused it with ketchup and tried holding her breath while swallowing the first bite.

"Oh, pssh. I faint all the time," Daisy said dismissively. "Last month it was at the Food Emporium, in the frozen food aisle."

"Was it a beautiful service?" Mary inquired brightly. "I love it when the boys' choir sings, but they never do funerals. Too upsetting for the little fellows, I suppose."

"I didn't see a soul I knew, Mims. I looked for Helen Dunham."

"Dear, Helen's been hooked up to a feeding tube at NewYork-Presbyterian for months. You know that."

From there the conversation turned to Charlotte Cummings, Mary exclaiming over the length of the obituary in the *New York Times*. "A full page! Can you imagine!"

"Did you know I was interviewed for Charlotte's obituary?" Daisy said.

"No, really?"

"This was"—Daisy paused with a forkful of cod ball in midair—"oh, many months ago. A reporter from the *Times* called and came up to the apartment. For important people, their obituary is written beforehand and updated from time to time. Well, we chatted for a good long while but nothing I told him ended up in the paper." Daisy smiled, almost coyly. "It's just as well. Somehow he got me on the subject of Silas and I'm afraid I wasn't very discreet. I said some awful things."

"I don't know why everyone was always so hard on Silas. He was always very pleasant to me." Mary dabbed her lips with a napkin.

"That's your problem, Mims. You think the best of everyone!"

"I do not!" Mary defended herself staunchly.

"Silas was dreadful." Daisy was addressing Rannie now. "Gas attacks that could wake the dead. And I never saw a hairier man in my life. At the club all the little children used to race out of the pool whenever Silas took a swim. He looked like a gorilla."

A bit of cod ball stuck in Rannie's throat. Daisy's descriptions of Silas had appeared almost verbatim in *Portrait of a Lady,* except in the book, "gas attacks" had been changed to the more vernacular "farts" and the "gorilla" had grown to "King Kong." Ret Sullivan taking literary license.

"Honestly, Daisy, how you love to exaggerate."

"Well, Mims, you won't deny that Silas's first wife palmed him off on Charlotte." Daisy launched into a long anecdote, one that Rannie already knew from having copyedited it only days ago. "Silas's first wife felt guilty leaving him—Lord knows why— and wouldn't start divorce proceedings until she'd lined up a replacement wife."

Mary was draining her gin, then said, "I never heard that."

"It wasn't common knowledge, Mims," Daisy said tersely. "Silas knew he was no picnic in the park. So he came to Charlotte with doctors' letters outlining all his medical problems. Swore he'd be dead within five years and his estate would be hers. Then they get married and Silas lives for *eons*! When it came to dying, Silas was almost as stubborn as Charlotte."

Rannie was ready with a plausible-sounding fib. "A friend of mine dates a guy at the *Times* who writes some of the big obituaries. Do you happen to remember who interviewed you?"

Daisy didn't, but her description nailed Larry. Tall, gray-haired, and "disheveled. He looked as if he'd slept in his clothes."

Surprise, surprise. Daisy Satterthwaite, unwittingly, had been one of Audeo's sources, a big, loose-lipped one! Rannie bet Larry had come with phony credentials that Daisy never thought to question. After all, Bibi Gaines had bought Larry's masquerading as an art scholar and Bibi seemed far less gullible than Daisy.

"I showed the reporter the album from Charlotte's one-hundredth birthday. What a party that was!"

Rannie didn't have to ask to see the album; Mary beat her to it.

Back in the bedroom, cursing how she had no memory left, Daisy finally unearthed the album and they all sat on the chaise, Daisy in the middle. The album was covered in sunburst yellow needlepoint. Charlotte Cummings's initials and the date were stitched in dark blue in the lower right corner. As they flipped through the pages that documented the gala held in the New York Public Library at Forty-Second Street, photos of Charlotte Cummings—looking pretty hale for a woman who had hit triple digits—showed her in a canary yellow evening gown. She had been decked out in yellow the other night, lying comatose in bed.

"Oh!" Rannie exclaimed. "Bibi Gaines wore yellow to the funeral, because it was her grandmother's favorite color. And the ushers. They had yellow freesia in their lapels."

From Mary: "Isn't that a lovely gesture."

From Daisy, grudgingly: "I suppose. She still looked like a stick of margarine. . . . I couldn't tell whether Barbara was"—Daisy hesitated, searching for the appropriate word—"*all right*, if you know what I mean. I only caught a glimpse of her."

"That's all ancient history," Mary replied. "Whenever I run into her, she seems absolutely fine. Has for years."

Were they referring to Bibi's alcoholism? If so, that was surprising given that Mary seemed to consider heavy drinking a birthright of the wellborn. Everyone she knew drank too much, so you couldn't call it a problem.

"Mims, you don't know the half of it." Daisy shut the album and addressed Rannie. "Did you notice there were no pictures of Barbara at the birthday party? That was because she came high as a kite. Kept trying to dance with a waiter, and she interrupted all the toasts." Turning back to Mary. "You'll notice she still always wears long sleeves. Even if it's ninety degrees out."

Hold on a second! Was this about drugs? Something administered with a needle and that left track marks . . . as in heroin or—even more unimaginable—crack? Bibi Gaines, an alcoholic. Okay. Understood. But jonesing, a monkey on her back? She was *so* not the type. But then, Rannie reminded herself, neither was Olivia's brother, Grant, equally fair-haired, equally privileged. And hadn't Tim told her that often people in AA had struggled with a double addiction—booze and drugs.

"You never liked Barbara. That's all there is to it," Mary stated with finality.

"How could I like her when she caused her mother—my best friend!—so much pain? If melanoma hadn't killed poor Madeline, worrying over Barbara would have. In and out of Silver Hill—"

Daisy didn't get the chance to finish her sentence.

"Daisy! Really!" Mary was aghast. "Why are you going on about this?" Mary rose and held on to the back of the chaise to steady herself. She was tipsy. "I think perhaps Rannie and I should be going." Her voice quavered. It was testament to Mary's good breeding that she didn't like to dish, but dammit, couldn't she let Daisy spill a little more?

Mary was gathering up her purse and muttering, "None of this is anything Rannie wants to hear."

Au contraire! Rannie definitely wanted to hear more. And Daisy could tell. Nevertheless, when Mary said stiffly, "Don't bother seeing us out, dear," Rannie had no choice but to follow. At the door to the bedroom, Rannie turned to wave good-bye. Daisy remained on the chaise, sulking, like a child whose party had ended too early.

Chapter 23

RANNIE RUMINATED OVER A PB&J SANDWICH IN THE SANCTITY of her empty apartment. Had Daisy "chatted" about Barbara Gaines to Larry/Audeo/phony *New York Times* obit writer? Most likely. Then Rannie changed her mind. Almost certainly. Yet there hadn't been one disparaging word about Bibi in *Portrait of a Lady*. She took another contemplative bite. Would there be any harm in calling Larry and pumping him about Bibi Gaines?

Do it! Her bad angel, appearing out of nowhere, started egging Rannie on. *Don't you want to hear everything Daisy told him? You know you do!*

Don't listen to her! She doesn't have your best interests at heart. Her good angel had arrived on the scene now. *Remember Larry Katz was hitting on you and Ellen barely dead. Stay away from him!*

Rannie wanted to listen to the counsel of her good angel. She really did. The trouble was she now pictured her good angel as looking a lot like Godelieve, or the way Godelieve would have looked before being strung up—the eyes not so bulging, but still a prissy goody-goody. A party pooper. Then, suddenly Rannie stopped with the good angel/bad angel nonsense and fixated on standing in Daisy's bedroom, encountering Godelieve, noticing the extra "frame" of brighter wallpaper around the painting. It wasn't a wave of déjà vu that had washed over Rannie: coming face-to-face with Godelieve had jogged a memory, Rannie now realized, a fleeting memory of entering Ret Sullivan's bedroom and noticing the painting of a sweet Madonna on the wall just an instant before absorbing the horrific sight of Ret murdered.

The Madonna in Ret's bedroom had been set against a frame of brighter wall paint, what, to Rannie, had appeared almost like a rectangular halo. According to Sister Dorothy, greeting card Madonnas were not to Ret's taste even when she was a child. Another painting had previously hung in the same spot in Ret's bedroom. Maybe that meant something.

Larry claimed never to have entered the inner sanctum. Whether that was true or not, Ret's steady Saturday afternoon date, the gym instructor with the police record, must have. Many times.

A quick online search of the first erroneous news reports about Ret's murder brought up the guy's name—Gerald Steele—and where he worked—the Equinox Club on Broadway and Fiftieth Street. What better time than the present to begin a new regime of physical fitness! Rannie called Equinox inquiring about membership and whether she might try out the facilities.

Of course she could, an eager receptionist told her. "I don't know if you're aware but, for a limited time only, an individual training session comes free for new members."

Oh, the stars were aligning! "That's wonderful. That's perfect. . . . Friends have raved about a particular trainer. Gerald Steele."

"Gerry. He's great. The best!"

"I know this is awfully last minute. But might he have something at around three o'clock today?" Rannie inquired. He no longer had a standing appointment with Ret, so there was a fair chance the time slot was open.

The receptionist suddenly sounded suspicious. "You have to sign a membership contract *before* you get the free session. And if you cancel after signing up, you owe us for the training session." She told Rannie the amount.

A hundred dollars. Gulp . . . "No problem."

Rannie was put on hold while the receptionist checked the schedule sheet.

"How does four o'clock sound?" It sounded perfect.

Rannie stripped off her navy suit and arrived ten minutes ahead of time, clad in Yale track pants that belonged to Alice and a pair of her high-topped sneakers. Once the paperwork was signed and her credit card cleared, she entered the vast expanse of machines—rows of people on treadmills and StairMasters and stationary bikes, everyone expending tremendous amounts of energy to get absolutely nowhere. In an adjacent room a group of old ladies in leotards were waving their arms over their head to the music of Donna Summer. "And again, ladies! To the count of ten!" a peppy instructor shouted.

At one point during her ten-year stint at S&S, Rannie had taken advantage of a greatly discounted yearlong membership at a sports club near the office, persuaded by Ellen that somehow it would be fun to sweat together at lunchtime. Rannie had gone exactly once, the inaugural week of her membership, managing to fall off an exercise bike during a spinning class. After that, she rationalized the money blown by viewing the yearly fee as something akin to vaccination: you paid and you were inoculated, the very fact of belonging to a gym being nearly as beneficial as actually using its facilities.

"Are you Rainy?" A stocky bowlegged guy in his midthirties carrying a clipboard was approaching her. He had either missed a spot shaving, right under his chin, or else sported the world's teensiest soul patch.

"Rannie. Rhymes with Annie."

"Gerry." He held out a hand. He wore a silver thumb ring. "So first why don't you tell me why you're here, what you want to work on?" Taking a step back, he gave her a quick head-to-toe assessment. "You don't look like there's an ounce of fat on you. That's good. Maybe for this session we do a general evaluation?"

Rannie had only an hour. She cut to the chase. "I don't want to work out."

He blew through his lips. "How many times have I heard that? Nobody does, not at first." He smiled. White even teeth that looked natural, not capped. "You haven't worked out in years, am I right? But now you've decided to do something good for yourself . . ."

"No. I mean it. I didn't come here to work out. I came here to talk to you. Look. I knew Ret Sullivan. I was who found her body."

The nice smile vanished.

"Are you shitting me? What the hell is this about?"

"Please! I just blew a hundred bucks. I figured if I called asking to talk about Ret, you'd hang up."

"You got that one right. I told everything I knew to the cops, who, you probably know, led me out of here in handcuffs."

"I paid for an hour of your time."

"An hour of my *professional* time," he countered. "And by the way, you have lousy muscle tone. Want to start with some upper-body strengthening exercises?"

"Please. I wouldn't be doing this except I'm scared. Another friend of mine was murdered. Just this past Monday. She knew Ret too."

He was shaking his head. "There's been nothing about anybody connected to Ret Sullivan getting killed." He tucked his clipboard under his arm and started walking away. Rannie kept pace with him and in a low voice said, "The runner who was attacked in the park. The police are keeping her connection to Ret quiet."

He stopped in his tracks. "For real?"

From her tote, Rannie produced her credit card holder, which still contained some S&S business cards. She handed him one. "All of Ret's books were published by Simon & Schuster. A new one will be out very shortly. I think the murders are somehow related to the book. . . . The woman killed in Central Park was Ret's editor and I was her copy editor."

"Copy editor?"

"Checking grammar, spelling, correcting dates."

He didn't look impressed; no one ever was.

"Listen. I'm scared I'm in danger, and the cops aren't doing squat to protect me." Exaggerating her fear factor and disparaging the NYPD seemed to be working.

He exhaled in a slow, resigned way. "I'm telling you, I know nothing. She and I weren't exactly close friends."

"Just a few questions."

At a table in the health bar up front, while sipping a smoothie the color of baby poo, Gerald Steele explained that before her disfigurement Ret had been a longtime member of the club. "She took personal training sessions with me twice a week, oh, for maybe three or four years. I've got autographed copies of all her books, not that I read any of them; a couple of times she took me to movie screenings. In fact, she took me to the screening of Mike Bellettra's last movie, the astronaut one."

"Far Side of the Moon."

"Yeah, that one. He was there at the party after. I had no clue Ret was writing a book about him. But I remember her going to me, 'He's not the good-hearted All-American guy everybody loves.' I figured it was just Ret talking, she had shit to say about everybody. Then her book comes out and—" He made an explosion sound. "I figured that was it, I'd never hear from Ret again. It was rotten what happened to her."

"But she got in touch with you?"

"Yeah. About a year ago. She called here, saying she was going nuts stuck in the apartment. It was like being in prison. She wanted to know if I'd give her personal training sessions—" He looked up at Rannie as if expecting to see a smirk. "And that's all it was for a long time. I'd get there. She'd have this mask thing on and she'd work out in the living room."

"Did she ever talk about the new book she was writing?"

"A little. She made it sound different from the others. She goes, 'I'm writing about somebody I like. I'm through trashing people.' I remember thinking to myself, 'Yeah, well, too bad you didn't decide that sooner. You'd still have a face.'"

Rannie nodded. "Okay. Look. I swear to you, I'm not inter-

ested in what went on between you two, but I need to know if
you were ever in her bedroom."

"Only a few times. It's not like how the papers said. That whole
boy-toy crap, which nearly got my ass booted here by the way.
Yeah, I fucked Ret a few times because I felt sorry for her. Okay?
I didn't get a cent. In my mind, it was kind of like a mitzvah—
you know what a mitzvah is?"

Rannie didn't believe him but nodded. "Yes. A blessing." She
watched him drain his smoothie. A disgusting foamy yellow-
green ring remained around the top of the glass. And the mini
soul patch, it had managed to catch a globule. "When you were in
Ret's bedroom, did you happen to notice artwork over her bed?"

"No. I wouldn't know about anything in there. She could have
had Elvis on black velvet for all I know."

"You didn't notice a painting? A religious painting."

"I just told you. I didn't see anything, as in nothing."

"I don't understand." Oh. Suddenly Rannie did. "You were
blindfolded?"

He nodded. "Ret didn't want her mask on during sex. But she
didn't want me to see her face and that was fine by me. She had
this sleep mask, the kind airplanes give out. She made me put it
on and then she'd lead me into the bedroom. She definitely got
off being in control. And I couldn't take the thing off until we
were done and I was back in the living room. In there she had a
whole wall full of crosses."

"Yeah. I know." Rannie slumped in her chair. Bummer.

He glanced at his watch. "So we done?"

"Almost." She'd bombed out on the painting angle, but she
wasn't about to kiss a hundred bucks good-bye without getting

her full sixty minutes. "Did Ret ever mention somebody named Larry? Larry Katz?"

"I met the guy. Several times. They were always doing work when I came. Ret had a thing for him. I could tell."

"You mean she was in love with him?"

"Love? Ret? I don't know if I'd go that far. But maybe. One thing I know is body language. Take shoulders. Everything I need to know about a person I can tell from the way their shoulders move. Most people look at faces to see what somebody else is feeling. With Ret, whatever was left of hers was all covered up by that mask. But it was obvious, just the way she moved when he was around, that she dug the guy. Then after he left, she'd act all pissed off. Tell me he was overcharging her. Cheating her. She'd go, 'Nobody cheats me and gets away with it. Nobody.' How many times did I have to listen to that? Then she'd peer at me through the little holes in the mask like she was giving me a warning."

His words tallied with what Sister Dorothy had said regarding Ret's veiled allusions to getting even with somebody.

Gerald Steele was drumming his fingers on the Formica table. Gerald. Gery. The other thank-you in the acknowledgments in *Portrait of a Lady* was "For Gery Antioch." "Steele" sounded made up, a buff, muscle-y name that a gym instructor would pick. "Is Steele your real last name?"

"No. It's Steiner. Why are you asking?"

"Ret knew a Gery Antioch."

"The name means nothing to me." He pushed the clipboard toward Rannie and stood. He was done playing "Twenty Questions." "Just sign at the bottom to verify you had your training session. And look. For your sake I hope you're wrong about being in danger. I mean, how can fixing a few commas get anybody murdered?"

"Thanks for your time. I really do appreciate it." Rannie signed the form while he returned the empty glass to the counter.

"One last thing," Rannie said.

His head swiveled back in her direction. He looked irritated.

She brushed her lower lip. "There's smoothie on your soul patch."

Chapter 24

THE BROADWAY BUS WAS APPROACHING 106TH STREET. THE next stop was hers. Rannie didn't want to budge. She wanted to stay seated right where she was until she reached the final stop at the George Washington Bridge. She felt totally wiped. Not that signing a couple of gym forms counted as a punishing workout. But she was mentally exhausted. Too many facts were bombarding her brain, caroming off in different directions before any sense could be made of them.

Larry had visited Ret's apartment the morning of the murder. Tim had told her that. But why had Larry gone there? In all likelihood, Ret's accusations about Larry bilking her stemmed from nothing more than typical Ret paranoia. Nevertheless, if Ret was convinced she'd been cheated, it wasn't that hard to imagine her threatening Larry, saying that she was going to go blab to Dusk about his role as Audeo. After all, *Tattletale* was the title she'd chosen for her autobiography. Or—here was another possibility: perhaps Ret wanted to punish Larry for spurning her sexual advances. Hell-hath-no-fury payback. Larry was forking out alimony; he'd told Rannie that. He couldn't afford to get fired from a job with a good salary. So maybe he'd gone to see Ret that morning hoping to calm her down but had had no success. So he went to Plan B. Murdering Ret ensured that he wouldn't be ratted out at Dusk.

But how could Larry have carried out the crime? Motive needed opportunity. Unfortunately, figuring out logistics was not Rannie's strong suit. It seemed a left brain ability, like understanding architectural designs or solving KenKen puzzles, talents totally alien to her. So she tried to imagine how Tim, a man blessed with a sharp practical mind, might approach the question. And that helped. She could almost hear Tim saying that murdering Ret wouldn't be all that complicated. In the many times Larry had been at Ret's apartment, he must have seen keys laying around. Maybe he'd pocketed a set last Saturday morning, and later that afternoon, while visiting the demented mother in Long Island, drove back to East Sixty-Ninth Street. Slipping past the concierge desk—first into the building and then out again—would be the highest hurdle to clear. No, wait. Tim would point out, "That's forgetting about security cameras." The cameras obviously had shown Larry in the building that morning. If there was any evidence linking him to the crime scene much later in the day, Larry would already be in custody.

So where did that leave Rannie?

On 116th Street and Broadway, unfortunately. Eight blocks past her stop. Hastily she exited from the back door of the bus.

When she arrived home, the apartment was still empty. She

flopped on her bed and tried—unsuccessfully—to ignore the message light blinking on her phone.

Peter, her ex-husband, had called. "Ran, hi. Give a call. We need to discuss Thanksgiving." Rannie stared at the phone. It wasn't fair that he had such an appealing speaking voice—low, relaxed, unhurried—when almost nothing out of his mouth was stuff she wanted to hear. He was canceling plans to come to New York. Rannie was sure of it. Alice had been predicting he'd bail for weeks. "Thanksgiving with the whole family at Uncle Will's? Dad can't stand being around his brothers." Yet Nate, far less cynical than Alice and far more invested in keeping up a relationship with his father, had gone online and ordered tickets for the two of them to see Steely Dan at the Beacon and to attend an exhibition tennis match at the Garden.

Schlepping to Will and Beth Lorimer's house in Chappaqua wasn't Rannie's idea of a jolly time either. Will, the eldest brother, had married late in life. He was a trusts and estates lawyer at a white shoe firm, whose disdain for ninety-nine percent of the world was masked by a bullying joviality that fooled no one, including his six-year-old twin daughters.

Harry, the middle son, taught statistics at Middlebury. Statistically, Harry was the most reserved—Rannie felt mean saying "boring"—person on the planet. A lifelong bachelor, Harry was sweet, unfailingly polite, yet after a twenty-year-long association with the Lorimers, Rannie knew Harry no better than she had after first shaking hands with him on the receiving line at her wedding reception.

During the early years of their marriage, Peter and Rannie would spend hours inventing unlikely talents and passions for

Harry: Harry won prizes dancing the Macarena, Harry's vast collection of Beanie Babies was now worth a fortune, Harry had seen every episode of *The Cosby Show* and was president of the Rudy Huxtable fan club.

Peter had a terrific silly streak but no gravitas whatsoever. He was unreliable and, without meaning to be, often cruelly thoughtless. He had quick bursts of enthusiasm, which were all-consuming while they lasted. But they never lasted long. At forty-five he was still floundering. And it embarrassed him. In all likelihood, in Chappaqua, Will would make sure to rub it in, clapping Peter on the back, and, all smiles, would inquire, "So, baby bro, what's the latest venture?"

But this Thanksgiving wasn't about Peter. Mary, who never made demands on her sons (hmmm, maybe that was part of Peter's problem), had requested that everybody celebrate the holiday together. "Won't that be fun!" Mary insisted cheerily nearly every time Rannie saw her.

A mile-long e-mail chain, mostly between Will's wife, Beth, and Rannie, finally determined that Will and Beth would host the dinner with everyone spending the night at their Greek revival house where the heat was kept so low that Rannie always pictured her young nieces with gooseflesh, chattering teeth, and slightly blue lips.

Rannie braced herself for the conversation with Peter. She knew exactly what she'd say. "There is no wiggle room. Not this time. You are coming." She punched in the number.

"Hey, Peter. I got your message. Listen. There is no wiggle room. None. You are coming for Thanksgiving and that's that."

"Whoa! Whoa! Whoa! Who said anything about not coming?'

"You did on your message. . . . Didn't you?"

"No. As a matter of fact, I didn't." Rather than taking offense, he seemed amused. "But now that I've been unjustly accused, I think you owe me. I called because I'm hoping you'll let me crash at the apartment."

"Nope. Sorry. It sends a wrong message to the kids."

"Come on. It'd just be for Wednesday and Friday night. I'm having a helluva time booking a hotel."

"You waited till now?" That was another irritating thing about Peter: he had amazing luck; without any effort on his part, plans almost always fell into place for him. But evidently not this time. She wanted to dig it in. She felt like saying, "Well, why would you have thought to make a reservation earlier? I mean, who ever wants to visit New York City at holiday time?" Instead, she said, "You can stay at Mary's." All three brothers' rooms had remained untouched since their boyhood. "You can commune with your tennis trophies."

"What put you in such a good mood?"

"Oh, let's see. A long day that began with yours truly escorting Daisy Satterthwaite to a funeral. She blacked out during the reading of the Twenty-Third Psalm. I thought she was dead."

Peter chuckled. "Charlotte Cummings's funeral?"

"Yes. How'd you know?" But of course Peter would know, and suddenly it dawned on Rannie that her former husband might be able to provide something other than child support payments. Namely information. "Peter, did you know the granddaughter? Barbara. Bibi . . . she's Bibi Gaines now, but that's her married name."

"Yeah. Of course. Since forever. One summer we hung out together. I'd take her sailing. Her mother had died pretty recently; the dad was long out of the picture. She was already living with her grandmother."

"What was she like? Bibi, I mean, not her grandmother."

"We used to get stoned together. Bibi always had epic dope. To look at her, you'd write her off as just another 'Polly Prepster' in a sundress. We'd show up at dinnertime in the clubhouse, and I'd be giggling and red-eyed, while Bibi, who was just as shit-faced as I was, would sit at the bar, sipping a wine spritzer and charming all the oldsters. I never understood how she did it. It was an amazing act. Fooled everybody."

"Daisy was making veiled comments about serious drug problems; I mean like crack or heroin, not just typical stupid teen stuff."

"That's exactly right. But I'd lost touch with her by then. She was at one of those junior colleges for rich girls. She sold a piece of pretty valuable jewelry to a friend, then reported it lost and collected from the insurance company."

"Double dipping?"

"Yeah. I forget how she got caught but that's when the shit hit, about the drug problem."

Not a word of this had appeared in *Portrait of a Lady*. "I've met Bibi a couple of times recently and to look at her, you'd never know. As your mother would say, she's 'a very attractive gal,' somebody who'd still look great in tennis whites. She seems fine, yet Daisy was hinting otherwise."

"All I know is she spent a lot of time at Silver Hill. Married a guy she met there. Another crackhead, or should I say 'recovering crackhead'? Isn't that how all serious twelve-steppers refer to themselves?"

Rannie winced at Peter's making light of addiction; Tim always called himself a recovering, not former, alcoholic. Tim would write Peter off as a total lightweight. "*Him?* Really?" she could hear him saying.

"So tell me. Why the sudden fascination with Bibi Gaines?"

"Morbid curiosity? You meet somebody. Chat a bit. She seems to have it so totally together . . . when of course nobody does."

"Listen. I grew up with lots of people who tarnished their families' good names. Let me stay at the apartment and you can hear all the stories. It'll be like Scheherazade."

"Nice try. The answer is still no."

I am flummoxed, Rannie told herself after hanging up with Peter. Only an hour earlier, when she was leaving the Equinox gym, Rannie's money was on Larry as "most likely" murder suspect. Now Bibi Gaines was . . . ooh, bad pun in the vicinity! . . . gaining on him.

Ret must have found out all about Bibi's past. Daisy hadn't had any compunction about bad-mouthing Silas Cummings to the quote/unquote *Times* obit writer, so why would she hold back about Bibi, whom Daisy didn't like any better? And without a doubt, Larry would have reported everything he'd heard to Ret. That's what Ret was paying him for. What if Ret had threatened to include Bibi's youthful transgressions in *Portrait of a Lady*? It was one thing for the tight-knit circle of your friends and family to know about your crackhead/scam artist days, quite another to have the whole world read about it in a blockbuster bestseller.

Then in the next instant Rannie recalled that this was just wheel spinning: she'd already discounted extortion as a murder motive. Before now she hadn't any clue what particular items of dirty laundry Ret might get the chance to air. Now that she did, it didn't mean murdering Ret made any more sense than before. . . . How would a conversation have gone?

> Ret: Pay me off or else you'll get your own chapter
> in the book about Grammy.
> Bibi: Okay, but you swear up and down that if I give
> you gobs of money, you'll only write nice things
> about me?
> Ret: It's a promise. We can pinkie lock on it.

No, it didn't matter how much money Bibi coughed up, she'd have no guarantee of what made it into print until she had a copy of the book in hand.

Also, Ret didn't need money. What she needed was a new face and that she couldn't get. Furthermore, Ret relished outing people like Mike Bellettra who were poisonous fakes, doing real harm while passing themselves off as upstanding and decent. That's what kept Ret shoveling for dirt. Smearing somebody like Bibi Gaines, a troubled social twit, was not Ret's M.O. And the proof was the manuscript itself. Bibi appeared on the printed page as a dutiful granddaughter.

In many ways, Ret must have envied Bibi. Bibi had essentially been adopted by her grandmother, exactly what little Ret had fantasized happening to her after meeting Charlotte Cummings all those years ago at the convent. So once again Larry was the front-runner. But why, even if he murdered Ret, did he have to go and murder Ellen?

Unless he hadn't. Was it possible that Ellen's death *was* unrelated? Though the timing was eerily coincidental, was it just an awful instance of random violence?

As if tuned directly into Station WRANNIE, Larry called that very instant. "I'm parked in front your building."

"What! Why?"

"I've got a scarf of yours. You left it at the deli."

"I—I—I can't come down," Rannie phumphered. "Just leave it in the vestibule. I'll get it later."

"Look. I need to talk."

"So talk."

"My phone's almost out of juice."

"Then talk fast."

"Aw, c'mon, Rannie, I wo—" On cue, cellular screeches and blips obliterated half of Larry's next sentence.

Rannie heaved a sigh that she hoped carried through to Larry's dying cell. "I'm coming down but only for a second. Larry? Larry? You hear me?" She pulled on a fleece hoodie over her head. Was it nutty to grab the blue metallic wand of Mace? Even if the answer was yes, she rummaged through a drawer and pocketed it in her fleece.

Larry was leaning against the car. As soon as he saw her he held out the scarf.

Rannie checked sidewalk traffic. A dad was barreling down the street with a double-wide stroller, one twin screaming, snot cascading down his upper lip, the other one out cold. Dad was a big guy, somebody who could subdue Larry if he tried anything funny, like shoving Rannie into the trunk of his car. Rannie took the scarf. "Thanks. Didn't even realize I left it."

Larry was staring at the Yale track pants. "Don't tell me you work out now! Weren't you the woman who once told me se—"

"Yes. I know what I once said." Her credo had been: sex was all the workout anybody needed. "Look, Larry, to be perfectly honest, I don't think we should be in contact."

"Why not?"

Rannie had no answer that Larry would like hearing, so she remained silent.

"Unbelievable. You still think I'm some homicidal maniac?"

"I don't understand why you're here."

"How about this? I'm scared. Ret, Ellen too, must have been murdered because of something in the damn book."

"Not necessarily."

Larry ignored Rannie and kept on. "Maybe I know something only I don't know what it is."

Almost verbatim what Ellen had said the very last time Rannie had spoken to her.

"You don't need to be in Mensa to figure out Ret had somebody helping her do interviews." He went on. "Who knows what that sicko did to Ret before strangling her? She was trussed to her bed, right? It wouldn't have taken much coaxing to get her to give out my name. . . . Ergo, I am in danger."

Rannie decided to throw him a bone. "Listen. You haven't read the book. I have and there are no bombshells, I promise. It is a tame, very un-Ret-like book. . . . You didn't uncover anything big and nasty, right?" Rannie looked at him, waiting.

Larry shook his head. "The granddaughter—Babsy? Boobsy?—was a druggie back in the day. All Ret said to that was 'big whoop,' that it was old news and wasn't worth wasting even a paragraph on."

"And she doesn't bring it up. It's not in the book. So there you have it."

"You're forgetting one thing. I only know what *I* came across. There's Snoop 2 in the mix. You told me that yourself."

"Gery Antioch."

"Yeah, him. Who knows what he uncovered."

Rannie didn't remember the exact wording of the acknowledgment but the gist was that the truth would always come out. "Wait. Even if this Gery Antioch did uncover something truly horrible, something that Ret kept out of the book for whatever reason—"

"Surely not out of the goodness of her heart."

"Let me finish. Even if Gery Antioch did uncover something, and even if the killer forced Gery Antioch's name out of Ret, he's the one in danger, Gery Antioch, not you. Have the police gotten hold of him?"

"They have no idea who he is or where he is. My guess is it's a phony name, to disguise his true identity, which, when I suggested as much to the sergeant, he actually started pondering . . . you know what I mean? Stroked his chin, eyes went all squinty, brow got all furrowed, lips clamped together." As he spoke, Larry mimicked each facial gesture. "And finally he nods a little and says to me, 'That's certainly an interesting idea, Mr. Katz.' This is the caliber of investigative mind that's going to solve a double murder?"

"Did you try playing around with the name? It's Gery with only one R."

"Of course. I tried anagrams, different codes. I got nowhere. I tried Gerald Antioch. Gerard. Geraldo. Zippo."

"It could be Gery as in Geraldine."

"Thought of that too. There's a writer who's done a couple of word puzzle books for me. I called him. He did no better. He said maybe Ret knew a Gery who went to Antioch College. That was a big help."

Once again, the more Larry talked, the more Rannie became convinced that his agitation was genuine, not an act to throw suspicion off himself. Then she remembered a nagging fact. "One more thing, Larry. What made you go see Ret the day she was killed?"

"I didn't! I merely dropped off an envelope in the lobby. I was on my way out to Long Island. I left the envelope with the concierge; I was in and out in less than a minute. This is why you're acting like you're gonna wind up chloroformed in my trunk? How'd you know, anyway?"

She ignored his last question. "What was in the envelope?"

"Duplicates of all the photos I took. Ret insisted on having them. God knows why. She said she paid me to take the pictures, so they were her property. Fine. What the fuck did I want with them?"

"What time was that?"

"No earlier than eleven, eleven thirty. I got a late start out to my mother's.... That's where I just came from. Today Mom and I went over the guest list for my bar mitzvah."

It was growing chillier and darker. Also, the couple who lived in 5B, the apartment directly under hers, was approaching the building. Now was the time to bring this tête-à-tête to an end.

"I've got to start dinner. Nate and a friend are upstairs waiting," she lied. "Thanks for the scarf. And for what it's worth, I'm really starting to think Ellen's death is unrelated."

"And what will Santa be bringing you this year, little girl?"

"I'm just telling you what I think."

The husband of 5B gave Rannie a stingy smile as he got his keys. There had been several calls as of late to inform her of the level at which Nate blasted music while she wasn't home. He opened the outer door for his wife, who had a large bag from B&N. Rannie half expected Larry to inquire whether a copy of *Tattletale* was inside it. He didn't and Rannie slipped inside her building before the door closed.

Upstairs, Rannie couldn't stop obsessing about the photos. What were the odds that they were still sitting in the package room at Ret's building? A long shot but, hey, you never knew. Ret avoided being seen, so she wouldn't have come down to the lobby for them. The concierge would have had to deliver the envelope himself to her apartment. And with only one guy on duty, that probably meant waiting until his shift was over to do so. By then it might have slipped his mind. Had it also slipped the mind of the police sergeant? Highly unlikely and, if he was dotting his i's, he'd have checked the contents.

Rannie had seen the photos and copyedited the captions for *Portrait of a Lady*. Most were of family members and famous close friends of Charlotte Cummings saying "cheese" with her on yachts, in boardrooms, at celebrations, and the like. There were photos of the various residences Charlotte had owned over the century-long span of her life, real estate porn for readers to drool over. And also there were four or five interior shots of the Cummings Fifth Avenue mansion—the dining room in which every president from Eisenhower through Bush 43 had been feted, the conservatory with a trove of priceless instruments, and the grand salon that housed the art collection Rannie had seen

Although the copyrights for all the photos of the mansion rooms were in Ret's name, undoubtedly Larry was the shutterbug. He must have taken many more than what ended up in the book. Ret already had a complete set. Why, on what turned out to be the very last day of her life, would Ret insist on having all the duplicates in her possession?

A compelling urge to see the photos—or at least attempt to see them—seized hold of Rannie. Was it worth making a special trip over to the East Side? Rannie was debating the issue when Nate texted her.

"O and I thinking about Paolo's. Wanna come?"

Translation: neither of us has a credit card or dough, so we'll let you treat us to dinner.

Cheap (for Manhattan) and convivial, a throwback to the days when small family-owned joints populated Lexington Avenue, Paolo's was renowned for thin crust pizzas—Rannie's favorite, clam with bacon. It also happened to be located on Sixty-Eighth Street, a meatball's throw from Ret's apartment building. Dinner for three? At the very least sixty bucks with tip. And she couldn't forget blowing a hundred dollars already for her nontraining session. But a little more snooping? In the immortal words of MasterCard, "Priceless!"

Rannie texted back. *"There in an hour."* Forty-five minutes of which were eaten up by public transportation, not bad for a Saturday, which evidently was a day off for ninety-nine percent of the MTA's workforce.

First stop, Ret's. Happily the concierge from last Saturday was not on duty when Rannie entered the lobby. A young skinny guy was at the concierge desk; the maroon jacket he wore, with 69 East Sixty-Ninth Street stitched on the breast, was swimming on him . . . was there only one uniform and all the security guys had to share it?

Rannie approached him, cleared her throat, and hoped the addition of her newly repossessed scarf and wool duffle coat made more of a statement than the Yale pants or Converse high-tops. All businesslike brisk she introduced herself. "I'm Miranda Bookman. A week ago, a package was left for me in care of Ret Sullivan. I'm here to pick it up."

His Adam's apple, a considerable one, bobbled up and down. "Ms. Sullivan? Uh, I'm afraid . . . maybe you don't know but—"

Rannie toned down the professional and assumed a just-sad-enough smile. "Yes. Of course I know about her passing." Rannie would have preferred the plainer, more forthright "death"; however, her hunch was that the euphemism would play better with this guy. "Just awful, awful, awful. I worked with Ms. Sullivan. I was her editor on the book she just finished." Rannie produced the S&S business card and hoped (A) the guy would be impressed with the title on it and (B) he would disregard its far-from-mint condition.

"Let me check if anything's still here," he said and in a moment returned with an 8½ × 11 manila envelope. Rannie's heart practically went into tachycardia at the sight of it.

"Gee. I'm sorry but it just has Ms. Sullivan's name on it."

"I've been away. She was supposed to hold it for me. That's why."

He was shaking his head. "I'm sorry but I can't—"

Rannie cut him off, returned to businesslike brisk, and threw some exasperation into the mix. "Look. This is important. Those are photos for Ms. Sullivan's new book. Is there someone else I can talk to? Is the building manager around?"

"Michael! I need help with my bags." A petulant voice pre-
ceded the entrance of a middle-aged woman who by the look
of her outfit—a real Barbour jacket, expensive "driving" loafers, and brandy-colored cords—had returned from her weekend place. She was cradling a yappy terrier in a pink cable-knit
sweater.

"Right with you, Mrs. Gordon." Then to Rannie. "You could
leave your card. I'll ask the manager to call you Monday." He
placed the envelope by the phone console.

Rannie nodded and he hustled off toward a brass luggage cart
stationed by the mailroom.

His back was to her. She snatched the envelope.

An adrenaline-infused "Go me!" rush acted like Super Pre-
mium Unleaded, propelling her out of the lobby.

Was it actually theft when the dupes had no value? Yes,
Rannie decided. To call it anything else was hairsplitting se-
mantics à la Bill Clinton and his famous definition of sex. At a
pace that was faster than trotting but still didn't really qualify as
running, she traversed the two blocks to Paolo's. At one point she
heard a police siren and looked back, convinced that in a minute
she'd be escorted via squad car to the nearest precinct to pose for
her mug shot.

Rannie had always prided herself on what till now had been
the unstickiest fingers among the Bookman sisters. As soon
as Amy, older than Betsy by twenty months, had her learner's
permit in hand, they'd head to the mall every Saturday to shop-
lift cheap cosmetics from Walgreens. Rannie, who was no more
than seven, was dragged along and forced to play decoy. Her sisters would generously steal a candy bar for her as payoff. Like
that Proustian madeleine, Rannie could still conjure the taste,

texture, and aroma of those purloined Snickers, how she savored their peanutty goodness but was simultaneously nauseated by waves of guilt. Tim was right: in another life, she'd definitely clocked a lot of hours in confessional booths.

Olivia and Nate had beaten her to Paolo's. They were at a table in the back under a garish fresco of the Bay of Naples. Examining the photos had to be put on hold.

"We already ordered," Nate told her and within ten minutes Rannie was gratified to see two medium-size clam and bacon pizzas arrive.

"I caught a glimpse of your parents at the funeral for Charlotte Cummings earlier today," Rannie said.

Olivia did the throat-clearing thing. "Yeah, my mother was totally stressing over what to wear. I'm like, 'Black, Mom. Black'll work.' She's at Mrs. Gaines's now. My mom is taking her on a trip next week maybe to Cabo."

"Your mother sounds like a good friend."

Olivia shrugged. "They haven't known each other very long. My mom thinks Mrs. Gaines is a big deal because of her family." Then, without Rannie having to resort to any unseemly probing, Olivia all on her own launched into a discourse offering up the fact, swaddled within layers of extraneous, forgettable information, that it was the Werners who actually owned Bibilots. Olivia didn't state it so baldly—"I think my dad bought the whole building or something ages ago" was how she phrased it—and she referred to Bibi and her mother as "partners." Yet since Olivia added, "Although I can't remember when my mother ever worked a day there," Rannie came away with the distinct impression that on some level, whatever livelihood Bibi Gaines earned from Bibilots came via the generosity of Carole Werner.

This was certainly not the larkish "working keeps me out of trouble" interpretation of her career delivered by Bibi that day Rannie had stopped in at Bibilots.

It was awfully hard to imagine Bibi Gaines needing to work in the same fiscally mandatory way Rannie Bookman needed to work. Bibi was rich . . . or rather she came from a rich family, which, Rannie stopped to remind herself, wasn't precisely the same thing. Look at Mary Lorimer. She came from money, piles of it. However, the stringent terms of Mary's father's will were such that even now at eighty-two, she was allowed access only to the interest on her inheritance. Mary could never touch so much as a dime of the principal. Peter had told Rannie all this: "My grandfather didn't think women could be trusted to handle money."

Up until this past Tuesday, when Charlotte Cummings finally checked out, whatever inheritance coming Bibi's way was theoretical, nothing Bibi could lay her hands on. Of course there was Bibi's late mother—Daisy's beloved friend—who must have provided for her only child. But Bibi was already getting into serious trouble before her mother's death. Straight from Daisy's lipstick-smeared lips had come the words "If melanoma hadn't killed Madeline, worrying over Barbara would have." So Madeline's will might have taken precautions to keep the purse strings pulled tightly on inheritance money, ensuring that Bibi couldn't squander it all on highly controlled substances.

Hard drugs were costly. An appetite for them would take a large bite out of anyone's monthly budget, even a budget with a lot of zeros after the dollar sign. Still, nothing about present-day Barbara Gaines whispered, let alone screamed, substance abuser . . . except for Daisy's comments about long sleeves and the one-hundredth birthday party.... Also, what was it Peter had said? Bibi had a knack for appearing fine when she was stoned out of her gourd.

"I'm going to walk O home," Nate said once the check arrived, which with tax and tip included was only three dollars over Rannie's earlier sixty-dollar guesstimate.

On Lexington Avenue, after waving good-bye, Rannie watched their two silhouettes head into the night, hand in hand, backlit by a streetlamp. She was happy for Nate, she was worried for Nate. But mostly she was hit with a sharp loneliness: almost like an amputee continuing to feel a phantom limb, she suddenly experienced the sensation of Tim's hand in hers, the comfortable, warm pressure of his grasp. Her fingers flexed involuntarily, yet all she grasped now was the envelope of duplicate photos.

The headiness of having done something that her bad angel would applaud had disappeared. Now remembering the way she'd cased the lobby so furtively, then hotfooted it outside made her cringe. It was pathetic, a little scary too. If she didn't watch out, thirty years from now she could wind up as "kooky" as her mother's friend, the one who interpreted messages from the beyond in pennies laying in the street.

Chapter 25

THE DUPLICATES, ABOUT TWENTY, WERE SPREAD ON THE COFFEE table; all were of the Fifth Avenue mansion, both exterior and interior shots. Larry was no Ansel Adams. Several were indecipherable blurs; one, taken at an odd angle, showed nothing more than a pair of feet, probably belonging to Bibi, in pink Tory Burch flats. All these went into a discard pile.

With a magnifying glass Rannie next inspected the photos she had seen before, the ones that were to be included in the book. *I have absolutely no idea what I am looking for,* she told herself. So how on earth would she know if she found it? It was a variation on the "what if I know something only I don't know it" theme. Still Rannie kept looking. There was a photo of an eighteenth-century harpsichord in the conservatory, a shot of the dining room with a chandelier worthy of Versailles, and photos of the grand salon that Rannie had been in herself. There were a couple of photos of martyred saint paintings and three of the gigantic fireplace that needed to be assembled side by side in order to view the whole. To the right of the mantel another painting of a martyred saint was partially visible. Rannie didn't recognize it from her quick tour with Bibi. She squinted. The saint was a young girl, her head yanked back savagely by a soldier in armor. The small brass ID plaque on the frame remained nothing more than a rectangular blur even under a magnifying glass.

Rannie leaned back on the sofa and, sighing, chalked off grabbing the photos as tangible proof that crime never paid. Then because the evening held nothing more urgent than waiting for Nate to come home, she searched through all the bookshelves in the living room for her copies of Ret's books. As expected, she found no mention of Gery Antioch on any of the earlier acknowledgment pages. Nor, by using an old set of Scrabble tiles, did Rannie get any further than Larry and his puzzle friend had in finding another name hidden in the same letters. . . . Unless— Rannie sat back and thought for a moment—Gery Antioch wasn't a name but a phrase, a phrase that was some sort of clue, in which case maybe adding in "For" to "Gery Antioch" would yield results. Rannie played with various letter arrangements. But no, all she came up with was

ANGRY FOOT REICH
OGRE FAIRY NOTCH
FRANTIC HOE ORGY

It was later, while hanging up her navy funeral suit, that Rannie noticed F. Anthony Weld's business card, printed in sober yet elegant Helvetica semibold, peeking out from her jacket pocket.

On Google Images, from the three photos that popped up, one showed F. Anthony with Bibi at some arts benefit. He'd mentioned having restored a painting in Silas Cummings's collection, so there was a professional connection between them. But their body language, which according to Gerry the gym instructor spoke more truthfully than words, said "We are a couple." A very attractive couple at that.

F. Anthony's career accomplishments were highlighted on a site called Art Discoveries. The information might have appeared on the curriculum vitae passed out at the Yale lecture but since she'd no more than glanced at it then, Rannie scrolled through the entire entry on Weld, learning that his cleaning of an eighteenth-century landscape painting had lifted it from the obscurity of "School of Constable" to the heights of genuine Constable masterpiece, one that subsequently sold for a whopping amount to an oil overlord in Dubai.

At ten, Nate returned looking dazed and confused. Not stoned; Rannie knew the telltale signs of that well enough. But something far more mind-altering. Love.

He sprawled across Rannie's bed on his back, his T-shirt hiked up, revealing the whorl of dark hair around his navel. That he was the official owner of a man's body still blew Rannie away. Staring up at the ceiling, Nate muttered, "I really like her, Ma. I *really* like her."

For once Rannie avoided the temptation to pepper him with questions, and trusting that whatever was happening was happening with safety precautions, she restricted herself to "She's worth liking."

Evidently that sufficed. Nate awarded her with an uncharacteristically joyful smile and went to his room. She was in bed shortly thereafter and half asleep when the intercom buzzer started sounding. "Nate, can you get it?" she croaked. "Nate?"

No response. More buzzing. As soon as she hauled herself out of bed and opened the door of her room, Rannie could feel the throbbing bass of the Decembrists through the soles of her bare feet. Oh, shit. The couple in 5B.

Yelling at Nate from the other side of his door to turn the volume down, Rannie hurried to the intercom. "Listen. I am *so* sorry," she said. "Really. This won't happen again."

"Rannie, it's Tim."

"Oh!" was all she said.

"I need to come up."

There was no time to think. All she could manage before hearing a knock at the door was to get her teeth brushed and throw on some clothes.

Tim looked grave. "I'm really sorry."

"Don't be."

"I came the sec—"

"Don't talk. Don't say a word. I'm just so happy you're here."

Grabbing him by the shoulders, she pressed herself against his chest. For a moment, Tim stroked her hair gently. Through the downy bulk of his parka she could feel the steady rhythm of his breathing. But way too soon, Tim took her by the arms, unclasped himself, and held her a few inches away. "I only just heard the news," he said.

Her body was still firing off "all's well with the world" pheromones, which was why it took a nanosecond for her brain to register that something in his words and tone was amiss. Rannie blinked. Her throat went dry. "What news?"

"You don't know?"

"Spit it out, Tim!" Rannie commanded. Nate was safe in bed. "Is it Alice? Is Alice okay?" Oh, God! There'd been an accident and somehow Tim was contacted to come break the news.

Tim looked confused "Alice? Your daughter?"

"What other Alice is there?" Rannie spat out frantically.

"It's not your daughter. Look. Larry Katz is dead."

Rannie's arms broke free from Tim's grasp and flailed about wildly. "No! You're kidding. That's impossible!"

"He was found dead an hour ago. The cops at the Twenty-Fourth want to talk to you."

"No!" Rannie insisted. "I just saw Larry. No!"

"Rannie, listen to me." Tim held her by the upper arms and forced her to meet his gaze. "A downstairs neighbor of his got concerned, because water was pouring down from his apartment. He didn't answer when she rang, so the super came ... and then the cops."

"No! He came to return a scarf. . . ." Suddenly Tim seemed very far away as if she was looking at him through the wrong end of binoculars; a flurry of white speckles began to descend like a snowstorm, clouding the outer edges of her vision. Her legs buckled.

Tim caught her before she dropped and got her on the sofa. "Put your head between your legs. Okay, now. Deep breaths. Just concentrate on breathing. Nothing else. In . . . out. In . . . out. Thatta girl. Keep your head down."

A cup of tea later, one loaded to the brim with sugar, Rannie felt steady enough on her feet to get her duffle coat. The reason Tim had come was to take her down to the precinct. That and only that. Rannie scrawled a note for Nate: "Grabbing coffee with Tim."

As they waited for the elevator he said, "I'm so sorry. I figured you already knew. "

In the car, except for Tim checking whether she was okay, to which Rannie replied, "If you mean, am I going to pass out, the answer is no," they didn't talk. Rannie was grateful. She was in no rush to learn the nitty-gritty of Larry's death—and even if she had wanted to know, Tim would follow protocol with some evasive reply like "The cops have all that information."

Larry. Rannie pictured water dripping down a neighbor's ceiling. An overflowing bathtub or shower. With Larry slumped in it. And blood . . . Lots.

Her gorge rose; Rannie put a screeching halt on this train of thought and breathed into the brown paper bag that Tim had insisted she take along.

"Need me to pull over?"

"No. I just want to get this over with."

In less than an hour, it was.

While Tim waited on the first floor by the front desk. Grieg took Rannie upstairs to the open pen of work spaces where only a few days earlier she'd read through Ret Sullivan's copy of *Portrait of a Lady*. He pointed to his desk chair and then, after fiddling with a tiny tape recorder, hoisted himself on the desk. The sergeant didn't waste time: around nine P.M., he told her, Larry had been found in his bathtub, both wrists slit. No note. No signs of a struggle. "Toxicology reports won't be in for a couple of days. But he had a bottle of Ativan in his medicine cabinet—"

"Who doesn't?" Rannie almost said.

"—that was nearly empty. And an open bottle of vodka in the kitchen."

He made Rannie go over each of the occasions when she and

Larry had met and relate verbatim, or as nearly as she could, their conversations. Unsurprisingly, Grieg drilled her most intensely on what had transpired that afternoon.

"Did Mr. Katz seem despondent? Was he acting remorseful in any way? Frightened? Was his behavior erratic?"

"He seemed frightened. Definitely. But not frightened in a guilty way because he was the murderer and you were closing in on him. I mean, he realized he was a suspect." She had to look up at Grieg while speaking, which convinced her that positioning himself on the desk had been purposeful, for a psychological advantage. "What scared Larry was that he'd wind up the next victim." Saying that made Rannie's eyes clamp shut and she swallowed hard. Larry had come to see her and Rannie had essentially blown him off, told him to get lost, sending him home to get murdered.

When she opened her eyes, Grieg was still peering down at her, his hands tented together at his waist. "And . . . ?"

"You're asking do I think he was killed? Or if he killed himself?"

Grieg nodded.

"He was killed. There's no doubt in my mind. Look. It was a long time ago when I knew him. But based on that, if Larry were going to commit suicide, no way would he slit his wrists."

Grieg's brow furrowed and his lips pooched together—the pondering expression described by Larry. He seemed to be waiting for elaboration.

"He was—squeamish." Rannie had been about to say "a big baby." "If Larry were going to kill himself, it wouldn't be messy," Rannie concluded. Then after a pause, she went on. "I'll be honest. I was suspicious of Larry. I mean, you know that. That's why I called you the other day. He worked very closely with Ret on the book for S&S. Doing that could have gotten him fired from his job at Dusk Books."

"Because?"

"Conflict of interest. When you work for one publishing company, you can't help someone write a bestseller for another company. So it crossed my mind that Ret might have threatened to tell Larry's bosses what he was doing—"

"Why would she do that?"

"According to Larry, Ret Sullivan accused him of overcharging her for the work he did. She'd keep repeating how she always got even with anyone who cheated her."

"So if he needed his day job, he had a motive to kill her."

"But I don't think he did. Kill her, that is. And there's nothing to prove she ever made threats. If anything, from what Larry said, it sounded as if Ret was in love with him."

"Ms. Bookman, were you in love with him?"

Rannie had been rubbing her temples. Now her head shot up. "No! Of course not!" Before Grieg cast her as a deranged, jealous ex-lover who killed Ret, Ellen, and now Larry, Rannie quickly moved on to how anxious Larry had been earlier that day. "He was angry because there doesn't seem to be any break in the case. He said, 'It's been a week; all that's happened is Ellen wound up in a body bag too.' And he brought up Gery Antioch, whether he'd been found and questioned."

No response from Grieg.

"Have you?"

"That's not something I can discuss." Grieg wriggled on the desk. Maybe his butt had fallen asleep. "So, Ms. Bookman, anything else, anything at all, you should tell me?"

Ooh. Now they were coming to the embarrassing part.

"Wellllll." Rannie strung out the word for as long as possible, then wet her lips. "Larry told me that on the morning Ret was murdered, he left an envelope of photos—duplicates of photos—at the concierge desk of her building. They were of the Cummings mansion. Ret used some in the book." Rannie wet her lips some more. "He couldn't understand why she was so insistent about having the dupes. So anyway—" How could she phrase what came next in a way that didn't make her sound like the newly elected mayor of Crazytown? "I'm afraid that, before dinner tonight, I went over to Ret's building and, uh, took the envelope."

If Poker Face 101 were a course at the Police Academy, Grieg would have flunked. Instantaneously, an "Are you shitting me!" expression consumed every feature on his face, even his nose. Nevertheless, he managed to ask, in a surprisingly level tone, "Why did you do that?"

"I thought maybe the photos would reveal a clue."

"Did they?"

"No." Did he believe her or suspect Rannie was covering for herself?

"Are the photos still in your possession?"

"Yes."

"Ms. Bookman, I don't get it. Are you trying to hinder this investigation or solve the case yourself?"

"The latter." She almost asked to get Tim up here; he'd confirm that indeed she was a meddlesome lunatic.

"Because you realize what you did is tampering with a homicide investigation."

Rannie held her tongue. Now didn't seem the moment to point out that if Grieg had been doing a thorough job, the photographs wouldn't have still been at Ret's building for Rannie to steal. "I'm sorry. What I did was wrong. I know that. But I'm scared. I was scared before I knew about Larry." Even if that wasn't exactly the truth, maybe stupidity was the only reason it wasn't.

"So before we go pick up those photos at your apartment, is there anything else?"

"I remembered something today, something in Ret Sullivan's bedroom. There was a religious painting above her bed, a Madonna and Child. I'm positive a different painting used to hang in the same spot."

"Hold on. According to the report, you'd never been to Ms. Sullivan's apartment until the day of the murder."

"Absolutely true, Sergeant," Rannie replied evenly. "What I remembered today was that all around the Madonna picture, the wall paint was much cleaner. A bigger painting hung there at one time."

"And this has exactly what to do with the murder?"

"I don't know. I am just trying to be as forthcoming as possible. Paintings of sweet Madonnas weren't Ret Sullivan's typical taste."

"You two liked to discuss art?"

"No."

"Because in the report you also stated there'd been no contact for years between the two of you."

"That's true, too." Rannie did not relish bringing up her trip to the convent or the conversation with Sister Dorothy. Nevertheless, she did. In full.

"So, Ms. Bookman. Attending the funeral? Were you just paying respects?"

"Not just that."

"More investigating?"

She nodded. Being the mayor of Crazytown was a 24/7 job.

Surprisingly, Tim was still sitting in a row of attached plastic chairs when Rannie descended the stairs to the ground floor of the precinct. Even more surprisingly, his car followed the sergeant's with Rannie in it back to the Dolores Court, where, possibly thanks to his much vaunted parking karma, his Toyota slid into a legal space even before Rannie had her keys out.

"You're coming upstairs?"

He nodded and Rannie didn't question why.

Five minutes later, Grieg left with the envelope of photos, Rannie thankful that Nate hadn't emerged to inquire about police presence in their apartment.

She faced Tim. He hadn't taken off his parka, which she interpreted to mean his departure was imminent as well. "You get a whole lot of mensch points for tonight."

He shrugged. His eyes looked tired.

The sight of him filled her with longing, not sexual longing, something more sorrowful and harder to bear. They could have belonged to each other. *I really fucked this one up,* she told herself. Then she reconsidered: that made it sound as if she could have behaved differently. Pure and simple, she was wrong for Tim.

She turned and headed to the front hall door.

"I'm staying," she heard him say from behind. At the same time she noticed a gym bag on the floor. Tim's gym bag.

"Really?" She turned back to him.

"I'm worried about you."

Rannie attempted a light tone. "My sanity, my safety? Both?"

A brief smile. He explained Chris was spending the weekend

at Amherst, attending some classes. "I'm solo through Monday. When I need to be at the bar, you'll come too."

"L. C. King Security's round-the-clock service?"

"A special deal for you, the friends and family rate." He rubbed his hands together, seemingly relieved that Rannie had put up no argument.

"Okay. I know where the pullout is. All I need is a pillow."

"Tim, do me a favor. Stay in my room."

"Not a good idea, Ran—"

"Not for me. For Nate. He was really happy you stayed over the other night. He barely says two words to me and the next morning, out of the blue, he told me how I deserve a good guy like you."

Tim was still shaking his head no.

"What if he finds you in the den? What am I going to say? We broke up but you're here playing bodyguard so I don't end up murdered?"

He blew through his teeth, looked undecided, then said, "Okay. In a crazy way I guess I get it."

Rannie unearthed the sole remaining air mattress from a disastrous family camping trip in Maine—Alice had ended up with infected spider bites the size and hardness of golf balls. Tim blew it up and spread a sleeping bag on top of it. "Maybe we can roast s'mores later," he said.

"And have a sing-along . . . I know all the verses to 'Found a Peanut.'"

It took a second but then Tim laughed and caught the pillow Rannie tossed.

By the time Rannie emerged from the bathroom, teeth brushed and flossed, fleece granny robe knotted over another

jumbo T-shirt, Tim had already slid inside the sleeping bag and
was lying on his back, his arms crossed behind his head.

"Comfortable?" she asked.

"Snug as a bug."

Rannie turned out the light. No surprise, sleep was not on
the agenda. All her untoned muscles decided to lock simultaneously; her eyes refused to shut and a digital news ribbon looped
through her brain over and over. Ret . . . Ellen . . . Larry . . .

Rustling sounds from the sleeping bag and occasional coughs
told her Tim wasn't off in Dreamland either. Finally she said,
"Can I ask you something? About what happened tonight?"

"I'm listening," he surprised her by saying.

Ironic that he'd dumped her because of her snooping and yet
now the murders were pretty much the only subject they could
discuss. "First of all, you don't think Larry Katz killed himself."

"No. I don't."

"Or anybody else?"

"No. Not anymore."

"The police were following Larry. So didn't they see who, besides tenants, entered his building tonight? It's a loft building. I
mean, there can't be that many apartments."

"I have no idea about surveillance tonight. Listen, Rannie.
Since your friend Ellen was killed, yes, I've tried to learn what
I can. But it's not like I get instant Twitter updates; I don't know
a quarter of what you think I do. . . . Let me ask you something.
What was in the envelope the sergeant took?"

A minute later he said, "You are out of your fucking mind,
you realize that." He wasn't angry; in fact, he almost sounded
amused, which Rannie didn't like, not one bit. Not becoming

enraged meant Tim was no longer emotionally invested in her, not past the point of seeing she remained alive.

"Listen, mister, you were the one who called about Larry going to Ret's apartment building the day of the murder. Remember? And I had my own suspicions about Larry. Someone told me Ret was troubled over something 'sinful' she'd done just a short time before she was murdered." Then Rannie explained her earlier erroneous theory that Larry had murdered Ret to keep his job at Dusk.

"So let me get all this straight. Ret Sullivan wrote her own life story under a fake name that Larry Katz's company published. And Larry Katz helped her write the new book, the one about Charlotte Cummings. And *he* used a fake name too."

"Well, I don't know if he or Ret came up with the Audeo name. It only appears in the acknowledgments."

"You're quibbling, Miranda."

"I figured out Audeo was Larry because that's the brand of hearing aids he wears—oh, God!—wore."

"What is it with you publishing people? Everything has to be an in-joke." Tim paused. "Wait. Just before, you said Ret was feeling guilty about something. How'd you find that out?"

Rannie let herself take some small pleasure in anticipating his reaction to hearing her say, "When I was at the Sisters of Mercy convent."

Tim sat up and guffawed. "I take it you're not considering the novitiate."

Rannie told him about Ret's childhood and her close friendship with Sister Dorothy Cusack. "I wondered why Ret chose Charlotte Cummings to write about. It turns out Silas Cummings purchased a painting from the sisters at the time the convent was in terrible financial shape. Sister Dorothy calls him their guardian angel. She also said Ret harbored this fantasy in which the Cummings would end up adopting her, like Little Orphan Annie."

Tim lay back down. "You have had one busy week."

"You haven't heard the half of it. . . . I have a theory."

"No, Rannie, I'm beat. This theory of yours can wait."

"Okay." In actuality, that was totally un-okay since sleep for her was not even a remote possibility. So she threw out a little bait and hoped Tim would bite. "Let me just say that all along I've thought the killer had to be a man . . . but what if it's a woman? I have a candidate."

"Sorry to blow your game changer, but it's a man."

"How can you be so positive?"

"Because of semen, semen found on Ret Sullivan's body."

Chapter 26

THE NEXT MORNING RANNIE SHAMBLED OUT OF BED AND FOUND Tim by the hall closet, stowing the sleeping bag and deflated air mattress in the front hall closet. His head swiveled toward her. "Jesus, you look like hell."

"Good morning to you, too." Rannie croaked. She felt like hell. It hurt to move her eyes, which burned in the same way they used to after pulling all-nighters at Yale. Yet she must have fallen asleep at some point or at least dozed off because she had jolted awake, the memory of the previous night walloping her with full force.

"You just missed Nate. He went to meet friends."

"He didn't see you putting away that stuff!" she exclaimed.

"Relax. I waited till he was gone. I saw him for all of two seconds. But I made sure to have a big satisfied smile on my face."

"Go ahead. Make fun."

"It's just not many mothers try to fool their sons into thinking they're doing the dirty deed. I made coffee."

Those were the magic words. Rannie plopped on the couch.

Her glasses were still on the night table, but for now remaining unfocused seemed preferable. In some way it kept what she wasn't ready to think about at bay. When Tim returned with coffee as well as toast, he glanced at the jumbled Scrabble tiles on the coffee table. "FRANTIC HOE ORGY???"

Rannie, squinting, reassembled the letters into FOR GERY ANTIOCH and explained. "He—or she—since it could be Gery for Geraldine, is the only other person besides Larry who gets an acknowledgment in *Portrait of a Lady.* I hoped scrambling the letters might reveal a name, a clue, a something."

They sipped and munched in silence, Tim scanning stories in the Sunday paper, Rannie allowing the caffeine to do its job. Then they each repaired to separate bathrooms to shower, Rannie finishing in record time because it was simply too unnerving knowing that directly on the other side of the tiled stall, with no more than a few inches separating them, an identical shower head, circa 1970, was fitfully spitting water down on a stark naked Tim.

She got dressed, donned glasses, and returned to the living room feeling as if she almost qualified for membership in the human race. "I know what you said last night, about the semen on Ret, but can I tell you my female murderer theory anyway?"

"Shoot."

"Barbara Gaines. Bibi." Rannie wasn't positive he'd immediately connect the name with the woman he knew from AA meetings. And if he did, she half expected a dismissive retort, something on the order of "No way, Rannie." Instead he put down the newspaper and waited for more.

"It's nothing concrete. Just a feeling. I told you I think Ret was blackmailing somebody. What if it was Bibi?"

"Why?"

"I'm not there yet. . . . Will you tell me this? Has she been in AA long?"

"I've seen her around for years."

Rannie needed a more specific time frame. "Longer than three years?"

"Way longer."

If what Daisy said was true, about Bibi's shenanigans at the one-hundredth birthday party, that meant Bibi was having "slips" while in the program.

Tim was frowning now and looked uncomfortable. He never discussed anybody in AA by name—it was always the generic "a person in the program"—yet Rannie could tell from his expression that something else was bothering him, something besides breaking AA confidentiality. She backtracked to what he'd said before about "seeing Bibi around for years." For Tim, showing up at meetings wasn't necessarily the same thing as truly being in AA, which involved a steadfast daily commitment to the program and its principles. Without ever naming who, he'd occasionally dismiss certain people in AA as being uncommitted. A few had to attend, a stipulation of probation. Others constantly fell off the wagon.

"Is Bibi serious about the program?"

"I've been known to be wrong. But no. I don't think so."

"She used to be a very serious drug addict."

"Rannie, there are no unserious drug addicts. That'd be a what do you call it? Oxymoron."

"Two points for you."

"Don't be condescending." Then Tim said, "The thing is, Barbara Gaines's problems with drinking and drugs were no secret.

I heard her qualify once and remember her saying that *Vanity Fair* or one of those magazines wrote all about her. So Ret Sullivan couldn't threaten Barbara with what was already very stale news."

"Okay. I get that."

"Then what's the motive?"

"I told you. I'm not there yet."

"And are you thinking she also murdered Ellen Donahoe and Larry Katz?"

"Not sure," Rannie said lamely.

"So you're without motive. What about opportunity?"

Rannie shot him a dirty look. Tim was making her feel like the student who comes to class totally unprepared and gets hammered by the teacher when Rannie had always been exactly the opposite, one of those obnoxious, smarty-pants kids whose hand was perpetually raised, bouncing in her seat, "Ooh, ooh. Call on me! I know the answer!"

A chorus of dings on her cell phone alerted Rannie to several e-mails that had popped up from S&S old-timers. News of Larry's death—"suicide," all the messages called it—was circulating. Ellen's assistant, Dina, had contacted Rannie too. "You think Larry was overcome with grief? He and Ellen never seemed a big thing, but if he was in love with her, it's so tragic."

Dina had punctuated the end of the e-mail with a teary-eyed emoticon. Rannie let out a groan—Larry deserved better than email-ese—and leaned back against the couch. Then something else occurred to her and made her groan again. "And what am I supposed to do now with the manuscript I copyedited for Larry?"

"Send it back with a bill. You finished the job and are owed the money."

"Yeah, but send it to whom? Larry?"

"Yes. It'll get to the right person." Tim was growing impatient. He stood. "I should get to the bar. Come on. You can drop the manuscript at UPS on the way."

"You're serious about this buddy system?" Serious seemed to be the word of the day.

At the Offbeat, Rannie made herself useful. She swabbed down the hexagonal tiled floor, laid out table settings, and corrected a misspelling on the chalkboard, which had advertised "dally specials."

Tim treated her to an early lunch—a decent chopped salad with chicken and a Diet Coke that he hosed up at the bar. That was where they ate. Although badly scarred, the bar was made of mahogany, had a brass foot rail, and faced an enormous gilt-framed mirror. Rannie caught their reflection in it; they looked buddy-buddy without giving off that "couples" vibe, not like Bibi and her art restorer guy.

Afterward while Tim caught up with paperwork, Rannie took some orders to help out the sole waiter, a retired cop whose customers had to endure a lot of corny banter. She could spot cops now, guys in windbreakers and khakis who, an hour from now, would be in uniform at the precinct two blocks away. Were any of them Tim's sources? The only way to find out would be to try some tough-waitressy banter of her own. . . . "So, big fella, got anything to spill on the Ret Sullivan case? That poor dame sure caught a raw deal."

By two forty-five the place was empty again; Rannie had pocketed almost thirty-five dollars. Cops were generous tippers. By three, Tim's car, almost as if it were holding its breath, squeezed into a tiny space within twenty feet of the Dolores Court.

Rannie shook her head. "You can wipe that self-satisfied smile off; the title is yours for keeps. Grand Poobah of Parking."

Nate was home, en route from the kitchen to his room with a plate of microwavable mac and cheese. Rannie and Tim resumed their former places on the living room sofa, and Rannie began tackling the Sunday crossword while Tim, legs stretched out on the coffee table, one sweat-socked foot rubbing against the other, skimmed the copy of the Sunday *Daily News* that he'd brought from the bar.

"Help me out here," Rannie asked. "The clue is 'Native New Englander?' There's a question mark, which means the answer's got a little spin, a pun or something. . . . Like it could be the name of a Native American tribe. It's long. Nine letters."

Rannie glanced up and realized Tim hadn't been listening to her. His eyes were fastened on the Scrabble tiles.

"What?"

"I don't even know what made me look again." He leaned over and nudged the R and G tiles closer to each other.

"Oh!" She clutched his arm, which sent all the tiles scattering. It didn't matter. She'd seen the same thing he had.

FORGERY ANTIOCH

"A forged will? Maybe Charlotte Cummings's will?" Tim said.

Rannie shook her head. "No, I don't think so." The photocopied manuscript for *Portrait of a Lady* still lay stacked on the console behind the sofa. Rannie reached for it and read aloud the complete acknowledgment. "'For Gery Antioch. I have come to appreciate how artful you are.' I think Ret chose the word 'artful' very purposefully. I think she was referring to an art forgery."

It had to involve the Cummings collection. Rannie decided to rule out the famous altarpiece. Ret's clue was Forgery Antioch. Even if Antioch turned out to be yet another scrambled word, Rannie felt sure it would bear no connection to the altarpiece. Why would Ret keep such major art world news a secret, buried in a cryptic book acknowledgment? She would have gone public as soon as her agent had secured a whopper of a deal—*The Counterfeit Masterpiece*—with Simon & Schuster. Yet not once had Ellen hinted about any other book from Ret.

"What's going on in that twisted mind of yours?"

"Shhh. I'm thinking." No, it was more reasonable that the forgery involved one of Silas's lesser paintings. The one purchased from the convent? Acknowledging the crime within a book acknowledgment seemed like a sadistic wink, an in-joke that only Ret and the forger would understand.

"Is there a St. Antioch?" she asked Tim.

"Not that I ever heard of."

"I'm calling the convent," Rannie said. The 914 Westchester number was long erased from her phone log, so she suffered through the prompts from the digitized voice and then punched in the numbers. But her hand had started trembling so badly, she misdialed twice. On the third try, she got through, only to hear another recorded voice saying that because Sunday was a day of prayer and silence for the sisters, to please call back on Monday.

"What about your mother? Might she know?"

According to Tim, Mama Butler was a font of religious trivia, crushing all competition in the annual Catholic Jeopardy Tournament held at her parish church.

Tim didn't answer. His own cell had started moaning. "Hey! How are you, man?" he said, nodding, and then a sudden clap to his forehead. "Good you called . . . No, it's fine. I'm there." He stood. "Rannie, I promised I'd lead a three thirty meeting down in the Village. I gotta go."

"Now? Right when we have a lead!" Still, abiding by the buddy system, she tossed the magazine and got up.

"No. You can't come. It's a closed meeting, strictly for us alkies."

"Swell. That means I stay locked in your car till the meeting's over?"

"No. You can stay here. But think of it like house arrest, Rannie. I mean it." He checked his watch. "I should be back no later than six. I'll take you and Nate for Chinese." Tim got his parka. At the front door, he turned. "Promise to stay put?"

Rannie crossed her heart.

First order of business: Google "St. Antioch." She didn't remember seeing a St. Antioch painting in the Cummings mansion, but that didn't mean one didn't exist. The search results showed numerous sites for a St. Ignatius of Antioch, martyred at the Colosseum in Rome by hungry leopards whose favorite dish was Early Christian Tartare. Ignatius's end met the required yuck factor common to all the paintings Silas owned. Rannie searched Google Images for paintings of Ignatius of Antioch. None belonged to Silas Cummings.

Bummer.

The setback necessitated the consumption of a perfect PB&J, and while confirming to herself yet again that Planet Earth offered no finer source of nourishment, Rannie considered whether she might be coming at the question of FORGERY ANTIOCH from the wrong starting point. What she needed was a checklist of all the paintings that Silas owned.

Back online, Rannie located a catalog of the Cummings collection, publication date 1976. By Rannie's calculation, the year postdated the visit from the Cummingses to the Sisters of Mercy. Whatever painting Silas had purchased from the nuns should be listed in the catalog.

A short preface written by a Met Museum curator in Northern Late Renaissance Art waxed eloquent on what Rannie already knew: the gem in the collection was the Crucifixion altarpiece by the Master of the Agony. Upon the death of Charlotte Cummings, it would become part of the permanent collection at the Metropolitan Museum, as would the rest of Silas's paintings, everything to be exhibited together in one gallery.

Rannie skipped past more stuff on the altarpiece and began scrolling more slowly through small-sized reproductions of martyred saints until—glory be!—she found her.

St. Margaret of Antioch. Ret had been born Kathleen Margaret Sullivan. The painting depicted a young girl in the clutches of not one but two Roman soldiers. Rannie recognized it. The St. Margaret painting had been partially visible in one of the photographs Larry had taken of the hearth, the dupes of which were in Grieg's possession now. Ret had seen the photo too.

The accompanying text explained that Margaret, an early convert to Christianity, had hailed from Antioch—present-day Turkey—and had been "grotesquely tortured." In addition to being strangled, she'd been plunged in boiling oil, beaten with clubs, and raked from head to toe with red-hot iron combs. Rannie enlarged the image. One of the soldiers had a club in

hand while the second soldier had Margaret's head wrenched
back by the hair, a great fistful of it in each of his hands.

The image of Ret's corpse, two hanks of hair tied to rungs
on the bedstead, would stay with Rannie for the rest of her life.
Now it made gruesome sense, sort of. But why bother replicat-
ing a martyrdom, as if Ret's murder was a copycat crime, only a
millennium later?

Rannie minimized the reproduction and read that Silas Cummings had purchased the painting of St. Margaret of Antioch in
1973 from the Sisters of Mercy Convent in Pound Ridge, New
York.

Yes! Yes! Yes! A match. No doubt St. Margaret was little
Kathleen Margaret's name saint. This was the painting that had
fascinated a morbid little orphaned girl. Rannie stared at the
computer screen, stunned by this eureka moment. Had Ret tried
to buy the painting? Was this the "important piece of art" she
boasted about owning but kept hidden in her bedroom? If Ret
had tried to purchase the painting, it seemed reasonable that she
might contact Bibi Gaines.

The big stumbling block, of course, was Silas's will, which for-
bade the sale of any paintings. Rannie imagined a conversation
between Ret and Bibi going something like this:

> Ret: For very personal reasons, I want to buy the
> St. Margaret of Antioch painting.
> Bibi: I'd love to help you out. The museum doesn't
> even want it but I'm afraid my hands are tied.
> Ret: I am willing to pay very handsomely for it.

No, that wasn't Ret-speak at all. Rannie revised Ret's line.

Ret: Look, would a million dollars—half for you,
half for the museum—change anybody's mind?
Bibi: Hmmm. Let me see what I can do and I'll get
back to you.

Bibi Gaines was a charming and persuasive person. Never-theless, the Metropolitan Museum would never agree to breach the terms of Silas's will and let her sell St. Margaret. Therefore, she needed to get creative.

Forgery struck Rannie as a reasonable option. Ret unknow-ingly bought a counterfeit. Ret was housebound, so what were the chances of her showing up at the museum and seeing the original displayed with all Silas's other martyred saints?

However, Larry's photo, the one with the painting partially revealed, had tipped off Ret to the fact that she'd been cheated, duped, screwed over royally. After that, getting even with Bibi would be easy-peasy: all Ret needed to do was call the cops, maybe insist on breaking the story to the media herself, and then be the star witness at Bibi's trial.

Rannie couldn't remember when she'd felt so pleased with herself. She looked around for her cell to call Grieg, then stopped. Something didn't compute. *Think like Tim,* she com-manded herself. Then it hit her, like a safe falling on an obliv-ious cartoon victim. If Ret had followed this last scenario, she'd still be alive and Bibi would have been under arrest. And an-other thing—notifying the authorities immediately consti-tuted the right thing to do; justice would have prevailed. Yet according to Sister Dorothy, Ret had been wrestling with her conscience over something she'd done, something sinful, mor-ally wrong.

Maybe it was time for Rannie to resurrect extortion as the motive for Ret's murder.

```
Ret: The painting you sold me is a copy, you twat.
Bibi: Excuse me. How dare you accuse me of—
Ret: Stop right there. I have proof. A photo of the
     real St. Margaret still hanging at Grammy's. So
     here's the deal. I keep my trap shut, but it's gon-
     na cost you.
```

So Grand Larceny Bibi. Extortion Ret . . . Rannie knew what Harriet Bookman would have to say about two wrongs. Furthermore, in Bibi's case, one wrong led to an even worse one—premeditated murder.

It was Bibi! It was Bibi! She killed Ret and stole the forgery. Rannie jumped up. "Go, me!" she cried and did a spazzy victory dance in the living room just as Nate appeared, with tennis equipment, and headed to the front door. He shielded his face with the racket. "Stop, Ma! You're hurting my eyes!" he cried and without breaking stride slammed the door behind him.

Rannie called Grieg and waited for the beep. Now she had a motive for Ret's murder. Of course, she still had no earthly idea why Ellen and Larry had ended up just as dead as Ret, but first things first.

When Grieg called back a few minutes later, Rannie tried hard to keep the giddiness out of her voice.

"This is all very complicated sounding, Ms. Bookman," he said at one point when she paused to take a breath. "I'm not following how Gery Antioch is really a Catholic saint named Margaret."

"I realize it's a little confusing."

"What about coming down to the precinct?"

"I can't. Not now." Breaking her promise to stay put was not an option. "Maybe later this evening. What if I e-mail you now? It'll be much clearer in an e-mail." The written word was her stock-in-trade, after all. Suddenly Rannie remembered a piece of evidence that she hadn't factored in. The semen on Ret's body. Rannie couldn't let on that she knew about it or how. So she added, "I know it must be hard to envision a woman committing the crime, but please consider what I'm telling you."

"Sure. E-mail me, Ms. Bookman. I'll read it."

Suddenly Rannie replayed a day years ago when she'd walked into Ellen's office as Ellen was ending a phone conversation with an unpublished writer, a friend of a friend. "Sure. E-mail me your manuscript. I'll take a look at it," Ellen promised, all the while rolling her eyes at Rannie and making the "let's wrap it up" roll with her free hand.

Grieg was taking Rannie no more seriously.

Undaunted, Rannie grabbed a legal pad and scribbled down the facts—okay, maybe not "facts" exactly but "likely suppositions," which she listed in a semilogical order. Then she started typing the e-mail. She stopped once, hit Save and returned to the site with the Cummings art catalog. The painting of St. Margaret of Antioch measured thirty-six by forty-one inches. In her mind's eye, the Hallmark Madonna that had hung on Ret's bedroom wall was smaller. Then returning to her e-mail, Rannie added, "I believe that after killing Ret, Barbara Gaines took the counterfeit St. Margaret and replaced it with the painting of a Madonna and Child that I saw on the day of the murder. If the Madonna is removed, my hunch is that the rectangle of cleaner wall paint will measure thirty-six by forty-one inches, the dimensions of the St. Margaret picture."

Rannie was still not finished typing when the landline rang. Rannie hit Save again and answered the phone.

It was Olivia.

"Sweetie, Nate's not here. I'll tell him you called," said Rannie, unable to disguise the impatience in her voice.

Olivia, however, did not disengage so easily. "Actually I was calling you, Ms. Bookman. I'm hoping I left a black silk reticule at your house."

A reticule? Was Olivia going through a Jane Austen fashion phase? Olivia said it might be in the den.

It was. Harriet had "tidied up" before leaving yesterday and, perhaps thinking the purse was Alice's, had hung it from a hook on the back of the closet door.

"Yeah, it's here. Nate'll bring it to school tomorrow."

"Um . . . could you do me one more favor and see if there's a Bloomie's charge card in it?"

Rannie pulled open the purse's drawstrings while keeping the phone cradled in her neck. "Yup, it's here. Also a piece of paper with an address and phone number." Rannie read it to Olivia.

"Oh, that's Mrs. Gaines's address. I don't need it. As long as the card's there. Thanks!"

After they hung up, Rannie was still holding the crumpled piece of paper with Olivia's round, surprisingly childish-looking print. A sickening little shiver wiggled up her spine.

Bibi Gaines's address was 69 East Sixty-Ninth Street. Same as Ret's.

Now Rannie could graft opportunity onto motive. Tenants' spare keys were kept, according to the handyman, in the basement of the building. Bibi could have stolen the set to Ret's apartment, slipped in and after killing Ret and switching the artwork, returned the keys to the basement. There would be nothing alarming about images of Bibi Gaines on security cameras. She was a resident.

When she calmed down after some more self-congratulatory victory dancing, Rannie debated whether to call Grieg right away or finish the e-mail with this astounding bit of late-breaking news.

She decided to finish her manifesto. Back on the sofa, she flexed her fingers and was about to resume typing when, to her mortification, she saw the long chunk of her message, which stopped abruptly in midsentence, had not been saved but sent to Grieg.

Rannie called and cringed waiting for the beep. "Me again! Rannie Bookman," she began. "I have critical information for you. Please call."

Grieg was dutiful, you had to give him that. "It's Grieg."

"Th-thanks for calling," Rannie stuttered. "Listen, I accidentally sent you an e-mail before I was finished."

"Is that your 'critical information'?"

"No. No. Of course not. Five minutes ago, I learned that Barbara Gaines and Ret Sullivan live in the same building. Well, *lived* in Ret's case. Barbara Gaines could have stolen spare keys and let herself into—"

"Whoa. Whoa. Whoa. Slow down. Tell me the address."

Rannie did.

There were a few moments of silence. Rannie could hear the clacking of computer keys. Then it stopped and he said, sounding weary and exasperated, "No, Ms. Bookman, Barbara Gaines doesn't live there. Her address is 302 East Seventy-Third Street."

"That's impossible!"

"Tell that to the New York White Pages. I looked up Barbara Gaines . . . 'B' as in 'Bravo,' 'A' as in 'Apple,' 'R' as in 'Rocket.' . . ." Grieg insisted on going through the whole mishegoss of spelling out the entire name. "What made you think she lived at 69 East Sixty-Ninth Street?"

Rannie wanted to cry. No way was she revealing her source was a teenage girl with a TCB tat on her tush. "I realize I have zero credibility with you now but I'm still sending the rest of the e-mail and I sincerely hope you read it."

Rannie wrapped up the manifesto, peppered with so many "possiblys" and "might haves" that if Grieg bothered wading through it, she tried not to picture him with eyes crossed, twirling a finger around his ear. Cuckoo bird. Cuckoo bird.

Rannie stared at the phone number that Olivia had written down and—what did she have to lose?—dialed it. An anonymous digitized voice answered. In frustration, Rannie flung her cell on the sofa, abandoned the computer, and felt so disheartened that even completing the Sunday crossword within an hour—"Wampanoag" fit for "Native New Englander?"—didn't lift her spirits.

The landline rang. Olivia again?

No.

"Hello, my name's Fred Rumson. I'm calling from Chaps. Is this Nathan Lorimer's mother?"

"Yes. Is Nate okay?" Rannie's breathing turned shallow, her heart rate jumped.

"He'll be fine. But he got whacked pretty hard with a racket. Right in the face. Got knocked out cold. My son and I were hitting balls in the next court. I waited till the EMTs came. They took him to Roosevelt Hospital."

"Who is this?" Warning flares went up. Someone—Bibi—was trying to get Rannie out of the house to waylay her.

"Fred Rumson. My son goes to Chaps."

"How'd you get this number?"

"A girl knew your son's name. And the security guard had a school directory."

"What girl? I want to speak with her."

"I have no idea who." The man sounded put out now. "Listen. I stuck around till the ambulance came because I thought if it was my kid . . ."

Were my kid, not *was my kid . . .*

" . . . I'd want a grown-up around."

Rannie needed verification. "Can I speak to your son? Or the security guard?"

"What! Look, lady, I was trying to be nice. I don't know what your problem is. Your son should be at Roosevelt any minute. Sorry I disturbed you."

The line went dead.

Oh God, what to do? She tried Nate, although he never answered once he saw her number on the cell screen. "Nate, please, *please.* If you're there, pick up." When he didn't, Rannie flew to her room and dumped out the night table drawer. In the Chaps directory, yes, there was the listing. Frederick and Clea Rumson, parents of Gabriel, a ninth grader. No answer at their number. Or Olivia's or Ben's.

Rannie tried Tim. She tried Chaps's main number, which predictably on a Sunday went straight to voice mail. She tried

Roosevelt Hospital and was shunted from one clueless person to another. In desperation, she tried Nate again. "PICK UP THE GODDAMNED PHONE, NATE!" Even before hearing the first word of his automated reply, Rannie hurled the phone at the wall, a pathetic girlie throw. The cell landed with a plop on her pillow.

Okay. Decision Time. In her head, she knew this was a trap and if she left, she was going to fall—*splat!*—right into it. But her heart wasn't so sure. What if Nate was hurt badly? A head injury? What if they needed to operate and she wasn't there to give permission?

She grabbed her fleece hoodie and tried to weigh consequences. In the end, her Nike-clad feet made the decision for her. She was powerless to stop them. She found herself propelled out the door to the landing, where her finger pressed the elevator button.

Chapter 27

NATE WAS FINE.

She wasn't.

Barbara Gaines had Rannie gripped about the waist. To passersby, unable see the knife held under Rannie's fleece, they probably appeared quite chummy.

Bibi had been waiting by the front door of the Dolores Court. "Hi there! I said to Tony the trick would work! And I was right!" she'd trilled as Rannie rushed out. "You're a good mom! Honestly, I would have made a *horren-dous* parent!"

A few doors down, between two buildings, there was a fifteen-foot-wide empty lot, where a structurally unsound brownstone had stood until the city finally tore it down. Bibi pushed her in there, stepping cautiously over fast-food containers, liquor bottles, beer cans, and more than one dead rat. They were many feet from the sidewalk on an unlit block, zilch chance of passersby taking notice of them.

"Who'd you get to call me?"

"Tony," Bibi said, sounding pleased.

"Tony? As in F. Anthony Weld?" Did it matter? No. But stalling for time did. "It didn't sound like him."

"Oh, that phony baloney academic accent, he can turn it on and off like a tap on a beer keg."

"You had him forge a St. Margaret." An art restorer was practically a euphemism for forger, "Tony" had said so himself. Rannie desperately tried remembering basics from the self-defense course she'd taken postdivorce, a single woman again. Fear of sudden death, however, was making it hard to focus: her head suddenly seemed stuffed with cotton candy, and her legs had turned as floppy as a rag doll's.

"Tony got the same wood, same paints. And he was meticulous about copying the painting. 'The woman has one eye!' I kept saying. 'It doesn't have to be so perfect, Tony!' Then in the end, I decided, 'Why not give Ret Sullivan the original?' So all her screaming about how I'd cheated her wasn't true at all. I planned to give the museum the forgery. They'd never bother to authenticate a painting they didn't want to begin with. I loved that part, the Met exhibiting the copy. I mean, how ironical."

Rannie's brain was functioning again; her inner copy editor autocorrected—*ironic* not *ironical*.

"Do you know, I was right on the other side of the door when you rang Ret's bell? 'Hello! Hello! It's your copy editor, Rannie Bookman.'"

Bibi was not as accomplished a mimic as Harriet Bookman.

"I was all set to leave. I'd wiped off my fingerprints and had St. Margaret in a Bloomie's bag. If you'd arrived a second later, we might have bumped smack into each other!" Bibi had Rannie pinned against a rough exposed-brick wall. She was wearing a black Burberry raincoat and black pointy-toed flats. Her eyes glittered and her smile was manic. "And after that you just kept popping up everywhere! The next night at Grammy's house and then at Bibilots. I thought to myself, 'Oh, Bibi. Watch out for this one.'"

The fog in Rannie's brain began to lift. Another self-defense ABC came back to her—the element of surprise. However, shouting "Boo!" probably wasn't going to cut it.

"Just before, when we saw your son leave, Tony followed in his car, and when it turned out he was going to Chaps, well, an accident at school, what better way to get you out of the house." Bibi's tone was weirdly convivial. "Tony went to Chaps, back when it was all boys. He has scads of friends with kids there now."

One of whom was Fred Rumson, no doubt. Rannie came to a decision: klutz that she was, her kicks were halfway respectable. The self-defense coach had even said so. Bibi was too close to manage a chorus-line high kick to the groin, but a kick to the shin, hard and sharp, she could pull that off. It might make Bibi drop the knife. "So all along the two of you have been in this together."

"Well, there are a few teensy things Tony doesn't know about," Bibi said at the same time Rannie's eyes fell on a wrinkly used condom near her feet.

"The semen on Ret. It was his," Rannie stated flatly.

"That's unpleasant. I don't want to talk about it." Now a dreamy expression flitted across Bibi's face. "I shouldn't have wasted time tying Ret's hair, but I couldn't resist. You know, it's the strangest thing, I had never murdered anyone before. I had no idea I'd be so good at it!" The remark was spoken blithely, as if she were talking about the accidental discovery of a hidden talent for macramé. Bibi glanced at her watch, then the street. Rannie's heart started hammering. She had to keep her talking. God, how she wished she could trade shoes; those pointy-toed babies could inflict serious damage. "I understand why you murdered Ret. But Ellen Donahoe?"

"That was absolutely not my fault!"

"You didn't kill her?"

"It was Ret's fault." Bibi sighed irritably as if now the topic of homicide was beginning to bore her. "When I had Ret all tied up, I—I *persuaded* her to talk. She said her editor had toured Grammy's on one of the days we open it to the public. Ret swore the editor was there just to get a few photos and didn't know anything about the forgery. But I wasn't taking chances."

The thing was, Ellen *hadn't* taken the photos. Larry Katz had. Then it struck Rannie. Ret had been trying to protect Larry. To do that, Ret had sacrificed Ellen.

"So the next morning you killed Ellen?"

"Ret told me about her morning exercise routine. I hung out by her building and followed her. It was no fun, let me tell you. *Pouring* buckets out. I sprinted ahead and by those pine trees pretended to fall. A minute later she came running up to see if I needed help. Sometimes people are too nice for their own good. What I can't understand: I left a scarf of Tony's nearby. The police should have found it."

"You're framing him."

"I'm protecting myself. And if I hadn't just happened to turn on the TV and see Larry Katz, he'd be alive, too."

Catching Larry on the talk show was how Rannie made the connection between Larry and Audeo. It was also how Bibi made the connection between Larry and Ret.

"I should have been more suspicious that day he came to Grammy's. He didn't look like an art expert, with those awful clothes and Brooklyn accent."

Actually a Long Island accent.

"So I called him last night, very teary, saying what a simply awful day I'd had, what with Grammy's funeral. He's tried several times to get together, so as I expected, he invited me down to his place. We were having drinks when I suggested a bath together might be relaxing. I tell you, the man practically started salivating. By the time he was in the tub all the Rohypnol was working like a charm." Bibi smiled again. "Jews think they're so smart, but that wasn't such a swift move on his part, was it?"

Okay. Not only a psychopath but also a raging anti-Semite.

Bibi glanced at her watch. "Listen, while it's been fun chatting, we have to wrap this up. You know, after getting mugged once, anybody in their right mind would have moved. I mean, here you are, getting mugged again, and this time you're going to lose more than a watch."

Bibi took a half step back, knife poised.

Now was the moment. Every muscle in Rannie's right leg tensed. Her eyes stayed trained on the knife, which was why it came as a shock to find herself lurching forward, then sprawled on the ground, a ferocious pain radiating throughout her body from ground zero, above her left hip.

Bibi had kicked her.

Rannie was stunned, barely aware of the shards of broken glass embedded in both her palms.

"Don't just lie there like a lump. Try to escape!" Bibi ordered.

She wants it to look like a struggle. Rannie groaned and, rocking in pain, clutched her belly. That was when she felt it, something inside the pouch on her fleece. A blue pencil? A blue pencil had come through for her once before. No. Something else. She grasped it anyway.

Bibi kicked her in the butt, more taunt than serious blow. "Get up!"

Rannie scrabbled to her knees. Her glasses had been knocked off. She was on all fours. When she gazed up, Bibi was coming toward her with the knife. Rannie reared back, ignoring pain so severe it put giving birth on par with menstrual cramps. Imagining Bibi in her black Burberry as a giant water bug, Rannie whipped out the pencil-thin metallic blue wand and sprayed for all she was worth.

A shriek. "You bitch!" Bibi was clutching her face with both hands. The vapor of peppery Mace made Rannie cough. Coughing was agony. The knife was gone, but without her glasses, it was useless looking for it.

Somehow Rannie struggled to her feet and lurched toward the sidewalk, hunched over like Quasimodo. On the street a man was getting out of a car. Rannie squinted. Tim? "Bibi's in the lot," Rannie rasped. It was no more than a whisper. Then she collapsed on the sidewalk.

Rannie heard rather than saw much of what happened next. Tim shouted—yes, unmistakably it was Tim—"Watch out!" There was the screeching of brakes, followed by a loud hollow thunk. Then Tim was at Rannie's side, telling her not to move.

Cries came from a gathering crowd in the street.

"Holy shit!"

"Call an ambulance!"

"No rush. That's one dead chica."

Later in the ER, Rannie learned the car that hit Bibi belonged to F. Anthony Weld. How ironical.

Epilogue

"IT WAS A MIRACLE. THE MACE."

"Sure. If you say so."

"Tim, I could never figure out how to turn the damn thing on and I never carried it around because I was scared if I did try to use it, I'd just end up spraying myself. And yet I got it to work on Bibi. Is there a patron saint of self-defense?"

"Yeah, but you don't want him. He's a favorite of the NRA."

Hmmm. Then maybe she should think of the Mace in the little blue wand as akin to the oil in the lamp that kept on burning in the Hanukkah miracle. In a desperate situation, it delivered. Rannie was in bed, a very comfortable hospital bed, at Roosevelt Hospital. The story for family and friends went as follows: Rannie had collided with a bike rider while crossing against the light. "Totally my fault, I wasn't paying attention," Rannie confessed to all, then listened to responses that ranged from sympathetic:

Mary: "No wonder; you have too much on your mind, dear."

To less than sympathetic:

Harriet: "I hope this teaches you a lesson! Next time—poo, poo—you might not be so lucky."

That was true. She had been lucky, all things considered. Rannie's internist Jim Lax informed her that she could have bled out—"exsanguinated" in MD parlance—almost instantly from a ruptured spleen. The day after laparoscopic surgery, she floated on a morphine-induced cloud.

"What's morphine like, Ma?" Nate asked with too much interest.

"Horrid," Rannie lied.

There was a lot to be said for drugs. There was a lot to be said against them.

The day before Rannie was discharged, Barbara Beauchamp Gaines's funeral took place in the small side chapel of Saint Thomas Church. Did it count as getting away with murder, Rannie wondered, if you wound up dead too?

Daisy Satterthwaite did not attend. Instead, she and Mary hired a car to pay Rannie a visit at the hospital.

"What on earth was Barbara doing up in that neighborhood?" Mary wondered aloud, neglecting to inform Daisy that "that neighborhood" was also Rannie's neighborhood.

"Probably a rendezvous with a dope pusher."

"Daisy, that's really uncalled for," Mary tut-tutted.

The NYPD had botched a triple homicide, a fact that they preferred not to publicize. Rannie was okay with that, for the most part. She had no desire for another fifteen minutes of fame. Ret had no relatives; the only one grieving for her was Sister Dorothy. Tim promised to drive Rannie to the convent once she felt well enough in order to tell Sister Dorothy a version of the truth: Ret's murderer was dead. Rannie planned to delete the part about Ret's extortion racket. Larry's mother was non compos mentis, incapable of understanding her son was dead, much less murdered. The publishing world would have no cause to question that his death had been anything other than suicide.

That left Ellen. In time, friends and acquaintances might become resigned to the awful truth that, in New York City, random attacks occurred and sometimes remained unsolved. But Ellen's family. Her parents and brother. They'd wake up every day for the rest of their lives to face that tragedy. Knowing Ellen's killer was dead couldn't provide closure—nothing could; still, it would erase an unbearable question mark. Rannie had elicited a promise from Sergeant Grieg. He'd tell Ellen's family, in person, the truth. It was then their choice whether to go public. A follow-up call from Rannie to the Donahoes would serve a dual purpose: to offer condolences and to ensure Grieg had abided by the deal.

Grieg had been right about one thing. Bibi did live at 302 East Seventy-Third Street. For the past three months, F. Anthony had been renting a studio apartment at 69 East Sixty-Ninth Street, where "his special friend" Bibi was a frequent overnight guest.

Weld claimed that, through Barbara Gaines, he'd received a quarter-million-dollar commission to create a copy of the St. Margaret painting for Kathleen Margaret Sullivan. All on the up-and-up. He knew nothing of Bibi's side scheme. Yes, they were involved with each other but not seriously; he was picking Bibi up for a dinner date when she appeared out of nowhere in the street; there had been no time to avoid hitting her. As for 108th and Broadway, Bibi had provided the address, claiming she was visiting an old friend that afternoon. Was that the whole truth? Who knew.

On the day of Rannie's discharge, Tim drove her to his house. She was to spend the next couple of weeks there, recuperating. Fine with her.

Nate, unsurprisingly, had proposed he stay at O's.

"Nice try, buddy," Rannie had told him.

"So, Tim? Once I'm all better, are you gonna send me packing?"

"Let's take it one day at a time, Rannie. Okay? See where we go."

They reached a stoplight. Suddenly Tim turned. "No. Who am I kidding? I need you. I want you with me . . . and if you're under my roof, I can make sure you stay out of trouble."

Rannie smiled. She didn't say anything. She didn't need to.

Driving up Broadway, they passed a Barnes & Noble store and Tim slowed down long enough for Rannie to catch sight of a big display window.

It was devoted to a single title: *Portrait of a Lady.*

Insights,
Interviews
& More . . .

About the author

2 Meet Jane O'Connor

About the book

3 Dear Reader

Read on

5 A Sneak Peek of Jane O'Connor's
Previous Novel, *Dangerous
Admissions*

11 More by Jane O'Connor

Meet Jane O'Connor

Jim O'Connor

JANE O'CONNOR, an editor at a major New York publishing house, has written more than seventy books for children, including the *New York Times* bestselling Fancy Nancy series. She is also the author of the adult mystery *Dangerous Admissions*. ∾

Dear Reader

If my name rings a bell, perhaps it's because you have a little girl in your life, a little girl who adores dressing up and being fancy in every way imaginable. I'm the author of the Fancy Nancy books and, no, I'm not wearing a boa and tiara as I write this.

My books for children are worlds apart—actually make that galaxies apart—from *Almost True Confessions* and an earlier mystery I wrote called *Dangerous Admissions*. And yet it strikes me that both Fancy Nancy and Rannie Bookman, the heroine of my "grown-up" books, do share one essential characteristic: they both love language. It's in their DNA. Fancy Nancy never misses an opportunity to drop a five-dollar word into conversation, and Rannie, a freelance copy editor for a major New York publishing house, is passionate about proper grammar and word usage. (She's passionate in other ways too.)

My characters' obsessions with language probably should not come as a surprise to me—I've been writing stories since I was Nancy's age; for decades I have been an editor at a New York publishing house; and on questionnaires requesting hobbies, all I ever come up with is "reading."

Since you've bothered to look at this ▶

3

Dear Reader *(continued)*

letter, there's a fair chance that reading is one of your primary pleasures as well. Fingers crossed that you found your time with Rannie well spent.

Jane O'Connor

A Sneak Peek of Jane O'Connor's Previous Novel, *Dangerous Admissions*

Mid-October, Tuesday morning

S.W.A.K. KILLER STRIKES AGAIN: PERV MURDERER STALKS UPPER WEST SIDE blared the headline of the *Post* lying on the front seat of the Jag.

Olivia Werner shuddered and fired up a Parliament. What a complete sicko, leaving lipstick kiss marks on his victims after slitting their throats. The only reason her parents had James chauffeuring her to school was because all the bodies had been found near Chaps. Olivia wasn't complaining: She got an extra half hour to sleep, and more importantly she could smoke. You could hardly do that anywhere in this city anymore.

Accelerating through a yellow light, the car shot across Fifth Avenue and into the transverse at 85th Street. She'd make it to school in time to catch Mr. Tut before some other senior having a panic attack got to him.

Last night her mother had barged into her room while Olivia was sewing. As soon as Olivia said, "No, Mom, I don't want to 'brainstorm' essay ideas now," her mother dropped her eager, helpful smile and went on a rant about the Princeton application being due in two weeks. ▸

"Mom, please. Face it. I'm not going to get in."

Being a double legacy didn't mean squat, not with her SAT scores and not when four brainiacs in the class were applying early. One of them—William Van Voorhees III—was claiming to be African-American because his grandfather came from Capetown. But that was Chaps kids for you, working every angle.

Olivia wanted to go to the Fashion Institute of Technology. Mr. Tutwiler understood. In fact, he "applauded her sense of direction." Those were his exact words. "Fashion does matter," he agreed. "The way we dress is the face we present to the world. With the exception of clothes, so little about our appearance is of our own choosing."

If a man over eighty got it, how come her parents didn't? At Werner family conferences, her mom's standard reply was: "We didn't send Olivia to Chaps for thirteen years so she'd end up in the Garment District."

The car pulled to the curb at 103rd Street and Riverside Drive. Shouldering her backpack, Olivia hurried through the gates of Chapel School—Chaps— a glowering, turreted hulk the color of chewed gum. She banged on the front doors until the guard let her in.

It was eerily silent in the Great Hall, a massive space that soared thirty feet to a barrel-vaulted ceiling. But in another fifteen minutes black Town Cars would be lined up outside, two and three deep, and seven hundred Chapel School students would come swarming through the doors, Lower and Middle School kids in Chaps uniforms, Upper School kids in anything that marginally passed Dress Code.

Her dad had gone to Chaps, class of '76, and complained about how the school had "changed," which Olivia understood wasn't about Chaps being coed or the way kids dressed. It was some sort of nasty code word for the fact that now the high school was twenty-five percent minority kids on scholarship. It killed her parents that practically all of them were guaranteed a spot at the Ivy of their choice.

From the Great Hall she crossed over to a neighboring brownstone known as the Annex. No need to check the wall directory; Olivia knew exactly where to find A. Lawrence Tutwiler, Director of College Admissions.

He was a Chapel School institution, the college advisor since way before either Chaps or any of the Ivies had gone coed. In a cover story last spring, *New York Magazine* had crowned him King Tut because he carried so much weight with college admissions offices. A lot of kids hated him. He didn't care who your parents were or how much money they promised your first-choice college. He could spot an application essay written by a high-priced tutor from the opening sentence. Some ▶

shrink suddenly claimed you were ADD and needed to take the SATs untimed? Uh uh. Didn't fly with Tut. It was one of the reasons Olivia liked him so much: Tut cut through the bullshit, judged you fair and square for what you'd accomplished at Chaps, and he let colleges know it.

In the Annex reception area, the new headmaster was talking to a couple whose little girl was sitting on the sofa, a half-naked Barbie on her lap. Obviously here to tour the school. Kindergarten had been so great; it was senior year that sucked. Olivia had loved school when she was little, everything about it—the school bus, lunch in the cafeteria, class trips, even the heinous maroon uniform. Her teachers had loved every single one of her art projects. Some were still displayed in the Lower School hallways.

As Olivia took the stairs to Tut's office, she worked at a hangnail on her thumb until it started bleeding. The Princeton application was in her backpack, the only part still blank was the space for the personal essay. *Tell us about something meaningful to you*, it asked. *Surprise us. Pick a topic that only you can write about.*

"Your brother's in rehab," Lily G. had said. "Just say how you want to devote your life to crack babies or something."

"She's right," Lily B. agreed. "Calm down."

What the Lilys didn't know (and never

would) was that lately the only way she could calm down and get to sleep was by masturbating. Coming always left her feeling peaceful, almost with a sense of well-being—it worked way better than the Ambien her mother was quick to offer. So how about "Teenage Girls Jerk Off, Too!" for her Princeton essay? Couldn't get more personal than that.

The door to Tut's office was shut, which probably meant he wasn't in. A floor below, she could hear the chirpy voice of the little girl, but on the other side of the office door, total silence like during an exam.

Sucking her bleeding cuticle, Olivia peeked through the little window in the door. Tut *was* there; she could make out the bulk of his head and shoulders through the wavy glass.

"Mr. Tut," she called tentatively. "It's Olivia. I hate to bother you, but I'm kind of desperate."

Tut was pretty deaf so Olivia rapped harder, then put her ear against the door. No, he wasn't on the phone. "Hey, Mr. Tut. You okay?" Olivia waited three beats before a tickle of concern made her turn the knob.

Mr. Tut, in a yellow bow tie and blazer, was sitting at his desk, facing her like some well-behaved first grader waiting for the teacher to say, "All right, class. Please open your books to page sixty-seven."

Olivia's eyes traveled from the mammoth pile of college brochures ▶

A Sneak Peek of Jane O'Connor's Previous Novel, *Dangerous Admissions* (continued)

and course catalogues on his desk to an overturned glass. It lay next to a bunch of soggy pink message slips all wadded together, the ink running. It was then that Olivia's gaze shifted back to Mr. Tut himself.

Something was wrong. His body was slumped, and his head tilted back in a funny way. Olivia could see bristly white hairs on his neck, spots he'd missed shaving. His mouth was hanging open with dried spit caked in the corners. . . . And Tut's skin was waxy, a little blue. Like skim milk. Still, her brain didn't fully process what she was seeing until Olivia focused on Mr. Tut's eyes—cloudy and yellow and open way too wide.

It was then that Olivia started screaming.

More by Jane O'Connor

DANGEROUS ADMISSIONS

Miranda "Rannie" Bookman—forty-three, divorced mother of two, with a recent love life consisting of a long string of embarrassingly brief encounters—is beginning to feel like a dangling participle: connected to nothing. Her career as a copyeditor is down the toilet (she makes one little slip—a missing "l" from the last word in the title of the Nancy Drew classic *The Secret of the Old Clock*—and suddenly she's Publishing Enemy #1!), so she's been forced to take any gig she can get. And that means giving tours at the Chapel School, the ultra-exclusive, ultra-expensive private academy that her children attend. Certainly not the most interesting of employments . . . at least until someone stumbles across the dead body of the Director of College Admissions.

Investigating a murder was never in her job description, but with her soon-to-be-college-bound boy, Nate, a prime suspect, Rannie has little choice. Besides, who better to dot all the "i"s and cross all the "t"s than a self-proclaimed "language cop"? Her diligence might even lead her to a brand-new love. Or to a killer. Or to another corpse—hopefully not her own.

Don't miss the next book by your favorite author. Sign up now for AuthorTracker by visiting www.AuthorTracker.com.